F

the Rain

• S M BARWANY •

Acknowledgements

Extracts on the Mongols are from Sir John Glubb's book, *The Lost Centuries* (Hodder & Stoughton, 1967), and he is also mentioned where quoted.
The '5th Line' of Hexagram 63 is from the Richard Wilhelm translation (the English translation by Cary F Baynes) of *The I Ching, or Book of Change*s (Routledge & Kegan Ltd, 1968).
The following extracts are from *Anthology of Islamic Literature*, edited by James Kritzech (Pelican Original, Penguin Books, 1964):

On Bribery by Sari Mehmed Pasha, translated by Walter Livingstone Wright;
The Purchase of Slaves by Kai Kaus (from The Book of Kaus), translated by Reuben Levy;
On Tobacco and Coffee by Katib Chelebi (from his Balance of Truth), translated by G L Lewis;
Advice to Governors by Nizam Al-Mulk (from The Book of Government), translated by Hubert Darke.

Omar Khayyam's quatrains are from the Edward Fitzgerald translation, *Rubaiyat of Omar Khayyam* (Collins, 1952).

About the Author

S M Barwany was born and grew up in Zanzibar Island, then a British Protectorate under the Sultan, where his seafaring ancestors had settled two centuries ago. When the Protectorate status ended in late 1963, and the newly formed government was overthrown weeks later, he was in England studying architecture. He pushed on to receive his postgraduate diploma from the University of Nottingham, and subsequently became a corporate member of the RIBA.

He registered as a UK citizen in January 1969, and in the following month left with his wife and son for Guyana, South America. This turned out to be the first leg of what became an extensive tour of developing countries, leading him to West Africa, the Middle East and East Africa, with periodic returns to Britain.

The author has two grown-up sons from his first marriage, and a ten-year-old son from a later marriage. All three were born in different countries: England, Guyana and Zanzibar. He is a lifelong aircraft and armour enthusiast.

To my father

©2004 S M Barwarny
Firefly in the Rain
ISBN 0-9549100-0-1

Published by:
Amethyst Publishing
46A Ruby Street
Leicester
LE3 9GR

The right of S M Barwany to be identified as
the author of this work has been asserted by him
in accordance with the Copyright, Designs
and Patents Act 1988.

All rights reserved. No part of this publication
may be produced in any form or by any means -
graphic, electronic or mechanical including
photocopying, recording, taping or information
storage and retrieval systems - without prior
permission in writing from the publisher.

A CIP catalogue for this book is available
from the British Library.

Design and production co-ordinated by
The ***Better Book*** Company Ltd
Havant
Hampshire
PO9 2XH

Printed in England

« PROLOGUE »

I was at a garden party in one of the lesser embassies in London, on an exceptionally warm evening in July, such as to remind me of early summer in my own country, Rivenia, some 3,000 kilometres away. One thing about these modest (for want of a better word) little embassies is that every now and then something unexpected and dramatic happens in their countries which can threaten the peace of the world by drawing in the big and powerful nations, which tend to be very touchy about their "spheres of influence". But such occasions are rare enough for some of these pocket embassies to have acquired quite a different and admirable reputation – that of holding the most swinging parties in town. The atmosphere is that of a private party, and normally sober diplomats literally throw off their jackets and "cut the rug" (as they would say in older times) with the friskiest of them, and no female under sixty is safe from groping hands.

Such then, was the pleasurable situation that evening, and I was making my way to the buffet tables at the end of the enclosed garden, from where mouth-watering smells wafted over flowerbeds and green lawn, which small groups of men and women were sitting on in preference to the garden furniture, when I was intercepted halfway by a man whose face was immediately familiar, but whose name I could not remember. Fortunately it came to me just as we smilingly extended our hands. Learning to switch on a smile is obligatory for a diplomat as it is for a politician, and much practice is done before the bathroom mirror to achieve the right degree of "genuineness".

‘Hello Francis!’ I gushed, ‘been to the Abu Dhabi show?’ I had just remembered that he was the Chilean military attaché.

‘Yes,’ he replied, falling in step. ‘Still looking for that perfect helicopter, one that will cost the same as a family saloon!’ I joined in the laughter, knowing that it was meant to be ironic. Nations were bankrupting themselves trying to keep up with the universal arms race.

‘We are converting VW Beetles into armoured cars in Rivenia,’ I responded; ‘you know their shape alone should bounce off shells!’

As we got to the buffet tables and took our turn he said, ‘By the way, have you seen Colonel Bertillot’s new book?’ I replied in the negative, not being particularly interested.

‘Well, I think you should, and I am surprised that it hasn’t been brought to your attention because you figure quite prominently in it.’

‘I what?’ I mumbled, my attention having been focused on the sumptuous spread on the table.

‘The book is entitled *“War, Witchcraft and Idealism in Rivenia”*, and I can tell you that he is pretty sarcastic about the “Firefly” ideology. He is no friend of your government, I assure you. Also, he singles you out for particular vituperation. Calls you a rabid warmonger, and says you were the leading advocate of war against your neighbouring countries.’

Needless to say, my evening was entirely ruined. I kept imagining people whispering about me and laughing behind my back or worse, though it was highly unlikely that many there knew me or had read the book. Nevertheless, if this colonel had any credibility in diplomatic circles he might very well destroy the trust it had taken me almost two years to build.

You see, as yet the Rivenian embassy had not reopened in most European countries, and neither our de facto ambassador nor I had an official position. I was operating as a “military envoy" from his business premises, a small office and a secretary being put at my disposal. This allowed me to circulate in diplomatic circles, which is where the search for recognition was carried out.

If all this sounds confusing, have patience, for everything will be made clear in the narrative.

My wife had not been accompanying me to these diplomatic dos in the last few months because of her physical state (also it must be said, her dislike of such functions!), but knew how important they were to my mission. So when I told her about the colonel and his book she was also furious and disturbed.

'Husband, you cannot allow this wicked man to get away with such lies about our country, and you in particular, you simply must write a book to straighten the facts out. You can't wait until the official history of the movement comes out.'

'Well, let us see what he says in his book first.'

Early the following morning I rang the office to say I'd be late and then went prowling the bookshops. To my relief, I did not see the book in the first two bookshops, but there it was, as large as life, in the display window of the third! And the cover was such as to attract attention. It showed a beautiful, scantily clad woman lying on her back on an elevated marble slab, her long neck arched as if welcoming the Indo-Persian dagger, all wavy and wicked, slicing down on it. It was held by a looming yellow figure, featureless, whose other hand was suspiciously close to her exposed left breast. Incongruously, there was a long line of battle tanks in the background, firing their long-barrelled guns against a purple sky.

I rushed through the book in the office, my blood pressure climbing steadily, and finished the rest over tea at home before handing it over to my wife. When both of us had read it the vote was unanimous...I had to tell of my part in the events of three years ago. My wife even said that she would not mind if I touched on my private life, provided I did not reveal too much.

This then, is the account of how I, a retired history teacher, came to be involved in the "Liberating Events", the rebellion that toppled the previous government. And also of the part I played in the brief regional war that followed, and its aftermath.

« ONE »

To put the political and military developments in Rivenia in their proper context, we have to go no farther back than the nineteenth century. Up to the last decade of that century, Rivenia was not a single country but a small empire, stretching from the desert north to the heavily forested south. To the west, it was within a day's march of three countries (as they were to become after colonisation; at that time they did not exist as such) bordering the Atlantic Ocean, and to the east the border was pretty much as it is today. Like most of the countries surrounding the Sahara Desert, the socio-political structure was predominantly Middle Eastern. The empire had grown through force of arms, coercion and persuasion, in the manner of all empires, old and new.

Of direct relevance to the "Firefly" saga, is the fact that the empire had reached the zenith of its power and prosperity under the rule of the legendary Twelve Elders, men who emerged from multi-layered council elections to form the Great Council at the imperial palace. The lowest administrative unit was the village council.

Empires, like all mortal things, are born, grow, mature, decline and die; there is no escaping this rule. In the case of Rivenia, however, our historians tell us that the empire was in its early maturity, strong and prosperous, when the European scramble for Africa assailed the continent. Among the historically-minded Rivenians, this fact aroused a feeling of resentment, as well as a kind of psychic nostalgia for what had been. The resentment moved forward and spread to encompass the succession of oppressive and corrupt regimes that followed "independence". The empire of Rivenia was colonised in this manner:

On the fourth day of July 1892, the lookouts on the north-eastern mountains of Central Rivenia observed an exceptionally heavy cloud of dust approaching from the north. The country had beaten off two invasions from a neighbouring federation of forces some three decades previously, and had learnt that any sign of mass movement coming from the desert boded ill. The dust cloud was still many kilometres away, so to speed up recognition, two men got on their horses and galloped towards it. When they were seen racing back half an hour later, the lookouts did not wait for them to arrive but reached for their bullhorns. Blast after blast echoed in the mountains and the valleys below, to be taken up by one village after another in an ever widening circle all the way to the imperial capital.

Able-bodied men dropped whatever they were doing to rush home for their weapons, horses and camels. Those with chain-mail armour and helmets donned them, and various types of rifles were in evidence, mainly flintlocks, but with a few more modern rifles. From the near villages came footmen armed with spears and bows and arrows. In the space of about an hour there were about three thousand men in the mountains, clustered round the critical mountain path, the only access route for an invading army, which indeed was what this one was, for it was within telescope range.

It was not long before the Rivenian forces realised that this invasion was going to pose a far greater threat than any so far. Several hundred horsemen were leading a long column of infantry, marching four abreast, which made it clear straight away that this was not a regional militia army, but a regular foreign army. As they got within firing range, the horsemen were seen to be Europeans, armed with carbines and pistols, and the infantry looked foreign, but not European, and were armed with bolt-action rifles. The Rivenian commander knew that without reinforcements from the capital, he could not hold out for long, and they would take several hours to arrive, but there were no other defensive positions farther back.

The first cavalry charge was beaten off, and then the enemy horsemen dismounted out of range and joined the infantry. The battle raged for most of the morning, with neither side gaining the advantage. Just as the enemy cavalry was regrouping, a small group of horsemen was seen approaching from a distance, escorting a mule-drawn covered wagon. Way was made for the wagon to come forward, and what was unloaded from it turned the tide of the battle. It was a Maxim machine gun, never seen in the region before. The shock effect was colossal, and the enemy's cavalry charge was conclusive this time.

By noon all resistance had stopped, and after a few hours' rest the enemy marched through the villages unhindered. The following day, with drums beating and trumpets blaring, the foreign army marched into the imperial capital, and the alien flag flew over the palace. The Twelve Elders bowed to the inevitable, and were treated with courtesy by the conquering general. They remained as titular heads and ensured a peaceful occupation until a formal colonial administration took over. It found no need for the institution of the Elders and they were pensioned off to various parts of the country. For Rivenia, it marked the start of a new and much troubled era.

It is not my purpose to dwell on this phase of Rivenian history, but must move swiftly forward to the twentieth century, to the set of circumstances that led to the entry of the "Firefly". Mention must be made, however, of the single most damaging act of the colonial period which paved the way for continuing conflict in the region, and this was to split up the Rivenian empire into four separate regions, which, with

Independence, became separate countries. As the boundary lines arbitrarily cut across ethnic, tribal and linguistic lines, the seeds of dissent found fertile ground. The policy of "Divide and Rule" can be said to have led to the endless chain of conflicts witnessed in all the former colonies since colonial administration ceased.

Having given the background against which the dramatic events of two and a half years ago were to take place, I have to complete the canvas with a very brief description of the geography of Rivenia, otherwise there will be unacceptable confusion in the reader's mind.

The Republic of Rivenia that emerged after independence actually occupied only the central core of the old empire. It formed an irregularly shaped mass, rather like an amoeba with a pseudopod extended, which was 360 kilometres at its longest divide, and 300 kilometres at its shortest (or "long" and "wide" respectively, if you like). A peculiar feature of the country is a range of narrow, ragged mountains which snakes down from the north-east, like a stretched "S", across the northern third of the country, to continue south-west into the neighbouring land of Xarcassia, which was once part of the Rivenian empire. The important thing to remember is that the mountains cordoned off (apart from the narrow passes) about a quarter of the country, which was heavily forested, and whose border is the Red River. It was this river that separated Rivenia from Xarcassia, and will figure much in our story.

Before the foreign invasion, the capital was known as "the Imperial Capital" in the Rivenian language, but the foreigners changed it to the name of the conquering general, despite wild protests. When independence was granted and the first Rivenian government was formed, the new name that was proposed was another imposition, as far as a large section of the populace was concerned, for it favoured the tribal affiliations of the president. Successive regimes kept changing it to glorify them in return, so that in the end, everyone took to calling the capital simply "The City", and so it remained to this day. Map makers, having become as fed up as the people themselves, have followed suit. A particularly oppressive regime tried in vain to force its choice of name on the country, even to the extent of imprisoning those who were heard to speak out against it, but the next president yielded and called a referendum. "The City" won.

At the last census, the population was put at just over four million, with 46,000 living in "The City". All the countries in Africa, which have old and historic links with the Middle East share the same basic customs and traditions, irrespective of ethnicity. Those located on the great trading routes of the past can boast of architectural traditions and culture going back many centuries. Rivenia is one of these.

And now to my personal narrative.

« TWO »

I lived in a suburb called "Bonelands", east of the City and about two and a half kilometres from it. I had moved there on retiring (early) from my teaching job at the Phoenix High School as a history teacher. I had been through a divorce, and had suddenly found life in the City unbearable. I wanted nothing more than to find some distant place to regain peace of mind. Bonelands was a fairly recently developed settlement, going back no more than ten years or so. The first residents were real pioneers because they had to dig wells and use oil lamps. Electricity and piped water did not reach the area until about a year before I moved there. I continued using my well for watering the garden and vegetable plots. My plot was 100 x 55 metres in size, and my bungalow was built of concrete blocks, plastered and painted, and timber, with clay tile roofing. (Cheaper bungalows had corrugated iron roofs.) It was a two-bedroom bungalow, with a nice, wide veranda, and I had a grand view of the distant mountains, a source of never-ending pleasure.

Nobody knew how the name "Bonelands" had come about, and theories ranged from the dryness of the land – it was semi-scrub – to the discovery of prehistoric bones somewhere there. Certainly truckloads of fertile soil and plenty of manure had to be brought in to start a garden, but the residents all tended to be quite well off, and status was reflected in the size and excellence of one's garden.

My bungalow was the very first one on the access road from the ring road, which formed a semicircle around the City. Next to me, about 100 metres away, was another bungalow, a lower-quality one, which had been unoccupied ever since I moved there, followed by another one farther down. And then the access road curved into where the bulk of the housing units were, forming a kind of street. Fine little villas were to be found here, surrounded by high stone walls and ornate iron gates. My own plot was enclosed by a wire-mesh and thornbush fence, as were the other two bungalows in my line. The fencing was to keep out casual burglars, as well as the wild dogs that came down from the mountains every night. These dogs never menaced anyone who chanced to be returning home late, and we rather welcomed their presence because they kept down the rat population. But nobody wanted them right in our compounds. And it was also wise to keep away from them during the mating season!

And then the first of the fateful events to follow happened one morning in mid-August. Destiny pointed a finger at me in the shape of a new neighbour moving into the decrepit bungalow next to mine.

I heard the sound of a heavy vehicle labouring down the dirt track and stopping somewhere near. I went out to the veranda and heard the screech of the gate next door. I hopped onto the veranda balustrade, holding onto a post, and peered over the separating hedge. I saw a furniture van which, when the gate was fully open, reversed towards the house. A tall man emerged and made for the door as two men opened the back of the van and started bringing out things. When they completed transferring all the things, the two men got back in the van and drove away. The tall man walked up to the gate and shut it, then returned to the bungalow.

He was wearing a white, peakless cap, and was dressed in khakis. I could not make out his features at that distance but I noticed how straight-backed he was, and how he walked with long, rhythmic steps like a military man. I hopped down quickly, lest he look in my direction and saw this peeping tom! Tradition demanded that I went to welcome him to the neighbourhood as soon as possible, but I had to give him time to settle down first. I wondered if he would soon be joined by a family, or whether he was a loner like me. If the latter, then he'd have the same problem getting to know the Bonelands' residents for they were all family men who did not welcome "rogue" males, of whatever age. I occasionally met one or two during my afternoon strolls but was never invited to their houses.

I went round to see him the following morning and found him already at work, uprooting weeds and generally tidying up.

I pronounced the formal "Peace" greeting, to which he replied elaborately as we shook hands. His grip was firm and dry. I have never been good at describing people, so I'll just say that he looked older that I had thought, with a deeply lined face and sharp, down-turned nose typical of the camel riders of the northern regions bordering the desert. He had a grey, drooping moustache, and what little I could see of his hair under the cap was the same colour, not white as one would expect from his age for I put him nearer eighty than seventy.

I formally welcomed him to the neighbourhood, and he surprised me by saying, 'You must, of course, be the man known as the Professor. I am privileged to be your neighbour. I am Sergeant Erion, formally of the 3rd Cavalry Regiment, 1st Division, National Defence Force, but much of my service was with the old Colonial Brigade.'

So I was right in my instinctive identification.

Actually I am not, and never was, a professor, but somehow the nickname had clung to me despite initial protestations. Not that I disliked it, but some of my fellow teachers seemed to resent it for it had started while I was still teaching history at Phoenix High. He must have made prior enquiries as to who his neighbours would be.

From then on I would go round to help him repair and tidy up his place, and afterwards have coffee at his place or mine. I enjoyed the physical exertion, having been too lazy to jog or exercise lately. And if he needed to get anything in town he would accompany me in my Morris Minor 1000 (which I had bought many years before from an expatriate returning to England) instead of catching the half hourly bus at the foot of our access road. When I bought the Minor it had only 20,000 miles on the clock, and now, a few thousand miles later, it looked little the worse for wear. I went all over it every Sunday, waxing, polishing, greasing and adjusting things. Black in colour, with shining chrome and white-walled tyres, it looked a dainty little lady indeed. Our roads were full of potholes, so its relatively high ground clearance and tough suspension were up to the demands. I hung on to it later when I could have had one of those powerful, four-wheel drive brutes.

As the days passed, I noticed that Serge (as I had come to call my neighbour, pronounced with an "eh" sound, not the more common "ah") often would not introduce me to particular men we would frequently bump into in town, though he seemed to take pride in introducing me to many others, for he had a wide circle of acquaintances. I did not mention it, of course, being none of my business. In the prevailing political atmosphere in Rivenia there was no such thing as innocent curiosity. Admittedly, things were not as bad as a few years previously, when you could be horse-whipped, or lose half your teeth for being too slow to brake to a halt when the President's motorcade swept past. Nevertheless, walls had ears and windows had eyes.

Serge had been talking of getting his own vehicle, but he could not afford the kind that would suit his intended long journeys. He said he had a plantation in the south (with a caretaker looking after it) and close relations to the north. In the end, he settled for a motorcycle (he had ridden bikes in the army), and one afternoon he came roaring in on a 500cc Honda.

'Heavens, Serge!' I said. 'That's a bit of a handful for you isn't it? Why not something handier?'

'Oh, nothing to it really. It's just a matter of balance. You need power for long journeys. And to get out of the potholes!' he replied, very pleased with himself.

From the very next day Serge took to riding out and returning at all sorts of hours. Initially, he would tell me where he had been, delighting in the telling. But then, abruptly, he stopped talking about his journeys, and on many an occasion I would hear his Honda chugging in late at night. It worried me that a man of his age should have been pushing himself that hard, even though he looked fit and tough. He was my only friend in Bonelands and I decided to advise him to slow down.

Months later I would discover just what had been going on.

« THREE »

I remember that Tuesday morning in May with great clarity, for the two events happened on that day which marked a turning point for both the country and me, though neither was clear at the time.

I was about to step down the veranda steps to go to the carport, when I heard the sound of Serge's motorbike, and instead of riding past he stopped at my gate, opened it and chugged in. He never went without his red helmet and goggles, despite complaining that his head got too hot for comfort. With a quick movement, he unclipped and took off the helmet, and I realised that he wanted to talk. In fact, there was an air of suppressed excitement about him which I had never seen before. Seeing me fully dressed, he asked if I could spare a minute, and he took a chair on the veranda as I went to fetch pineapple juice from the kitchen.

'I have just witnessed something pretty crazy in town, Prof,' he said, after a sip, 'and I don't know what the hell it was all about!'

He had been driving down Main Street, he said, when suddenly there was a screeching of brakes as the traffic came to a ragged halt, some cars bumping into the ones ahead. Fortunately, they had been moving at a snail's pace and so no great damage was done. Then he heard the sound of shouts and women's screams coming from several car lengths in front, and he pushed forward between cars to see what was happening. People were running helter-skelter all over the place, and he soon saw the reason why – three men, wearing only loincloths, were charging from one side of the street to the other, waving machetes and flinging small bundles of leaflets into the air, which went fluttering up in the brisk wind to fall all over the place.

'But who were these people?' I asked, astonished.

'Let me tell you what they looked like, first. They were shaven-headed, clean-shaven, barefoot and painted bright yellow from head to foot! Never seen anything like it. They reminded me of the Snake Men of Bussota, thirty years ago.' Bussota was south-west of us, after Xarcassia. Both of these were once part of our empire, and the Forest People of Bussota forced the Twelve Elders to send a punitive expedition on more than one occasion, because of their intransigence.

'May the Almighty protect us!' I said, aghast. 'Did anyone get hurt? Did the police get them?'

'By the time the police appeared, they had smashed the glass front of the Zedex supermarket and that of the shoe shop next to it, and then disappeared down the alley on the right, just past your favourite Corner Café.'

The Corner Café was the regular meeting place for old friends and colleagues, and I will have more to say about it later.

At this point, Serge reached in a side pocket of his khaki jacket and pulled out a crumpled sheet of paper of foolscap size. He smoothed it out and handed it to me.

'This is one of the bits of paper they were flinging about.'

I looked at it with some interest, noting that the words were in green ink, in block letters, and placed dead centre on the page. Each letter was about two centimetres high and stamped on. The message was an old Rivenian saying:

WHEN YOU ENTRUST GAZELLES TO THE CARE OF HYENAS,
EXPECT TO FIND HOOVES AND BLOODSTAINS,
BROTHERS AND SISTERS! THE FIREFLY IS HERE TO RETURN
YOU TO THE WAY OF THE TWELVE ELDERS.

This struck me as being a political statement, but I could not conceive of any of our dispirited political parties as having put on this weird charade of a demonstration. They would not dare, to begin with! Secondly, to link this tasteless and frightening melodrama with the hallowed memory of the Twelve Elders was bound to infuriate people.

'Drug addicts or members of a witches' coven, I think. I am afraid the high unemployment rate is sending many of our young people astray,' I commented, not really much interested and about to tell Serge I was going into town.

'I am not as sanguine as you are about these people. Unlike the Snake Men, these characters seem to be politically motivated, and such people do not give up easily. I smell trouble ahead.'

'Oh, come, Serge!' I retorted. 'If these are political, why don't they come out into the open and register as a party? We have a democracy here, after all, even if it is somewhat flawed.'

'I envy your trust in our system, Prof, and wish I could share it with you. No doubt you and your friends do not know what life is like in districts like Fishtail and Flowers, otherwise you would not be so complacent. Anyway, whatever happened to the New Era Party? Remember how close it came to winning the general elections six years ago?'

Like many of my class (the old middle class which had survived the pogroms of three decades ago and regained a precarious foothold again) I had turned my back on politics and was leading a fairly comfortable life on my investments and pension. It was not pleasant, therefore, to be reminded that the leadership of the once vigorous NEP still languished in prison on trumped-up charges, causing the party to fragment.

'Politics is a dirty game, Serge, you know that.' It was the best I could think of saying and it sounded pretty hollow, even to me. 'I assumed you were a government supporter, Serge, being a former military man and all that. Anyway, you are receiving a fat little pension, aren't you?' I was trying to make light of things, as the atmosphere was becoming a bit strained. I wanted to go into town, at any rate. He smiled faintly and stood up. 'How is your book coming along?' he asked, as he got on his bike. I envied him the sound of his exhaust as he rode off. I wished my Morris sounded like that.

Serge had just cleared the gate when a car stopped in front of it and a man and two women came out and walked towards me. I was in front of the veranda, about to make for the carport. The man led, with the women a few steps behind, and he seemed in a hurry. I had seen the car, a white Toyota, several times driving past, but only in quick snatches between the gaps in the thornbush fencing, too quick to make out the occupants. But as the man got nearer, I recognised him as the man I had been introduced to, many months before, at a wedding reception. He was the Permanent Secretary of the Ministry of Defence, and lived in a cul-de-sac off the bottom of our access road. His villa was one of the larger ones.

On my afternoon strolls I never had cause to go in the direction of their villa, as it was a cul-de-sac closing off the eastern end of what was developing into the main street of our community, the western stretch going on to join an out-of-town road. So there had been no contact whatever since that one and only meeting, and I had even forgotten his name. He was a plumpish man of medium height, clean-shaven, with a receding hairline and just a suggestion of a paunch, which every senior government official was expected to develop.

Never having been visited by a Bonelands family in the two years I had lived there, I was secretly delighted and hoped it was about to mark an end to my isolation. Even my old friend had more visitors a week, friends and relations, than I had in months. 'Greetings, neighbour!' he called, when still three paces away, 'I hope you'll forgive our butting in like this. Have to make an urgent phone call, and you are nicely placed here to save us having to go back to the house. Must phone before eleven, just five minutes to spare!'

I led the way to my study, where the telephone was, and made way for him. 'Not for me, it's for my daughter,' he said.

Just then his wife and daughter walked in. It is not our custom to introduce our womenfolk to strangers by name, and one just says 'My wife/daughter/aunt/sister/etc.' We consider names to convey intimacy, and not to be made available to all and sundry. Meeting him, one would never guess that he was a cog in a most corrupt machinery.

His wife was pretty much what one would expect of the spouse of a high-ranking civil servant with extra income from other sources, attractive, well-dressed and exuding ease and contentment. I had hardly acknowledged the introduction with a polite smile, when the daughter appeared from behind her, and I was thrown into utter confusion. I could not remember ever having seen her, let alone met her, and yet I had this overwhelming feeling that I had known her for a very long time. So strong was this feeling of familiarity that I very nearly made to embrace her and kiss her on both cheeks. And then, as she looked up at me with a startled look on her face, no doubt because of the way I was staring at her, my memory was jogged and I realised why she had affected me in that manner. It had to do with a dream I had had many months before. I must tell about this dream because it was to play a key role in shaping my life.

It was one of those astonishingly clear dreams, in full colour and consistent from start to finish. I was at a large party in a building like you would find in the old sections of the city, with thick walls, tall arched windows and ornate balconies. I was circulating among the guests and moving from one room to another, arranged in an open-plan. The faces, though of strangers, were clear enough and the snatches of conversation that I could remember, on waking up, were as you would expect at a party. And then came the one break of sequence: I was suddenly on the ground floor, at the foot of broad stairs leading up, feeling desperately anxious to get back to the party. I ran up the stairs and was two steps short of the landing, when I was brought to a halt by a woman blocking my way. She was dressed in a long black dress with small yellow flowers, and I marvelled at her beauty and the length of her hair, which came down to her waist.

I was about to step to one side of her, wondering who she was and if she was somebody's wife, when she reached out and placed her hand on my left shoulder. My head was level with her stomach, and my gaze was drawn to a yellow flower precisely where I guessed her navel to be. I felt my face being pulled gently towards it. And then she spoke, softly but clearly above the buzz of conversation drifting down from upstairs.

'Why go back in there? They are all dead, you know!'

I looked up at her pensive face and moved up a step to wrap my arms around her and bury my face in her bosom, when I was snatched out of sleep by the alarm clock.

Well, this young woman standing in front of me that morning was the living twin of the one in the dream, though her hair was not as long, and she dressed differently. There is no country without its beautiful women, and though criteria vary widely across the world, there is a kind of beauty which cuts across cultures, and such a woman attracts attention wherever she goes. Such was this fellow neighbour's daughter.

She stepped past me to reach for the telephone and I returned to the front room. They came out after a few minutes, a look of obvious relief on their faces. Apologising that they could not stay, I accompanied them to the veranda. To my surprise and delight, she paused to say, 'You have so many books in your library, more than I have seen in any private home. I'd like to borrow one or two, if I can persuade father to bring me.'

Like in the countries in the region, all the way to the Middle East, a woman did not visit a man's house unchaperoned if he was eligible to marry her, unless she happened to be a housemaid. To my annoyance, her father chipped in with, 'No, you'll only make a nuisance of yourself.'

'Not in the least!' I jumped in so hastily that her eyebrows went up in surprise. I tried to cover up my embarrassment with, 'We are neighbours, after all, aren't we?' which sounded pretty flat in my ears, but seemed to reassure him. They promised to ring first.

When they had driven off I got in my car and made for the city centre in a bit of a daze. However hard I tried to shrug off the remarkable coincidence, I had a terrible feeling that I was not going to put her out of my mind that easily. I had "that old feeling", as the song goes, and having thought that the divorce (not the first one, but we need not go into that) had cured me of all illusions, it was not pleasant to realise that I could still be unbalanced by the flashing of a woman's eyes.

The Corner Café was the regular hangout for our group of former schoolmates and colleagues, mostly retired or running their own businesses. Members would start trickling in about 10.30 a.m., and the number present on any single morning would range from six to nine. The manager had come to know us well, and always linked a couple of tables with a "Reserved" notice, in anticipation. Despite its rather common name, which the new proprietor had not bothered to change, the café was an upmarket coffee-house in the traditional Turkish mould. It had been extended to face both the old Main Street side and, rounding the corner, Sulak Street. This Egyptian entrepreneur had spared no effort and expense to create a genuine Turkish atmosphere in the decor and layout, even to the extent of importing curtains, carpets and furniture from Turkey. The result was that one paid through the nose for a cup of coffee and sweetmeats, and the old customers had had to give way to a new crop of habitues, consisting of the intelligentsia and the financially stable. The nice thing about the place was that one could stay as long as one liked without having one's empty cup snatched away by a scowling waiter, though few abused this concession. There were nuts, dates and cookies available as well.

This particular morning, I was keen to hear of the peculiar events that had taken place earlier, which Serge had told me about, but none of the seven present could add to Serge's account, and at second-hand at that. Members of the group were always wary of discussing politics anyway, at least in public. As we turned to the usual gossip (and there was always there somebody better informed than the rest), I found my mind drifting back to the Permanent Secretary's daughter, much to my annoyance.

What came to be known as the "Yellow Men Incident", was not mentioned in the one o'clock news (government controlled) but gave the independent papers much amusement the following day. One lucky paper, which soon sold out, had the photograph of a running "Yellow Man", flinging a bundle of leaflets. Taken by a tourist, the picture showed the man frozen in motion, looking like a statue, facing the camera. Nevertheless, despite the drama, the papers treated it lightly, with even a suggestion that it had been to advertise a musical group called "The Firefly", about to come from Xarcassia.

But then a woman living in Ikram Street came forward and claimed that she was absolutely certain that the photo showed her son, Majid, a trainee carpenter, reported missing four months before. Over the previous seven months, many young men had been reported missing, but since most of them were unemployed, or known layabouts and drug addicts, it was assumed that they had made their way to the coast, to stowaway on-board ships bound for the Middle East or Europe. The police certainly had shown little interest, and apart from three or four who had had no compulsion to leave, like this Majid (if that was who the photo showed), even their families had not shown much concern.

As the days passed, the incident was quickly forgotten, and it was not until three weeks later that a member of our group at the Corner Café brought to our attention that he had been keeping an eye on the back pages since (he was an avid reader of detective stories) and had noticed an increase in the number of disappearances, including that of older men. Effect of the publicity, we opined.

About a month later, I was at the café when, to my surprise, in walked my neighbour, Serge, accompanied by a short man in a well-cut suit with no tie. In Rivenia, like everywhere else nowadays, north or south of the Sahara, men and women dressed in many different ways, from shirt and trousers to robes and long shirts. Suits, with or without a tie, were by no means uncommon, but were usually "official". Serge's companion, with his well-trimmed moustache and polished shoes, looked more like a company director or bank manager. Serge was not the café-going type, preferring fruit juice at a stall, in the shade of a tree. He said that he could not stand the smoky atmosphere and the incessant gossip, though I suspected other reasons, frugality being one.

He did not see me as they made their way to a corner table, where they were soon deep in conversation. I wondered if he was selling his pineapple plantation, or was negotiating some business deal. They were still there when I got up to leave, so I walked across to say salaam. He looked up in surprise (which I was to discover later was actually feigned).

'Well, well, Serge!' I said, 'this is a rare privilege. Let me see if I can get you a gas mask!'

Serge laughed, with his companion quick to catch on.

'We were just talking about you, Prof. Mr James here is a freelance journalist on military affairs. I mentioned to him that you were writing a book on the Mongols.'

Mr James had the short, curly hair and high cheekbones of the central part of the country, though with so much intermixing it was never easy to identify ethnicity or tribe. He had the calm, confident air of your favourite GP, and I felt immediately at ease with him. What vaguely puzzled me was why Serge kept calling him "Mr James" when they were obviously close friends.

'I contribute an article to the *Military Journal* every now and then,' he said, 'and if you can spare the time, I'd like to hear about the Mongols' tactics. Our public library has hardly a thing.'

I said I'd be delighted to provide him with a bit of information, and we arranged for him to come to my place at 4.30 p.m. the following Thursday. Serge would bring him round. As I was driving home, I reflected that Mr James must be a pretty highly paid journalist to afford a suit like that, but perhaps he was a rich man, just doing it as a hobby. It was to be some months before I saw, in retrospect, how that meeting in the café had been yet another nudge by Destiny to push me off the beaten track.

•••••••

A matter which had begun to assume increasing importance was that of my finding a wife. A bachelor's existence had little charm in a society, and with a religion, that strongly favoured the marital status for both men and women. We had our playboys and our unconventional females, but these operated outside the mainstream of society, and ultimately found it difficult to marry into a respectable family. On the other hand, those who remain single through no fault of theirs, for instance the divorced, the widowed and men who are too poor to afford a wife, receive no blame whatever. On the contrary, relations and friends will go all out to help them secure a willing and suitable mate. Indeed, matchmaking is a popular pastime for reasons both religious and social. The successful matchmaker receives God's blessings as well as the gratitude of the families of the bride and groom. And, should the arranged marriage break down, no particular blame attaches to the matchmaker since mutual consent had been obtained. Much adverse comment is directed against arranged marriages in the West, but there are vital differences in procedure between one culture and another. For instance, in the Hindu system, it is the bride who pays the dowry, whereas in the Muslim it is the bridegroom. Forced marriages are very rare, in that the cleric who conducts the rituals has a religious obligation to ensure that there is mutual consent. And the marriage institution itself is seen in a very different light from the West, being considered a religious, family and social obligation. It is not just a respectable arrangement to allow a man and woman to live together.

Having made up my mind, I had let it be known to my café group (not having any close relations, particularly female, who usually do the scouting around) that I was considering remarrying. Within a matter of days, no less than three of them said they had got to know (through their female relatives) of just the woman for me! The one that sounded most likely to interest me was suggested by Adam, an engineer in private practice. He said he could arrange for me to meet her at his house the following Saturday. His wife would find an excuse to invite her. I agreed.

These meetings are arranged in such a way that they appear to be accidental to the object of scrutiny, so that there would be no loss of face should one not take to the other. Thanks to careful preselection, (a good deal of discussion between the matchmaker and close acquaintances of both sides first take place) a surprisingly high percentage of first meetings result in a measure of some interest being shown, which provides material to work on. After the meeting, both would be privately asked for their impression of the other, and, if both are favourable, then the man wastes no time sending a formal proposal and things pick up pace from that point on. If, on the other hand, one is not too keen about the other, then withdrawal is smooth and painless. Men and women look for different things in a partner. In our society, a man of rank or means has little difficulty finding a wife. Financial security and/or a good family background top the list of eligibility, though physical appearance does count, as does reputation. Age differences play a far lesser role than in the West. Where a large differential exists, it is compatibility that determines success or failure. And there is always support and encouragement available. Computer-matching, which is steadily gaining popularity in the industrialised world, is just another form of arranged marriage, but lacks that vital element of instinctive selection. I put it on a par with consulting the *I Ching* by computer, which shows a lack of understanding of the psychic forces operating when one throws the yarrow sticks or coins.

When Thursday arrived I had an early lunch, my indispensable siesta, and then had tea and biscuits all ready for the coming of Serge and Mr James. Some liked their tea with lemon, others with milk, both with sugar, so I filled a large flask with neat tea for them to choose. I had it with milk myself.

They arrived at 4.30 p.m. sharp, in Mr James' Land Rover, and as I greeted them at the bottom of the veranda steps, the journalist swept his eyes to the distant mountains and clucked in appreciation.

'Lovely view you have here! All I can see from my house in the City are the soulless new government blocks of flats, but I live in more pleasant surroundings abroad.'

'You live abroad as well?' I enquired.

'Mr James actually spends more time abroad than here,' explained Serge. 'His work demands it.'

Mr James (whose first name was Jonathan, but as Serge never used it I did not either, feeling that perhaps he was one of those people who did not encourage intimacy) did not appear to want to talk about himself, though he was not taciturn or unfriendly. I asked him why he was interested in the Mongols, and he said that he wanted to give his readers something different from this and that episode of World War Two, and reports on new war machines. There were always lessons to be learnt from history, he said. I was a bit at a loss to know where to start, but he simplified things by asking me to describe their organisation and tactics.

The history of mankind is one which would be read by morally superior beings with horror and loathing, for it is drenched in blood. Historic figures who fascinate mankind are those who were responsible for terrible destruction and bloodshed, creating never-ending cycles of aggression, repulsion, and counter-aggression. And among these glamorised but essentially monstrous figures, none, until the twentieth century, was more demonic and destructive than Genghis Khan, or, as modern historians prefer to spell his name, Chingis Khan. He left a vast trail of devastation through the Near East and south-eastern Europe, destroying old civilisations in the process.

But to a military historian, Chingis Khan's army displayed many remarkable features and is considered, in fact, to be the first army in history to have been organised along what we call "modern" lines. In fact, it is said that Field Marshal Erwin Rommel, among others, was an enthusiastic student of Mongol tactics at the military academy.

Mr James was scribbling away on his notebook as I spoke,

and even Serge made the odd note. As a result of colonisation, the history being taught in schools tends to echo that taught in European schools, which is predominantly Eurocentric with a bit of local history thrown in. So, much of what I expounded on was unknown to my guests. Mr James, for instance, wanted to know if it was the sheer weight of numbers, the "Golden Horde", which was responsible for the incredible Mongol invincibility which lasted three or four generations. The truth was that they often won despite being greatly outnumbered. (It was not Chingis Khan's army which was called the "Golden Horde", but that of his descendants who conquered Russia and much of eastern Europe.) They prevailed through superior tactics and specialised weaponry, dividing and reuniting their spearheads at will. The ability to maintain communications between widely dispersed forces was crucial to their success.

There was a bit of a question and answer session after that, and then they thanked me and left, Serge looking very pleased, like a proud uncle. I wonder how I would have behaved if I had known that Mr James was anything but a journalist, and that the whole exercise had been to size me up for a future role.

•••••••

The very next day, Friday, came the second appearance of the "Yellow Men", and this time their aim was unmistakable, for they burgled the Ministry of Finance. According to the two watchmen, it was around 4.30 a.m., with dawn just about to break, when shadowy figures jumped over the wall round the car park and were on one of them (the other one was on his round, out front) before he could blow his whistle. They gagged and tied him up and went for the other watchman, whom they soon brought back with them. There were six men in all, described as wearing shorts and canvas shoes but nothing else, and painted yellow all over. They then broke into the building through a window, levering out the iron grill, and opened the back door from inside. The two watchmen were then carried in and dumped in a small store room amid brooms and buckets. After that, they heard occasional splintering and breaking noises echoing down the staircasewell, and assumed that the "Yellow Men" were breaking into rooms and locked cabinets.

The watchmen estimated that they went out of the building about half an hour later, but it was not until the cleaners came at seven o'clock that they were released. The police statement mentioned only that the burglars had ransacked some offices and carried away a few items. No further information was released, and it was left to the two independent newspapers to provide some details. It appeared that the "Yellow Men" (not mentioned by the police) had carried away files and nothing else, and had turned the Minister's office on the third floor upside down, though they had not cracked the safe.

Needless to say, the City was disturbed by this new development, as the "Yellow Men" could no longer be shrugged off as cranks and drug addicts, or members of a witches' coven. And why steal files, unless their purpose was blackmail? Or could it be they had a political aim? The City was rife with speculation and nervousness.

Serge came just as I was finishing my afternoon tea, and burst out straight away, 'The plot thickens, Prof! Do you know who owns the Zedex supermarket, which the "Yellow Men" attacked the first time? None other than our beloved honourable Minister of Finance! Interesting, isn't it?'

'Very interesting indeed, Serge.' I responded. 'Do you think it is a vendetta against the minister? Maybe another minister is trying to undermine his position?'

'Anything is possible, Prof, even a high level conspiracy. Taking away office files suggests that someone expects to find some financial hanky-panky somewhere.'

'So it's blackmail then?'

‘Could be, though I think all that “Firefly” business indicates a political motive to me.’

‘It is the wrong way to set about achieving political ends in my opinion, Serge. Politics means winning the people over, and I don’t see theatrical antics and burglary as likely to achieve that. At any rate, the police will soon be on to them.’

‘Quite right, Prof, quite right.’

There was a glint in his eye that made me suspect he was pulling my leg, and it was probably over my mentioning the police, whom everyone knew were pretty corrupt. Also, their heavy-handed conduct in dealing with demonstrators has not endeared them to the people.

As Saturday arrived, I woke up looking forward to going to Adam’s house to meet the woman recommended as a wife prospect. The feeling of anticipation continued all day, and when the time to go came, I had led myself to believe that she would be a ravishing female, and we would take to each other like a house on fire. But the powers that be seemed to have decided not to let me meet the woman that day, for my faithful Morris absolutely refused to start! No matter what I tried, (the batteries, plugs, carburettor etc. were fine) the engine just would not fire. I returned to the house and rang the nearest garage but they could not spare a mechanic. Another one farther down promised to send one “before sunset”, and I had to settle for that. Ringing Adam to tell him was most embarrassing, and we ended up arranging another day. I had seldom felt so disappointed.

They say that God works in mysterious ways, but for those who do not hold that He interferes personally in the petty affairs of every creature, one may substitute “Destiny” or “Fate”. For, had I gone to Adam’s house, I would not have heard a man on the radio, in a chat programme, suggesting that perhaps the “Yellow Men” came from one of the outlying villages, and that the yellow paint washed off easily and they emerged as ordinary people after a raid. This struck me as being unlikely, unless the entire village was behind them, for in a village everybody knew everybody else, and there were no secrets. In fact, there is a saying which goes, "If you want a faithful wife, marry a village woman, and live there." I could not see, therefore, how all those missing men could have quietly seeped into a village, however large, without the village gendarmerie getting to hear about it. So, if not in the villages, where then?

It was at this point that a little flame of curiosity flickered into life in my mind. As the police seemed to be acting completely in the dark, it might be because they were short of trained detectives. A lot more brawn than brain was being used, and surely, if I brought cold logic and a whiff of psychology to bear, I might crack the riddle. A bit of the old Sherlock Holmes stuff and, who knows, I would receive accolades for meritorious public service!

First I had to get a large-scale map of the City and its environs, and I waited with some impatience for the mechanic to arrive. He arrived an hour later and, to my chagrin, had the car going in no time at all! Damp leads or something, apparently. I still believe it was Fate at work. Soon after breakfast the following morning, Sunday, I spread out the map I had bought on the carpet, where I lay to survey it, chin cupped in hands. With a felt pen I circled the two areas where they had appeared, and then tried to work out possible escape routes. The first incident had been in Main Street itself, and the Ministry was just round from it. The leaflet throwers were the more interesting of the two groups in that they had appeared in broad daylight, down a very busy street. The sheer audacity of it was breathtaking. Now this group was reported to have disappeared down a narrow side street just off the Corner Café, little more than an alley actually, and it joined up with another which ran behind a row of houses, making one long garden wall. In other words, only the residents would be using it and not general traffic. Now if we followed this other alley, it curved back to feed into Main Street several blocks down. So Main Street had to provide the focal escape point. But then to where?

Main Street emptied into Central Square at its inner end, and its distant end bifurcated into Stadium Road and Mountain Road. The former curved towards the sports stadium (erected about fifteen years ago) and Two Sisters suburb beyond; the latter went almost straight up to the ring road, on which one could drive north or south to towns and villages. Surely they must have come in a vehicle which lay in wait somewhere just off Main Street, and then driven up to the ring road, and away to some town or village. For on the other side of ring road was nothing but waste ground with the mountains about a kilometre beyond. The ring road had been constructed on a raised embankment, the ground falling unevenly beyond.

But would they get into the habit of using the ring road with the police closely checking enclosed vehicles at random since the first incident? They must long have come to the conclusion that the raiders had come in a vehicle, probably a van.

I looked at the map again. Could it possibly be the mountains? The western forest, grim and forbidding, was behind them.

It is said that fools walk in where angels fear to tread. Well, I was about to do precisely that.

« FOUR »

It was not until the following morning that another arrangement could be made for the woman and I to meet at Adam's house. It was for "casual" tea this time (with sugar, but no milk), and while chatting with Adam his wife emerged from the kitchen with the tea tray, and just behind her came the woman I was to look over. Adam had already told me that she and her husband had divorced many months ago, their marriage having been childless. Well, this was all right by me as I had no particular desire to father more children, though it could of course have been the husband who was lacking. Her former husband was a policeman, and it is never easy to be the wife of one, the world over.

She proved to be quite an attractive woman in her late thirties or early forties, with a well-looked-after figure and smartly dressed. We did not look directly at one another as that would have been impolite among strangers, but I kept sneaking glances at her. It was obvious that she had not been tipped off as to the reason for my visit, for she showed no particular curiosity about me, talking and laughing quite naturally.

The ladies disappeared upstairs after a while, and I got up to leave.

'Well?' asked Adam, at my car.

'Nice,' I said, 'but give me time to think. I'll ring tomorrow.'

Back at my place I sat back and reviewed my impression of her. As was my custom since the divorce, if I met a woman who struck me as being a good wife prospect – and that had happened about twice before – I'd imagine her in various domestic situations. Like how she was likely to look first thing in the morning, fresh from sleep, with not a trace of make-up and all rumpled up. And then see her moving about the house, attending to household chores, and so on. Also the way she laughed or giggled, and whether she would be an intelligent, attentive listener, or would bore me to death with constant chatter. Was she good-natured, or a regular shrew?

It may sound as if I was being too demanding, and that I was looking for perfection. Perhaps I was, but I had experienced all those things and so knew what to look for. Or thought I did.

Well, this woman at Adam's seemed to pass on most of those points, yet I found myself hesitating. Some instinct told me that the right one was yet to come, and I was now faced with the awkward and difficult task of telling my good friend Adam that I needed more time to think, which he would rightly interpret as meaning no.

I rang Adam in his office the following morning and he said he was most disappointed, and his wife even more so, but added that he understood my reservations. I felt really bad about it, but at least the woman would not be losing face, having been told nothing. I hoped she would find a suitable husband soon.

Gentle rain started falling, but when I looked at the eastern sky I saw that patches of blue were breaking through the dark clouds and I knew that it wouldn't last. The rain had stopped by the time I arrived in town, and I walked to the open-air market to buy fruit and vegetables. It always pained me to see how fruit sellers would bring mountains of mangoes, bananas and pineapples, and then progressively see them rotting away rather than lower the price. They would stick to the same price from the time the fruit was fresh to the time it rotted, which struck me as being very bad business. They would rather sell thirty-nine mangoes at a high price than two hundred at a lower one. The very poor could not afford these prices and were thus deprived of readily available sources of vitamins. Beggars abounded.

I mentioned this fact to fruit sellers (as well as fishmongers), and their answer was always the same: "If I lowered my prices I'd be ostracised!" It should have been up to the government to control prices to help the poor, but it never did.

I stopped off at the Corner Café for a coffee with the group, and as always returned home refreshed.

Then came the midday news, to remind us that something was happening beneath the superficially placid surface of life in Rivenia. The report said that "Yellow Men" had attacked a police station in Fishtail, one of the poorest districts consisting of mud huts and corrugated iron shacks. This station was the largest building in Fishtail and even had detention chambers, often packed with young hooligans and drug addicts.

The "Yellow Men", six of them, had suddenly piled out of a closed van parked just off the building, and had come charging in wielding pistols and revolvers. They rounded up the policemen present and locked them all up in the general office, ripping out the telephones. They then broke open the arms rack and carted away rifles and boxes of ammunition. They released the prisoners from the cells, taking away with them five or six, after which they drove off at high speed. A police car returning from a routine patrol gave chase but lost them in the maze of side streets (if they could be called "streets").

Naturally Fishtail was turned inside out by the police and more people were arrested on suspicion of having helped hide the raiders. The van (stolen) was found abandoned on the outskirts of the district. Only a pair of old sandals and stubbed cigarette butts were found in it.

I climbed the veranda railing to see if Serge was in, but his motorbike was not there in its usual place under a tree. He was hardly ever home these days.

Superstitious people began to link the yellow colour with

magical practices, maintaining that only through witchcraft could the "Yellow Men" have been managing to disappear so swiftly. Some maintained, and the local newspapers were quick to jump on the rumours, that they had the power to make themselves invisible at will, the yellow colour fading away to transparency. But that did not explain the disappearance of the prisoners as well.

Since they had so far posed no threat to civilians, the feeling of the man on the street was one of fascination, rather than fear. In fact, the denizens of the poor districts were beginning to view them as heroes as more "Firefly" graffiti appeared on walls. Little boys would shout "Firefly!" at policemen and women, and then scurry back among the shacks. The chief of police vowed to bring them to heel, or his name was "Horseradish", the choice of which name puzzled people. In fact, it proved to be a mistake on his part because that became his nickname henceforth!

In the days that followed, more young men were reported missing, including a high school student. A general feeling of unease swept through the country. Something very unusual was happening and nobody knew just what. Things seemed to be getting out of hand, and one could sense that the government was beginning to worry. Extra policemen were brought in from the south, and a Special Squad was set up to combat the "Yellow Men". Some of the methods they used soon came in for criticism by the two independent papers.

I returned to the map of the City and its environs, and marked another red circle on where the "Yellow Men" had struck. Once again I worked out the escape route – and again it pointed to Mountain Road, this time detouring past the swampy, uninhabited area to the north. Surely the police would already have worked this out? But judging by the areas they were still pestering people in, they seemed way off. Should I go and see the Commissioner? No. The behaviour of the Special Squad had not endeared itself to me. I'd keep any discoveries I might make to myself, and then discuss what to do with Serge.

As I stood looking at the map I felt the familiar itch left by a stripe-legged mosquito on my ankle, and waving my hand under the table just managed to catch sight of it, abdomen swollen with blood, slowly flying out. I ran round the table and swatted it with my hand, making contact, but I couldn't see where it had fallen on the carpet.

Mosquitoes are really the most remarkable of creatures. If an attack helicopter could do half the things that a mosquito can, it would be an exceedingly formidable machine. Its aerobatic capabilities alone would impose unbearable G-forces on a human pilot, but that is only part of its specification. Just consider this: a mosquito can see in bright sunlight as well as in pitch darkness, which it prefers for security reasons. It can smell its prey from astonishing distances, singling it out from a myriad of other smells that pervade the air. Though its sense of hearing seems to be used mainly to locate the humming of a potential mate, it is said that among sleepers it will make for the one who is snoring gently or making other sounds of deep sleep.

But it has other skills which border on science fiction. For instance, its infrared vision, with which it detects a warm body from a distance – say an animal sleeping under a bush. And, even more fantastic, it singles out those with a high level of lactose in their blood! Now, how does it do this?

I had been seeing Serge on and off over the weeks, helping him patch up his bungalow, and with new veranda supports and a coat of paint it was looking quite respectable.

'If I had bought it in this condition I'd have had to pay twice as much!' he said proudly. His army pension could not have amounted to much, but he never complained. Nor did he ever try to borrow from me.

I had learnt during our conversations that there was hardly anything going on in town that he didn't know about, and the few times I bumped into him in the City he was always talking to somebody. Some called him "Mr Erion", others "Sergeant". More people visited him in a week than visited me in a whole month, but I was to blame for that because I had cut many old ties after moving to Bonelands. I had lost the zest for socialising after the divorce.

Well, one fine morning over coffee at his place it struck me that he might know something about our neighbour's daughter, since she had been drifting in and out of my mind since they came to my place. I could not get over her remarkable resemblance to the woman in the dream.

'Serge,' I asked, making it sound casual, 'are you acquainted with all our neighbours here?'

'A few,' he replied, 'you know people with daughters do not welcome rogue males dropping in uninvited.'

'Do you know the Permanent Secretary and his family?'

Serge had sharply observant eyes, and the way he turned to look at me showed that he was already way ahead.

'You are not getting interested in Zain's daughter, are you? Well, my friend, there is quite a queue for that one, though I find her a bit too thin for me if I have to say. And cold as ice.'

'Well, Serge, I just wanted to know —'

He cut me short, 'I'd advise to forget her, Prof. She is a strange female and no mistake. Thirty years old and still keeps turning down proposals of marriage. You know our girls begin to panic when they reach twenty-five without being hitched up, so how come she is not bothered?'

A sudden anxiety seized me, 'You don't suppose she is not interested in men, do you?'

'Not to my knowledge. No rumours, as far as I know.'

I decided to let the matter drop, and changed the subject.

As coincidence would have it, I returned home two days later to find a folded sheet of paper wedged into the doorframe. When I unfolded it I saw that it was a short letter addressed to me as "Teacher" and signed "A Z". One of my old students, no doubt. I sat down and read:

Dear Teacher,

I made the mistake of mentioning to the girls in the office that you have lots of books, and they have been pressing me ever since to bring them to have a look. Would you let us borrow one or two? I will guarantee their return.

Please let my maid, whom I'll send after lunch, know whether Friday afternoon at about 5 p.m. would suit you.

Sincerely,

A Z

Who else could it be from but my neighbour's daughter? The "Z" stood for Zain, of course, but what did the "A" stand for? A dozen possible names sprang to mind. What a lucky, lucky break, I thought. Here was a golden chance to get to know her, and on my own territory!

When the maid came round – a girl of about fourteen, with a cheeky, flirtatious smile which seemed to suggest that she knew something was afoot as I wished there was! – there could only be one answer, of course. I tipped her handsomely, and that seemed to confirm her suspicion!

Friday finally arrived, and I made sure everything was spotlessly clean in the house. My prized Afghani carpet was given a thorough going over with a soft brush, and then I went into the study and removed any book with naughty illustrations!

For some reason I had butterflies in my stomach and severely rebuked myself for beginning to let matters get out of hand. After all, I was just "Teacher" to her, wasn't I? But why had she not called me "Professor" like everybody else?

When they arrived, leaving the car outside the gate, I went to the end of the veranda to watch them sauntering in, in the manner of our women. They never hurry. My eyes immediately focused on "A Z", noting the upright, smooth-limbed way she walked, and the way her ankle-length yellow skirt swayed with each step. They were all in long skirts and wearing headscarves, hers matching her skirt. A long-sleeved white shirt completed the outfit. To this day I can't remember the colours of the dresses of the other two!

As they got near I moved back to the veranda steps to welcome them. The woman who was probably their office senior was the first up the steps, and gave me a firm no-nonsense handshake. Strictly in order of seniority, next came "A Z", and her hand was soft and cool. And then came a girl of about nineteen, probably just finished school.

They all sat side by side on the sofa, the senior woman in the middle, all smiling expectantly. I could see they were aching to dash into my study, but first had to come tea and chocolate biscuits. To my delight, the moment I mentioned tea "A Z" said, 'We'll look after it. I can see where the kitchen is.' She was followed by the girl, while I exchanged banalities with the woman.

There was no doubt about the effect that "A Z" had on me. That dream must have come up from some unexplained depths of the subconscious, where fantasy and reality, and something else, flowed into one another.

I was careful not to look too long at her, and tried to share my attention equally. When conversation began to show signs of flagging I suggested they look at the books and they literally ran in!

I had been such a hermit that female voices in the building sounded like distant music. What an abnormal life I had been leading! The very bungalow seemed to rejoice.

They came out after quite some time, and I had in fact been helping myself to more tea. Wide smiles emerged from the study, each hugging a volume to her breast. The first one to show me her choice was the girl, and I couldn't help smiling when I saw that it was my thick volume of Gothic horror stories. Then the woman showed me hers, and it was on Japanese gardens. Gardens were a status symbol in Rivenia, and the prettier and more unusual it was, the more cultured the owner was considered to be. I did not take my guests round the house to see mine! "A Z" came up looking a bit apologetic – she was carrying two books. She could have borrowed ten and I'd not have minded!

'Sorry, Teacher, but I couldn't make up my mind,' she explained.

I said I didn't mind at all, seizing the moment to touch her hand as she handed me the books. One was on psychic experiments in Russia, and the other was *Song of the Mystics*. This young woman was searching for something in life, I thought. Perhaps that was one of the reasons she kept turning down those handsome, rich young men who came courting.

As they got up to leave, she asked me a question whose significance emerged only many months later.

'Teacher, were you ever in the army?'

'No. Why do you ask?' I asked in surprise.

'Oh, no particular reason. It's just that you have so many books on war,' she replied, with a rapid flutter of her eyelashes. I watched them all the way to the gate, willing her to look back. But she didn't, and they all got in the car and drove off in the direction of "A Z's" villa.

I stayed on the veranda gazing at the mountains until dusk, feeling a peculiar sadness almost sweet in its intensity. And since it was customary for a woman to introduce herself or another woman as so-and-so's wife, mother or daughter, I was left still not knowing her name!

On the night of 20 October I had a dream which was to shape events. It was another of those very rare dreams which are distinguished by their utter realism and lucidity, the identity of everything being retained to the end.

In this dream, I seemed to be a monitor lizard crawling on the sand, my head about fifteen centimetres above ground. While I was crawling, skirting boulders and carefully avoiding large, hairy desert scorpions, I suddenly noticed two unusual objects in front, like two marble pillars. They turned out to be human legs, barefoot, but I could raise my eyes no higher than the knees.

An arm then appeared, holding a stick, as the man bent down (as he must have done, though I could still not see the upper part of his body) to place the longer tip of the forked stick on the sand. He then drew a perfect circle, and laid the stick across it.

Just then a gust of wind blew up and I had to shut my eyes and look away to protect them. When I looked back the legs had disappeared, as had the circle and the stick. I stood on my hind legs and looked all round, but all I could see was sand and round boulders of various sizes, stretching to infinity.

I woke up knowing that my psychic faculties had been at work and, in highly symbolic form, were trying to tell me something. But however hard I tried I simply could find no meaningful interpretation of that dream.

On the following Sunday, I woke up late and missed the morning news on the radio, so it was Serge who came strolling round to tell me. I was having breakfast at the time. Serge didn't stay any longer in bed than was absolutely necessary, and often the sudden roar of his motorbike as he started it would briefly interrupt my sleep, very early in the morning.

'Heard the news, Prof?' he asked.

'What news?' I enquired. It had to be important for him to have come at that unusual time.

'The "Yellow Men" have broken into the Rockside high security prison and released about forty prisoners, most of them political. There was quite a firefight with the guards. Blew holes in two walls with dynamite. It happened just before dawn, as usual.'

This was astonishing news, indeed. It was a dramatic escalation of their assaults, and revealed much increased strength and advanced planning. He said that some seven guards had been killed and wounded, but the "Yellow Men" had carried away their casualties so there were no figures for them. We chatted a bit, had a coffee, and he left.

I went to look at the map to locate Rockside prison. It was a high-walled complex just north of the Two Sisters suburb, built on former marshland. Main Street, the Ministry of Finance, Fishtail police station, and now Rockside prison. What did they have in common, location-wise?

Suddenly the dream overlapped the map. Was this the answer?

I realised that it was all wildly imaginative, but if we took the circle as representing the ring road, the forked stick would be Main Street splitting up into Stadium Road and Mountain Road. Now the former curves round and then links up with the Two Sisters suburb, the abode of the nouveau riche, so no joy there. If we took the longer side of the fork as being Mountain Road, this in the dream went over the circle. Elementary, my dear Watson. Beyond the road were the mountains, and the forest behind. If we paid any attention to the dream, the answer was here, and it made sense. Only in the mountains and the forest could a group of men hide away and yet be within a short distance from the city centre.

Well, if it was so obvious and logical, then the security forces will long have figured that out, so what was new?

Nevertheless, I thought I should discuss it with Serge and walked across to his place. I stopped at the gate when I saw that his motorbike was not in the shade by the side of his house.

Then I thought of finding out more about the mountains from the Forestry Department, where one of my café group worked, and dressed up and drove down. "Forestry and Mines" was on the ground floor of the Ministry of Natural Resources, and I soon found the "greenhouse" where he worked. After expressing surprise to see me we went into his small office and sat down.

'Now Prof, what brings you to the jungle? We are the least visited ministry in the world, I think!'

'I have become deeply interested in entomology, Raufi, and have learnt that the mountains teem with some pretty rare types. Any info you can give?'

'The mountains, Prof? Our own protectively dressed men are not too happy when we send them there twice a year to collect snake venom. Last year a small team – about six of them, I think – came here from America to collect specimens. They were so insistent that we finally gave them permission to go. They said they had been in the jungles of New Guinea and Brazil, and knew how to look after themselves. We didn't know then, alas, that the "green demon" had much increased in numbers.'

'The green demon?' I asked. 'What's that?'

'It's a green spider which must have evolved fairly recently there, perhaps coming from the forest behind. It certainly wasn't around forty years ago when mining was going on. Zinc, but it soon became uneconomical and they packed up and left.'

This was getting interesting. Mines. What better place to hide in?

'I suppose all the tunnels and things are still there?'

'No. The government had them all dynamited when they became the favourite hiding place for assorted criminals and smugglers. Some gun battles took place and, in fact, the tunnels were sealed up with some of them still inside, refusing to come out. The mountains are said to be haunted; people walking on the ring road still claim to hear distant screams on some nights.'

A grim picture, indeed, on which I did not dwell.

'What happened to the entomologists?' I asked.

'When they did not return the following day as arranged we sent out a suitably clothed search party. They were found scattered among the bushes at the foot of the mountains, all dead.'

'Dead? Why?'

'They were covered with rusty-brown blotches, and our men had to brush off some spiders, green in colour, from their bodies. It was fortunate they were wearing heavy gloves because when they brought one of the spiders back for investigation we discovered that it carried a toxin which killed a rat in a few seconds. Even that of a large viper takes several minutes!'

Well, puff went my theory of the "Yellow Men" hiding in the mountains. Not with those spiders about.

On the drive back down the ring road I slowed down to a crawl as I took a long look at the mountains, a bare kilometre away. Rocky outcrops and scrubland lay in-between, reputed to be full of snakes. Then I stopped the car as I saw a group of animals in the distance and could just make out that they were mountain goats. Surely if goats could meander round the mountains, and probably on them, those spiders must be restricted to a small area? It could have been pure bad luck that the Americans had bumped into a nest of them.

In a fit of daring I made up my mind right there and then to visit the mountains. I'd do it suitably dressed, and with utmost caution.

I chose Sunday morning, very early, for my trip. All geared up in my hunting jacket and baggy trousers tucked into high boots, and with a wide-brimmed hat on, I carried a travelling bag which had, in addition to my picnic basket and a flask of tea, an insect spray, a bottle of antiseptic and a sharp-pointed commando knife. I also had my 8 x 35 binoculars around my neck.

Finding a place where the embankment was just about a metre high, I stopped the car, locked it, and jumped down. The bushes were widely scattered and formed no barrier, but I was on the lookout for the reported venomous snakes. And I soon saw one, basking in the weak early morning sun on a rock. Snakes at that time of day would be too sluggish to attack, so I just made sure that I did not step on one.

From the ring road the bushes had not revealed that the land kept dropping as one went towards the mountains, so that halfway down I looked back and couldn't see my car at all!

Clearing the last clumps of bushes I found myself standing on the lip of a steep but short drop to a flat and smooth area, about one hundred metres to the mountain foot, which, when I scrambled down, I discovered to be made of baked clay cracked into irregular shapes. As it stretched all the way from the thick foliage in the east, right across the mountains, to disappear into the forested west, I assumed it was an old riverbed. Just the odd shrub grew from the fissures, so perhaps the stratum of clay did not go very deep. I wondered how long ago the river had dried up, and why.

I stood in the middle of it and with my binoculars surveyed the mountains all down the line. There was no indication anywhere of where a tunnel might have been, or any trace of irregularity in the mountain face which was quite steep, becoming almost perpendicular from about a third of the way up. The mountain range was highest in the far north-east (which I could see from my bungalow), and at this juncture it was about five hundred metres high in places, but generally lower.

Bushes, shrubs and creepers grew all the way up to the top, and I noticed an unusual plant with heart-shaped red leaves growing from cracks in the mountain face.

Up the mountainside a bit off to the left I suddenly saw what appeared to be a terrace (like they cut for rice planting) and after searching a bit (I had completely forgotten about the snakes and the spiders!) found a gradient shallow enough to climb up, with the help of a thick stick which I cut and trimmed from a smooth-branched bush. Feeling like an old-time explorer, I heaved my way up and with some difficulty made it to what proved to be indeed a terrace, wrapped round the mountain-fold and about three metres wide. Like the riverbed, its floor was of cracked clay, with tiny little flowering plants growing in the fissures. I wondered if long ago some medicine man had cultivated special herbs on it.

I chose a place where the mountain face was smooth and I could sit leaning against it. I was about twelve metres from the bottom and was astonished when I looked in the direction of the ring road and could just make out my car roof! From that height I had expected to see all of it, the bushes in-between being quite low. I could not understand how dry scrubland could be literally within sight of thick foliage, but it probably had to do with type of soil and subterranean streams.

I was beginning to feel relaxed and peaceful, the purpose of my trip forgotten, as I had a cup of tea and dipped into the picnic basket. I intended to walk down all the way to the forested western side and to continue looking for the old tunnels.

It was at this point that a momentary, tiny flash, like a drop of rain reflecting the sun, on a bush on the lip of the terrace caught my attention. There it came again, as a small creature jumped down and came rapidly towards me. I recognised it when it was about two metres away. It was a spider, and it was shining green. Ah, I thought, so this was the "green demon"!

Well, I had seen it, and was fully prepared.

Protected by my high boots, and with the stick in my hand, I watched it with interest as it slowed on getting near, crouching low, and proceeding step by long-legged step. From head to abdomen it must have been about five centimetres long, and it was all green apart from its legs, which were jet black. Spiders, even the notorious black widow, are not aggressive towards people so this one must be just curious about this strange, giant visitor, and would soon turn back. It stopped just a step away, and I stamped my boot by way of warning. For a moment it seemed about to turn away, when it suddenly drew its legs in and leaped into the air! I lurched back, making painful contact with the mountain face. It landed on top of my left boot, a matter of two or three centimetres from my trouser leg! As I bent down to hit it with the stick I saw that it was biting into the leather, and its mandibles seemed to have achieved some penetration. That took care of my complacency and I knocked it off with the stick. It fell down and lay on its back, its legs clawing at the air and its mandibles working. I bent down to have a closer look, having to admit that it was a beautiful creature, shining like a green jam. Admiration stopped when it righted itself and turned to face me! I quickly crushed it with the stick.

I packed the picnic things, keeping a sharp eye open for any little glints and movements, and scrambled down to the riverbed. To prove to Serge that I had actually been to the dreaded mountains (why was I so keen to prove to him that I was just as adventurous as he was?) I eased off one of the red plants which was already flowering. The leaves looked, and even felt, like plastic, thick and smooth, and the flowers were the shape of tulips, yellow on the outside but greenish inside. I knew next to nothing about plants, but I thought this one could be a type of orchid. I carefully gathered the soil on which it had been growing, as well as bits of rock around it. I had to make it feel at home in my greenhouse.

It was already beginning to get hot, so after my experience with the spider I did not now want an encounter with a fully awakened snake. I carefully trod my way between bushes and around boulders, breathing a sigh of relief when I was finally sitting in my car.

It had been a bit of an anticlimax, in a way, because I had seen nothing to suggest human presence. No wonder the security forces had long discarded the possibility of the "Yellow Men" hiding in the mountains or the forest behind. So it was back to the drawing board for me, for I intended to pursue my investigations.

As I drove back, what I didn't know was that I was carrying a passenger and a most unwelcome one!

Hospital Road is roughly halfway between Mountain Road and Bonelands, and this fact was to save my life.

I had just driven past it, on my left, when I felt something land lightly on my left shoulder, like a bit of sponge. Wondering what it could be – perhaps a small twig falling off my wide-brimmed hat – I turned to look. Just then what felt like a red-hot needle plunged into my shoulder. I gave a half-scream of agony and saw what it was. A green spider, large and glossy, was firmly fixed to the back of my shoulder so that I had to raise my chin and twist my neck to see it fully. My right hand instinctively left the steering wheel and swiped it off. My left hand had also followed the lowered shoulder so that the car swerved on to the grassy verge, nearly turning over. I quickly got the car back on the road and braked. Then I jumped out, leaving the door open, and quickly looked around for a stick or a largish stone but could not see any.

I returned to the car and peered carefully under the seats and the dashboard. Not a trace of it. Nor was it under the back seats.

Finally I found it wedged between the passenger seat support and the door, glistening like a precious gem. I took out my commando knife, went round to open the door, and as it righted itself to leap out I skewered it through the thorax. Its legs waved wildly as I looked closely at it, noting that its underside was really black and not green. I took it to the verge and, placing it on the ground pushed the sharp point of the knife deeper into it. The movements were already getting feebler, so it had to be dying. I propped it carefully on the passenger seat and returned to the driving seat.

In my excitement I had forgotten about the pain, but now it returned, a dull, throbbing ache. I couldn't bring myself to believe that a single bite could really kill me, but I had no idea what to do when one was bitten by such a venomous creature, so I decided to go to the hospital and swung the car round. It was when I was shifting to top gear that I began to feel a certain numbness in my left fingers. When I was at Hospital Road, changing down to swing into it, my entire arm felt stiff. This won't do at all, I told myself, the numbness seems to be accelerating.

I made straight for the emergency entrance, over the protests of the gate attendant, and came to a juddering stop for I could brake but no longer change gear. When I showed him the skewered spider he ran round to help me get out, for my left leg had also lost all feeling.

At the reception counter I just had time to blurt out, 'Spider!' and place it and the knife on the counter when my legs gave way, and the attendant caught me. I was out to the world after that.

When I came to I was in bed in a private room, with only another bed in sight which was empty. I was totally naked (one never quite gets over the humiliation), with a sheet covering my lower body. A drip was sticking out of my arm. I couldn't remember how I had got there for a few minutes, and thought it was another of those lucid dreams. I must have been on the first floor for I could see the top of a small tree outside the window, with the sun playing on its leaves. Then memory flooded back, and I quickly looked at my left shoulder. It was not bandaged and looked swollen and purplish. I rued the impulse that had made me go on that stupid trip.

A few minutes later a nurse came in, all smiles and goodwill (unusual in our hospitals where nurses seemed to resent patients), and took my pulse and blood pressure.

'Almost back to normal,' she said, giving me a pat on the cheek. A motherly sort. 'I'll call the doctor. You are lucky he is here. The best in the country on venoms.'

The doctor, a beefy-looking man who wheezed a bit as he talked (probably smokes too many cigars, I thought, for he certainly smelled of tobacco), came in and checked the bed chart. Then he examined my eyes, grunting.

'Well, you seem to have got away with it. How did you come to get involved with these spiders? They are only found in the mountains.'

I explained that I was an amateur botanist and had learned of strange plants there.

'Don't you know that it is forbidden to go there? There is a large notice off the ring road.'

I swore I hadn't seen it.

'Ah well, we shan't inform the police, don't worry. But I don't want to see you here again!'

I asked him how long I had been out, what else there was to be done, and when I could go home.

He said I had been unconscious for two hours, and that they had done all that was necessary.

'You'd not have liked some of the things we did to you to clean you out. Ha! Ha! Ha!' The man was a monster.

'You'll be having your lunch in a few minutes. We'll see if you can keep it down, before deciding whether to release you. By the way, there is a small charge to pay for the room. Oh, another thing,' he added, 'your khaki jacket and vest absorbed much of the venom. That's a pretty big specimen you brought us. Worse than a large viper.' And with these reassuring words, he left.

Lunch came and I got it down without much difficulty. I was not sick afterwards, so in the late afternoon they brought me my clothing and I got dressed. They had cleaned the jacket and vest, and they were spotless. A resurgence of pain was controlled by painkillers ("It'll go away in a day or two") and they released me at 4.30 p.m.

I complimented them on the efficiency and friendliness of their section. The doctor told me to take it easy for a couple of days.

The first thing I did on getting back home was to place the travelling bag right in the middle of the garden, and then take out one item at a time, ready to jump back at the first flash of green. It was clean, so I went back to the car and peered and prodded everywhere. Then I thoroughly sprayed insecticide under the seats, the mudguards, and anywhere likely to provide a hiding place. After that I took the plant to a pot in the garden shed and carefully surrounded it with the mountain soil and small rocks. The roof of the shed had transparent plastic panels, so I placed the pot where it'd get the kind of sunlight it received on the mountainside, no more, no less. Plants are sensitive things, and you can be sure that the rarer the plant, the more sensitive it'd be. So I was only half-hopeful that it would catch.

How was I to know that that plant would play a most crucial role in my life? No instinct had warned me.

As far as my investigative work was concerned, I was virtually back to square one. I had seen for myself that no human being could survive for long in that area. The spiders, more than the snakes, were the guardians of the mountain and forest in that area. So I had to go back to the map and look at the City even more closely, but to my knowledge no underground drainage or sewage system was of such a size as to accommodate even stooping figures, let alone upright ones.

So they had to be collecting outside the City but, if so, what about the police checkpoints? And where outside the City? Certainly not in a village where even a stray dog would soon be noticed.

A possible hiding place for scores of men would probably be in the caves of the ravine north of the ring road, but I had to rule them out because of the steepness of the sides. Anyone on the Northern Bridge had a clear view down both ways. Even if the "Yellow Men" themselves were fit enough to go up and down the ravine, the forty released prisoners from Rockside prison most certainly would have baulked at it.

Perhaps the man who might throw some light on this whole "Firefly" business was Serge. Up to then we had only talked about the incidents without going any further than that, but Serge was the kind of man who had his ear close to the ground. Very little happened in the country which he didn't know about.

It was not until days later than Serge returned, and I was particularly keen now to know if there was any chance of the "Firefly" incidents being linked with the continuing stories of young men reported missing. Parents were petitioning the police for official information. What if there was a terrible serial killer of young men on the prowl? People were getting frantic and it was getting more embarrassing for the government. The radio and many newspapers were under state control, but calling the "Yellow Men" drug-crazed thugs and criminals did not deceive or impress the man in the street. The proliferation of "Firefly" graffiti alone showed that this man or group was emerging as a kind of Robin Hood. People were at first appalled, and then increasingly delighted as the weeks passed and no "Yellow Man" was caught.

So when Serge came round next I wasted no time in broaching the subject.

'Serge, do you think there's any connection between this "Firefly" thing and the missing youths?'

We were out on the veranda and had been gazing at the mountains. For some reason, I could not (and still can't) look at mountains without feeling a pull towards them.

He turned and looked at me humorously.

'And how am I expected to know that, Prof? Your guess is as good as mine.'

'Oh, come, Serge!' I retorted, 'you move around a lot more than I do, and have your ear to the ground. Surely you must know something?'

He thought for a moment and said, 'Tell me what you think first, and then I'll give you my honest opinion.'

'Well, either these young people are stowing away on-board ship at Port Clearwater, or they are being kidnapped by these Yellow characters.' The port was 400 kilometres away and belonged to our western neighbour. (Not to be confused with our south-western neighbours, who were to cause such conflict the following year.)

'That makes sense,' said Serge, 'except that there has been no evidence of kidnapping. Wherever they have gone, I think they have gone voluntarily and the police know it. They must have seen the leaflets circulating in the poorer quarters.'

'What leaflets?'

'Leaflets recruiting for the "Firefly" movement, with instructions on what to do.'

I had not heard of the leaflets even from my café group.

'If so, surely it'd be child's play for the police to follow those instructions and nab them? It sounds most peculiar to me.'

'Well, I'm only telling you what I know. I have no idea how they manage to get recruits and escape surveillance at the same time. They must have a pretty efficient system, nevertheless, to have got away with it so far.'

I had to let it go at that, but was curious to know if Serge knew anything about the "Firefly".

'Is this "Firefly" a real man, or just a cover name for a group? Is he one of those characters setting himself up as a future warlord?'

To my utter astonishment he replied, 'The "Firefly" is a man, all right. In fact, I met him about ten years ago.'

'What? You know him?' I couldn't help shouting.

'Easy now, Prof. We don't want passers-by to hear.'

My mouth must have been gaping open, because he looked at me with amusement. All these months and Serge had not said a word about knowing the "Firefly" but I was so anxious to hear about it that I felt no resentment.

'All right, I'll tell you all about it. I didn't really think it would be wise to do so, as you might misunderstand and probably tell somebody else. Our jails here are not for gentlemen, I assure you.'

I waited, breathless, for him to continue.

'I was in the northern village of Isfahar at a meeting of the elders to discuss the digging of new wells. I had just married my second wife, so I remember the precise day and month. We heard a commotion outside and when it went on I got up and went to see what was happening. There was this thin, scholarly type of man with a beard, struggling with two of our men. When he saw me he shouted, 'They are stopping me from addressing the elders. I *must* speak to them!' Well, he had a cultured voice, and did not look mad, so I asked them to release him. I told him to wait and went inside to tell the elders.'

He paused and was deep in thought for several minutes. I was inwardly rejoicing. At last I had an idea what the "Firefly" looked like.

'Unfortunately the elders declined to admit him, saying that it was nearly prayer time, and we had to complete the agenda. It was a decision that they were to bitterly regret in the years to follow.'

As it seemed to be a painful memory to him, I sat still and said nothing until he resumed.

'You see, he went from one village to another, preaching a return to our ancestral ways, to the time of the Twelve Elders. In the end he fell foul of the police and they took him in. He was to spend the next four years in jail, without once being brought to trial. His wife died while he was in prison. She happened to have come from my own part of the country.'

It was the only time I was to see Serge close to tears, and to save him from embarrassment I asked to hear what happened next.

'When they released him he was given assistance to go abroad. He returned two years ago and disappeared. Nobody knows where he is, but we can see he is alive and well, can't we?' he concluded, enigmatically.

'Serge, are you on his side by any chance? The man is going to end up on the gallows, you know. There is no way he can overthrow this government. The army and the police are solidly behind it.'

'Well, I consider myself on the side of the people. I ask myself, are the people behind this government? Anyway, Prof, I have to be going.'

He left me in some state of confusion, having had to revise my view of the "Firefly". Did I still want to find out where he was hiding? To what end? To see him and his followers hanged or shot?

I intended to continue with my investigations, no longer with the aim of presenting my findings to the security forces, but as an intellectual exercise.

I mulled over what Serge had told me about the "Firefly" (and, in the process, revealed that he had been married at least twice) and I began to feel some sympathy for the man. Up to then I had not really thought of him as a human being but as a symbol of rebellion, justified or not. While I was not one of those who actively benefited from the regime, I was not too unhappy with the status quo as I was living my life pretty much as I wanted. Like all my colleagues and friends, I had little or no contact with the likes of Fishtail residents, and shut my eyes and ears to their suffering. In fact, we blamed them for the rising crime rate and accepted corruption in high places as an unavoidable fact of life.

•••••••

I was meticulous in my care of the mountain plant, and daily I checked its condition and even spoke to it, knowing that there was much evidence to indicate that plants have astonishing sensitivity, bordering on the psychic. They seem to know when they are loved or disliked, and react accordingly. My plant had shed a few of its glossy red leaves, but it appeared to be holding its own. Two fresh blossoms had emerged, and that was a good sign. If it was of the orchid family then I had been doing the right thing in giving it very little water, just about the amount it would get from overnight condensation on the mountain spot.

But if it was an orchid, where was the special kind of ant that mysteriously appeared where there was an orchid growing, seeming to provide some vital service? I could see none, and it had been there many days. In fact, I had feared that the large, voracious black ants in the garden (which fortunately attack just about anything except human beings and the larger animals) would be drawn to the nectar in the flowers, and maybe chew them up. But they were totally disinterested, ignoring the plant's presence and not even bothering to climb up the pot to investigate. There was often a bee or a butterfly on the flowers of the other plants in the shed which I was using as a glasshouse, but I never saw one on my orchid. Perhaps the nectar was not sweet, or appealed only to a certain kind of wasp or fly.

That particular morning I noticed that the largest, and hence the oldest, flower was beginning to droop, and I could only hope that this did not mean the plant was too homesick to survive. I gave it a bit more water, just in case I had been giving it too little.

I was strongly tempted to show it to Serge, but then I'd have to tell him the whole story, including the spider bite, and I feared that it might make him change his opinion of me. After all, I had acted in a most juvenile manner, like playing chicken.

I decided to say nothing to anyone.

« FIVE »

With a peculiar sense of humour, but effective timing, the "Firefly" chose 31 October, Halloween, for his next armed raid against the government. And he chose a risky target – the large precinct police station at Two Sisters. With an estimated thirty men he stormed the complex at his favourite time of around 4 a.m., finding practically everybody fast asleep. The "Yellow Men" were well armed this time with assault rifles and pistols, and their objectives seemed to be the administrative building and the armoury. Only the sergeant at the reception desk and a constable saw them rushing in but had no time to raise the alarm. Since there can hardly be a safer place than a Police Headquarters, there was no guard on watch. They forced the sergeant to open the armoury door and also ransacked offices. Not a shot was fired during the whole raid, and they faded away as swiftly as they had come, leaving the two policemen tied up to be discovered later by a returning patrol car.

Halloween meant nothing to the vast majority of Rivenians, but the choice of the Two Sisters Police Headquarters was significant in that it was a suburb inhabited almost exclusively by the bourgeoisie, the new rich, the cosmopolitan crowd, who would definitely know about Halloween. Many, in fact, would have gone out to parties, some reputed to be pretty wild!

So this was a message directed at the complacent well-offs, of that I was sure. It also made the security forces (and hence the government) look totally weak and inept. The newspapers would certainly seize on the Halloween angle, and it might even now appear in the foreign media and cause a few titters.

I was impatient for Serge to come, having gone to his place only to find that he was not in. I had heard the news at twelve noon, so I went on with my usual routine of prayer, lunch and siesta. His motorbike roared in as I was having afternoon tea.

'Well now, Prof, I have brought you a present for once!' he said, handing me a little parcel.

I opened it and found raisin cookies.

'Home-made,' he added, 'straight from my niece!'

He was in high good humour, and I had a shrewd suspicion that "niece" wasn't the right word. The old man had some head of steam left. But I was anxious to talk about the raid, and asked him if he knew.

'Oh, yes, a bit of excitement at Two Sisters. Perhaps the police will now pay more attention to their own security! They have been going round arresting people right, left and centre, beating up some. Closing the gate after the horse has fled, I call it.'

'The radio didn't give many details, as usual. For instance, how did thirty men get into town and out again without anyone knowing how?'

'Well, Prof, I understand you know the police Commissioner very well, so why don't you go and ask him? Also one or two of your café friends is sure to have inside information.'

I had not expected this response and protested. 'The Commissioner is no friend of mine. The last time I met him was two years ago at the club. I can't say I liked him much. He has an air of arrogance about him. My café friends are more interested in the good things of life, and care only about what impacts on their lives. They know only what they hear on the radio and read in the papers.'

'Is that so? Ah, well. Perhaps there is hope for you yet,' he said with a straight face.

'This "Firefly" seems to be a tactical genius, Serge. Or

maybe just exceptionally lucky. He has got away with raid after raid, leaving the security forces floundering like the Keystone Cops. Is he using magic?'

Serge gave me a strange look which I could not decipher. He stood up as if to leave, then changed his mind and sat down again.

'Prof, troubled times lie ahead. I look upon you as a friend, so I am giving you some solemn advice. Let things be. Do not seek to know too much. And watch your tongue at the café.'

I found these words quite astonishing. What had I said or done to require these warnings? Just a minute! Had Serge somehow found out about my trip to the mountains? He couldn't possibly have, or he would have berated me for it. So he had to be talking generally.

'I mind my own business, Serge, but that doesn't mean I should not be interested in what's going on in the country.'

He placed his hand on my shoulder in placation. 'I didn't mean to offend you, Prof. It is just that we are sitting on a bit of a time bomb at the moment. Soon brother may be pitted against brother.'

'I think you are taking this "Firefly's" challenge to the government far too seriously, Serge. Believe me, every man has his price. Having made his point, he will be just ripe for a deal with the government which will see him well provided for, for the rest of his life. And the "Yellow Men" will be happily paid off, and that will be that!'

To my relief (for the atmosphere was a bit tense), he smiled.

'You may be right, but I very much doubt it. Which reminds me, a good friend of mine found your exposition on the Mongols of great interest. He'd like to meet you in the next few weeks. He's out of the country at the moment. He thinks you'll make a good historian.'

'What does this friend do?' I asked.

'He raises camels,' he replied with a laugh.

When Serge drove off I was left wondering what all that had been about. I seemed to remember his telling me weeks before that he had a friend in the police, which was why I assumed he'd have inside information. Quite apart from the fact that he had a wide circle of acquaintances. But we all have our moods, and he'd add something later, perhaps.

The builder who put up my bungalow must have misread the site plan or something, because the gate and driveway were directly in line with the side of the building. This was a real nuisance as there was no way I could see the gate without first having to go to the western end of the veranda, the side wall being blank. The windows in my sitting room and study all faced north, looking over the veranda floor. To reposition the gate and drive would be quite a costly exercise, so I thought of placing a suitably sized mirror in the front court in such a way, and at such an angle that I'd see the gate from either the study or where I normally sit on the veranda. Such an arrangement was, in fact, in use for drivers in a couple of our streets which met in a "T" and were very narrow. I had put up with the inconvenience because I seldom had visitors, but after the hibernation I intended now to return to a fairly active social life, and not put off people from visiting me. Since I spent most of my time indoors in my study, or out on the veranda, it'd be good to have a sneak view of whoever was coming without having to expose myself. Just in case I had to put on a shirt over my habitual vest.

So I drove into town the following day and bought a large mirror, 110cm x 60cm and took it round to a carpenter's for framing and subsequent mounting on site. He brought it in his van in the afternoon, and after many trials found the best spot and height for it, about three metres in front of the veranda. It certainly looked odd, perched on its two legs dug into the ground, but it worked. Later the legs would be hidden behind flower plants. The top of the mirror was protected from sun and rain by an aluminium canopy.

The mirror gave me an extraordinary feeling of security. Whoever came (beginning with the noise of the creaking of the steel gate) would now be known to me long before he or she knew whether I was in or not. For a car in the carport is not a guarantee that the owner will be in.

I was not to know that the first person I'd see reflected in that mirror would be a most unwelcome individual, a veritable "bird of ill omen", as the Elders would say.

Monday is a hateful day for those who go out to work, but it is a welcome day for the retired and the unemployed. It is Sunday that is ironical to the latter, a day of rest for those who least require rest.

And so it was for me that Monday morning in November, when I was preparing to go and join my café group. I heard the groaning of my front gate and I took a peep in the mirror. I saw two men coming through the gate, one slightly ahead of the other in a manner that suggested authority. Having been regular with my income tax, electricity bill, and so on, I had nothing to worry about, but fretted at this inconvenient timing.

I received them at the veranda steps and, after the customary greetings, asked if I could help them. The obvious senior of the two, a broad-faced man of average height, with a stubby nose and receding hairline, spoke.

'We are sorry to disturb you, sir, but we are making routine inquiries. This is Corporal Slana, and I am Lieutenant Zuki of the Special Squad, anti-terrorist section.' His voice was low and respectful, and yet I had heard stories of the brutality of this squad.

'I fail to see the connection with myself, Lieutenant.' I was annoyed and curious at the same time. Perhaps I'd learn something new.

'Well, gentlemen like you are very observant, so you may have noticed something unusual in the area. A new face, a change in someone's routine, an unfamiliar car, and that kind of thing.'

He was watching me closely, but I thought the whole thing quite ridiculous. What "Yellow Man" would pick on Bonelands to hide in?

'I can't say I have noticed anything unusual in this area. Bonelands has nowhere for anyone to hide, and a stranger would stand out like a giraffe among camels.'

'That's very good to hear, sir, as we now can eliminate this area. But just for the record, would you mind if we looked round a bit? The captain said to look for anything picked up in all innocence at the scene of the assaults. It'll just take us a couple of minutes.'

'I'm sorry, Lieutenant, but I am getting late for a meeting in town, so if you will excuse me…' making to go inside the house. But he made no move to leave.

Suddenly his expression changed as he lashed out, 'And what were you doing in the mountains?'

This came as such a shock that I was nonplussed for a moment. So somebody had seen me after all. But in an instant I decided to brazen it out.

'But I have never been to the mountains!' I replied.

Quite unexpectedly the corporal came to my rescue, just as I was wondering how to explain it away. My mouth was going dry.

'Your car was seen on the embankment, at its lowest point,' he blurted out. A look of acute annoyance appeared on Zuki's face.

The corporal had obviously spoken out of turn and received a stern look which made him take a step back. Zuki had wanted to keep me guessing how they had come to know about it. My own fear had been that somebody at the hospital had told the police. I now knew where I stood, and my mind switched on its afterburners.

'Oh, you mean about two weeks ago? Or was it a week?' I said. 'I stopped there because I was feeling sick in the stomach and did not want to vomit in my car. So I ran down to the bushes.'

'The bushes, eh? No fear of snakes? Brave man!' he said, sarcastically.

'Now look here, Lieutenant Zuki. I was a hunter in my youth and know more about wildlife than you'll ever know. Snakes are harmless if you leave them alone. If they bite you it is poison wasted as far as they are concerned, since they can't eat you.'

'I'm grateful for the lesson in nature, sir, but what were you doing that early in the morning? Not you usual habit, is it?'

He nearly had me there, but it is amazing how inventive the mind can get under duress.

'Well, Lieutenant, I am almost afraid to tell you. You see, I was carrying out speed tests.'

He did a double take, an incredulous look on his face.

'Speed tests? In a Morris 1000? Why, had you had it souped up for racing?'

'No, I have had one of the new variable-pitch fans installed, and I wanted to see how much it added to the top speed.'

'Oh, I see. And does it really work? Could you manage say, 150 kph?'

The speed limit on the ring road was 100 kph, but I doubted if he'd take any action even if I mentioned exceeding that.

'Well, my car is an old one, and I haven't had it souped up, so the best I got out of it was 110 kph.'

'Hardly worth all the money you wasted on the fan, was it?' he added, quite reasonably.

'The engine sounds happier, and there is a slight increase in acceleration, so I'm not complaining.'

‘May I see it?’ I had expected this question and knew that the worst was over, for I had indeed had one fitted a couple of months before.

After seeing it he said they might have to come round again in the fairly near future for random searches. The captain wanted it.

When they had left, I got in my car and drove to the City to the Corner Café. That mountain trip, totally unnecessary, had so far brought me nothing but danger and anxiety. But that was not the end of the story. Far from it.

After the Halloween raid the City as a whole began to exude a certain amount of nervousness. If these bandits could attack a large police station and get away with it, then there was no knowing what else they could do, was there? They could blow up the parliament building, or the electricity generating station, or drug the water supply! Anything was possible.

This nervousness was reflected at the café in the way everybody carefully kept away from the subject of the “Yellow Men”, which was a pity, for I was dying to know how they viewed the whole business. And at least one of them had a close relation in the security forces.

As everywhere in the world during times of uncertainty, there was a sudden re-awakening of interest in what are loosely called the “psychic sciences” and much of the conversation that morning revolved round such things as the tarot, cartomancy, astrology, and so on. Even the *I Ching* was mentioned (mispronounced as usual, as it overwhelmingly is in the Western world. I always judged the seriousness of the advocate on the basis of how he or she pronounced “I Ching” and wrote off as mere dabblers those who called it “Eye Ching”) but I did not rise to the bait.

I found Adam the most interesting of the lot with his new-found interest in numerology. As an undergraduate I had been keenly interested in Chinese numerology, and had even worked out my own system, which one day I was going to take out and re-examine.

Adam, earnestly trying to convince bored sceptics, chose to quote from Pythagoras, a revered figure in mathematical lore: "Number is the essence of all things, and is the metaphysical principle of rational order in the universe."

I agreed entirely and made a mental note to invite Adam for tea and discussion one day.

Driving back to Bonelands, I saw a group of municipal workers washing off "Firefly" graffiti from the side wall of an office building, surprisingly high up. The penalty for defacing public property was quite severe.

Back at home I felt an urge to speak to Serge, and seeing that his bike was there I went straight away. He was so elusive nowadays.

'There is plenty of fine, long-grained rice cooking in the pot,' he said, 'so you can stay for lunch.'

I thanked him, but had to decline. I had a leg of chicken and olives waiting for me.

'Serge, I was visited by the law this morning.'

His eyes narrowed, but he sounded casual. 'Oh? And what did they want? Caught speeding again?' his expression changing little.

I briefly related what had happened, giving Serge the same story I had given the police. He looked at me with a quizzical expression.

'I know you were a sports car fanatic in your young days, but really, Prof, aren't you getting on a bit for that kind of thing?'

'You are a fine one to talk, Serge, with your 500cc job!'

'Ah,' he smiled, 'but I have to travel long distances, and don't want to spend all day getting from A to B. I seldom exceed 100 kph actually. Does the new fan actually work?'

'Adds about 5 kph to the top speed, I think. And the engine sounds happier, or I may be imagining it.'

Then he returned to the policemen's visit. 'I know Lieutenant Zuki. Troublesome man, very ambitious. Wants to make captain. I knew his father, in fact. An army man, died a few years ago.' He paused for a moment and then resumed. 'Our security forces are in a highly nervous state. They are losing face and can't stand that. They are now beginning to suspect that the middle classes may be sheltering them, so be very careful what you say among your friends. The fact that they came to you, and not to anybody else in Bonelands, shows me that you are not above suspicion. But then you have to admit that leaving your car opposite the forbidden area would make anyone suspicious! Next time get sick on this side of the ring road!'

'Serge, everybody knows I have no interest in politics. I have never belonged to any party, which some of my colleagues believe is a mistake. I'm losing out, they say. There are financial benefits to being a member of the party.'

'That's why I feel I can trust you, Prof. You are a man of integrity,' he replied.

I was beginning to wonder about Serge's allegiances, but decided not to probe. Nevertheless, I was still keen to know more about the "Firefly" and felt that Serge had not told me all he knew.

'This "Firefly" character reminds me of the Scarlet Pimpernel. "They seek him here, they seek him there..." You know, the fictional hero of the time of the French Revolution.'

'Oh? You must lend me the book if you have it.'

'I have been trying to put together a sort of psychological profile of the man, so why don't you tell me more about him? He really interests me. His exploits have been quite remarkable so far, but I suppose he will slip up one day. It's inevitable.'

'Really now, Prof!' he said with mock surprise, eyes glinting. 'I thought you were a historian, not a psycho-whatsit! Leave the poor man alone. Like you said, he'll soon be brought to book and you'll see what he is like.'

That was a clear hint that he was through with this line of conversation, but I was not finished yet. I was convinced that he was a "Firefly" sympathiser, if not a supporter.

'Stop pulling my leg, Serge, and tell me more. I am really consumed with curiosity. This man has brought a bit of excitement to our hideously boring lives.'

'You know what they say about curiosity and the cat, don't you? How do you know this man who calls himself the "Firefly" isn't going to turn his attention to blowing up the power station or something? We do not really know his true intentions, do we?'

These remarks puzzled me. They were so contrary to what he had said earlier.

'But Serge,' I said, 'you seemed to harbour a certain sympathy for him. Surely what you told me suggests that he is not that kind of man? He has not harmed a single civilian up to now, and down at Fishtail they look on him as a kind of hero.'

'Perhaps, perhaps,' he replied laconically, and then changed the subject. 'How would you like to attend a "spirit deliverance"? My relations in the village of Maroon are going to hold one for one of my nieces tomorrow afternoon. Poor girl has been behaving in a most peculiar manner and they'll be taking her to a healer for a check-up.'

I had never been to a "spirit deliverance" session, though everybody in the country knew about them. In other countries it would be called "exorcism", and it is the common belief that many forms of mental disturbance are due to "possession" by one of the many different types of assorted spirits, demons and jinns, and a trained and experienced "healer" can quickly identify the kind of entity present.

Now what is remarkable is the fact that a severe mental disturbance which in industrialised countries would be diagnosed as schizophrenia, manic-depression, and so on, requiring many months and years of psychotherapy, not to mention enriching psychoanalysts, is far more often than not cured here in a matter of weeks or very few months through "spirit deliverance". And a good healer can tell very early if the cause is of pathogenic nature and treats it with herbal concoctions and mineral compounds instead, though not guaranteeing a cure. Should he, on the other hand, identify it as being a case of "possession" he goes through the procedure of "deliverance" with very high prospects of success. The speed of recovery depends on the healer's skill, and the type of possession. Some "entities" must be driven out, whereas others are less virulent and can be persuaded to remain in the patient only on condition that they cause no harm or disruption, being offered the periodic sacrifice of a goat or chicken, say once or twice a year. This type, it is believed, can actually be of benefit to the host and so to force them out would do more harm than good. It is quite a complex psychic science and needs very many years of study and practice.

So I accepted Serge's invitation with pleasure and much anticipation, my scientific curiosity awakened.

Serge's village was about eighty kilometres from the City, and it was astonishing how different the sights and sounds became after one crossed the Northern Bridge. Trees became sparser and the country opened out, so that one began to catch glimpses of an undulating horizon. In the City and its surroundings one never saw the horizon, only distant trees or mountains.

The architecture also changed from modern and characterless concrete block housing, with its corrugated iron roofs, to traditional earth and stone or sun-baked clay blocks. Windows became narrower and higher off the ground, and roofs became flat. By the time we reached the village, the transformation was almost complete, and one saw the odd camel under a tree. People were also dressed differently, with long shirts and caps and turbans predominating, though shirt and trousers were not uncommon.

We made for a small house which had an enclosure for goats behind it, with some small-leafed trees rearing up behind the matted fence. On knocking we were let in by a turbaned, white-bearded man who was obviously the "healer", for he had that calm, friendly look that the better medical practitioners have. We exchanged the traditional greetings, and he led us into a medium-sized room which was devoid of all furniture but for a small table placed against the outer wall, between two narrow, louvred windows. A worn but good quality carpet covered the floor, leaving a narrow margin round the walls.

On the table were all the implements required for the "deliverance": an old and much used copy of the Holy Book; a bowl of water in which special prayers written in saffron ink had been dissolved, giving the water its colour; an incense burner made of clay; a small china bowl containing gum araby, and a silver rosewater dispenser.

The healer looked like a man well advanced in years, and stooped a little, but he could sit down and get to his feet quite smoothly. Men (and women) of his calibre were getting rarer and rarer, very often leaving no successors. Modern young people did not seem to have the necessary self-sacrificing spirit to sit at the feet of a master year after long year, for very small rewards. For traditional healers depended entirely on voluntary contributions from their patients. They never mentioned payment. They were performing a service in the name of the Creator, and expected their reward elsewhere.

'Come over here, gentlemen,' he said, indicating an area at the end farthest from the door. 'I suppose I need not tell you that you are not to say anything or make a sound during the proceedings. I pray you not to draw attention to yourselves in any way.'

For some reason I shuddered slightly at these words. This was totally unknown territory to me, and I hoped I'd not make a fool of myself by an involuntary exclamation or something.

We had hardly been there twenty minutes when there was a knock on the front door, and the old gentleman got up (he had been reading from a small book) and went to open it.

In walked a man and a woman, accompanied by a young girl of about eighteen. Serge rose and embraced them in turn, but I remained seated. He explained to them that I was a very close friend of his, who also happened to be deeply interested in the supernatural.

With the healer seated against the wall next to the little table, and the family in a semicircle in front of him, the girl in the middle, he asked them to describe the symptoms. Father and mother looked at one another, and it was the woman who spoke.

'Honourable sheikh, a month ago my little girl started waking up at night screaming. She said she had dreamed of a face with glowing eyes staring at her from an arm's length away. She woke up when it got nearer.'

The girl was looking quite calm, as if it was about somebody else.

'The following night the same thing happened. The same face, except that this time a hand reached out to touch her. Nothing happened in the following week, and we thought they had just been ordinary nightmares. And then one morning, when my husband was out to work – he gets up very early – and I continued sleeping, I was snatched out of deep sleep by somebody shaking me strongly by the shoulders. May the Almighty preserve us! It was her, my daughter, and her face was terribly changed. I sat up and drew her to me, holding tightly to her and reciting from the Holy Book. She struggled like a demon, but did not hit me, the Creator be blessed! After a time she calmed down and fell asleep. She woke up an hour later, and was quite normal. She had no memory of what had happened.'

The girl was now looking very concerned and was close to tears. She reached for her mother's hand and held it.

'You can continue the story. There is nothing to worry about,' prompted the healer.

'Well, nothing else happened until a few days ago, when one of her cousins came to spend the day with us. I don't know how it happened, but I was in the kitchen when I heard a scream, and running to the front room saw my poor Zeinab with her hands round her cousin's throat. I cannot describe to you what she looked like! Even her hair was changed, all twists and ringlets, not a straight strand in sight! And her voice – the Almighty preserve us – was that of a man, deep and strong! I nearly fainted.'

The daughter now hung her head and was crying softly.

'And that,' added her father, 'was when we arranged to come and see you.'

I have to admit I was thoroughly shaken, and felt deeply sorry for them. I hoped the healer could effect a cure, for not every case yielded to treatment. If the ailment was of an organic, and not psychic/psychological nature, then the sheikh could do nothing about it. She'd have to go to the mental hospital where she could be interned for years, if not for the rest of her life.

Without saying a word, the healer stood up and went out of the room. We could hear him speaking to someone in another room, and then he returned.

'My wife is bringing the live coals so that we can start.'

A veiled woman came in with only her eyes and hands showing, bringing live coals in a metal container, and quickly put some pieces with practised fingers into the incense burner. She then transferred the silver tray containing the requisites from the table on to the carpet in front of the healer. Her job was done for the moment, and she left the room.

The healer put some incense into the burner, and wisps of smoke curled lazily upwards. He had drawn the curtains just before, and the room was now dim, but he did not need much light to begin reciting from the Holy Book as he undoubtedly knew most, if not all of it, by heart. Many people did, right down to gifted children as young as ten and twelve.

He read in a low monotone for what seemed a long time, and with the growing heat and smoke in the room I felt myself getting drowsy. I loosened the top button of my shirt and sat up straighter, legs crossed. I looked at Serge and saw that his eyes were closed but his lips were moving, probably reciting along with the healer. The girl's eyes were also shut, but her parents were looking on.

When he had finished he told the girl to sit nearer to him, and the veiled woman reappeared and draped a white sheet over her so that she was fully covered, with not even a toe showing. More incense was added. The real business was now about to start, and the atmosphere had suddenly grown tense. All feelings of drowsiness left me.

The healer started chanting words with which I was unfamiliar, and which seemed to include strange names. He went on like this for a while, and then leaned forward and placed his right hand on her head. I heard a small gasp of surprise, but she remained still. He continued his chanting, very gradually raising his voice until it was just above a normal conversational tone.

This went on for some minutes when there was movement within the sheet. The healer now raised his voice higher and seemed to press more firmly with his hand, and suddenly the movement within the sheet became more agitated. The sheet bulged out in front as if she was pushing against it.

With a cry that made everyone jump, the sheet was thrown off. What was revealed shocked me to the core and made her parents rear back. For she was changed beyond recognition. Her face looked harder and wider, her jaw jutted out like an aggressive man's, nostrils flaring. But it was her eyes that convinced me that this was certainly not a normal psychiatric case. They glowed in a way which I can only describe as nakedly malicious. And the story of the hair was true: her normally straight hair was hanging down in springs.

I was watching her so intently that when the healer spoke I jumped again, even though his voice was in normal pitch.

'You have exposed yourself, evil one. And now prepare to leave, in the name of the Ever-Lasting!'

The face worked furiously, and she/it spat out a reply in a deep rumbling voice which sounded most weird coming from such a pretty girl.

'You silly old man! Is this the way to treat an honoured guest? This delightful young woman invited me. How could I refuse?' This was followed by a tut-tutting sound. It all sounded so normal and reasonable.

'In that case,' said the healer, smiling strangely, 'please remain fixed in place, in the name of your master, while I continue with my recitation.'

He resumed in a chanting voice, eyes closed, his voice rising and falling and soon the girl appeared to be making an effort to get up, pushing herself up with her arms and almost unlocking her knees, but repeatedly sinking back. I could not bear to look at her face, and her mother had buried her head between her knees, sobbing. Her father looked fearful but determined. There came a shout which was more like a scream, a string of words pouring out:

'ENOUGH OF THAT! ENOUGH, I SAID! LEAVE ME ALONE YOU FILTHY OLD QUACK! THE WOMAN

LOVES ME, DO YOU HEAR? SHE LOVES ME!'

For the first time the healer cast a glance in our direction, and there was no mistaking an air of triumph in it. I looked at Serge, and he nodded.

'You are misguided, and your gain will be temporary. This girl is under the protection of the All-Merciful and His angels. Leave now before they take action against you, action too hideous to contemplate!'

Was I dreaming? Here was a man arguing with an invisible entity as if it was the most ordinary thing in the world. But the truce was about to end, quite dramatically.

'You can't frighten me, old man,' the voice said, sniggering. 'This young woman is a bag of sensuality, so what angel would bother? Just leave us alone, my love and I.'

'In that case, stay a while and listen to the rest of my recitation,' and he immediately resumed the chanting. (He explained afterwards that it was the final chapter of the procedural text entitled 'The Wrath of the Master of the Universe, Seen and Unseen', reached only in the case of a particularly well-entrenched entity, as this one seemed to be. In the majority of cases the entity would have offered terms – like the sacrifice of a goat – long before now. This chapter had its dangers, and healers resorted to it in trepidation. If it failed, there might be a rebound reaction on the healer himself.)

Events now took an unexpected turn. The girl leaped to her feet, fists clenched, and eyes blazing, and seemed to be preparing to fling the tray at the healer, for her gaze flickered rapidly to it and back to the healer. But he must have been prepared for this moment, for he suddenly picked up the bowl of saffron water and flung the water at the girl, at the same time shouting at the top of his voice, 'IN THE NAME OF THE GIVER OF LIFE, THE PROTECTOR, THE GIVER OF DEATH! DEPART THIS INSTANT TO WHERE YOU CAME FROM!'

Suddenly I realised that all of us were on our feet, staring in horror at the girl.

And she closed her eyes and went limp! She would have collapsed on the floor if her parents had not caught her and gently lowered her down.

'Let her sleep,' said the healer, 'and let us go outside.'

As we made our way out to the porch, the veiled woman came in to pull back the curtain and placed a pillow under the girl's head.

Coffee and sweetmeats were brought to us in the porch as the healer explained some aspects of what had transpired.

'That was a Wandering Entity, but a shrewd and powerful one. In a way it was true that your daughter had invited him, for our thoughts draw down on us things that are good and things that are bad. Innocent but highly imaginative young women in their teens and early twenties are particularly susceptible. As are some young men. The occasional older person who comes to me usually carries a "directed entity", that is one deliberately sent to him or her by one who has gone through the whole complex procedure with an unscrupulous witchdoctor to harm the victim. The aim is usually to break up a marriage or disrupt a business or official position.'

I had always maintained an open mind about things I knew nothing about, so I did not listen with cynicism.

'Is she now cured?' asked the mother.

'We shall have to watch her in the coming days and weeks. I shall write down for you specific protective prayers which she is to recite every day early in the morning and in bed. I have also prepared a soothing herbal mixture which she is to take morning and night, for one month.'

The girl came out not long after, and apart from a still slightly damp dress she looked none the worse for her experience, but she was obviously offended.

'Mother, why did you let me fall asleep in front of the sheikh and Uncle's guest?' Her mother just hugged her as we all smiled, and said it was because the treatment was over. She could not remember anything that happened after the reading of the Holy Book.

Serge and I said our thanks, and made our way back to the City. It had been quite an experience for me, but Serge said that he had been to quite a few "deliverances", some short, some long. They were always stressful, he said, but very seldom physically violent. The character of the entities varied greatly, and there were times when a decision was made not to try to forcibly remove it but to exact certain concessions from it and allow it to stay as long as it behaved itself! Which many of them apparently did, and no problems sprang up. But some, like his niece's, were too malevolent to be allowed to stay.

When all is said and done, one cannot argue with results, can one? Cure is effected in almost all cases which do not have a physical, pathological basis, and a good healer can quickly diagnose this. Unfortunately, the odd quack does exist, and sometimes lack of experience can cause a wrong diagnosis. But experienced healers like the one we went to fail but rarely, and they'll be the first to terminate a session if they are not absolutely certain of what they are dealing with.

« SIX »

Unknown to me, something was happening in my garden which was to affect my life profoundly. It was, in fact, destiny's final push to get me on to the new path it had chosen for me.

It concerned my red mountain plant. One morning, towards the end of November, I went to fetch a rake to clear leaves which had fallen from the old fruitless tree at the northern end of my front court, and entered the garden shed. As always, I looked at my plant to check its condition – it was still unhappy, but alive – when I noticed that the flower which had been gradually drooping lower and lower, shrinking, was now perpendicular to the concrete floor, and was dripping nectar. There was a small pool directly under it, and it was brownish-yellow. I dipped a finger in it and rubbed it between my fingers. It felt oily, and when I sniffed it there was no discernible smell. For some reason I had expected it to have a sulphurous whiff. I rubbed if off on the wall.

And then I noticed something unusual. The voracious black ants, which should have been all round it for a sip (for I assumed it was nectar, and hence sweet), not only were not interested but a column of them were avoiding the pool and keeping far away from it! They didn't do that even with spilled petrol or drops of oil.

My scientific curiosity was aroused! I pulled off the flower and squeezed a couple of drops as close to the marching lines as I could, short of hitting them, and stood back to watch. To my astonishment, they scattered like I had dripped hot oil! For about five minutes the two lines were totally disorganised, and then discipline reasserted itself; and they pulled away to continue in a semicircle round the drops!

This was very interesting indeed! Had I discovered an unknown and potent insecticide? Here was the chance of fame, at last!

I took the flower to the kitchen, put it in a jam jar, and then washed my hands in warm, soapy water, just in case it was poisonous. I wiped my hands on a towel and made for the sitting room to sit down and think things over.

I sat, pen in hand, to record the event in my diary, when I received a shock. My right fingertips were yellow! I went back to the kitchen and this time used a detergent and a sponge to scrub my fingers. The yellow remained however, even after two thorough scrubbings.

A thought struck me like a thunderbolt: was this the stuff the "Yellow Men" painted themselves with? As a protection against the spiders and all other insects in the mountains and the forest? It was a fantastic thought, and I felt shivers running up and down my spine. But common sense told me not to jump to conclusions. I had to carry out a series of tests yet, on different kinds of insects, including large spiders even if not of the venomous green variety.

But first I had to get the yellow off the fingers of my right hand, for repeated scrubbing failed to remove it. What to do? Imagine the lieutenant dropping in and seeing them! He would undoubtedly come to the conclusion that I had touched one of the "Yellow Men"! The blessed stuff seemed indelible, and I had no spirit in the house to try on it.

I had two small bottles of drawing ink, one red, one black, which I used on my charts, and I dipped a finger in the red ink and then spread it on the other fingers. It looked exceedingly untidy, but it did the trick. I'd say that the bottle had slipped in my hand, or something.

That done, I put on a dishwashing glove and gingerly picked up the flower. There was a trail of the tiny, aggressive red ants running down the corner of the kitchen nearest to the rubbish bin, and I never interfered with them because if I had sprayed them they would have found other ways to get to the rubbish, and they would have been all over the place. Their bite is exceedingly painful, amazing for such tiny creatures.

Well, I placed a drop about two or three centimetres from the line, and waited for one to break rank and investigate. Sure enough, a big-headed soldier-type did after a few minutes make a rush for it. It recoiled so violently that it dropped off the wall! Others gingerly coming forward rushed back into the ranks, spreading a warning, for within seconds there was wild confusion before, as with the black ants, they formed a semicircle and resumed their march.

So it did work with other ants, but now I had to go after bigger game. There was a community of spiders of the "Wolf" family which had spread their webs over and between the thornbushes of the fence behind the house, and I went out to try it on them. These spiders are large and fierce-looking, but are quite harmless if left alone. They did an excellent job controlling the insect population, so most people left them alone even in gardens if they did not intrude too much.

I chose the web of one large specimen, sitting right in the middle, gently swaying with the wind with little bound-up bundles of insects dotting the web. I placed a drop well away from it, but that light contact sent a signal which it interpreted as an insect. It came rushing towards it, ready to wrap it up in silk strands. It stopped short just before touching it perhaps to make sure it wasn't one of those spider-stinging wasps. An insect would be frantically trying to get away but this thing just sat there! The spider was puzzled, and gently inched closer.

What happened next was quite astonishing. The spider

literally leaped off its web, and unreeling its exuded thread lowered itself rapidly to the ground. It had given up its web altogether! The nearby spiders must have caught the panic because they started heaving at their webs, up and down, to scare off whatever it was that was threatening them. The movement spread all along the fence.

Here was my proof! The yellow nectar or sap was a most powerful deterrent, even if it did not kill. Or did it, as well? It seemed to me that it didn't matter, for the critical thing in the mountains would be to make sure no insect touched one's skin.

Scientific fervour now seized me, and I reasoned that the raw sap was too thick and slimy to apply directly to the skin, and furthermore there would not be enough of it available at one time for possibly hundreds of men. So it had to be in a very dilute form.

A drop of it in a glass of water simply floated, so it had to be some other solvent, cheap and readily obtainable. Like cooking oil, for instance.

Three days of experimentation – hiding everything in the larder every time the front gate creaked (almost invariably it would be Serge, but I didn't want him to see either) – gave me what appeared to be the optimum proportions if one wanted to retain the yellowish tinge. The ratio was: one drop of sap from the nose-dropper to three tablespoons of vegetable cooking oil.

I repeated my experiments with my unfortunate guinea pigs, and the terror it spread was the same, though not so swiftly as with the raw sap. QED! At no time did I consider going to the security forces with my discovery.

Serge had long noticed my red fingers, but had easily accepted my explanation. On completing my experiments I had hardly any sap left, having squeezed the flower dry and then thrown it away over the back fence where there was only bush.

I now waited for the other flowers to mature and then collected the sap in a small medicine bottle to take with me when I went abroad, which I planned to do in about three months' time.

But, "Man proposes, and God disposes", the enlightened say, and so it proved. I never got round to making that trip. Or to becoming a millionaire.

Serge was a keenly observant man, and he must have noticed a certain smugness in my behaviour towards him. For once, I was feeling that I knew more, much more, about the "Yellow Men" than he did!

'I detect something going on in your mind this morning. If I didn't know you better, I'd say that you have fallen in love or something. Who is the unfortunate woman?'

In a flash my thoughts turned to "A Z" and I decided to confess my secret interest in the neighbour's daughter. Perhaps he would think of a way to get to know her better. Serge had many relations, and one of them might be working in the Ministry of Defence, where "A Z" had joined her father.

'Serge, there is indeed a woman who has been on my mind on and off ever since I saw her. She is our neighbour's daughter. Zain's.' I braced myself for the ridicule that would follow, for my chances with her were like those of a butterfly in a forest fire.

His eyebrows arched, and a shadow of a smile played on his lips.

'Really? That weird young woman? Prof, she has been turning down one man after another, and the Minister's son, Zahor, has been wooing her for months now, from what I hear. He is a very handsome young man, and owns a BMW. Also shines in sports. My advice is to forget her. At your age you should know better.'

He was right, of course, and any sensible man would have faced facts and gracefully retreated. But the heart is blind to reason; and there was the dream to spur me on. How many people first meet in a dream?

'Serge, I must tell you this. I saw her in a dream many months before seeing her in real life. I'm absolutely positive I had never seen her before, even from a distance. What do you think that means?'

He looked at me in surprise, before replying, 'A strange coincidence, certainly. But can we depend on dreams? And how can you be so sure that you had never seen her before? She might be on some photo in one of your friend's houses. Many families here are related, as you know.'

I must say I had never thought of that possibility and was abashed.

On leaving Serge, I was feeling somewhat deflated and drove straight to the Corner Café. About four of the group were already present, and there was a stranger among them, a young man in the uniform of our air force, with a pilot's wings on his breast. Did we really have an air force? I had seen the odd Dakota DC-3 flying overhead in military colours, but nothing else as far as I could recollect. On paper, we were supposed to have jet fighters and even attack helicopters, but if we did they must be restricting their flights around their aerodrome in the south for certainly none came over the City.

A retired fellow teacher introduced him with a flourish: 'My son, Flight-Lieutenant Seif, of the NAF.'

Being a lifelong air enthusiast (with particular emphasis on World War Two aeroplanes), I was more than happy to meet a flyer and instantly planned to invite him to my place for a good, long chat. He had his father's friendly aura, and I immediately asked him what he flew.

'At the moment, nothing but old DC-3s and Fokker transports. Nothing glamorous, I'm afraid.'

I was a bit disappointed since we were supposed to have jet fighters and helicopter gunships. I figured him for a fighter pilot, but I decided to leave it for later to ask him more questions. Anyway, if I could wangle a flight in a DC-3, probably the longest-lived of all aircraft having been designed before the war and still serving today in many parts of the world, it'd still be a thrilling experience for me. (I expected it would be very noisy, draughty and uncomfortable, but that would be a small price to pay!)

I invited him to drop in the following morning after 10 a.m., telling him about the aircraft books and magazines I had.

The moment I got home I did something I hadn't done for very many years: I pulled out the trunk in the spare bedroom which was full of the memorabilia of my old student days and carefully unpacked cardboard boxes containing the plastic aeroplane models which I had built myself. The familiar and beloved old friends were all there, in immaculate war paint, all in 1:48 scale. I had foolishly given away the far more numerous 1:72 scale ones when I was packing to return to Rivenia.

There were just nine models in this larger scale, and I hung them up by means of black string loops on the inner wall of my study. The four-engined B-17 was the largest in my collection and took centre spot. On either side were the single-engined Spitfire, A6M5 Zero-sen, Fockewolf 190, Messerschmitt 109, P-51 Mustang, Yak-3, F4U Corsair and, leading the formation, a DH Mosquito. As model-making knew no age limits, I intended to add a few more in future, though I was sure that most of my countrymen would think I was going through my second childhood!

As a result of the new display, my study now was a happy, cheerful place, and I couldn't care less if Serge or anybody else thought it was childish.

Actually, many of these aircraft were engineering marvels of their time and were superb works of art. And the remarkable thing, for a discerning enthusiast, was the way the specific shapes of the aircraft revealed the character of the nation that made them! A Heinkel 111 would never have been designed by a British or American engineer, nor a Mosquito by a German one. And this applied to the Russians and the Japanese as well. Each nation had its characteristic design criteria.

The following morning the first visitor to my gallery was Flight-Lieutenant Seif, and he was absolutely thrilled by the display! His remarks were, 'I must buy some kits when I go abroad again. I can see what fun they must have been to make. Lovely stuff. How I envy the pilots who flew these!'

Over tea and chocolate biscuits we talked about aviation in general, and he was particularly glad to see my aircraft magazines because they had stopped getting them at the base about a year ago.

'I assumed a man with your overseas training would be flying a fighter-bomber or a gunship. So why transport?' I asked.

'What fighter-bomber? What gunship? They are all grounded, and have been for over four years. No spare parts.'

'But that's unbelievable,' I said, genuinely surprised. 'I remember the publicity about expanding our air force over two years ago, when we were supposed to be forming a complete jet squadron.

'Well, Prof, I'm not in a position to comment on that. In fact, I trust you'll say nothing about what I have just told you.'

As things went, this titbit of information was to prove of great interest to some people in the land. The air force base was several kilometres from Granitetown in the south, and it was a high security area.

As he was leaving, with a bundle of my magazines, I asked him whether he could arrange for me to have a ride in his DC-3 one day, and he said he thought he could persuade the station commander. They had two DCs and one Fokker, which ferried top government officials about.

My good mood was disturbed an hour later when the twelve o'clock news announced that the government was about to grant concessions to a logging company for the area adjoining the Red River. We were assured that the area would be just ten per cent of the rich forest, and that hundreds of jobs would be created for the unemployed. Work would start after the preliminary surveys, now expected to take place in February next year.

I had no idea where the "Yellow Men's" camp was situated, but it stood to reason that it would not be far from the river. So any activity in the area would make things pretty difficult for them. It was also to be supposed that the loggers would come in with flame-throwers to burn the undergrowth for safety reasons, like the miners had done, and that would remove all cover. Access to the river would be cut off.

There was no organised environmentalist movement in the country so I expected no opposition to this scheme. "Foreign currency" were magic words, and none would dare raise a voice.

Serge's only comment was, 'Ten per cent? It is more likely to be sixty per cent. The top people will want their cut, and it'll have to be a big one.'

Incidentally, he did not laugh when he saw my aeroplane models. He even picked one, the gull-winged Corsair, off the wall and flew it around a bit!

'You actually made these yourself? How long did these small ones take?'

I had, not for the first time, misjudged my people.

I think it can be demonstrated mathematically that time does speed up the older one grows. Consider this, for instance: at the age of ten years, a year is one-tenth of one's life; but move on to sixty and it dwindles to one-sixtieth of one's life! Work your way down and surely this fraction affects the hour and the minute? Nature should have compensated by making one become mentally and physically faster as one grew older! For some reason nature has only singled out the shark for special favours. The older a shark grows, the bigger and stronger it becomes! And then provided it with the enviable ability to keep growing new teeth throughout its life, and how long can this be? To my knowledge no one has been able to establish how long a shark can live.

I mention time because it was absolutely dragging that morning when I wanted it to fly. I was waiting for Serge to come and provide me with more information on my "dream woman", "A Z", at 11 a.m. as promised, and it was still only 9.45, curse it. I kept pacing to and fro on the veranda.

A diversion unexpectedly came a few minutes later when the phone rang. Having more or less withdrawn from society for over a year, apart from the periodic meetings at the café, hardly anyone rang any more.

'Hello, Prof. Having an early breakfast for once?' It was Tony, a chemist by profession, and an occasional member of our group.

'What's up, Tony? Run out of drugs again?'

'Not the kind that would interest you. Anyway, listen, I am holding a party on New Year's Eve. How would you like to come? Who knows, you might strike gold!'

With "A Z" and the divorcée on my mind I was not particularly looking for yet another woman to add to the list.

'Tony, I really have lost interest in parties. I know yours is always terrific, but I'm getting too old for that kind of thing.'

'Well, in that case you will miss being introduced to next year's presidential hopeful. He is considered a sure thing, you know.'

Now this made me sit up and pay attention. Not because I wanted to be known by him, with a view to future favours, but because I'd be interested to hear his views on the "Firefly", and what he intended to do should he win. (Though, to be realistic, no genuine opposition party would ever be allowed to win.)

'All right. I'll come.'

It would certainly provide a welcome break from my self-imposed hermit's existence, and perhaps return me to a normal social life.

Serge did not come until almost noon, and he looked unusually tired.

'When are you going to stop scampering all over the place and relax at home every now and then? You'll kill yourself, you know,' I said.

'It's my plantation down south. Pineapple harvesting time, you know, and if I'm not there in person they'll take away the big ripe ones and leave me with grade two. The bastards can never be trusted.'

I went into the kitchen to make coffee, and when I had placed it on the table could restrain my curiosity no longer.

'Well, Serge, what did your woman relation at the Ministry find out about her?'

'Who?' he asked, his thoughts still far away. 'Oh, you mean your witch? Nothing much, really.'

I sank back in acute disappointment.

'Surely she must have found out something?' I persisted. 'What about this Minister's son, Zahor? Surely he must be dropping in at the office?'

'My relative didn't say. Sorry, Prof, but I'll ask her to do better next time.' Without waiting for me to say anything, he continued in a different, more serious tone of voice.

'Prof, I'm going to ask a favour of you. You remember Mr James, the journalist, who was interested in the Mongols? Well, he has just had to leave the country, but will be back in two weeks' time. Now he was contracted by the *Military Journal* to write an article on the special parade in ten days' time of the 1st Armoured Regiment, at Brigade Headquarters at Killini. It is some kilometres north-west of Granitetown.'

He paused, and I just could not see where I fitted in.

'So?' I asked.

'Before he left he begged me to persuade you to attend this parade on his behalf and write a detailed, technical article for him. He said only you could do it, for the *Military Journal* is a fussy magazine.'

'But Serge,' I protested, 'I am not an accredited journalist. They'd never let me in without security clearance. Sorry, but rule me out.'

'You needn't worry about accreditation Prof, he thought of that. The man has initiative, you know, and made prior arrangement. Just let me have a passport photograph and you'll get your card tomorrow.'

He didn't tell me then that the name on the card would be a false one!

'To be doubly sure of getting in, why don't you go across and ask Zain to provide an invitation for you? The Ministry of Defence is co-hosting it. Surely he will understand your interest as a historian?'

I must say this suggestion had its attractions. I was going to see "A Z" as well as get to see the parade as a VIP, in case Serge got me a limited access one. I was already looking forward to moving in among the armour at inspection time. While I knew a lot about AFVs, it was from books. I wanted to actually step inside a tank and see what it felt like.

I determined to go and see Zain that same afternoon.

I walked to their villa at the magic hour of 5 p.m., when everything was soft and subdued, the sun about to touch the peaks of the mountains west of the City, the sky reddening. Often I went out for walks in that direction, but I turned off at the junction with their access road and went left instead of right past their house. This was because their road ended in a cul-de-sac and anyone going there had to be going to one of the three houses, whereas the left turn led all the way to connect with the main road.

As I approached their villa I was surprised to find how nervous I was. I almost lost courage and turned back. Quite ridiculous, really!

Their villa had been built just four or five years ago, and I doubted if it had been designed by a qualified architect. Too many frills, and a facade which did not balance but the front garden was well landscaped, complete with a fountain just off centre.

I saw them as I was to see them many times in the traumatic days ahead – sitting in their wide, decoratively grilled balcony, with just their heads appearing clearly over the balustrade. As I got closer "A Z" stood up and went inside, coming down to open the door.

And there she stood in front of me, her hair tumbling down all over her shoulders like a desert woman's. There was no doubt about it: I had not just magnified her looks in my imagination. She was, truly, a beautiful woman. But what made the hairs at the back of my neck prickle was the dress she was wearing – a black dress with little yellow flowers! The only difference with the one in the dream was that this one was shorter, being halfway down her legs. In the dream it was full length, but it made no difference to the coincidence. I stood staring silently at her until her eyes fluttered in embarrassment.

'Please come in, Teacher,' she said, opening the door wider. Behind her I could see Zain and his wife coming down the stairs.

'Well, well, this is a surprise, neighbour! Do come to the front room.'

I could not come straight out and bluntly ask for an invitation, so I followed him to the sitting room. "A Z" had disappeared down the entrance hall, to be followed by her mother. Soon after they came in with a tray of coffee and sweetmeats, and "A Z" looked just once at me, as if in puzzlement (perhaps at my having stared at her), and then left the room.

Zain and I discussed this and that, with Mrs Zain contributing little, but that didn't matter as it was standard men's talk. Looking at him, I found it difficult to believe that he worked in a ministry that was supposed to be one of the most corrupt in the country.

Finally I casually mentioned my interest in the forthcoming military parade, and he pre-empted my request by saying, 'We shall have to invite you then, shan't we? Just come round and see my secretary tomorrow morning, and bring a photo. You'll have your invitation within the hour.'

Would you believe it? As simple as that!

"A Z" had not come into the room again, though I had prolonged the conversation. I left with a certain amount of disappointment, despite reminding myself that a well-brought-up woman was not supposed to hang around a near stranger, though I was developing into a family friend.

I was turning to close the gate when I chanced to look up at the balcony, and saw her standing there. On an impulse, I waved, and she waved back. But surely that meant nothing at all. If only I had not had that dream I'd not have been getting myself so worked up! And then there was the coincidence of the black dress.

The following morning I drove to the Ministry of Defence, up three flights of stairs, to Zain's office. His secretary was expecting me and immediately disappeared with my photograph, asking me to return in an hour's time. Down the stairs again – feeling sorry for Zain with his leg problem – to pass the time window shopping. I returned precisely an hour later to have a smiling secretary hand me my VIP card, plus a sticker for the windshield. The average citizen wanting something done would have had to run up and down those stairs for a week or more before being attended to. And with great arrogance, at that. People hated civil servants.

In the afternoon Serge came with my press card, and I was disturbed when I saw another name next to my picture.

'What is this, Serge? Why give a false name? This could cause me no end of trouble if found out. Sorry, I have no wish to commit a criminal offence!'

'Just take it easy and listen, Prof. They will have a list of registered reporters, and they are bound to refer to it. Your name is not on it, whereas that name is. He happens to be a colleague of Mr James but knows nothing about armour. He has agreed to let you use his name this time. At any rate, you now have two cards to use at will, but VIPs are not supposed to go in among the tanks, inspecting and interviewing crew. So after the parade slip on your reporter's identity and leave your comfortable seat.'

He reminded me that Mr James wanted a detailed, technical report and not the kind that he, Serge, could write.

'But why does he want that? What's the point?' Wisps of suspicion drifted at the back of my mind.

'To be frank, he intends to expose the true state of our armoured forces to put the government to shame. Surely our army deserves better?'

I had a feeling that Serge was not quite telling the truth, but could not think of an explanation.

« SEVEN »

Christmas came and was celebrated in the traditional manner by those of the Christian faith and friends. The rest of the populace enjoyed two days of public holidays, biding their time for the more general celebrations of the Muslim Eid, which was not due until the following February–March.

I shall relate an incident to show just how obsessed I was becoming with my neighbour Zain's daughter.

I was driving slowly down Main Street when I saw a woman walking hand in hand with a man, and I could swear it was "A Z". They were on the pavement, on the opposite side of the road, but there was no mistaking that delicate profile and slim figure. I was so taken aback that I very nearly drove into the car ahead. I kept twisting my head round so as not to lose sight of them, while looking for a place to park. Just as I found a place I saw them going into a department store.

I hopped out of the car and made for the store across the road, dodging in and out of four lines of slow-moving traffic. Some blared their horns in disgust at this jaywalking, but my eyes were focused on the store entrance. When I got to it I stopped to look right and left, in case they had come out, and then I went in. I walked up and down the rows of display shelves and cases, and finally saw them, their backs turned, at a shoe shelf. I had seen "A Z" in that headscarf, and as I crept up to them, not really knowing what I was going to do (for what right had I to do anything at all?), she sat down on a stool to try a shoe on. I didn't recognise the man, but he was definitely too young to be an uncle, and he had a hand on the back of her neck.

I hesitated about three metres from them, pretending to be looking at some shoes on a side rack, but moving gradually closer.

I decided to just walk up to them and say hello, and was about to do so when the woman put the shoe back in its place and they turned to walk away. It was not "A Z"! In fact, this close there was very little resemblance full face, though this woman's figure was not far off, and the way her hair came down from the head shawl was very similar. There must have been something peculiar in my facial expression, because they looked back once as they hurried away.

To preserve my dignity, I was forced to buy a pair of shoes, of a type that I'd never normally pick. Quite a bit of money gone down the drain because of my upsurge of unreasoning jealousy! I still wince to this day when I remember the incident.

The days that followed to the end of the year were a bit of a drag in that Serge had gone to his village and nobody called, either physically or on the telephone. My red plant's flowers seemed to take a long time to mature, and that delayed further experiments. I was going to try different kinds of cooking oil, cold and hot. There is a scientist buried deep inside most of us, I think, and that's how mankind discovered a million and one things. Just imagine the first person to bite into an onion – surely the natural reaction should have been, "Ugh! Poison!"

On New Year's Eve I was one of the first to arrive at Tony's. There were about eight or nine people already there, none of whom I was acquainted with. Tony had a chain of little chemist's shops ("pharmacies" was the term preferred) throughout the land, and was reputed to be very rich. His house was certainly a veritable mansion, with no less than five bathrooms. The room we were in seemed to have been designed for large parties, for with the furniture pushed to the walls there was room in the middle for twenty or more couples to dance in. The building was pretty old, and was said to have belonged to an Emir favoured by the Foreigners when they ruled the land, and Tony had spent much money renovating it.

As those present were all strangers to me, I didn't feel very comfortable until more people trickled in, some of whom I was acquainted with. Then Tony switched on his hi-fi set and the party really started going. His taste in music was wide, and there would be jazz one moment, pop music the next, and Arabian belly-dancing rhythms after that! It was a lot of fun, and I was glad I came. I had a few dances myself, the first in many years. This was a cosmopolitan crowd, and almost everyone had lived abroad for varying periods of time. The general populace would not have approved of this kind of conduct, but most of those present were the picture of orthodoxy in their day to day lives and did not challenge the established order.

But for me this was not to be just an ordinary, enjoyable party night, for two strange things were to happen to me:

The first one happened as I was chatting with a veterinary surgeon about the diseases of camels, animals which may strike most people as being well-nigh indestructible.

Out of the corner of my eye I saw this female figure, sitting just off to my left, rise and make straight for us. She joined us with a greeting, and then stood there listening. She was a flamboyantly dressed woman of late middle age, wearing enough gold jewellery to sink a small boat. Her fingers were covered with rings encrusted with stones of various colours. I knew nothing about gems, so I couldn't judge whether they were genuine or fakes. Round-faced and plump. Was she a performer of some sort, I wondered? Definitely in the entertainment business.

When the vet and I were about to go our separate ways she placed her hand on my arm and said, 'Wait!' and I turned to her. 'I'm Madame Solika,' she said, 'and that's my husband looking at us. So don't worry!'

I looked at the man sitting against the wall, and he smiled and waved. This is all very curious, I thought. Why hadn't he come with her?

'I want to tell you something in utmost confidence, as such things must be, and it is up to you to believe or not.'

All I could manage was, 'Oh?' but it was enough to make her proceed.

'You are carrying a "guest", did you know that? It is a female entity, and she is wagging her finger at me right now!' Involuntarily I looked over my shoulder, and she laughed.

'No, no! She is in your aura, and only mediums like me can see her. Unless, of course, she chooses to reveal herself to you.'

What was this woman trying to do? Scare me into going to consult with her for a fee? She had got the wrong person.

'I'm afraid I don't believe in that kind of thing. I have never detected a "presence" in my life, nor have I, to my knowledge, suddenly started speaking in a woman's voice!'

The music was so loud that we had to stand very close to one another, and I wished it were "A Z"!

'If only you could see how smug she is looking! Tell me this, do you tend to shun people and have no women friends, or are you a married man with many friends?'

I reflected carefully, and replied, 'Divorced, and I have few friends because I have much writing to do.'

'Of course,' she said, beaming benignly, and changed her line of questioning. 'This guest of yours – no, I will *not* shut up, and you behave yourself! – is trying to lead you in the direction she wants. I don't know what it is, but keep what I'm saying in mind if you should find yourself going against your common sense.'

This woman must be mad. That annoyed aside seemed to have been directed at someone just above my head. Certainly I had not told her to shut up.

'Madam Solika, I appreciate your concern, but perhaps you'd like me to call at your place for consultation?' This was what she was angling for, after all, wasn't it? That should end this conversation, and I'd resume dancing.

'Oh, no!' she replied, 'I am a medium, and I also practise the tarot, but I'm not a healer, an exorcist. If you wanted her removed you'd have to go to somebody else. But looking at her, I think you'd find it very difficult to get rid of her. Strikes me as being a sort of priestess in her world, pretty powerful. Well, I have kept my husband waiting long enough.' She looked up again at the space just above my head and shook her head.

She left me deep in thought – what had been her purpose in telling me all that and then refusing to offer help if it was needed? Nor had she offered me her card, or asked for mine. I jumped when I felt a hand on my shoulder. It was Tony, extra merry with the amber stuff.

'Come on over and let me introduce you to the next president of our country!' he shouted above the beat music. "Hard rock", I believe they called it. Waltzing round gyrating figures we finally got to the bar at the end of the room, where about five or six people were clustered round this figure in the centre. He was a portly man, of medium height, with a slight paunch and a way of rocking on his feet as he spoke. But he was reputed to be a charismatic speaker, so his appearance belied the man. Nevertheless, somehow he didn't strike me as likely to be the strong, dedicated and scrupulously honest head of state that the country was crying for. He seemed cut of the same cloth as the incumbent president. The people were about to be fooled again.

I shook his limp hand, and he immediately asked me why he had not seen me at any of his rallies. I said jokingly that as a historian I had to avoid political entanglement.

'Oh!' he said, with open disdain. 'No intelligent man can afford to ignore politics. Come and register with my party in the new year, and you'll be glad you did.'

After which he turned his back on me and resumed his conversation with the prominent businessman he had been chatting with. I could see that Tony was a bit embarrassed. But I wasn't going to let this arrogant little bastard shrug me off that easily, as if I was one of his minions.

'Excuse me,' I said, and he looked over his shoulder, annoyed. 'What have you got to offer the people that is going to raise their standard of living? Any programme to deal with corruption and poverty?'

He could not believe his ears! One did not ask such questions in Rivenia, and frankly I realised that I risked going down in somebody's little book as a potential dissident. He turned to face me again.

'My New Reform Party is absolutely dedicated to eliminating poverty in our land. Read our manifesto and attend our meetings and all your questions will be answered.'

But my blood was up, and the loud beat music seemed to have switched on a rebellious streak.

'And how do you intend to deal with the "Firefly" challenge?'

Tony was gently pulling at my shirtsleeve from behind as a warning, but I was prepared to stand my ground.

'The "Firefly" is a pest and a criminal. He will hang, with the rest of his evil gang.' He turned to the businessman again, and this gave Tony a chance to drag me away.

'What came over you, Prof?' he asked in shock. 'You really must be extremely careful what you say. I have no wish to lose a good friend. Now, let me introduce you to that sumptuous female over there. Comes from Peru, of all places!'

The Peruvian lady had her eye on a young man dancing with great abandon, barely looking at me while we were talking. It was just ten minutes to the New Year, and I excused myself and hurried to the lavatory downstairs. There was somebody in, and

I could hear the sound of vomiting. Curse it, I thought, he'll probably be in there ages. The minutes were ticking away, but I came out of it just as they were counting the seconds upstairs.

I ran up two steps at a time, and was at the landing when "Auld Lang Syne" started. It is quite remarkable how one hears this Scottish strain all over the world, in countries as far apart as Chile and Japan. I was turning to take the next flight of stairs when, over the words '…and ne'er brought to mind…' I distinctly heard another voice, '…are you? They are all dead, you know!' Just as in the dream.

I arrived just in time to join the circle, and the hugging and pecking of cheeks that followed. (The Peruvian woman had her man.)

I left for home soon after, wishing my dream sweetheart were there.

I went round at ten o'clock the following morning to offer Serge New Year greetings (we celebrated both the universal new year and our own) and found him gardening. He dropped his implement and we went and sat on the veranda.

'One year nearer to meeting our Maker,' he said, sombrely.

'You shouldn't let that worry you, Serge, if you have led a good life, full of sincere good deeds,' I said, tongue in cheek.

'Ah! If angels came down, they'd make for my house first before coming to yours, I can assure you! Hell will be brimming over with the bourgeoisie, not us humble folks!' He was teasing, of course. Well, partly. I told him about the party the previous night, mentioned Madame Solika's assertion, and then my meeting with the presidential candidate. He was more interested in the latter.

'Well, Prof, I'm glad you saw for yourself that we have been ruled by the same clique, the same old gang, practically since independence. They put forward "opposition" candidates from within their circle, and then put on a show of maligning them.

It's a no-lose situation for them. Genuine opposition candidates are very quickly crushed. Don't expect any change in the set-up for the foreseeable future.'

He said he had heard of Madame Solika; she ran a clinic off Main Street. Couldn't tell whether she was genuine or fake.

'Anyway, you are already "possessed" by a female, and you don't want to get rid of her, do you?' he said, laughing. Then he quickly added, 'Which reminds me, you know I forgot to ask my relative in the Ministry your witch's name. By pure chance I got to know it yesterday.'

He stopped and looked smugly at me, waiting for a reaction. I was filled with unreasonable anxiety lest it be one of those hideous names that "clever" parents inflict on their children, just to be different from the common lot.

'Oh? What is it, then?'

He took a deep, deliberately theatrical breath, and said, 'Aida.'

"Aida" pronounced like the famous opera. I couldn't remember any other woman bearing that name. Perhaps one of her parents had seen and been impressed by the opera. It was a very unusual name for us, but it was not bad at all. In fact, I thought it suited her perfectly.

'How did you find out?' I asked.

'I was chatting with their next-door neighbour in the garden, when over the wall between them I heard her mother calling her, "Aida! Aida! Come down a minute." And that was it. Unusual name, isn't it? But fit for a witch!'

At last! I could now stop thinking of her as "A Z", like she was some kind of android. My lovely, beautiful Aida, now I had your name to send telepathic messages to!

'I invite you to a wedding a few months from today, Serge. That woman is going to be my wife, the Almighty permitting. I'm sure of it!'

Serge looked most concerned and placed his hand on my shoulder.

'Now look here, Prof. Don't start building castles in the air. A woman that young can change her mind six times between sunrise and sunset. She'll break your heart as easily as sew on a button. Women have no conscience, you know. And even if, for her own reasons, she comes to prefer you to a horde of rich young men, you'll find yourself having to watch her like a hawk every time some handsome young man hovers around. Look for somebody who will be grateful for the shelter you give her. A divorced woman or a widow.'

Serge was talking sense, I knew it, and the elation of knowing her name faded. But deep down I knew I was prepared to risk anything to have her as mine, even if only for a short while. One cannot reason with an obsession. Surely the dream had not come to me for nothing? There was a psychic bond between us, of that I was absolutely sure.

The midday news commentary had a surprise in store. After its summary of notable government achievements in the year gone by, the reader came out with this statement:

'I cannot speak for the government, but one cannot but be astounded by the sheer cheek of this criminal, who calls himself the "Firefly", for sending new year wishes to the government, and asking that he and his band of scoundrels be granted an amnesty, and be allowed to register as a political party. The man must be out of his mind. His letter to the President is an affront to the citizens of Rivenia!'

The "Firefly" must be playing a political game of some sort, I thought. He must have known his peace feelers would be rejected.

The Minister of the Interior gave the official government response later in the evening. The "Firefly" and his men were to surrender themselves unconditionally to the security forces, and were assured of an open and fair trial. 'They need not worry about the treatment they will receive, for we are a just-minded people, with a long tradition of fair play and mercy. They shall not be wronged.'

Well, perhaps it could mark the beginning of a dialogue. Every man had his price, as I had told Serge, and this could be the preliminary to his being quietly bought off. It couldn't be fun sweltering and scratching in the forest, and a nice settlement would make all the suffering worth it. At any rate, they'd have to come out once the loggers got going.

Serge had been becoming increasingly disinterested in what was going on in the country, seeming preoccupied with other things. He had no comment to make about the "Firefly's" peace offer except an 'Uh!' then went on to remind me of the military parade the coming day, Saturday the third. He didn't have to worry because I was looking forward to it. It would form a nice picnic down south, quite apart from the pleasure of watching the tanks in action. They are the modern equivalent of the armoured knights of old, and never failed to impress. (If rhinoceroses learned to gather and attack en masse, no hunter would dare fire on one!)

When Saturday came, I put on my best lightweight suit and the new pair of shoes I had been forced to buy in my fit of jealousy. I was now as "VIP" looking as I was likely to get as I stepped into my strenuously waxed Morris and made for the open road, directly opposite the one I always took to town.

The journey south was never as interesting for me as the one north because very soon all you saw were trees and thick undergrowth on both sides of the road. No animals could be seen except the odd monkey, and one felt a measure of claustrophobia. Only at night did one see animals caught in the headlights, or shining eyes peering out of the foliage.

I wondered why the Armoured Brigade should have been

stationed south, in country unsuitable for tank warfare, instead of in the open north. In jungle warfare, as happened in World War Two in South-East Asia and the Pacific, light and medium tanks were used but in handfuls, to support infantry.

Somehow I didn't see the low-slung T-54s and SU-100s as befitting jungle warfare. Perhaps the reasoning was that any likely threat would be from the south and south-west rather than the north.

Signposts led all the way to the Armoured Regiment's headquarters, which was way in from the main road, about five kilometres from Granitetown. I showed my card at the first and then the second iron gate, and was directed to the VIP parking. My little Morris Minor looked completely out of place among the limousines, and I received quite a few peculiar looks! I made my way between little groups of soldiers, and when I got to the stands found that the three rows from the bottom were already packed, apart from the seats in the centre of the second row, reserved for the President and his entourage.

We faced what must be the landing strip for military aircraft, with open ground to the distant barbed wire fence. Behind the stands was a complex of army buildings, and the armoured vehicles must have been behind them for there was none in sight.

Half an hour after my arrival the military band, located just off centre, struck up the national anthem and everyone stood up as the President's cavalcade arrived. No sooner were they seated than there was the growing sound of heavy engines and the clattering and screeching of steel tracks, and the first of the armoured vehicles appeared coming round the stands on our right. The first to appear were actually wheeled armoured cars, seven of them, arrange in a V-formation. I didn't recognise the leading car, but the three on one side were Soviet-built BA-64s, and on the other were French-built AML-245s. Then came ten armoured personnel carriers, two abreast, followed by four specialist vehicles of various descriptions.

They were keeping the tanks for dessert, for next came machine-gun-mounted jeeps and about half a dozen motorcycle combinations with light machine guns. (I thought they were stretching the description "armoured parade" a bit!) Finally came the crunching of the tracked vehicles: three trusty old Soviet-made SU-100s self-propelled guns, three T-54s, and three French-made AMX-13s. The dominance of Soviet and French vehicles was due to their having been bought at throwaway prices through a Middle Eastern dealer. Quite legitimately, after every flare-up out there, for history seems to have singled out that area for permanent strife. All the vehicles had seen combat, and many of them had very little mileage left. But reconditioned and repainted, they still looked workmanlike, and moved and fired.

As we were sitting back waiting for more vehicles to appear, hoping to see perhaps much newer models, there came an announcement over the speakers regretting that the rest of the parade had to be cancelled because the President had to return to the City immediately to receive a direct call from the head of a major state. All the guests were requested to proceed to the specially prepared canteen where lunch was about to be served.

The vehicles which had paraded had meanwhile turned round and were now parked along the runway, so I waited until my nearest neighbours had vacated their seats, looked carefully around, and substituted the reporter's card on my coat pocket. Then I made my way down to the armoured line-up, keeping an eye open for anyone from the *Military Journal*, whom I'd make sure not to get close to.

I made straight for the SU-100s, relics of World War Two and yet still effective in their limited role of assault gun. I had always pictured them as being very low so that one could easily look over them, and was astonished to discover that they were well over two metres in height! In fact, the T-54 tank was lower, and so was the AMX-13. Seeing one with an open top hatch, I climbed on it and was about to lower myself into the interior – after all, they were here on display, weren't they? And I didn't think anyone would object to a military reporter inspecting a vehicle, nothing about them being secret – when a voice hailed me.

'What are you up to, up there?'

I looked down and saw that it was a captain. I introduced myself, and told him that I knew what the inside of many tanks looked like, having built 1:48 models, with inside detailing of them, but I had no idea what the interior of an SU-100 looked like.

'All right,' he said, 'but don't fiddle about with anything!' It was, as you'd expect, a tightly planned steel box affording the barest room to move around for its crew of four. But actually as the gun was fixed in place (tilting only a few degrees up or down) there was quite a bit more usable space than in an average tank.

I got into conversation with him when I got out and we got on like the proverbial house on fire. The pity was that I could not invite him to view my collection of 1:48 scale tanks because I could not give him my real name and address.

I asked him if there were other types of vehicle he'd like to have, and he said several, from PT-76 amphibian tanks to Centurions. As for armoured cars, there were so many good types he just couldn't decide.

I then asked him to take me to the vehicles which had not paraded and was taken aback when he snapped, 'Well, you can't see them! They must be under tarpaulins by now, parked in a high security area. I suggest you go straight to the canteen before they run out of delicacies. Quite a treat waiting, I assure you!'

His sudden eagerness to get rid of me rather spoiled our budding friendship and I thanked him and strode round the stands towards the canteen, which I easily picked out because it was decorated with pennants.

Halfway down the quadrangle I looked to the right and saw the missing tanks, a whole line of them, all under canvas but with the turrets showing. They were about one hundred metres away, on the open ground at one end of the compound. I did not see any unfamiliar outline and figured they must be more of the same three basic types.

On a sudden impulse I turned sharply right and started walking briskly and purposefully towards them just in case somebody was looking my way. Pure curiosity drove me: I just wanted to know if perhaps they had a different camouflage pattern on the hull, which the army was keeping as a surprise for next time.

I got to the first T-54 (there were two of them) and lifted a corner of the tarpaulin as far as the glacis plate. I was appalled by the filthy condition of the bogey-wheels and the tracks. What I saw of the hull was dusty and oily. Lifting the corner further, I saw no bow machine gun, only its mounting. I went quickly to the next tank, and its condition was the same. Also no bow machine gun.

Instinct told me to get away from there immediately, but I had to resist the urge to run. There were small groups of soldiers drifting here and there, obviously waiting for the guests to leave so that they could have their lunch but nobody paid attention to me. Nobody, that is, until I was close enough to the canteen to smell the rich fare.

'You there! One minute!'

I made the mistake of looking in the direction of the voice and saw this man striding towards me, and he was not even in uniform. But everything about him screamed "Security!" and I stopped and turned to face him. He scrutinised my identity card and said, ‘Why aren’t you with the others in the canteen? Have you been to see those stored vehicles?’

So he had not seen me peering under, thank heavens. I’d have found it very difficult to explain that!

‘I had to have the total number of tanks, assault guns, armoured cars, and so on for my magazine. People who read the *Military Journal* expect technical detail.’

‘Yes, of course,’ he said, a cunning look coming into his eyes. ‘I can understand your going right up to inspect the tanks.’

I wasn’t to be caught that easily! ‘Identify and count them, not inspect them. I had a chance to inspect the ones at the parade, and even went inside one.’

For a moment he seemed undecided as to what to do, but a glance in the direction of the tanks confirmed that one had only to go slightly nearer to be able to identify the different types from their uncovered turrets.

‘All right, then. Let me just note down your personal details and you can go for your lunch.’

I was convinced that he’d start checking up as soon as he got back to his office, so I had no option but to make myself scarce without delay. I went into the canteen, made my way between tables stocked with all manner of delicious smelling dishes, envying the bulging cheeks and chomping teeth of blissful-looking eaters, and got out through the back entrance.

In the car I switched identity again and drove out as a VIP, receiving salutes at the gates, and dubious looks at my non-VIP Morris 1000. Once on the road I built up to a steady 100 kph all the way to the ring road, slowing down to my customary 90 kph on it.

There was no doubt in my mind that those T-54s, SUs and AMXs at the depot had been out of action for a considerable period, perhaps years. The money released for their repair and renovation was regularly going into somebody's pocket. The allocation no doubt included maintenance and fuel charges, not to mention salaries and allowances for the ghost crew.

And the President and Ministers concerned must have been getting the lion's share. Leaving the parade at that juncture had been planned in advance.

After what now looked an exceptionally boring little lunch in comparison, I sat down to write my report, dividing it into two distinct parts. The first one was a description of the parade, as a newsman would report it, fit for publication; the second was strictly confidential, for Mr James' information only. This included my suspicions, and he was free to ignore it if he wanted.

When Serge came in the late afternoon for tea he surprised me by his eagerness to see it. His cup was still half-full when he started reading it. He went quickly through the pages until he was stopped short by the "Strictly Confidential" opening to part two. He looked up quickly at me over his half-moon glasses and then resumed reading. He read it over again, slowly, before putting the article on the table.

'I don't understand this thing about the bow machine gun being missing. What's so important about that? Isn't there supposed to be another one? And isn't that adequate?'

'Yes, the co-axial machine guns were in place, but then the co-axial is right next to the big gun and had to be in place for the tank to look functional. They had to leave it in place. But to answer your question, it is the bow machine gun that has freedom of action in a wide arc in front. The co-axial points where the big gun is pointing.'

'I see what you mean. But are they complete write-offs, or do you think they could be repaired fairly quickly?'

'Well, I didn't go down the whole line – there were about ten of them, the same three types plus an armoured car at the far end – but I should think a few could still be done up. Spares are easy enough to obtain in the region. But it seems to me they won't part with the money that easily.'

It was obvious to me, of course, that Mr James and Serge were looking for something to beat the government with, so his consuming interest did not surprise me. But I couldn't help adding, 'Serge, if Mr James goes ahead and publishes this he might end up in the chain gang. And also his colleague, whose name I used!'

He laughed, his exceptionally light brown eyes glinting.

'I hope you won't take offence, Prof, but that man doesn't exist. It is a false name!'

I was surprised and offended, and told him so in no uncertain terms. He did not try to defend himself but pretended to be examining the lines in his left palm. When I had finished letting off steam he looked up and put his hand on my shoulder.

'Prof, the country is being bled dry, and the vultures and hyenas are getting greedier by the day. Anything that'll help bring this government down is to be grabbed with both hands. You have made your contribution, and it may scare off a hyena or two. The end will justify the means.'

'And what if I had been arrested and put in prison, my reputation in tatters? Thought of that?'

'The end justifies the means, Prof. It is the end you must keep in mind.'

That statement by no means mollified me, and I resented having been deceived and used. But there was nothing I could do about it. And I had to admit to myself that I had enjoyed taking risks. After all, Mr James had not asked me to peer under tarpaulins, had he?

Serge, satisfied that we were still friends, collected the article and went back to his place.

It was Act III.

Just three days later, on Tuesday morning, I received

another visit from Lieutenant Zuki of the Special Squad. This time he was accompanied by a police sergeant armed with an AK-47, which he kept jerking up and down as if it was a walking stick. I disliked him on sight.

'Prof, I'm sorry about this, but the captain has been making my life a misery by insisting that I search every house in this neighbourhood. We have already searched Two Sisters and Orange Grove, and you know that some heavyweights live there. So please don't be offended.'

He was the epitome of courtesy and friendliness, so I saw no reason to insist on a search warrant. After all, I had nothing to hide.

They began with the front room, even looking under the furniture, went into the two bedrooms, the kitchen, and even the bathroom, ending up in the study. Here Zuki spent a long time picking off a book at random, and then riffling the pages as if hoping for some bit of paper to fall out. He then asked me to open the drawers of my Victorian writing desk, and I warned him not to touch anything. Every time I opened a drawer he would bend down and peer into it, and then ask me to lift this or that.

I remembered the City street map, with its circles showing where the "Yellow Men" had attacked, just in time to lift it out with a bundle of notes!

About forty-five minutes later he was through, and I breathed a sigh of relief. But now would come a most serious development.

'I'd like now to look around outside, if you don't mind,' he said, and made for the back garden. Where the garden shed was. Where the mountain plant was!

When I suddenly remembered my red plant my blood turned to ice. What an utter, suicidal idiot I was, not to have got rid of it! It was the strongest possible evidence that I had been to the mountains!

First they went round the perimeter, probably looking for openings in the fence, and then poked at a heap of broken bricks before entering the shed. As they did, I rushed through every little prayer that came to mind, but knowing that it was too late for any of them to be answered. Zuki was already fondling the leaves of the plant.

'This is a very strange plant,' he said. 'It looks and feels almost plastic! Where did you get it from?'

Could it be that he really didn't know? Or was he playing with me?

'A friend from the north brought it to me,' I replied, after having to clear my throat. 'One of those weird desert plants.'

The sergeant was also touching the leaves; surely he was bound to know where it grew? But he just grunted.

'Prof, may I ask a favour of you? Could you give me a cutting to plant in my garden? I have really fallen in love with it.'

'Well, it is a very fussy plant, and I doubt if a cutting will take. But I can write to my friend and ask him to send me another one.'

'That'll be fine. But meanwhile perhaps you could let me take this small branch to show my wife. This flower is fantastic.'

And without much ado he took out a flick-knife and cut off a branch. There was no way I could stop him, but I was so overcome with relief at neither of them knowing where the plant was from that all I wanted was to see the back of them. I'd worry about the possibility of somebody else at the station recognising it later.

When their car drove off it seemed as if a little miracle had happened, but then I surmised that since no one ever went to the mountains, except maybe a forestry and mines inspector once a year, it'd be just plain bad luck if there was anyone around who knew about it. This type of plant must have started growing fairly recently, perhaps a mutation of some sort, because it was not even listed in the encyclopedia of regional flora. The major worry was that the flower was going to shrivel up sooner or later and begin dripping the yellow sap.

I now had to get rid of that nemesis plant, but I was reluctant to kill it. So I took the pot to the back fence, behind which was rocky, bushy ground all the way to the Eastern border, and threw it over. Then I walked out of my compound and round to it. The pot was not broken, and I took it among the bushes until I found a rocky outcrop. I emptied it out under a shaded overhang, about a metre above ground, carefully consolidating its familiar earth and little rocks against it, safe from sun and rain. It might even do better there that in my garden shed.

It was as if a load had been lifted off my shoulders.

In the late afternoon a very annoyed Serge came and said his house had been searched as well, but by a different pair. Somehow this put me in good humour, for it proved that Serge wasn't invincible after all! He said they hadn't gone into the villas of civil servants or party members, and I felt some resentment as well as relief at hearing this. I'd hate any man entering my Aida's bedroom. (My heart skipped a beat at the thought.) Serge surprised me by saying that the policemen who searched his house were "rank amateurs" – they didn't know where to look!

'What do you mean, Serge?' I asked him. 'What have you got to hide?'

He burst out laughing until tears came to his eyes. What could be so funny?

'Oh, nothing much. One or two small items which might have given them the wrong impression, that's all.'

I was far from convinced, but I let it pass. I wondered if my little secrets were not, in fact, much bigger than his! Perhaps he had some diamonds, or a pistol, hidden away, but I had the secret of knowing where the "Yellow Men" camped!

What with all the tensions of the day I felt the need to get away from it all, even if only for a couple of hours or so, and in the early evening I toyed with the idea of going to the club, which I had not been to for over two years though I had kept up the subscription. But the place could be exceedingly boring on some nights, and on an impulse I decided to go and see a movie. There used to be three cinemas in the past, but now only one, the Movieland, remained. It was a reasonably good cinema, with comfortable seats and air-conditioning. Naturally the patronage was almost exclusively middle class. I didn't know what film was showing, and I hoped it wouldn't be one of those karate ones.

There is something about watching a film in a movie theatre which is very different from seeing that same movie on a wide-screen TV. The excitement starts the moment one steps inside the cinema, and one sits down in acute anticipation. This is shared with several dozen others, and for a well-known movie the atmosphere becomes electric.

I had seen at the gaudy entrance that the film on that night was *Hangmen Also Die*, an old war movie which I remembered seeing very many years go. It was in black and white, made, if I'm not mistaken, while World War Two was still in progress. What I like most about these old war movies is the authenticity of the equipment shown. Every weapon, every vehicle, every aircraft shown was authentic, unlike in films made long after. For instance, when I went to see the 1970s film *Battle of the Bulge*, I lost interest from the beginning when I saw that the "German" tanks were nothing but slightly padded American tanks. They made no effort to try to preserve the boxy character of the German Tiger tank. For me it was an absolute farce to see American Sexton tanks fighting against other Sextons painted with the German black cross!

The night's film was about the famous assassination of the man whom Allied propaganda called "The Butcher of Czechoslovakia", by Czech resistance fighters trained in England, and dropped by parachute. The victim was, to give his full rank, Obergruppenfuehrer Reinhardt Heydrich, of the SS. It was an exciting film, and I actually enjoyed it more the second time than the first, for one who knew the true story (which emerged long after the war) could now tell fact from fiction. For instance, the fact that Heydrich had to be eliminated was not because he was any more cruel than other SS governors, but because his programme in Czechoslovakia seemed to be gaining the support of many Czechs! Obviously this could not be allowed to grow!

On the way back I had the second experience that month of returning home after midnight through almost deserted streets and dark roads. As I drove down the access road to my bungalow I was confronted with a unique sight. A pack of wild dogs was sitting in a circle, which spanned from one side of the road to the other. There must have been at least sixteen of them, an exceptionally large pack. The immediate impression I received was that they were in conference.

As I got nearer, with my headlights full on, they continued to look in my direction but made no move to get out of the way. I slowed down but kept moving towards them, flicking the headlights several times. I must have got to within three metres of them, and could see that they varied in size and colouring, brown, white and grey predominating, when one of them, probably their leader, got up on its haunches and yawned widely. I had stopped the car and was watching. Then it trotted off into the bush, and the circle unreeled and followed. Not one of them looked back. Their arrogance was magnificent.

The film of Heydrich reminded me of the time when I was much preoccupied with such things as the *I Ching*, the tarot, cartomancy and, in this particular instance, numerology. I had discovered something which, to my knowledge, had escaped the attention of numerologists, for I had never seen it in print. In fact, I have not seen it to the present day, so I feel I should point it out. I am referring to the extraordinary preponderance of the letters "G" and "H" in the surnames of practically all the key figures (with just two exceptions) who shaped and ran the Third Reich and its Nazi ideology. Beginning with those who shaped the Nazi ideology, we have "H":

Hans Horbinger – with his "Wesltelehere" doctrine of "Eternal Ice".

Karl Haushofer – the mystic who, it is believed, introduced Hitler to the Swastika emblem and Aryan lore.

Frederick Heilscher – Founder of the "Ahnenerbe", the Society for the study of Ancestral Heritages (which was later incorporated into the SS).

And then we move on to the rulers of the Third Reich:

Adolf Hitler.

Rudolf Hess – his Deputy until his mysterious flight to Britain in 1940.

Heinrich Himmler – Reichfuehrer SS, who needs no introduction.

And somewhat lower down, the likes of:

Dr Werner Heyde – responsible for the Euthanasia Directorate.

Hoess – Auschwitz commandant.

Heydrich – who many expected to succeed Himmler.

Hugenberg – Head of GNP.

And many others right down to the Luftwaffe's highest-scoring fighter-pilot, Hartmann.

We now move on to the second letter mentioned "G":

Herman Goering – Reich Marshal, who moulded the Luftwaffe into the most powerful air force in the world in the early period of World War Two, a vital element of the Blitzkrieg.

Joseph Goebbels – Minister of Propaganda, and probably the father of modern propaganda techniques.

Heinz Guderian – creator of the German armoured forces, the Panzer sledgehammer, the ground element of the Blitzkrieg.

Again here we find a fighter-pilot of outstanding merit, Adolf Galland, who rose to become Inspector-General of Fighters.

And what could be more closely linked with the Third Reich than the – Gestapo?

A remarkable coincidence was that the letter "H" manifested right across to Germany's major ally, Japan, where we had:

Emperor Hirohito.

Tojo Hideki (as it is written in Japanese, and not "Hideki Tojo") – Minister for War.

And, one need hardly say, Hiroshima.

The names one found on the Allied side covered the entire alphabet.

But let us look at the two letters, "G" and "H", more closely in numerological terms. "G" is the 7th, and "H" is the 8th letter of the alphabet. Now 7 + 8 = 15. Any numerologist will tell you that "15" is also known as the Number of Destiny, whose "divine principle" is predestination! It would appear that Omar Khayyam was not far off with this quatrain:

'Tis all a chequer-board of Nights and Days
Where Destiny with Men for Pieces plays:
Hither and thither moves, and mates, and slays,
Any one by one back in the Closet lays.

The wild dogs paid me back in good measure that night for having broken up their conference. They gathered on the open ground behind my bungalow and set up an almost continuous howl most of the night. There was no doubt about its having been positively orchestrated, for whenever it started to die down there appeared to have been a "conductor" who started it all up again with a few angry growls! Three times I went out with a torch right up to the back fence and threw stones in their direction, and each time they stopped – until I was back in the bungalow! Done out of pure revenge, I was sure of that.

I was reminded of the time, when I was living in the City, when I heard a most unusual and seductive warbling in the garden, one night, which I attributed to a frog for it was in the rainy season. Well, after several tries I must have got very close to imitating its call because it suddenly stopped. It resumed after a while and again I went on imitating it. It stopped again, and then started up such an ear-piercing shriek which went on for so long that I could bear it no more. I went out into the garden with a torch to try to find it, but the garden wall bounced the din in all directions and I failed to locate its source. It started to rain but that didn't stop this banshee, and after another fruitless, and dripping wet, search I returned to switch on the radio to block it out. It must have been almost an hour later when, on turning down the radio, I heard that it had resumed its seductive warbling and I could retire to read in bed. I had learned my lesson, and minded my own business when I heard it the following night. I never heard it again after that.

On the last night of January the new moon was sighted, so the Holy Month of Fasting coincided precisely with 1 February. Now this month, despite its severe demands – no food or drink from just before dawn to sunset; no sex during the day; and no speaking ill of another person! – has its compensations. Family bonds strengthen, the crime rate drops, and night is turned into day with family and friends visiting one another to either share in "breakfast" or afterwards for table games or strolls in moonlight. Children are allowed to stay up later than usual, and every “breakfast” becomes a little feast, even among the poorest because of handouts. It is meant to be a month of good deeds and tranquillity, and to treat it otherwise is to commit a grievous sin.

So it was this very first day of the month that Serge came staggering to my door looking very sick indeed. He slumped into a chair on the veranda as I asked him what was wrong. He looked up with bleary eyes and mumbled, ‘Just my rotten luck! I think I have caught malaria. Can’t remember the last time I had it, curse it!’

I brought a thermometer, though his forehead had already told me he was running a high temperature, and it registered just over 40°C. The fever had to be lowered immediately, and I told him to go into the shower for a sponge-down. He said he preferred to do it in his own place, but meanwhile to get him some tablets. I gave him two of the single-dose variety, hoping it was not one of those resistant strains of malaria which can be so debilitating.

As I was accompanying him to his bungalow he suddenly said, ‘Prof, I want you to do me a favour.’ Without giving me time to say anything, he continued. ‘I have received reports of a build-up of security forces in the city, and even that two armoured cars have moved up from the south. I want you to find out from your friend Zain what they are here for.’

I had a feeling that my vague suspicions were now about to be confirmed.

‘But why should that bother you, Serge? They must be about to swoop on some gang of criminals, and you know their numbers are increasing by the week. So you should be glad the government is about to take some action at last!’

‘Not criminals, Prof. You know the top cats are in league with the regional mafia. They are after some friends of mine, and they, Prof, are no criminals, I assure you.’

'You mean the "Yellow Men", don't you, Serge?'

We were at his veranda steps when I asked this question, and he said nothing as he concentrated on climbing the steps. It is astonishing how swiftly a severe bout of malaria can weaken one.

Without waiting for an answer – for I knew it already – I bullied him straight to the shower to have a sponge-down. The temperature had to be brought down without delay. I asked him not to lock the door, and sat to one side of the door ready to rush in. After a time I heard the shower running.

When he came out, wrapped in a bath towel, his eyes looked a bit clearer and I took his temperature. It was down to just under 39°C, which was still high but tolerable. The pills should be starting to circulate, and I left the thermometer with him, with specific instructions.

'Look, Serge. You people have already used me once, and I have no intention of getting involved. I have nothing against the "Firefly" but I am not cut out for this cloak-and-dagger kind of thing. Sorry, but rule me out.'

'Well, it's entirely up to you, Prof. We will cope, whether you get me that information or not. All I'm asking you to do is to have a chat with Zain, that's all. Not to assassinate him or steal something.'

And when I remained silent he resorted to cunning.

'By the way, when are you hoping to see your witch next?' he asked, with a sly look.

He had me there. I fell for it.

'But I have no reason to go and see Zain,' I pleaded.

'Oh yes, you do! My malaria. Go get some pills for me!' He was smiling now, knowing that he had got me.

'Zain will be at work until late afternoon, so I can't go before then.'

'I'll survive until then, don't worry!'

Since he was going to use me on behalf of the "Yellow

Men", I felt I had every right to find out precisely where he stood in all this.

'Serge, how did you come to get mixed up with this weird lot, at any rate? Are you an active member or just a sympathiser? You know what the Special Squad will do to you when they find out, don't you?'

To my surprise, he burst out laughing. Which probably lowered his temperature a further degree or two, because there is nothing like a happy frame of mind to aid healing. It is an established fact that laughter is worth half a bottle of vitamins.

'Listen, Prof, I have already warned you about what curiosity did to the cat. Let us just say that a close relation of mine has chosen to throw in his lot with this group, and I wish no harm to come to him. All I'm concerned about is his survival, whether I agree with the aims of his group or not.'

'But, Serge, why do they have to give people the impression that they are a crazy bunch, with all that theatrical yellow paint and shaven heads? How do they expect people to take them seriously?'

I waited for his reply with acute interest, for it would reveal just how much he really knew about the "Yellow Men".

'I agree with you, it's certainly very strange. Well, the next time I meet them in the supermarket I'll ask them, okay?'

That was a signal for me to leave, and I advised him to take plenty of fluid. He was one of those people who very seldom caught malaria, unlike the rest of us who considered ourselves lucky if six months passed without an attack of some description. That a mosquito net afforded all the protection one needed was a myth propagated by "experts" living far away from infested areas. One has to be under cover for twenty-four hours a day to avoid getting bitten. A net reduces the chances of catching malaria, but does not eliminate them.

After my afternoon tea I made my way to the Zains'.

Butterflies fluttered in my stomach as I turned the bend towards the right, instead of the usual left, and soon came on their house which was the first in a line of three. Opposite and around them was quite thick thornbush, waiting to be cleared by whoever bought the plots for the entire area was already a jigsaw of plots on the survey map at the Ministry of Housing. I supposed that within a few years most of them would have been snatched up as the City became increasingly congested.

Being the Month of Fasting, I did not expect to see them catching the breeze on the balcony at that time, and they weren't. They'd all be busy doing various things. Aida was bound to be in the kitchen helping her mother, the maid being no cook.

So I was pleasantly surprised when she was the one to open the front door.

'Why, Teacher, this is a surprise!' But her smile was suitably restrained. 'Father is in his study, over there,' she said before disappearing round a corner to where I presumed the kitchen was.

Zain was equally surprised to see me, and not looking too pleased about my intrusion either, having been writing down something. I apologised and told him about Serge's acute attack of malaria, pretending I had no drugs at home and there was no time to rush to the City and be back to complete preparing my own "breakfast". This put him in a sudden good mood as he realised how lucky he was to have three women ministering to him.

'You'll just have to find yourself a wife then, neighbour. How many more years are you going to waste?'

I answered him in my mind: 'Just let me marry your daughter, Zain, and not even an extra week will be wasted.'

'I already have somebody in mind, neighbour. It is just a matter of getting down to preliminaries,' I replied boldly. He'd never guess I meant his daughter of course.

He stood up and went out of the room, returning to say that his daughter was bringing the pills. She came in with a whiff of garlic and spices, a cheap cotton scarf protecting her hair, and a stained apron on. (This is the woman I'm in love with, Zain; this is *she*. She seemed to have caught something of that involuntary but powerful mental pulse because she paused and looked at me for a second instead of turning straight round.)

But how now to get round to getting the information Serge wanted? 'My friends at the café say the City is teeming with security men and soldiers, and even armoured cars have been seen moving up. Everybody is worried about what might be going on.'

'Where did they get that information from? There seem to be too many idle tongues around.'

It struck me then that it was not supposed to be common knowledge, and somebody in the security forces, but of low rank, must have tipped off Serge. I had to immediately reassure Zain that my café mates were firmly loyal and very discreet.

'Well, I'm glad to hear that. It'll be in everybody's interest to have these scoundrels eliminated.' And then he became very indiscreet by adding, 'We now know the track they use to bypass our checkpoints. Clever as mountain goats, they are, but they are in for a surprise. Very, very soon indeed!'

I dared not go any further, and got up to leave.

'Oh, by the way, she wants to say something to you.' He went to the corner and shouted down what must have a short corridor, saying, 'The neighbour is leaving.'

This was a really promising development, and no mistake! What could she want? Not so fast! It had to be a book. Accompanying me to the door, she said, 'Have you got any books on dreams? I can't remember if I saw any.'

'Any particular aspect of dreams?' I asked, my heart leaping.

She turned and looked behind her; her father had remained

in the hall.

'Oh, vivid dreams, repeating dreams, that kind of thing. You know, interpretation.'

I asked her to send her maid to collect it tomorrow morning, and she thanked me and I let myself out.

I went straight to Serge and found him having already prepared his modest "breakfast". I still had to prepare mine. He should have eaten, being so sick.

'I have just been to see Zain, Serge,' I announced dramatically.

He hardly moved and just said, 'Well?'

I repeated everything Zain had said almost word for word.

'I feared as much. Well, we'll see what we can do. You have done well, Prof, and it will be remembered.'

Back in my bungalow I dwelt more on the little exchange with Aida than on what might or might not be happening to the "Yellow Men". None of my business, really, and the next time I was asked to do something I'd give a flat no. Enough was enough. I valued Serge's friendship, but not to the extent of jeopardising my own life.

The Month of Fasting, despite its blessings, is not one for single men. Certainly not those living alone, outside a family context. It is very much a family thing; at least there must be a woman living in the house, and better still if one can invite, and get invited back by, another couple. For me the month had become twenty-nine or thirty days of sheer hardship and tedium, to be endured with gritted teeth. Serge was single, but I expected him to start making frequent visits to his village during the month.

My thoughts went back to Aida's interest in dreams. It would be stretching wishful thinking and credibility too far to speculate that her dreams had anything to do with me. I did not recollect a single instance when she showed the slightest sign that I was anything more to her than a respected teacher figure. She might even grow to look on me as a family friend and sort of "uncle" figure, and be shocked to learn of my feelings. Not specifically because of the age difference, since our women are brought up to value family status, respectability and material security more than transient physical attraction (though a modicum of it must be present, for one cannot live with someone whom one finds unlikeable from the start), but because I simply was not the type of man she'd want as a husband.

On this matter of age difference, it puzzles me that in industrialised countries it is found quite acceptable for an elderly man to maintain a mistress (unless he happened to be a Minister of State or something!) very many years younger than himself; but should he choose to marry her he becomes the subject of much disapproval and malicious gossip! This also, of course, applies to older women with young men. To us this is a reversal of morals. And societies which imprison people in watertight age compartments, so that a thirty-year-old young man is considered too old for an eighteen-year-old girl, also happen to have the highest divorce rates in the world. Throughout nature, creatures mate according to ability and availability. Ever seen an old tomcat, with one ear chewed off, being turned down by a nubile she-cat? Or a cat which has already produced ten litters lacking suitors?

One talent that women the world over possess is that of being able to make a perfectly intelligent man behave like a rank idiot. You will catch a renowned scientist or professor of theology doing cartwheels over a woman of neither intellectual nor physical distinction. To you, that is; to him she is Nefertiti and Helen of Troy combined.

In view of what was to happen that night, there was an ironic prelude when the 10 p.m. news had a commentary, after the news, which stated that the government was appealing to the “misguided rebel who calls himself the Firefly” not to disrupt the lives of civilians and destroy property in the Holy Month. The “Firefly” must honour its significance, it preached.

I woke up for a small meal at 2 a.m. as was customary, only the time changing according to one’s wish. From experience I knew that the fast the following day would be no easier because of it!

About three kilometres away something had already happened which was to turn my entire life upside down and change it irrevocably.

« EIGHT »

I woke up that Thursday morning with a strong feeling of unease, which I put down to probably having had a bad dream. With no breakfast to prepare, and the long day stretching ahead, I decided to do some gardening while the sun was still not too high. My tomato plants were beginning to produce fruit, and I looked forward to what promised to be a rich harvest. Much money would be saved as tomatoes were unreasonably expensive, and yet were needed in so many dishes, from salad to curry. I went to the shed, checked the experimental grape seedlings (what a relief not to have the red mountain plant any more!), and returned to the house in time for the 10 a.m. local news. I was in for a terrible shock.

'Last night, just before midnight, our security forces ambushed a gang of the criminal "Yellow Men" in the foothills of the Western Mountains. In a firefight that lasted half an hour it is believed that at least ten of the rogues were killed, and others wounded. Our men lost two men killed, and two wounded. The "Yellow Men" dragged away their dead and wounded into the side bushes, and our men are in hot pursuit. The President has sent his congratulations to the police and the army.'

My life turned nightmarish as of that moment. I looked around desperately, hoping that it was all a dream and I'd wake up any moment. But everything remained in place, and the sun continued to pour in.

I had no doubt in my mind that it was my red plant and flower that had brought about the discovery of the secret nocturnal visits to the mountains. The flower which Lieutenant

Zuki had taken would have ripened, drooped, and started exuding the yellow sap. A single phone call to the Forestry Department would have established where it grew. A discreet watch with night glasses over a period of several nights would have discovered the harvesting cycle.

The feeling of guilt was overwhelming, and I literally retched. And then came fear. They should be coming to take me in any time now. In fact, they were overdue, it seemed to me, but perhaps they were watching and waiting, to see who came to see me, or whom I contacted in town. A desperate urge to pack a suitcase and race for the airport seized me. It seemed to be my only chance of escape. To just move to another town in the country wouldn't work.

What stopped me was the thought of losing Aida for ever. There was a chance that with a good lawyer I could claim to have been used unwittingly, or something. Or leave that out altogether, and stick to the story I had told at the hospital – foolhardy, but scientific curiosity.

And then I remembered Serge. How could I possibly ever face him again? Well, you can take the bull by the horns right now and go to see him. You don't have to blurt out the truth. Just find out what he is thinking.

I found him sitting in his veranda, a small radio by his side playing soft music.

'Peace be upon you, Serge. How's your fever?'

He had risen to shake hands, as was customary, and showed no signs of disturbance, sadness or anxiety.

'Haven't you heard the news, Serge? About the mountains?'

'Oh, I have,' he replied casually. 'I have indeed.'

'I don't understand,' was my reaction. 'Weren't they your friends?'

'They were, they were.'

He never usually repeated words, and this suggested to me

that he looked calm but was actually highly stressed. And there was something else on his mind. I could sense it.

'Prof, the information you gave me yesterday saved us from disaster last night. We had two parties going into the mountains, one of fifteen men from the north, and one of seven from the smaller southern camp. I telephoned our, er, liaison point and managed to stop the main party from going. Unfortunately he could not contact the smaller group. So how the police and two armoured cars got to kill ten men when only seven were present remains a mystery!' But he was not really smiling, for he went on to say that two were killed and were carried away into the bushes by the others, one of whom was also wounded.

'The security forces were too eager. Or maybe plain jumpy, for they were lurking behind the camouflaged armoured cars on the bushy plain, and knew there were snakes around! Anyway, they started firing the moment our men appeared instead of waiting until they had put their assault rifles down to collect the herbs with small torches.'

'Well, thank the Almighty for that!' I said, while writhing with shame and guilt inside. Saved them? I had not saved them. They'd not have been fired on to begin with, but for my plant. I was responsible for two deaths. Four, including the security men.

'Prof, how would you like to join us? The Ancestor is very keen to meet you.'

I was flabbergasted. In fact, I did not want to get involved at all. But I was already, wasn't I? Deeply involved. The police were just marking time to pounce on me, and the "Yellow Men" would kill me if they found out. A fine situation to be in.

'Who, under heaven, is the Ancestor?'

'"Firefly" leader. His close aides call him the Ancestor. He represents the spirits of our ancestors.'

'I see,' I said, my mind befogged.

I still had three options: pack up and immediately leave the country; go the police and explain everything, and hope for the best; or seek refuge with the "Firefly" people. All three looked like pretty bad choices, with the last one probably the worst, for I might end up on the gallows. I cannot understand to this day what made me say, 'Right. Count me in.'

'I shall take you to meet the Ancestor in the next few days, God willing, but meanwhile do absolutely nothing which might interest the police. And drive safely!'

Serge had not even blinked, or shown pleasure. If you only knew, Serge! Any day now Lieutenant Zuki would come for me, and that might lead to betraying you as well!

Perhaps the best thing was to pack up and go abroad while I still had the chance. I could see no other alternative. My world had turned into a living nightmare, in which I was up to my waist in quicksand. Movement in any direction would lead to sinking deeper. By agreeing, was I not playing for time?

I was briefly rescued from my pit of despond by Aida's housemaid coming for the book. I had selected two, one on the nature of dreams (as if anybody really knew!) and the other on popular interpretations. What was needed was really a heart-to-heart talk between us, for I had a feeling, a hope, that our dreams might be connected in some way. I refused to dismantle my castles in the air.

I could not figure out why the police didn't come for me as the days passed; perhaps they were shadowing me and waiting for me to lead them to the big fish. And I thought they did not bring in artillery to shell the forest because they did not know precisely where the "Firefly" camp was. The forest stretched all the way to the Red River, and north to within ten kilometres of the town of Mirage.

It was not until the weekend that Serge came to see me about going to meet the "Firefly". And it happened with hardly any warning, for he came at 4.30 p.m. on Saturday afternoon and said a car was coming round to collect us at 7 p.m.! He would not reveal the destination, of course, and I had visions of our ploughing through dense jungle by torchlight.

When he left I sat back as if in a dream. I was actually, actually going to meet the now near-legendary "Firefly". It seemed unreal, like being told one was going to see a real live unicorn.

I was ready to go long before the appointed time, all dressed up in my khaki hunting jacket and baggy trousers tucked into high boots, and the only thing missing was a peaked cap! Serge came in at about twenty minutes to seven, carrying a small bag. He smiled tolerantly when he saw my outfit.

'We are not going into the jungle, you know,' he said, 'but you look good!'

Then he unzipped the bag, and brought out two handguns which he handed to me. I was no stranger to guns, but I hadn't been near one for about ten years and I was quite startled.

'Pick one,' he said.

They were a .38 Smith and Wesson revolver (probably stolen from the police), and a 7.62 mm Tokarev automatic pistol. I weighed each in turn in my hand, and pointed them at various objects in the room. Both were good guns, tried and proven, but my cautious nature made me pick the revolver. If one round failed to fire, the following one would not; if an automatic jammed, it took a minute or two to get it going again. And also for reasons best known to the Russians, the Tokarev lacked a safety catch or grip-safety, though this did not seem to have worried the soldiers on the Eastern Front!

'Prof, playtime is now over. If at any stage we are stopped by the security forces we'll have to shoot our way out. And should either of us be unable to get away, the other will have to shoot him. I'm sorry to have to say this, but you also possess information, though it is still little, which must be protected.

And certainly in my case you must shoot me without hesitation, do you understand?'

I think it was only at that moment that it sank in on me that I was plunging into very deep water indeed. To relieve the pressure in my head, I tried to make light of it.

'Where would you like it to be, Serge? Heart or head?'

'Head,' he said, without smiling.

Almost on the dot we heard a car stopping outside my gate, and we went out to it, leaving the lights in the house on.

The driver just turned once to shake my hand, and Serge and I sat in the back. The gun was in one of my bottom pockets, with five rounds in; the hammer was resting on an empty chamber, safety catch off. We drove south for about seven kilometres, then turned into a dirt track for several hundred metres. We stopped when we saw a large four-wheel drive car, and two men stepped out of it and made for our car. Serge nudged me, and we got out and went to meet them. One said something like, "Number thirty-three," and proceeded to our car. We moved into theirs, and it turned round and back to the main road.

To my surprise, we returned towards the ring road. There was a police checkpoint just where it curved right to link up with the Northern Road, so I was wondering why we were going that way. We slowed down at the barrier, and an armed policeman came forward. I found myself gripping my revolver. But he flashed his light on the number plate, and without looking inside the car waved us on! I was astounded and looked at Serge.

'Diplomatic number plate,' he said. 'Northern country.'

I had to rest content with that!

Once we crossed the Northern Bridge we drove carefully through the unlit streets of several villages, and suddenly stopped by a group of houses. The driver got out to talk to a small group of turbaned men, looking shadowy and mysterious in the light of hurricane lamps. The smell of strong coffee and tobacco wafted into the air.

The driver returned and said, 'All clear.'

Serge said to leave my gun under the seat and step out. The group then led us down a narrow lane to a high-walled compound. There were three houses in it, their high, narrow windows casting beams of yellow light from their oil lamps against the ghostly white of the buildings. The whole scene was almost like a three-dimensional painting. This is real "ancestor" country, I thought. It was just like this a hundred, two hundred years ago.

I could hear goats bleating somewhere off to the left, and for a brief moment I thought I saw the outline of a camel, lighter in colour than the black background of the moonless sky.

We approached the middle of the three low houses, where a hurricane lamp hung on one side of the door. There was a man sitting on the traditional raised platform, built against the wall on either side of the entrance. We greeted him, and he rose and went inside. After a moment he emerged to welcome us inside, leading us to a room which was lit by two ornamental oil lamps hung on opposite walls. The lighting was a subdued yellow, but one with good eyes could read beneath one of the lamps.

The room was devoid of furniture, but a wide carpet and two smaller ones covered almost the entire floor, and there were colourful cushions propped up against the walls. We sat just off centre of the wall facing the door. Serge had withdrawn into himself, and hardly a word was exchanged while we were waiting. I was beginning to feel increasingly nervous as the minutes passed and nobody appeared.

Then suddenly and silently a man stood framed by the door, dressed in the manner of the people outside, in a long white robe and turban, shadows shifting across his face as the flames of the lamps danced in the faint breezes. No one had to tell me: I knew it was the "Ancestor", the "Firefly" himself. He slipped off his sandals and moved swiftly towards us, eyes fixed on me for a moment before turning to Serge whom he embraced. He then shook my hand, a normal firm handshake, not one meant to impress.

He fixed his eyes on me again, and I can only say that as from that moment I became his disciple. For there was something priest-like about his expression and his manner, accentuated by a wispy, philosopher's beard and bushy eyebrows. He was slightly taller than me, and I'm slightly above average, so it cannot be said that he was a tall man. But he appeared to be, and this is a general rule with charismatic people.

He looked from me to Serge, and back again, and his next words caused all the tension of the moment to dissipate.

'So this is the Armoured Professor! I have never met one before!'

I couldn't help it – I burst out laughing and was joined by both of them. The ice had been broken, and conversation flowed freely after that. He said something about his aims and aspirations, about Serge being his right arm, and how interesting he had found my exposition on the Mongols, and my reporting of the military parade. Our "Mr James", it was revealed, was the head of the "Firefly" military intelligence, and was currently in another country recruiting agents.

I marvelled at the way, even at this very first meeting, that the Ancestor seemed to trust me implicitly. And I swore inwardly that I'd die rather than betray his trust.

Just then a man came to the door and held out a hand, palm facing us. The Ancestor said that our car would be ready in five minutes. He left the room and returned with two baskets of ripe red dates, handing them to us.

'From Marmar,' he said.

'Naturally,' said Serge. 'Where else?'

I was struck by this mention of Marmar, where I had grown

up from the age of three and lived right up to when I went abroad to study.

'Why, are you from Marmar, Ancestor? That's where I was brought up! Both my parents are buried there.'

'Really? What a fine, exciting town it used to be, so full of merchants and caravans coming and going. And the music of the troubadours.'

He had sidestepped my question but I did not repeat it. He had mentioned quite a bit about his aspirations and programme for fundamental reforms, but with time running out I felt I had to know something of his political stand. So I asked him what political system he was going to adopt when in power.

'Professor, I think I'm going to shock you a bit. You see, all my life I have resented having the quality and direction of my life determined by semi-literate leaders kept in power by a combination of a repressive state machinery and the votes of easily fooled illiterates. Look at the countries on this continent; with two or three notable exceptions, they all practise one of these three forms of dictatorship. There is the one-party, brazen dictatorship, with its shop-window elections of unopposed candidates. Then there is the unvarnished military dictatorship. And last, but by no means least, there is the fashionable so-called multi-party form of dictatorship, in which one party is so dominant and unscrupulous that opposition simply withers away.'

He paused, looking at me enquiringly, probably expecting a comment or question. Remembering a controversial remark by the historian Sir John Glubb, the former commander-in-chief of the Royal Jordanian Army, to the effect that a "benevolent monarchy" was superior to "democracy" as practised in the developing countries, in safeguarding the rights and interests of its citizens, I asked the Ancestor for his opinion.

'Well, times change, and what was appropriate yesterday

may be unworkable today. So many new pressures have been added to life, from within and from without a country. Nevertheless, as a historian you will know that only the maddest of monarchs ever turned against his or her citizens with the viciousness shown by present-day party-based regimes. I have dedicated myself to restoring, in essence, the reign of the Twelve Elders. My concern is the people of Rivenia, not what they'll say in foreign capitals. I place freedom from want and from fear at the top of my list of priorities.'

Just then the man appeared again at the door and we all stood up. The Ancestor showed us to the gate and said he would see us again soon. We returned to Bonelands by a different route.

Now that I had committed myself to their cause (of which I knew hardly anything at all) Serge no longer had to put on an act with me. And for the first time I dared ask more direct questions, while knowing that I was not yet going to receive direct answers.

'How many men have we got hiding out?' I asked.

'We are in three camps, spread over the forest. The men had to be where they can fire guns without the fishermen on the river hearing it. The mountains block all sounds this side of the forest, of course. All I can tell you at present is that there are several hundred men at each camp receiving intensive training from somebody whose name you'll probably recollect.'

'Oh? And who may that be?' I asked.

'Bluebeard.'

'What are you talking about? Bluebeard died a generation ago.'

Bluebeard was a legend in Rivenia, having been a constant thorn in the side of the foreign rulers for many years with his river piracy and cattle-rustling. There was a huge reward on his head, but no one ever collected it because the Red River claimed him in a thunderstorm. His body was never found.

'Bluebeard Junior, formerly Colonel Bluebeard before he published an article criticising the High Command. He was kicked out of the army and was about to be hauled in on a trumped-up charge of treason when he disappeared into thin air, until we found him just over two years ago where you'd least expect to find him!' He chuckled, but did not explain. Bluebeard was actually his father's nickname because of his piracy, but it had completely replaced the family name, as occasionally happened in the country.

'I suppose the men are training with stolen police weapons and wooden guns?' I asked, dubious about the whole business.

'I'll overlook the insult, Prof. We are better organised than you think. But you'll learn that in due time. Sooner, in fact, than you can imagine because the discovery of our mountain trails means that we may have to come out of the forest in a matter of weeks rather than months.'

'Come out of the forest? And go where?' I asked, deep guilt giving me a pain akin to that of angina.

'There is only one direction from the forest, and that's the one we'll take. Our programme has been totally messed up, curse the man who betrayed us!'

I think that if I had courage I'd probably have gone out to the bushes and shot myself.

About two days later Serge started getting nocturnal visitors. A car would drive up and stop halfway between his gate and mine, and about forty-five minutes later would drive away. I decided not to mention it. I was very much on probation, and too many questions would have made Serge consider me too indiscreet.

I think it was on the sixteenth of the month that the whole situation was abruptly transformed, and the countdown began.

Serge put in a surprise appearance at about 10.30 p.m., just after his visitors had left, and I knew that something was up.

Without preamble he said, ‘Prepare yourself for a shock, Prof. We are moving out of the forest within three weeks, and the Ancestor has several courses of action open to him. One of them is to attack the City.’

I was not shocked so much as astounded. I seemed to be entering a sort of Never-Never Land, a world divorced from reality.

‘Are you people mad, Serge? Attack the City? With a few hundred poorly armed dropouts and former drug addicts? You must be joking, Serge!’

He did not look the least bit annoyed or disturbed. He continued as if I had said nothing at all.

‘The Ancestor wants you, as a military historian, to describe in detail how you personally would plan the seizure of this city. Towards that end, I have brought you a factual deposition of government forces in the City and its surroundings; and a hypothetical breakdown of our own forces and weaponry. He regrets that as yet you cannot be given the factual breakdown, but his interest is in the way you would approach the problem. The actual plan of operations will be prepared by us.’

‘Are you seriously telling me that storming the City is an option?’ I asked, already knowing from the look on his face that it was.

‘One of the options, yes,’ he replied, cagily, but I had a dreadful feeling that it was top of the list.

As he stood up to leave, he said, ‘You have precisely three days to complete the exercise.’

Well, this was a real turn-up for the books, and no mistake! But I was the man responsible for having got them to this stage, so there was no honourable way of getting out of it. I’d never be able to live with myself if I were to catch the next plane out of the country. And the image of Aida would haunt me for the rest of my life.

I had a closer look at the papers he had left me, and spread out the City map on the carpet. I marked in the strongpoints which they had identified: City barracks, police HQ and stations, the presidential Palace. Then just five kilometres away was the 3rd Battalion camp, close to the Northern Bridge spanning a crevice. In the short term one could ignore the scattered units of the Northern Division, not only because of the distances involved but also because all we had to do was to blow up the bridge, and that would keep them away several days.

But the Southern Division around Granitetown, a mere thirty kilometres away, was the biggest danger. Not only was it much better organised than the much neglected Northern one, practically all the armour was down south. My most optimistic estimate (which I later discovered was precisely that arrived at by the "Firefly" planning team) was that we should have to capture the City within just two days, before the southern armour mobilised and streamed north. According to the "hypothetical breakdown" we had available just over 1,000 combatants armed with an assortment of weapons, from assault rifles to heavy machine guns and hand-held anti-tank weapons. We were also said to have a "5th Column" in the City, and it was hinted that we had "friends" in one or two of the National Army battalions. The enemy strength in the City was put at approximately 2,000 men, including the armed police.

I did not go out that day, nor the next, but enjoyed myself hugely placing one tracing paper after another on the map and drawing in those symbols beloved of generals – little squares, triangles, sweeping arrows in different colours, numbers and symbols, and otherwise producing highly colourful sheets which would have greatly impressed a layman. But I had no illusions that they would impress the real military men, and I really did the exercise purely to show the Ancestor that I had taken his request seriously. A few pages of notes accompanied the operation plan.

With a sense of achievement, I neatly arranged the sheets in a folder, rejoicing at having done it with a day to spare and looked forward to seeing the surprise on Serge's face.

And that's when disaster stared me in the face. The doorbell rang, long and loud. No ordinary visitor of mine ever rang like that, for it revealed a total lack of concern or manners.

I grabbed the folder and ran with it to the study and shoved it under a pile of aircraft magazines. Just in time I remembered the City map folded up on a chair and shoved it under the carpet.

I was not surprised on opening the front door to see that it was Lieutenant Zuki, again accompanied by a policeman holding an AK-47. Without waiting to be invited he pushed into the room. And he did not give the customary greeting, and this gave me a chance to put him in his place.

'Didn't they teach you proper manners at the Police Academy, Lieutenant?' I asked him sternly.

He had no option but to apologise, but then quickly rounded on me.

'It is very naughty to lie, Professor. People get into bad trouble for lying to the police.'

'I don't know what you are talking about. I'm not in the habit of lying, so say what you have to say and then come round with a search warrant next time. I'm very busy at the moment.' He dug into his jacket pocket and came out with a bit of paper, and I knew I was in trouble. He showed it to me. It was a formal search warrant.

'Now,' he continued, 'you can make things easy for yourself and get off with just a small fine and a warning. Or you can force me to take steps which I'd normally not like to take with a gentleman like you.'

As yet I was more angry than scared, but that was to change with his very next remarks, after I had protested yet again that

I had no reason to lie.

'In that case, you'll have no objection to our searching your house again. Corporal, you start with the bedroom and then take the bathroom. I'm doing the study.'

He wasted no time at all with the sitting room this time but went straight into the study. Like the last time, he peered behind rows of books, occasionally withdrawing the fatter volumes, which he opened and shook, and then asked me to unlock the side bottom drawers. Nothing there, of course, and I was about to breathe a sigh of relief when suddenly he made for the pile of magazines. Under one of them was the plan of operations.

A major crisis was suddenly upon me. If he saw the plan, under no circumstances was I going to let him go away with it, with or without me. And that applied to his companion as well, of course.

I started edging away towards the door because the .38 Smith and Wesson that Serge had given me was hidden in one of my tall hunting boots in the spare bedroom. The moment he found the folder under the pile of magazines I was going to run for the gun and come out shooting. I had no alternative. I could hear the corporal in the kitchen as Zuki went to the first pile of magazines. It happened to be the one with the plan.

He picked up the top magazine, riffled through it, and then picked up the next. I was at the door, my heart chugging like Serge's motorbike. I hoped I wasn't going to get a heart attack. There were just six magazines in that pile, the latest ones which I intended to go through again. He was down to the fourth when, miracle of miracles, he stood up and looked at the aeroplane models on the wall.

'What makes you so interested in aeroplanes?' he asked, with what sounded like a tinge of suspicion. It was as if it wasn't the kind of thing a Rivenian of my age should be preoccupied with.

He lifted off the large B-17G and shook it, before replacing it clumsily. Had he expected to hear the rattling of diamonds, perhaps? He grunted and after glancing briefly at the ceiling, made for the spare bedroom, which had a trunk full of memorabilia, a chest of drawers, and all manner of little parcels. And, against a side wall, my hunting boots with the gun. While he was looking through the trunk, the corporal came in and at last I knew what had brought Zuki round this time!

'Corporal, go round to the garden shed and bring the red plant. We'll take the professor and his plant to the station with us.'

I had been hoping against hope as time passed and he did not mention the plant that it had not been the cause of their discovering the mountain trails, but now there could be no doubt.

'You see, my dear Professor, this plant is living proof of your having gone to contact the "Yellow Men". I saw the plants close up with my binoculars when I went the next day to see the scene of the action. Some of my men – wearing boots just like yours there – went right down to the mountains to look for dead bodies.'

And then came the next crisis: the corporal came running in to say that he could not find any red plant in the shed. Zuki gave me one searching look and then went running out and round to the garden. When he returned his face looked murderous.

'Destroying evidence is a most serious offence, Prof. You are coming with us to the station. Corporal, bring those boots as well for laboratory examination.'

I was standing by the boots, and I was not going to let them take them or me to the station. The two had to die. I bent down as if to zip up the left one, and slipped my hand in to grasp the revolver. The butt fitted my hand like it was tailor-made for it. I had kept it loaded, as usual with the hammer resting on an empty chamber. I was straightening up when all hell broke loose!

My front door was flung violently open and a wild figure came charging in, wielding a heavy stick with both hands and giving the cry of a soldier charging with a fixed bayonet.

It was Serge, and he was halfway into the room before he saw me, frozen in position with one hand in the boot. The two startled policemen reeled back against the chest of drawers. I straightened up, leaving the gun in the boot. Serge's impetus had carried him forward to within a metre of Zuki, the pointed end of the stick almost touching his throat. For a few seconds the tableau held, then gradually Serge pulled back and lowered the stick. Zuki looked petrified.

'Zuki, you son of a twisted goat, from now on I want you to leave the Professor alone, do you hear? You have already searched his house and found nothing. Why do you keep pestering him?'

The voice was icily calm, but at that moment I knew that Serge had come in prepared to kill, had he found that Zuki had discovered anything incriminating or had me in handcuffs ready to take me out.

After repeatedly clearing his throat – the corporal seemed to have forgotten he had a rifle – Zuki gave vent to his fury.

'Sergeant Erion! You have threatened a police officer and interfered with official security investigations. You have committed very serious offences for which I'm placing you on charge. Corporal! Take him to the car.'

Once again I prepared myself to dip for the revolver should the corporal make a move, but he hesitated, and Serge spoke up.

'Go and ask your captain to come and arrest me, Lieutenant. Tell him Sergeant-Major Erion sends regards to his family, and to the Commissioner and his family.'

By the way Zuki was taken aback, I surmised that family bonds were involved, and this could make things very unpleasant for Zuki since he had nothing tangible to pin either on Serge or on me. Had he discovered the plan or the stolen Smith and Wesson it would have been a very different situation.

To save face, Zuki turned on me.

'Prof, I am absolutely certain you have much to hide, and I swear in the name of the Almighty that I will not rest until I see you where you belong – behind bars!'

With this parting shot he stormed out of the bungalow, viciously banging my front door behind him after the corporal had slipped out. A minute later we heard the police car screeching off with wheels spinning.

I told Serge I was making coffee and he went and sat out in the veranda, where I joined him a few minutes later. Both of us were dripping with sweat and my knees felt weak.

'Serge,' I said after a few minutes in which neither said anything, 'if providence had not brought you in like the proverbial 7th Cavalry as the Yanks would say, I'd have shot both men.'

He looked at me pensively and punched me lightly on the shoulder.

'The Ancestor was right about you,' he said, before relapsing into silence. Then he added, 'Call it an old soldier's instincts, but when I heard a car stopping outside your gate I felt I had to see who it could be. When I saw it was a police car I knew you could be in very serious trouble, knowing you'd be working on the attack plan. So I came round and sat behind your car, waiting to see if they came out with you. If they had I'd have killed them.'

'With the stick?' I asked, smiling.

'Quite easily, but I also brought the Tokarev.'

He reached under his loose-hanging shirt behind his back and pulled it out from his belt.

'Anyway,' he continued, 'when twenty minutes passed and no one came out, I sneaked up to the veranda and hid under it. That was just before the corporal went round to the back of the house, to be followed by Zuki on his return. From his steps I could tell that some sort of crisis was at hand. That's when I decided to come in.'

He then asked me how far I had got with my ideas, and I brought out my plan. He flicked swiftly through it, and his only comment was that it looked interesting.

'Serge, I had very limited information to go on with, so I must have left out many important things. And I still have not been given the exact number of men we can put in the field.'

'Oh, don't worry about that. The Ancestor will be interested more in your approach than your figures. Bluebeard heads the planning team, and he'll be your critic, not the Ancestor.'

That Zuki had not mentioned the red plant in Serge's presence had saved me from a potential catastrophe, and I was thankful to providence.

One thing which was firmly fixed in my mind was that the "Firefly", the Ancestor, was neither a self-seeking politician, after power and money, nor an aspiring warlord. In fact, I feared for his future even if he should succeed, for he struck me as an idealist, a dreamer. The stories he had heard as a child sitting at his grandfather's feet had sunk deep into his subconscious and were not to be rooted out easily. What I feared was not that he would change, should he succeed in overthrowing the government, but that he would die of bitterness and disillusionment. Or be assassinated.

•••••••

I was most pleasantly surprised when at about 9.30 p.m. two of my café group came to see me. When I heard the creaking of the gate I thought it was Serge, for nobody else ever came round in the evening.

'I keep telling you to get married, and you keep putting it off,' greeted Adam at the veranda steps. 'Look at you! Thin as a pinstriped mosquito!' The other man, Abdullah, was his brother-in-law.

'You two should be entertaining your wives instead of prowling about at this time of night. Looking for somebody to pick up, no doubt!' I retorted.

It really was good to see them, and the next hour was spent as if we were at the café (which, being the Month of Fasting, was shut all day, and we had never taken to meeting there in the evenings), drinking coffee and eating Turkish delights.

Towards the end Adam brought up the subject of the wife prospect whom I had met at his house.

'I think she likes you, Prof. My wife tells me she has mentioned you several times. She really is a fine woman, and I think you two would get on well.'

The image of Aida drifted across my mind, and she would have to reject me first before I could consider anyone else. But by then this woman might have got snapped up. I had to tell Adam the truth.

'Adam, there is another woman on my mind, and she was already there even when I came to your place. But there are complications, and I may not know for some time if I am just imagining things.'

'Well, it's your life, my friend, but I am not going to mention this to my wife. How about coming out for an ice cream? This is the month of night revelling, if you remember. You are turning yourself into a hermit.'

I was tempted, but declined. They promised to drop in again before Eid.

Much cheered by their visit, my mind turned to Aida. I had read somewhere that if one concentrated one's mind on a person of close acquaintance, positively or negatively, actual and measurable physical changes take place in the other person, the intensity varying according to the power of the transmitting mind and the extent of the emotional bond between them. This gave me the idea of sending a telepathic message to Aida, beginning with a wave of love, and then begging her to phone me. I did so, feeling slightly foolish afterwards, then I took to bed with a view to waking up later for a pre-fast meal. I was soon asleep and had a vivid dream.

In the dream, I was in a large dance hall, softly lit, and there were many couples dancing to a waltz. I was standing on the side, and pair after pair of handsome men and beautiful women pirouetted past me. Then I noticed a man and a woman who were patently very much in love, lost in one another, moving as one. They whirled nearer and, to my utmost horror I saw that the woman was Aida! And the man was the Commissioner of Police! Seized by blind fury, I lurched towards them, but they were already past, and she looked back and laughed.

I woke up in a foul mood, not helped by the knowledge of the long, hungry day that lay ahead. It was a bright, sunny day, but with no café to go to it might as well be dark and wet.

And then unreasoning suspicions started creeping in. What if the dream revealed the true reason for Aida having turned down one proposal after another? Could she and the Commissioner, a married man, have been carrying on in absolute secrecy for years? Perhaps on the occasions when she spent weekends with relations? Easy to slip out and say she was going shopping. I called myself all manner of fools for maligning her that way. The events of the last few days, plus the terrible burden of guilt, were obviously affecting me badly and I had to watch it.

Out on the veranda, watching the shifting kaleidoscope of colours on the mountain, the phone rang. Another morning call? Tony again?

'Hello, Teacher!' It was Aida! I could not believe my ears.

'Why, Aida! What a lovely surprise!' I exclaimed.

There was what sounded like a gasp, and then silence. I was

suddenly filled with anxiety. 'Hello! Hello!' I said, pressing the earpiece tighter.

'What did you call me?' she asked in a cold voice.

'Why, Aida, of course. That's your name, isn't it?'

'That's my name at birth. Mother changed it to Aisha when I was two years old, lest they teased me at school. So how did you find out?'

I was thunderstruck. Serge had got it wrong, the two names sounding so similar, with the same double "i".

'I honestly don't know. It just came to me. I can't explain it. Perhaps in a dream, or something.' I couldn't mention Serge.

'That is very strange, Teacher. Very strange indeed.'

Her voice was cold and distant, and I feared she was going to put the phone down. There goes your little castle in the air, I told myself. The woman was offended. A stranger had revealed a family secret.

The silence that continued started getting painful, though it was probably only a matter of half a minute. But she had not put the phone down, and I had to say something, fast.

'Aida… Aisha… where are you ringing from?' Anything to re-establish contact.

'From home. Father and Mother have gone next door. I wanted to ask you if you have other books on dreams. These two are interesting, but I can't find the things I'm looking for.'

Should I not now find out, once and for all, if we had some tenuous link in the dream world? Life was short, so why not come right out and settle the matter? If she burst out laughing, that would restore realism, wouldn't it? For imagination to get out of hand at my age was a dangerous thing.

'Aisha…' I started.

'You can call me Aida. But not in front of anybody else.' These words gave me wings! Suddenly some intangible thing began to take shape and moved closer.

I told her about the dream, stopping short only of confessing that I had fallen hopelessly in love with that woman in the dream, and hence with her.

'Weird,' she said. 'Most strange.'

But she wouldn't be drawn, and when I mentioned that I did have another book on dreams, this one on precognitive dreams, she said, 'I must hang up. I can hear footsteps on the gravel.'

I went to the study and wrote down as much as I could remember of what she said. In the course of the evening I repeatedly went over the words, but failed to find anything to hold on to. Except one – that she wanted me to go on calling her Aida. Surely that was pregnant with implication. Or was it? I made up my mind to put all my cards on the table the very next chance I got. A stanza from Omar Khayyam sprang to mind:

Oh, come with old Khayyam, and leave the Wise
To talk; one thing is certain, that Life flies;
One thing is certain, and the Rest is Lies;
The Flower that once has blown for ever dies.

I had to ensure that Serge never referred to her as 'Aida', so the next morning I went round to see him, pretending to be in a huff.

'Serge, you nearly made a fool of me. The woman's name is Aisha, not Aida. You know we don't use that name here.'

He was genuinely apologetic, admitting that he had misheard it, and that was that. In fact, I was very grateful to him indeed for having got it wrong!

Before I left, I asked him how things were progressing and he said that a deadline was looming up, but he'd let me know in good time. He stressed again that under no circumstances was I to allow myself to be taken to a police station. To my horror, he gave me a small paper envelope with a couple of blue tablets in it.

'Put these in your pocket every time you go into town.

You'll be the judge of when to take them, should there be absolutely no way out. Don't take your gun in your car. I suggest you wrap it up and bury it in the garden for the time being. I know all this is hideous stuff, but you now possess information known only to the planning council. You must be prepared to sacrifice yourself for the sake of the country, as all of us are.'

'But if I bury the gun, what if Zuki calls again?'

'They have nothing on you yet, though they have been watching your movements. And, in fact, mine. But soon you won't have to worry about them.'

It wasn't a pleasant feeling going round with poison pellets in one's pocket. I wondered if I'd have the courage to take them, should the moment come. And when would that moment be anyway? They could arrest me just in order to harass me, and then let me go. Serge was overdramatising things perhaps. I knew that this was the month when the Firefly Army would move out of the forest and attack the City, and it was this knowledge, above all, that made it so critical for me not to fall into government hands. No, Serge was not overdramatising. On the contrary, he was showing astonishing faith in my loyalty to the "Firefly" movement. Much later I learned that it was the Ancestor himself who had told Serge that I had struck him as being a man to be trusted.

As to the exact date for the attack, that evening's local broadcast put it to within a day or two. For there was going to be a conference of regional heads of state on 26 February and this was bound to be a major factor in the choice of date. Would it be better to storm the City before or after the President's departure? I speculated that the Ancestor would opt for before. Outside the country the President would devote his full energies to raising support among the international community, and would get it.

It was the eighteenth of the month, so there were about six or seven days left. I waited for Serge to confirm this, but he did not return from wherever he was for four days, leaving me feeling terribly exposed.

In the days until he came back I found it almost impossible to concentrate on anything for long. In the process I discovered a new source of comfort – poetry. I had three or four books on the poetry of the old masters, stretching across the world from Shakespeare to Pushkin to Hafiz to Li T'ai-po and Tu Fu. But I had never been too interested, and had only bought them under the influence of a girlfriend long forgotten. The trouble was that many of the great works were associated in my mind with certain periods of my life, happy periods whose memories kept coming back to haunt me. Happy memories make me wish I could return to those days, and that can be depressing.

So I was pleasantly surprised to find I had a poetry book whose contents I could not remember at all. In fact, it was quite likely that I had never got round to reading it. This was a collection of early Middle Eastern poems and was a bit of a discovery for me. Love and the transience of things seemed to be the common theme running through the book. Opening a page at random, I chanced on a poem which made me smile – a rare thing, that! And it brought Aida to mind, and that added to the pleasure.

It was composed by little-known Abu Al'Ata Al-Sindi, a few centuries ago, and seems to have been written tongue in cheek:

I dreamed of you
As tawny spears
Between us shook,
With twin bloods
Spilling on the roasted sand.
By God, I do not know the cause of that.
It must be either Love or Magic.

Supposing it is magic
Let us assume it is love
If not magic,
Then, of course,
It is no fault of yours!

In view of the threatening situation, the reference to blood spilling on the sand was a bit disturbing, but I liked the general tone of it. And, in my case, the magic had certainly been in the dream!

When Serge returned from his long sojourn he was looking pretty depressed.

'Prof, I don't know what we are going to do. We may not be ready to act before the President leaves the country. The equipment we ordered is scheduled to arrive on the twenty-fifth, the very day that we must attack. To attack the Palace without blasting equipment would be foolhardy. I have never seen the Ancestor so disturbed. Suddenly everything has started to go wrong.'

The presidential Palace occupied several acres, surrounded by a high, very thick wall built almost two centuries ago to withstand a long siege. A parapet protected by battlements ran all along the top. Powerful explosive charges would have to be placed repeatedly against it, in the same spot, to be able to make a breech. A heavy steel gate was its weakest point, but it would no doubt be heavily covered by rocket-propelled grenades and machine gun nests. And possible anti-tank weapons.

I was getting more and more distressed as Serge went on talking, for was I not the man responsible for having created these almost insuperable difficulties?

And then suddenly I remembered something that Lieutenant Zuki had said. He had seen the red plants on the second day through binoculars when they returned to the site. In other words, it was not my plant that had tipped them off! No wonder no one had come round to haul me in for questioning! I was innocent of any treacherous act, after all, and bore no responsibility for the present drastic situation.

The relief was tremendous, and I fervently thanked the Almighty for the release from terrible guilt. But had not that feeling of guilt been responsible for pushing me whole heartedly into the "Firefly" camp? Well, there was no going back now. It had to be to the very end.

« NINE »

Serge had warned me to be on standby for my "marching orders" one day before "S-Day", which was the storming of the City, but without being specific about the day itself. I had the impression that the Ancestor had still not decided whether to attack before or after the President's trip abroad. The date announced on the radio had been 26 February, in order to allow him to return in time for the end of the Month of Fasting (which, it being a leap year, should be on 1 or 2 March, there being a chance of the new moon being spotted on the twenty-ninth of the month.)

Well, today was the twenty-fourth, so if the attack was going to go in before the President flew away it would have to be tomorrow night. And yet it was nearly twelve noon and Serge had still not returned from wherever he was. After the shock of Zuki's visit, and the equally shocking realisation that I had come within a whisker of shooting two men in cold blood, I had been sort of drifting through life like a somnambulist, almost a zombie, just waiting for the order to do whatever needed doing. My intellect had died, and my emotions gone into abeyance.

When Serge did come I felt great relief, for I was beginning to develop neurotic symptoms like biting my nails and getting ectopic heartbeats which refused to yield to the usually effective "Valsalva manoeuvre" breathing technique. He was looking absolutely worn out, and his greeting was mumbled.

'Prof, we have received as yet unconfirmed information that the President may postpone his trip to after Eid. Let's hope and pray that it is true, for we are simply not ready to attack tomorrow. The blasting equipment has not yet arrived, and how are we going to breach the Palace wall without it? The National Army battalion which we expect to join us in the attack has also told us they'll require an additional two days to secure mortars from the north.'

'So we do have an NA battalion absolutely committed to join in? You are one hundred per cent sure about that?'

'Yes,' he replied simply and did not elaborate. 'Leave the radio on until the one o'clock news. I'm going back to my place for a minute. Have to be near the phone.'

The news came, and the miracle had happened! The President was postponing his trip until after Eid!

Serge was a very different man when he returned, having heard it on his radio, and been in touch with "Liaison". He performed a little northern jig at the foot of the veranda steps, humming one of those desert songs which bore a weird resemblance to the sound of the winds whistling over sand dunes.

'Prof, the powers that be surely want us to succeed!' he said, when he had caught his breath. 'Everything will now click into place very nicely indeed.'

Then he gave me some more information: 'This is now the time of maximum danger, Prof, and you must remain alert twenty-four hours a day. "Security" have a way of smashing into houses in the small hours, and just because Zuki went away that time don't get the impression that they are through with you. The man has the instinct of the Devil, and it tells him that you have information of interest to them. So keep your gun under your pillow, and prop a heavy chair against your front door, and the iron bar across your back entrance. Should they break in, don't waste time talking but start firing. And aim to kill, do you hear? If there are many of them don't get discouraged. Just keep firing until I come round.'

It was a sign of the astonishing change in me that I took his words quite calmly, almost as if he was asking me to make tea for a group of friends dropping in without warning.

The following day he just rang to say he was going away for a couple of days or so, and he gave me a telephone number to ring should "what he had pointed out" happen. He said a cousin of his would then come to fetch me to his village to, as he put it, enjoy the remaining days of fasting in a family atmosphere.

A strange stage of calm now replaced the whirring of the butterflies in the stomach and the missing heartbeats. I started thinking of hoarding some foodstuffs and other necessities in case, as seemed inevitable, shops closed and power and water were cut. I started going into town for tinned and bottled stuff, making sure that I went to different shops on different trips so that I'd not arouse suspicion. For there was a good chance that I was being shadowed by the security people.

And then I began to worry about Aida and her family. I could not think of any way to tip them off and make them stock up. Well, I'd just have to buy a bit extra and share with them when the time came. And that included paraffin for stoves and lamps, which everyone in Rivenia possessed because of periodic power cuts.

The matter of their security was also beginning to exercise my mind. What would happen when the police disappeared from the streets and all law and order broke down? Would not prosperous areas like Two Sisters, Orange Grove, Bonelands, and so on be singled out for special attention by renegade troops and gangs of criminals and hooligans? It was something I must discuss with Serge with great urgency.

In the calm before the storm, so to speak, bits of conversation with Serge, which I had attached little importance to, now surfaced in their true light. For instance, Serge's interest when I mentioned the visit of Flight-Lieutenant Seif. And, as it appeared at the time, how delighted he was to hear that our national air force had no working war planes or attack helicopters. 'Are you sure he said that?' he had kept saying. Now I knew what a relief it must have been to the "Firefly" command to know that they did not have to worry about aerial attack. On the other hand, it had also suggested to me that their intelligence service was a pretty poor one if it did not even have that basic knowledge of what weapons the government had or did not have.

And then there were those remarks of Serge's, soon after our meeting the Ancestor, to the effect that the Ancestor was in regular touch with the spirits of the Twelve Elders. I had been rather disturbed by this and had wanted clarification from Serge. 'What is this about spirits, Serge?' I had asked. 'Surely you know our religion forbids this dabbling with supposed spirits?' Serge had pointed out patiently that the Ancestor did not "dabble" in anything; the images appeared to him unbidden during moments of contemplation.

Once I had thrown in my lot with them – under the weight of a terrible guilt which, as I have narrated, I had had no reason to feel, having been misled by a false premise – I had smothered all my misgivings.

I had always been confused as to the difference between "Destiny" and "Fate", uncertain, in fact, as to whether either actually existed. No student of history can avoid this uncertainty and confusion. All great historical figures reveal a consistent series of "coincidences" in their lives which defy pure mathematical odds. A certain "guiding hand" is seen in their affairs which makes them get in and out of dangerous situations, and places them in the right places at the right time, as well as providing them with the companions and the means to accomplish their allotted tasks, good or evil. In the light of history, these two terms "good" and "evil" tend to get blurred, merge, and then become interchangeable.

As far as I was concerned, I was mentally prepared for mayhem to break out before the Eid celebrations, which would be on 1 or 2 March. My reasoning was that it would be a mistake to start shooting when the streets would be crowded with revellers, family groups visiting one another, and much traffic from the outlying villages of people coming to enjoy the festivities and the shops packed with toys and seasonal things. There would also be the fairground with its roundabouts and amusement stalls. Far better to storm the strictly identified targets – this was not going to be a general attack on the city, with shells and rockets screaming in – before the end of fasting, with people sticking at home and the streets almost empty.

One thing was certain: the people would be deeply shocked and bitterly resentful. The Firefly Army was going to lose the moral high ground, at least in the short term. It would certainly be no way to seek popularity, and we had to believe that the end would justify the means. No doubt all this was greatly exercising the Ancestor's mind.

Despite Serge's instructions to start shooting should Zuki and his lot come for me, I did not believe they would do so as yet. Perhaps I was deluding myself, but I reasoned that since they had nothing really tangible they could pin on me (as well as the unspecified knowledge of Serge's family links with the captain and the Commissioner) I'd be safer if I hid my revolver, and so I went and buried it in the garden.

As a historian, how was I to categorise this action being contemplated by the Firefly Army? Every greedy warlord or army-supported gang of politicians used the word "Revolution" when overthrowing a government, though in most of their cases it was not the people who had risen. The people would peer out of their windows after the firing and the massacres had died down, leaving only the rounding up of followers of the overthrown government (in some cases elected quite fairly and squarely), and be told that they, the people, had triumphed. But the word "coup" also carried its negative implications, so I was to suggest the word "liberation". In fact, my suggestion was later accepted, and the developments that took place became known as the "Liberating Events", soon shortened to just "The Events".

While waiting for Serge to return, I actually managed to put in some work on my book on the Mongols, and for the nth time was struck by how incredibly heartless the Mongols were. It was as if from the Great Khans downwards they were all rabid psychopaths. (This phenomenon has, alas, been witnessed in quite recent times in our very century, even very recently.) Just note these recorded remarks by Chingis Khan:

"Victor and vanquished can never become friends. The only safety for a conqueror is the complete extermination of the defeated."

And again, after failing to get a satisfactory answer from his intimates who, incredibly, tended to be learned men. Thus, he was always accompanied by cartographers, poets, historians, philosophers, artists, medical doctors, engineers, and so on. Among his closest associates were Nestorian Christians, Chinese, Arabs, and he even had a Jewish minister of state! The answer he wanted was to the question as to what the greatest happiness in life was, and he offered his own, not being satisfied with the other answers:

"No, the greatest pleasure in life is to defeat your enemies to chase them before you; to rob them of their wealth; to see their dear ones bathed in tears; to ride their horses, and to clasp to your breast their wives and daughters."

What made this remarkable man, who hungered for knowledge and was fully aware of his historical position, perpetrate such heinous acts, such diabolical crimes against humanity? His was not a crusade against a religion or a race, or an ideology. His aim was very simple – to conquer the world.

And there are many historians who will tell you that he and his sons came very near to conquering the entire civilised world of the time. What saved it was his death, and the extraordinary Mongol custom of all armies having to return to the capital, Karakoram, for the inauguration of a successor, the new Great Khan.

I had been busy stocking up with tinned foods, bottled drinks, oil, sugar, rice and so on, but from different shops and in small lots. I knew I was being shadowed, but I had nothing really to hide, had I? I was not doing the slightest thing subversive. But my store was already filling up, and things could get tricky if Lieutenant Zuki chose to call.

A surprise lay in store for me that lunchtime, and a lovely one! Aida's maid came round bearing a small plastic carrier bag. Eyes shining, lips curled up in her usual little smile, she handed it to me. This girl was convinced that there was some secret liaison between her mistress and myself.

'She says she hopes you like them,' she said, with a giggle. Her parents had better get this girl married off quickly, I thought, or she may fall into unscrupulous hands.

I felt here was a chance to find out if Aida had shared confidences with her. 'So how is your mistress?' I asked. 'I suppose she must be going out a lot with her friends at the office?'

'Oh, no. She reads a lot and watches TV. I sit and watch it too when I have no work. She lets me. It is upstairs in the family room. Master Zain and Mistress Salha are usually downstairs with guests. We get many visitors in the evening. I now sleep in the house. I have my own room,' she ended proudly. In her own home she probably had to share with several sisters or very young brothers.

Now how was I going to get more intimate information?

'I suppose she must be thinking of getting married soon?'

She looked up at me with eyes twinkling with mischief.

'Mistress Salha is always on to her about it. Some fine

gentlemen come a-calling sometimes, and her mother calls her down. Mr Uddin came again yesterday.'

'The one with the big grey car?' I asked. This man was reputed to be pretty rich. Owned a supermarket. Had one wife already, and five children, but could add another, of course, with his wife's permission. I remember reading that in Imperial China a rich man could have up to nine wives, and the first wife actually helped in the selection of subsequent wives. In our society the number was restricted to four, but again with the approval of the first wife, and on the strict condition that they should be treated equally. But by the nature of things, the first wife retains dominance. Actually, I have known of only a handful with more than one wife, the main reason being not only economic but the sheer difficulty of fulfilling all the terms and conditions.

In the Soviet Union, at the end of World War Two the country was left with twenty million more women than men, and one can assume that a high percentage of these never married or remarried. This was the kind of situation that cried for polygamy, surely?

Unless I am very much mistaken, the Mormons in the United States permitted a limitless number of wives. I am not in a position to say whether they still do or not. The maximum of four is pretty modest by comparison, and was actually aimed at war widows, and to unite families and tribes.

I had to ask the maid one last question, knowing that everything I said would be repeated to Aida. No harm in her knowing of my interest.

'I suppose your Mistress Aisha has already got somebody in mind, and so is not bothered by the others?'

'She hasn't told me,' she said, giggling away, walking down the veranda steps with hips swinging. She was smarter than she appeared. I sat back and unwrapped the parcel in the bag.

Cookies, delicious smelling, home-made cookies with sultanas. To thank me for the books?

I think that a man or woman in love – perhaps infatuation would be a better description, for the emotional storm may soon blow over; the word "love" should be used for something abiding – regresses both mentally and behaviourally to childhood. You'd catch a sophisticated, mature individual playing games like "she loves me, she loves me not" with a flower, or a packet of sweets or whatever can be easily counted; or smile at the wrong time during conversation, simply because the mind is far away. One's entire behavioural pattern changes.

And so it was that I found myself counting the cookies, looking for some hidden intimation as to her feelings towards me. For the record, I ended up with "she loves me", which gave me quite ridiculous pleasure. Needless to say, not since my grandmother was alive had cookies tasted sweeter.

But the wheels of Destiny were grinding their relentless way, and that near-idyllic day was to be shattered early in the evening by the unexpected return of Serge. He went home first, and must have had a shower and something to eat, for he looked clean and relaxed. It was 8.30 p.m., not his usual time, but I had recognised his ring on the doorbell and knew in advance.

'And how is our wandering minstrel?' I greeted him.

'About to blow charge on his trumpet, Prof, so you had better make some strong coffee. If your blood pressure will permit, that is. Mine is that of a camel.'

I went to make coffee for him, and a pineapple juice for myself. He asked me to fetch pen and paper.

'Prof,' he began quite casually, 'we are moving in tomorrow night.'

The absence of drama made me doubt that I had heard correctly, and I said, 'Pardon?'

'The Ancestor has ordered the attack to go in tomorrow

night, Thursday 29, at 0100 hours. Not all the weapons have been delivered, but we feel that to wait any longer would be extremely dangerous.'

'You mean the President flying off sooner than scheduled?'

'Yes, but there is also something else. We have an enemy agent in our midst.'

'What?' I was seized with sudden terror. Could I be the one they were referring to? But why should I feel so? There was no reason to worry.

'He is the one who gave away our mountain trail, and he may very well be on the point of revealing our invasion plans. No evidence of any government preparations, or unusual activity of any sort so far, so we are not too worried. Nevertheless, a close eye is being kept on the fairly recent recruits.'

Having already found out that my red plant had played no part in the discovery of the mountain trail, I really had no cause to feel uneasy. But it was with great relief that I heard him say, 'A small wireless transmitter was found deep inside a gap in a baobab tree, some distance from Camp B. By chance one of our men had noticed a monitor lizard going in, and you know they provide good meat. He saw the set when peering in.'

'But if so, then the government must have known about the forest hideout all along!' I said, aghast.

'Only from quite recently,' he said, 'and they must be thinking of ways to get us out without having to shell the forest. They have to preserve it for the loggers. One way would be to use poison gas.'

'You think they would go to that extent? There would be an outcry throughout the world!' I exclaimed.

'You think the outside world would know? They would send a few people in with protective gear and a bulldozer, and bury all the bodies in the marshes. Shouldn't take more than a couple of days.'

He said all this in a matter-of-fact voice, with no trace of bitterness. Anyway, the government was running out of time. Then he got down to the purpose of his visit.

'Tomorrow night, an hour or two after the attack goes in at 0100 hours, someone will ring you and say one of these code words: "Moonlight" or "Solar Eclipse". We are going to attack the army barracks first, mopping up police outposts on the way, and you should hear the fireworks from here. Now listen carefully. If you hear "Moonlight", it means that we have taken the barracks, and you should then go out and round up the neighbours and organise the defence of Bonelands against the gangs of hooligans who, I'm certain, will try to take advantage of the confusion.'

'But defend Bonelands with what, Serge? Just my single revolver?'

'Well, our neighbours are mostly quite well off, and are bound to have a twelve-bore shotgun or two. Perhaps even a pistol. Otherwise think of something else! Plenty of other things you could do.'

'Anyway,' he continued before I could protest, 'in the event of the second code word being used – "Solar Eclipse"– it means that the outcome is becoming uncertain, and we are considering pulling out. In which case have a suitcase packed because a car will come round to collect you. Never mind where we go, but it would be to carry on resistance and not return to the forest. Got it?'

On an impulse I asked him why I could not go along with him and join in the fighting, instead of hanging around here waiting. He smiled.

'What! And lose our official historian on the very first night? You'll do far more good looking after Bonelands. We won't fail, don't worry. Our men are highly motivated.'

Then he reached into his pocket and brought out something

which he placed in front of me. It turned out to be two brass discs, each about two and a half centimetres in diameter, which I picked up and examined. They were engraved with a star whose points touched the circumference, and in the middle was a large insect with wings outspread, obviously meant to be a firefly. At the back was a pin arrangement for attaching to something. They glinted when turned towards the light.

'What are they for, Serge?' I asked in puzzlement.

'They, Prof, are your insignia of rank. Pin them to on to your lapels, and never go out without them,' he replied.

'What do you mean "rank"? And what rank would that be?' I had quickly deduced that I was being drafted into the Firefly Army, probably being made a lieutenant or captain because of my age and qualifications.

'As from this minute you are an honorary Commander, Second Class. The Ancestor insisted on it despite Bluebeard's objections. He said he wanted you at the top table so as to be able to record everything at first hand. He – we – also value your advice, which has proved sound so far.'

'I still have no idea what rank I'm supposed to be, not having heard of "commanders" in the army. It is a naval thing.'

'The Ancestor wanted to create our own ranking system based on our own old one, though we found it inconvenient to change the standard system from corporal up to captain. Anyway, you'll learn more about it in due time. Your rank is the same as our Mr James', and only Bluebeard and myself are Commanders, First Class. So that makes the two of you – actually Mr James has gone abroad on a mission – number four in the military hierarchy.'

Had I heard right? I was subordinate only to Serge and Bluebeard, the Ancestor's oldest and closest associates? I didn't know how to take it.

'Serge, this is really too much for me. Surely the other

officers, the real military men, will resent this? I'm quite prepared to take a lower rank, even if an honorary one.' And I sincerely meant it, for I was going to be outside the command structure at any rate.

'You will have to complain to the Ancestor, Prof. I was just obeying instructions. And he is not a man to change his mind once it's made up. You'll have plenty of time to earn your high rank, believe me!'

He picked himself up, rolled his head round to stretch the neck muscles and made for the door. Then he suddenly stopped and turned.

'Oh, I nearly forgot. Here's the yellow handkerchief to tie round your neck for distant recognition. You never can tell. God willing, we'll meet again soon after "Moonlight"!'

A short while later I heard him returning up the road and making for the ring road.

I hid the discs under a pile of magazines, just in case. There would be plenty of time to fix them on my hunting jacket the following night.

I peered at the dawn of Thursday, 29 February, a day which could only be celebrated every four years, with eyes full of grains of sand. Two tranquillisers had failed to grant me a restful night, and I had kept waking up. I must have had many dreams, but could not remember a single one. Tonight the Firefly Army was going to storm the City, and yet I felt neither excitement nor fear. All I wanted was to get back to sleep, and preferably never wake up again.

I closed my eyes and lay listening to the chattering of birds on the tree in the front court, and the more distant exchange of information by crows. And then I found myself wondering how several hundred men, loaded down with weapons and ammunition were going to be collected from three separate camps in the forest, and then brought into town to assault the extensive City barracks, and then the equally extensive Palace complex. It had never occurred to me to ask Serge how it was going to be carried out, and kept me mentally busy until sleep overtook me again.

When I did open my eyes again the sun was high in the sky, and the bedsheet was damp with sweat. With no breakfast to prepare, and nowhere to go, I was relieved to find it was nearly noon, and I took a leisurely shower and then sat out in the veranda with the radio. Like all my "Firefly" brethren, I listened to the one o'clock news with trepidation, lest we heard that the President had left that morning for somewhere or other, but the news was all routine. Government-controlled media in many developing countries seem to live in dread of the people forgetting who their rulers are if they are not mentioned or shown on TV every single day, in every news item. The President has but to inspect a leaking tap, or visit a chicken farm, to take precedence over a massive earthquake in some part of the world, or a new medical discovery.

With my late getting up, siesta had lost its relevance and I got down to my Mongols notes for practically the whole afternoon. Then I went out to the garden and dug up my revolver, wrapped in layers of plastic, from under a rosebush and took it to the garden shed for test firing. I shoved the muzzle between two bags of fertiliser to muffle the sound and pulled the trigger. There was a satisfying "Vhoomph!", the bullet burying itself in the ground. I threw some water on the bags and the smoke stopped.

Sunset, and time for "breakfast"! A light but nutritious one, intending to supplement it with another at zero hour, 0100. How was I going to spend the time in between?

Just then I heard the unusual but unmistakable whirring clatter of a helicopter, coming low and fast, and ran out to look at it. It was a large machine, with a row of lit-up windows. It soon disappeared behind the hills in the direction of the City, and I assumed it was bringing official guests for the Eid celebrations which could conceivably be tomorrow if the moon were sighted tonight. (Which was something our army most sincerely hoped would not happen, unlike everybody else in the entire country.)

The helicopter was bringing guests all right, but not of the usual kind. Had we but known who they would be, the plan of operations would have had to be modified. And yet for me, personally, it was to strengthen my position in the Firefly Army and provide the long-awaited breakthrough in my relationship with Aida! Such are the twists and turns of fate!

Still many hours to go, and I tried to imagine how "Bluebeard's Boys", who had been through many months of hard training in a most hostile environment, must be feeling, waiting to be unleashed. It is the common experience of all fighting men, whether they be on land, at sea or on an airfield with engines revving, that the period of waiting is the hardest one to bear. Once the flare goes up or the whistle blows, shaky knees soon regain their strength, and saliva begins to flow again in the mouth.

I tried to calm myself down with my clarinet, but found that I could not concentrate. Also my right hand was trembling slightly, which made me keep missing keys. I gave up in disgust and searched the wave bands for classical music of any kind, preferably with plenty of percussion. But commercialism ruled the world, and it was pop music everywhere. The Founding Fathers of the United States of America feared "the tyranny of the masses", and I tended to share their anxiety. The word "popular" has come to be associated with what is the lowest in taste and standard. That a very high percentage of human beings can be so easily influenced, deceived and manipulated surely bodes ill for the future of mankind?

I took mosquito coils out to the veranda and lit them, even though there were still two hours to go. The first target, the City barracks, was north-west of us, away from any big buildings, so when the shooting started we should be able to hear it at Bonelands, though faintly, there being hills and trees in between. I was going to sit out with something to eat and coffee, and hear the action. The attack on the barracks was going to be a commando-style raid, swift and disruptive, so that troops could regroup and attack the Palace, while smaller detachments spread out to take care of minor targets. Success depended almost entirely on speed and surprise, for we could muster (as I learned later) a mere 1,100 men, some of whom would not come into the City at all but would proceed directly to the Northern Bridge to lay charges and stop all traffic; while others, the anti-tank unit, would block off the southern road. This would be a company, armed with anti-tank rifles and bazookas,

Then at about 11.30 p.m. the phone rang. It was the last thing that I expected and I literally jumped. Not a last minute change of plans, surely? Something must have gone wrong. With great relief I heard Adam's voice at the other end.

'Prof, just one more night to go, so why don't you come over for a game of cards and then have "pre-fast" with us? You have no work to get up for tomorrow morning.'

I had a sneaking suspicion that the woman he was keen for me to marry was there that night.

'You left it very late, Adam. By the time I get dressed and get down there it'll be well past midnight.'

'So what? Forgotten which month it is? Actually we have just got in from a visit to sister-in-law, and my wife's cousin was left here babysitting.'

I knew it! It must have been his wife's idea to ask me over. Had he rung a few days earlier I'd have been delighted to go, not so much because of the woman (though with Aida still a big question mark she'd have been an added attraction), but because it'd have made a welcome change. But tonight, of all nights? Ironic.

'Listen, Adam. What about inviting myself to the last "breakfast" with you and family tomorrow? Then I can spend all evening there.'

'Excellent idea! We'll be expecting you before sunset.'

I felt strongly tempted to prepare him for the night's events, but there was no safe way I could do it. Anyway, they lived south of the city, near the fairground, and so were in no danger of stray bullets.

My insignia of "Firefly" rank were already pinned to my hunting jacket, and the other gear flung over a chair. I had also decided to put on my hunting boots, for if I was going to start issuing orders to the residents of Bonelands, as I'd have to do to organise a defence, then I might as well look as militaristic as possible. Being a warm, humid night, I wasn't going to put them on until I heard the "Moonlight" report.

With about forty minutes to go I got tired of sitting down or pacing to and fro, and went inside to do stretching exercises on the carpet to relieve the tension. Begin with the toes, now… nice, easy breathing… up the legs…

And I fell fast asleep!

What returned me to full consciousness were vague vibrations in the air, as if a flock of birds was circling the house. I was lying on my back on the carpet, and looking at the ceiling wondered idly for a moment whether bats had sneaked into my roof. Then in an instance memory was restored and I jumped to my feet and looked at the watch. It was 1.46 a.m.!

If the attack had gone in as scheduled, I had slept through forty-six minutes of it! I then began to identify the aerial disturbances as being caused by little explosions and rattles and boom-booms. The fighting was going on longer that it should, having been meant to be a commando raid lasting about half an hour or so.

I rushed to the bathroom for a quick wash, put the kettle on, and then got dressed. All that completed, I went out to the veranda with the tea tray and chicken sandwiches. There was a faint reddish glow over in the direction of the barracks, and I assumed that vehicles and buildings were on fire. The longer the barracks resisted, the more time the Palace would have to reinforce. Things were not working out as well as planned, and I started preparing myself for the "Solar Eclipse" call, meaning we had to clear out, and placed my suitcase, already packed, next to the door.

The intensity of the distant din of battle suddenly died down, just before 2 a.m., with only the occasional muffled explosion and cracks of something or other thereafter. Then silence reigned. The attack was over, one way or the other. My worry now was that Serge might have forgotten my existence in the heat of the battle, and no phone call would come.

I sprinted to the gate and looked in the direction of the "street", where most of the Bonelands residents lived. From the glow above the trees and hedges I surmised that the lights were on in all the houses, and no doubt they would be out in groups wondering what was happening. I returned to wait for the phone to ring – and it soon did.

'Hello, is that the Professor?' It was a young voice, and female! I had not known that there were female "fireflies" operating in town.

When I replied in the affirmative she said, 'Do you still want the Moonlight lamps for Eid?'

'I do indeed!' I replied, hand trembling; 'Would you deliver them personally?'

She laughed and rang off.

So there we were: the barracks were in our hands; the first major obstacle had been overcome. Now for the Palace!

Ideally, and included in my proposal, barracks and Palace should have been attacked simultaneously, but there weren't enough troops for the tasks. Already platoons had been sent to the airport, the Northern Bridge, and – with hand-held anti-tank weaponry – to seal off the ring road at its southern junction. And then there were the squads taking care of Police Headquarters. It could not be helped that the Palace was given over an hour's notice of impending attack.

With a positive feeling of exhilaration I walked towards the neighbouring houses.

I was not surprised to see that all the houses had their lights on. As I got to the turning into the "street" stretching from Aida's villa's cul-de-sac right on to join a secondary road, I looked left and saw a small group of men at the gate of one of the houses. There was no street lighting but the gateposts had those weatherproof electric lamps on top; and there was also the light from the houses. I had meant to go to Aida's house first but decided to make for the group instead.

There were about five men, and they turned to look at me as I approached. They looked scared and shuffled nervously until they recognised me. Then, as one, they moved forward to meet me. Eyes spotted the revolver in my belt as we got within talking distance. The first one to burst out was a man who I knew to be a civil servant.

'What's going on, neighbour? What's all the shooting about? Do you know what it's about?'

They clustered around me, and first there was the ceremonial shaking of hands. I decided to tell them the truth, including where I stood, for I was taking over the neighbourhood on behalf of the Firefly Army. I was quite prepared for their condemnation, insults, angry outbursts, or whatever.

'I want all of you to go and tell all the men in the neighbourhood to collect in my front court, and do it immediately. Those with guns of any description should bring them. Do you understand?'

In a time of confusion, an authoritative voice will almost invariably be obeyed, and they were hurrying off without complaint when I turned to look back, I had not hung around for questions.

Aida's villa's gate was bolted and locked on the inside, so I had to bang it with the external bolt. A figure in silhouette appeared in one of the first floor windows, unmistakably that of Zain's.

'Who is it?' he shouted. He was scared too.

'It's your neighbour, the teacher, Zain,' I shouted back. 'Come and open your gate!'

He disappeared inside, and his place was taken by the outline of his wife. He came running to the gate, inundating me with questions even while fumbling with the lock. I wanted to see Aida – and wanted her to see me, cutting a heroic figure! I'd have been less than human if I had not wanted to impress her, wouldn't I?

'Let's go inside, Zain. I have things to explain,' I said, taking the lead, with him trotting behind me.

('This tiny bit of power you have been granted is already making you lose your natural humility?' asked the voice of conscience. 'Already you are becoming pompous and arrogant!')

We made for the sitting room, and were soon joined by his wife. Aida was not in sight, curse it! I couldn't wait for her, so I began telling them the bitter truth.

'Zain, my old neighbour, and you, Mrs Zain, must prepare yourselves for a shock.' I waited for that to sink in.

'Wait!' said Mrs Zain. 'Aisha must hear this.' She went out. I quietly blessed her.

A few minutes later there were sounds of rapid steps down the stairs, and they came in breathless. Aida was in a house robe, her hair in that undisciplined tumble which so delighted me. This is a desert creature in spirit, like me, I thought. We belong to the limitless horizon.

I gave them a few moments to settle down, and began: 'Zain, you are the most senior public employee in this area, and with immediate effect I'm appointing you District Officer for Bonelands.'

He didn't catch what it meant, or, indeed, what I was talking about.

'The Firefly Army is taking over the country, and we expect the City and central Rivenia to be in our hands in a matter of days. The old government is now defunct.'

All this, of course, was highly speculative on my part, but the defeat of the City garrison had filled me with confidence.

Zain appeared to be a man slow to anger, but this anger had been building up while I was speaking, and now it burst out.

'I think you have gone totally mad! I feel sorry for you. I always figured you as a respected intelligent man, and now you come out with this monstrous nonsense! I totally reject everything you have said, and if you don't get out this minute I'll ring the police and have you thrown out!'

'Father! Please!' cried out Aida, in deep anguish. She did love me, I was sure of it.

Fuming and spluttering he went to the phone and dialled.

'Hello? This is Permanent Secretary Zain. Get me the captain at once!'

There was silence for a while, and then I could hear a voice at the other end.

'What do you mean?' asked Zain. 'That's ridiculous! I'll have you reported for this, I promise you! Stupid bastard!' he added. He dialled another number. 'I'm sorry to wake you up,

Mrs Kadan, but I must speak to your husband most urgently.'

A voice talking, and then clicking off. Slowly Zain turned to us, and returned to his seat. He avoided looking me in the face until I said, 'Well?'

'What did they say, husband?' asked Mrs Zain, with fear in her voice. Aida was looking steadily at me, her expression indecipherable.

'The man at police HQ said the building had been vacated and then laughed. The Commissioner was not at home.'

My heart leaped with joy. Secondary objective secured.

'All right, Zain. I want you to get dressed quickly and join the other neighbours at my place. I have to organise the defence of our neighbourhood against rampaging gangs from Fishtail and other slums.'

Nobody stood up to accompany me to the door, and I left husband and wife comforting one another. But, strangely, Aida did not look dejected but followed me with expressionless eyes. I could only hope that she was not in a state of shock. (Much later I was to find out the reason for her behaviour, and it had nothing to do with the events of the night.)

When I walked into my compound there was already quite a crowd assembled, upwards of forty men and older boys. As I got nearer I saw a shotgun here and there. I hoped that was no hothead among them who'd take a potshot at me for having gone over to the enemy.

I stood on my veranda and surveyed them. I asked them to wait a few minutes until everybody was there, and the hubbub of conversation resumed.

As if on cue, the sound of a tremendous explosion came from the direction of the City, and a section of the sky glowed red. Lesser explosions followed in short order, and a giant-size plume of think black smoke rose behind the hills. There were startled exclamations from the gathering. Now they'll pay more attention to me, I thought, while guessing that only the blowing up of an ammunition dump could have produced an explosion that big.

After perhaps two or three minutes Zain showed up with a large torch in his hand, accompanied by his nearest neighbour. I asked him to come up on the veranda, and he automatically stood on my left, either by accident or design. I had the impression that he had very quickly accepted the situation, though he was far from happy about it. It was a pity that he was probably on the "Firefly" list of "exploiters of the people", depending on his involvement in the misuse of public funds.

I now turned to face the expectant crowd of neighbours, most of whom had benefited from association with the party or government. My veranda lights were switched on, and I could make out their faces.

'Neighbours!' I began. 'The Firefly Army is in the process of liberating the country, and has just defeated the City garrison.'

There were immediate exclamations and outcries, and chaos reigned as everybody tried to speak at once. I raised my hand, palm outwards, for silence, but nobody paid the slightest attention and there was a concerted movement to get nearer to me. Fear and confusion were beginning to turn into anger, and things were beginning to get tricky. An ordinary group of sane, decent family men can change into a lynch mob with shocking speed. The anger did not appear directed at me personally yet, but it soon would be if I did not calm them down.

I held up both hands and shouted, 'Now shut up and listen!'

It might not have worked with a crowd from the slums, but it worked with this one. The shuffling forward stopped, and a shotgun was lowered; I had noticed two others. A tall, angular man pushed his way to the front and stood directly under me.

'What sort of infidels are these who dare launch an attack and cause bloodshed on this penultimate night of the Holy

Month? They must be demons from the depths of hell!' he shouted, turning to include the others in his just protestation. There were angry shouts of acclaim. It was a bad situation, and one which I had anticipated. As the Ancestor must have done.

'Neighbours,' I replied, raising my voice, 'you must listen to me and believe what I say. "Firefly" Leader had no other option. The future of the country is at stake, but there is no time now to go into that. What you must understand is that, come dawn, rioting mobs may pour out of the slum areas – slums created by the present government – and loot, rob and kill. They will come to Bonelands and break into our houses. Do you think they will spare your wives and daughters? Remember that!'

That got them, as I knew it would, and there was uneasy mumbling and muttering. I gave them a few more seconds and pitched in again.

'Now this is what we have to do. Get old boxes, tyres, logs, old furniture or whatever, and block off your street from the main road. Pile up thornbushes in front. A man with a shotgun will sit in the balcony of each of the two houses overlooking the barricade. A group of vigilantes will form round the third shotgun and patrol the entire street in case some hooligan braves the wild bushes and creeps in from the side. Also to come to my assistance, should I need it, for I am looking to keep an eye on the access road. It'll be an easy thing to do since whoever comes must arrive by vehicle from the ring road.'

I had their full attention, and they were already beginning to move to their stations. I concluded the gathering with final instructions.

'One moment! I have appointed Zain as your district officer, and he will supervise the preparations. When the mobs come – I think they'll realise by about 6 a.m. that there is no policeman in sight – first fire a warning shot over their heads. Should they charge, aim lower than the head, for the twelve-bore can blind, and our aim should be to scare them off and not kill them. And may the Almighty protect us!'

Zain slipped down and joined them without comment. I told him to advise everyone to return home for their customary "pre-fast", but first to get the barricade completed to his satisfaction. He nodded solemnly.

I returned to my own place for another shower, for I discovered that I was sweating profusely. Then I intended to have a bit more to eat, followed by coffee. It was only for one night, after all.

Our first unwelcome visitors arrived at 6.30 a.m., shortly after I had come out to wait in the car. Unexpectedly, they came down the access road, and not in a vehicle but on foot! We had all forgotten the ramshackle settlement of "Revolution" just over a kilometre south of us off the ring road, because none of us ever went in that direction.

My eyes were smarting a bit and I had closed them, reclining on the back seat of my car. They were barefoot or wearing canvas shoes, and they would have slipped by me unnoticed if they had not stopped in front of my gate, and I heard low voices.

'What about this one?'

'Maybe afterwards. Let's make for the big ones first,' replied a maturer voice.

I eased myself out of the car and crept up to the gate. They were walking swiftly towards the street, nine men and one boy, all carrying various kinds of weapons, long and short. No guns.

'Where do you think you are going?' I shouted.

They stopped as if electrified, and then whirled round as one. Apart from two of them, who looked in their forties or fifties, they were young men in their teens. Machetes and home-made spears predominated. The little boy of twelve or so was carrying a hammer. They talked among themselves for a minute and then returned in my direction, those in front smiling widely. I did not trust their smiles and told them to stop when they were about three metres away.

'What do you want? What are you doing here?' I enquired.

One of the older men, a short, powerfully built man, stepped forward and came to within conversation distance. He was holding a machete, but my hand was on my gun.

'I'm sorry if we disturbed you, sir, but we are here to help. Many rough people about.' He was smiling, but the arm with the machete was swinging ever so slightly back and forth. A well-meaning person would have transferred it to his left hand and offered to shake hands with the right. And I remembered their words.

'Thank you very much,' I said, 'but we do not need help. As you can see, we are all armed here.'

He went back to his companions and they argued in low voices, then returned the way they came, giving me a wide berth.

I found a flattish stone in the shade of my hedge, a few metres from the gate, and reflected on what was happening. Fatigue was beginning to overtake excitement, and I was hoping Serge would ring soon.

Just then there was the sound of a shotgun blast from the neighbourhood, quickly followed by another. I had specifically instructed them to fire a warning shot, so it must have been ignored. Two more shots rang out. They must be in trouble over there, I thought, so I might as well go and see what was happening. I stood up and stretched, and that's when I came within a couple of seconds of being turned into mincemeat!

I had left my gate open, and the last thing I expected was somebody coming from within! I had a blurred image of a snarling face, a white shirt, and a rusty machete, high up, outlined against a blue sky, and the man was upon me. I fell back against the hedge, pulling out the revolver at the same time. I fired as the machete began its downward arc. For a split second his forward momentum was checked, but then he toppled forward at my feet. A flicker of movement caused me to look up and a homemade spear just missed my left shoulder, and disappeared into the hedge. The young man who had thrown it was now standing petrified, not knowing what to do. I lifted up my gun and pointed it steadily at his face, noting that my hand was not shaking. Shock was yet to catch up, and I was totally emotionless. I could have killed him without compunction.

'Come here!' I ordered, repeating the order when he made no move. He came with dragging steps.

'Why did you want to kill me?' I asked.

The first man had fallen on his chest, head twisted to one side and one arm hidden under his body, legs straight out and close together. Blood from the exit hole had spread to stain almost his entire back, as if he were wearing a red shirt. But he had hardly moved from the moment he fell, and struck me as being dead.

The young man seemed unable to answer, and I had no desire to shoot him, so I told him to run and get his companions and carry the body away. He ran off like an antelope and returned barely a minute later with his group. They had been waiting under the trees just around my plot. Later I discovered that they had lifted up a corner of my wire-mesh fence and these two had crept under it and the hedge.

I sprinkled earth on the splash of blood on the ground, debating whether I should remain at my post or go inside the house in case of a phone call from Serge. I first walked across to the street to check that all was well and, seeing just a couple of men conversing behind the barricade, was reassured. If there was any rioting going on it would be in the shopping centre, and I didn't think that anybody else would dare come from the "Revolution" settlement. I returned to my place to stretch down, and to wait for a possible phone call. Later I'd go round to the Zains.

When the phone did ring, well past nine o'clock, I was already fully dressed and about to go out. It was Serge.

'I hope you had a restful night, Prof,' he said.

'What's going on, Serge? How are you doing?'

From his calm voice I knew at least that we were not in precipitous retreat.

'A bit rougher than expected. We have succeeded in making a breach in the front wall with repeated satchel-charges, but just poke your finger through it and it gets sliced off! No end of machine gun nests in there. They had more than an hour to prepare while we were attacking the barracks.'

'So what next?' I asked, wishing I could go to see what was going on. My wish was about to be granted without asking.

'We are working on it. Which brings me to why I rang you, though I'd have done it later to know how's things at that end. The Ancestor wants to see you. We are sending an APC round to collect you in half an hour, so be ready.'

'An APC, Serge? Where in the name of the heavens did you get one?'

'Ask the driver when it arrives. See you, God willing.'

There was time for me to visit the Zains, so I walked out briskly to their place. I was pleasantly surprised to see that there was still someone at the barricade. Bonelands was obeying my orders.

Zain's gate was open, and I found him sitting on the front steps. I noticed the bags under his eyes when I got closer. He was taking his responsibilities as a "district officer" seriously, and had just returned from an inspection tour. I made up my mind to get him off the list of "exploiters of the people", which he most probably was on, being the permanent secretary of the Ministry of Defence, as soon as I had the ear of the Ancestor. He was co-operating fully with us, even if with reservations.

‘What was all that shooting this morning? I heard four shots.’

‘We were rushed by a pretty wild crowd who wouldn’t stop. I think they were criminals and drug addicts.’

‘Anyone killed?’ I asked, though knowing that a twelve-bore is not a killer gun, except perhaps at very close range. But it can still blind or cause bad little wounds.

‘No. They got within ten metres before retreating, some screaming their heads off.’

‘Well, I don’t think they’ll make another attempt. I had to shoot a man myself. He was about to chop me up for firewood.’

‘Yes, we heard the shot, but hearing no others we decided it must have been a warning shot.’

All the time I was hoping that Aida would come down, but she must have been catching up on her sleep. I had a sudden, incongruous vision of her wielding an assault rifle, her long black hair flowing behind her as she charged; followed by a nastier one of her lying on the ground, the same long hair matted with blood. The human mind works in peculiar ways at times.

Time was running out for me to return for the APC, and there was still no sign of Aida or her mother. In the end I could not help asking whether he had sent the family down south to a relative. To my great relief he said that they were asleep upstairs. It was, of course, the last day of fasting, being the thirtieth day of the month, whether the moon appeared or not. The last two or three days tend to be as long and tough as the first two or three! The middle days are the easiest to bear.

I waited at my gate for the APC and it soon scrunched down the access road, looking reassuringly chunky. A soldier in combat gear was manning the heavy machine gun on the roof, a trace of yellow still on his face and arms. I was wearing my insignia of rank and I received my first salute. When it stopped, the driver who came out proved to be a lieutenant, but he was in olive green and showed no trace of the yellow dye. I sat by his side, surprised that the view through the front slit was wider than one would expect. The engine was pretty noisy, though, and the clutch was rather harsh.

'How is it you are in the uniform of the National Army, and have no yellow dye?' I asked my driver.

'I belong to the 3rd Infantry Battalion, sir, stationed at Gumtree Creek. We came down to join in, about two hours ago. Our commander is Major Aziz.'

'Oh? And what made you do it?' I was curious to know.

'Major Aziz had spoken with Commander Erion before.'

So everything had been prearranged, as Serge had hinted.

'What have you brought down with you?'

'Three APCs, trucks, heavy machine guns and mortars.'

I whistled. The mortars would be particularly useful. We were gaining momentum. And the armoured personnel carriers were a real gift.

There was a checkpoint at the junction with Mountain Road, manned by a squad with rocket-propelled grenades but we were let through straight away. Moving down Main Street I saw that a few shops had been broken into, and the pavements were littered with glass. Must have happened before the police were allowed to deploy again, and I saw them now in twos and threes, with riot shields and batons. They were not allowed to carry arms for the time being, our own men being seen periodically passing by in trucks.

We went in a roundabout way towards the Palace, and ended up behind a three-storey building which I recognised as the Ministry of Trade and Tourism. An enterprising little trader had already set up a kiosk selling bottled drinks from cold boxes and packets of biscuits and nuts, making good business.

'Army Headquarters, sir,' said the lieutenant, and he led me through the back door and up to the top floor. At the end of the inevitable corridor he knocked on a panelled double door, and we went in. I found myself in a very long room which looked like it had been formed out of three office rooms, partition framing still visible on the walls and ceiling. All the windows down the long side and in the left wall were closed and shuttered, but the ones on the right end wall were open, letting in bright sunshine which showed eight men in various uniforms sitting around two linked tables. We walked up to them and my guide saluted smartly and announced, 'The Commander Professor, sir!'

I picked out Serge's beaming face just as a figure stood and came round from the head of the table. Despite the camouflage uniform and the red beret there was no mistaking him. It was the Ancestor, smiling broadly.

'I knew the whiff of battle would bring you running, Professor!' he said, in reply to my general greeting.

'This, gentlemen, is our future official historian. I assure you he knows more about armour and guns than many a general!'

This introduction seemed to make me immediately acceptable to all present; except, apparently, one. This was the man introduced as "Commander Bluebeard". He was a tall, taciturn man with a moustache – but no beard! Imagine being called "Bluebeard", admittedly his father's nickname, when one had no beard. And why didn't he have one, to begin with? All the rest of us did, of various descriptions. Even Serge was now sporting a stubbly sort. Bluebeard did not smile when we were introduced.

I slipped into the empty chair next to Serge, who was next to the Ancestor at the head of the table. Bluebeard was opposite Serge. That was to be my position from then on, wherever we sat. My hierarchical position was already established: I was number four.

Even while coming up the corridor I had kept hearing

periodic bursts of machine gun fire, and the cracking of rifles, and now I heard it more clearly in the room. The shooting must be coming from somewhere very near. Seeing me turn in the direction of the firing, the Ancestor said, 'There is a bit of a lull at the moment. Those are enemy machine guns trying to get our snipers, and our men are preparing for the next attack. The 3rd Battalion is deploying its mortars on the north side of the Palace, and our Foresters are planning a frontal attack to coincide. There is something else I want to tell you, but first let me show you something.'

I followed him to the other end of the room where an object was resting on a table pushed up against a shuttered window. One of the louvres was missing however, and was a slit of light with something silhouetted in it. I saw with some surprise that it was a telescope, which just stopped short of projecting outside. The Ancestor gestured to me to look through it, and after I had made a slight adjustment I beheld what was beyond. It was the Palace, the eastern wing of it, and it looked like it was next door. I could even see figures moving behind the windows on both floors. The Palace garden separated it from the very thick mediaeval boundary wall, which was just about forty metres from us, and I looked down on its two-metre parapet with the naked eye, battlements adorning its outer edge. In the old days bowmen would be lining behind them, and there would probably be piles of rocks to throw down. The wall was about seven metres high, and add another one and a half metres for the battlements, closely spaced. But the construction had not been designed to cope with snipers placed in high buildings about two hundred metres away, so there was nobody on the parapet. The sandbagged machine guns were spread out right down there in the garden, and snipers in our building could have taken them out. But that would have brought RPGs and mortar shells pouring on us, which is precisely why all the windows were shut, and no movement of any sort was permitted in front of the building. When night came, all the front rooms would be vacated, and everybody moved to the middle rooms so that no light would be seen.

'Having our HQ right under the noses of the enemy is a bit risky, isn't it, Ancestor?' I ventured.

He laughed. 'I was inspired by what the Japanese did when attacking Singapore. You no doubt know all about it.'

I did indeed. In February 1942, when the Japanese forces had pushed British defenders all the way down the long Malayan Peninsula to the narrow strait of Johore, preparatory to crossing on to Singapore, their commanding officer, Lieutenant-General Yamashita, committed what was patently great military folly. He chose for his observation post and HQ the imposing and majestic Palace of the Sultan of Johore. Now this Palace was on high ground in full view of British forces in Singapore, and within range of heavy machine gun fire from them, let alone artillery. Yamashita and his entire High Command could have been wiped out with just a few shells. And yet no shot was fired, and the Japanese went on directing the onslaught on the island to its successful conclusion. How did he manage to get away with it? First of all, through not revealing their presence in the Palace; and secondly, because the British went by military logic and good sense it never struck them that any commander would be so foolhardy as to place his HQ in such a location!

So this, then, was what had given the Ancestor the idea and it seemed to be working. So far.

When we got back to the table the Ancestor turned to me and said, 'And now, as to why I sent for you so urgently. I want you to get some information for us.' He looked knowingly at Serge, half-smiling. 'You see, just after we breached the wall – the gate is covered by all manner of weapons, dug in – our men received a bit of a shock. About a dozen or more of the enemy unexpectedly came charging out of the hole firing machine pistols and throwing grenades. They also used a kind of weapon which we had not seen before; a kind of fat Tommy gun which fired highly explosive shells. Now, our men swore that the men had their faces daubed in war paint, and they wore a different kind of camouflage jacket from the local army's. In other words, they were sure that the attackers were not local men but were probably foreign mercenaries.'

He paused, and looked round the table.

'We share that view, and we want you to find out without delay who these men are, how many there are, and how they had got in without our being tipped off.'

I was absolutely flabbergasted. Where on earth would I go for that information? Surely it was work for the intelligence section? Why me?

'Ancestor, where am I going to get that information? Surely I am not being asked to sneak into the Palace?'

There was what sounded to me like nervous laughter, and Serge cut in.

'From your neighbour, Zain. Being permanent secretary of the Ministry of Defence he is bound to have approved their coming, on his Minister's directive. He'll have done the paperwork.'

Of course! It was more than likely that Zain would have the details.

'Zain has been co-operating fully with me, but my impression is that he still believes the old government will be re-established. He may refuse to reveal anything.'

'In which case,' added Bluebeard, 'we'll send a squad to collect him and we'll hand him over to intelligence.'

Serge touched me on the shoulder and said, 'Come over here a minute.'

We went to the other end of the room, and in a low voice he

said, 'The Ancestor and Bluebeard know of your interest in his daughter. I had to tell them once you became a member of the executive council. This is why we ruled out dragging Zain in for questioning, to spare your relationship with the family. We do wish you well, you know, Prof. So I ask you to use all your skills to get this information out of him. You can go straight away.'

We returned to the table and one of the Assistant Commanders (it would take me many meetings to get to remember all their names) went out to arrange for an APC to take me.

I was thankful that the lieutenant was not the talkative type because my mind was fully occupied with what I was to say to Zain.

By the time the APC stopped outside Zain's villa I knew the approach I should adopt. Neither threats nor inducements but an appeal to his loyal civil servant's heart.

A neighbour chatting with another in front of a gate stared in our direction and quickly went in, perhaps not recognising me for I had been given a red beret to wear. Also our machine gun on top of the vehicle must have looked pretty intimidating.

The throbbing of the heavy APC outside their gate caused faces to appear at various windows, and it was Zain himself who opened the door, a frown on his face. He might have been hoping it was a government vehicle signifying that the City had been retaken. His greeting was lukewarm.

'Zain, I have come on a most urgent mission. Let's find a quiet spot in your house.'

He led me to a room on the right of the small entrance hall, which proved to be his study. I saw two rows of books on shelves, but there was no time to see what kind of books he read. As soon as we had sat down on a couch I began.

'The Firefly Army is about to occupy the Palace, and negotiations for its surrender are in progress.'

He had passed the point of being shocked and he just stared dumbly at me.

'Now the point is, "Firefly" Leader is fully prepared to grant the President full amnesty, but the mercenaries are refusing to leave until they are paid all the money owed to them, plus a bonus of twenty-five per cent for extra hazardous duty. Otherwise, they'll kill the President and blow up the Palace. There are thirty of them in there, and very heavily armed. We were prepared to let them go to save further bloodshed.'

He believed my lies implicitly, and suddenly he stood up in fury, almost shouting as he said, 'I warned my Minister about those monstrous bloodsuckers, having read about their atrocious deeds, but he said the President had insisted. And we approved only eighteen of them, so who authorised the additional twelve? I have the receipts to prove that they were paid in full, and it cost us an arm and a leg. The dirty bastards!'

First bit of information: there were eighteen of them.

'But why bring them in at all?' I asked. 'Surely our own forces are more than adequate?'

He looked wryly at me, and commented, 'Obviously not so adequate, with or without the mercenaries.'

I had to secure more information, so having got over the first hurdle I could now move straight ahead.

'Why were they brought in, anyway? And how did they get in?'

'We brought them in to track down the "Firefly". These are the same men who followed the rebel leader, the notorious and elusive Feraika, into the bush in Bussota four years ago, and brought his head back.'

I remembered reading about it, but nobody had felt sorry for Feraika, an exceptionally brutal warlord. Nevertheless, the image of our Ancestor's head on a plate roused fury in me and my next question was brusque.

'Did you know that the Firefly Army was going to attack the City or were the mercenaries to go into the forest?'

'We expected an attack sooner or later, but the mercenaries would have gone in within a week of arriving.'

'Didn't you know about the spiders?' I continued.

'Yes. They would have gone in fully protected in gas-proof suits and masks.'

'Gas-proof?' I asked with some shock. So Serge's assumption had been right after all. The government was going to use some kind of gas.

He said nothing, but that was answer enough for me, and I asked one more question. 'When did they come in?'

But even as I spoke I suddenly knew the answer. They must have been in that helicopter which had flown over my bungalow. What rotten luck!

'Sorry, neighbour, I really have no idea. They were just due this week.' And then the Permanent Secretary reasserted himself. 'Look, take me to the Palace – under a white flag or something – and let me negotiate with the mercenaries. The Minister of Finance is there and we can arrange additional payment for them. Anything to get them out.'

I felt some admiration for his courage and dedication, but the whole story having been pure fabrication I could not very well take him up on his offer, could I? I thanked him and said we would sort it out eventually. Just then the door opened and Aida peered in with anxious eyes.

'Anything wrong, Father?' she asked, looking pleadingly at me.

'Just a minor matter, Aisha. Nothing to worry about,' he replied, his face shining with sweat despite the ceiling fan.

With Aida there I felt a sudden impulse to declare my feelings for her. I had a feeling that there was no longer time to lose for the two of us to understand one another.

'You are a brave man, Zain,' I proclaimed, grandly. 'I shall be proud to have you as my father-in-law.'

I passed an open-mouthed Aida at the door and touched her lightly on the cheek. I did not look back as I let myself out.

Outside I was amused to see quite a crowd inspecting the APC with awe, a beaming machine-gunner looking down benevolently at them. A boy of about twelve or thirteen shouted as I was about to step in, 'Is this your battle car, sir?'

I replied that it was only for general visits and shopping; I had a much bigger one for battle! This drew admiring exclamations from the children and smiles from the grown-ups.

I drove back in high spirits, marvelling at how easily I had secured all the required information. I toyed briefly with the idea of studying law, so glib had been my lies. Why, in a courtroom…

Over an hour had elapsed since I left army HQ, but I found everyone in place when I entered. Eight curious pairs of eyes looked at me as I took my seat, my expression as deadpan as I could manage.

'Well?' barked Bluebeard, unable to restrain his impatience. The Ancestor gave him a reproving look.

I told them all that I had learnt, and there were mixed sounds of anger and relief.

'Only eighteen of them? That's not too bad. I feared there would be a whole company,' commented the Ancestor.

'I met their leader once. A Captain Enrique, retired from the French Foreign Legion. He was our guest for a couple of days, which shows you the kind of company our President kept,' narrated Bluebeard.

'Mercenaries or not, I want the Palace in our hands not later than tomorrow morning. Already southern armour may be about to roll up to relieve the cursed place. We must reinforce our southern defences before dawn.'

Just then a man came from the temporary radio room next

door to say that the 3rd Battalion mortars were in place north of the Palace. At this everyone sprang up to go to their various command positions. Bluebeard was to drive to the northern sector. The Ancestor and Serge made for the radio room, after telling me to keep watch at the window to report any substantial movements.

The order to start would be given when every commander reported in place and ready.

I was at the window peering through the telescope for about twenty minutes when all hell broke loose. Bangs, thumps, cracks, the constant stuttering of machine guns, and just about every sound you could imagine. Unfortunately for me, all the action was away to the left, where I could not see it, or behind the Palace from where I could see clouds of dust rising soon to be replaced by smoke and the odd tongue of flame. Once I saw two enemy soldiers running hard on the parapet, going from right to left, stopping to throw grenades over the side. A sniper caught one of them and he lay writhing. The other, crouching low, dragged him back the way they had come, passing right under me.

One of the machine gun nests in the garden, incongruous among the bed of sunflowers, started opening up, tracer arcing towards my left where the Palace gate was. Almost immediately I heard a very different sound, a sort of overlapping "boom-boom-boom", slow and methodical, which I figured had to be from heavy-calibre cannon, probably a twin unit. It sounded very close, and must be from where the machine gun was directing its fire, and therefore must be ours. But what on earth could it be? The 3rd Battalion lieutenant had not mentioned bringing in cannon. This went on for barely three minutes when I saw three figures jump out of a ground-floor Palace window, carrying machine pistols, and they started crawling vigorously towards where the booms were coming from. One of them was dragging a bag. I recognised them immediately as mercenaries, and the bag most likely contained an explosive charge or grenades.

I ran to the radio room and reported them to the Ancestor and Serge, who immediately ordered an urgent withdrawal from the gate, which was acknowledged. Serge then explained to me.

'That was a ZSU firing through the gate. Just brought out of the barracks workshop.'

The mercenaries must be going to try and knock it out. The ZSU-57 was an armoured anti-aircraft vehicle with twin, long-barrelled 57 mm guns, which could be lowered right down to horizontal. It was being used in that mode here, against the Palace front fortifications. There were only two in the country, the other one being down south with the Southern Division.

I returned to my observation post, fearfully waiting for the explosion to indicate that the mercenaries had destroyed it with their charge or grenade cluster, but the firing had stopped and the ZSU must have withdrawn. A few minutes later I saw the three men running back in a crouch and jumping back into the window. One of them seemed to have been hit in the arm or shoulder, and was holding on to it.

Under cover of the ZSU's fire, a company of our men had dashed in through the breach in the wall and had run along the wall to occupy a storage building at the western end of the Palace grounds, from where they kept a steady fire on the narrow windows of the Palace wing. This was a major tactical move, for we could now make another breach at their end of the wall under the cover of their guns and RPGs.

Bluebeard radioed to say he was moving the mortar company to the western end as enemy mortars were beginning to zero in on his position, and received approval. It was getting on towards sunset, and the decision was made to launch another attack in the evening. Sporadic firing was still continuing, mainly between the defenders and our men in the storage building. We were going to reinforce them as soon as it got dark.

For the first time we felt we were getting somewhere.

Sunset saw the end of the Holy Month, and we all gathered and had the final "breakfast" in a middle room, sitting on mats spread on the floor. The food had been ordered in advance from a restaurant nearby, but minds were too preoccupied to really enjoy it.

Afterwards we formally wished each other a happy Eid, though we knew the word "happy" could hardly apply under the circumstances. We could only hope that all over the country the people would celebrate as normal in their homes, at least, and not hold it against us in the long term. We were thankful that no civilians had been caught up in the fighting so far, though that might not be the case if the southern armour moved up and started flinging shells about the place.

« TEN »

We had just finished our "breakfast", reflecting that it was the gloomiest of any that I could remember when we were startled out of our wits by the whirling roar of a helicopter directly over our building. By the time we got to the observation window, having run up the stairs with torches from the lighted middle room, the helicopter had already landed behind the Palace. Its landing sparked off a hail of machine gun fire seemingly from everywhere in the Palace, aimed at nobody in particular since our troops had disengaged. It must have been meant simply to keep our heads down to prevent us firing at the craft from wherever we happened to be, or maybe just throw us into confusion.

Frantic orders were sent to the mortar squad to shell the back of the Palace, but it was still on its way to the west end and was in no position to open fire. And even our snipers could not get at it.

All the commanders were recalled to an immediate emergency meeting, and meanwhile somebody remembered the ZSU, our only anti-aircraft weapon with a chance of bringing it down when it took off. But the vehicle had withdrawn a street back for safety, and it arrived in the Avenue just in time to hear the helicopter revving up for take-off. Racing round the Palace wall to find an open spot free of tall trees, it never caught sight of the machine as it swung low and fast over the orange grove north of the Palace.

The questions before us now were: did the helicopter bring in reinforcements, probably mercenary? What else did it bring?

It was a large, twin-engined affair, quite capable of bringing in quite heavy weaponry and abundant ammunition. Should tonight's attack go ahead, or should we wait for the promised arrival of a Major Elba and his 2nd Infantry Battalion (motorised) tomorrow morning?

Bluebeard had no doubt as to what should be done: attack straight away and not give them time to organise. But that opinion was not shared by all and Major Aziz (who had brought in the 3rd Battalion) was of the opinion that the 2nd Battalion would considerably enhance our firepower, being a motorised unit with perhaps even an anti-tank cannon or two.

The Ancestor kept out of the discussion, as did Serge (who was virtual Chief of Staff), his expression carefully controlled so as not to reveal which side he favoured. But suddenly he looked up from the notes he had been jotting down on a pad and asked Aziz, 'What guarantee have we got that the 2nd Battalion will arrive tomorrow morning?'

There was no answer to that.

'All right, then,' he decided, 'we attack in one hour!'

But yet another dramatic development was to take place, very soon indeed.

The Ancestor had gone to his private room and office, an army cot having been brought in. When things quietened, and adequate security could be set up, he would move elsewhere.

Serge remained in the room, the only inner room large enough to accommodate two linked tables for the whole Council, though it was a tight fit. Our usual conference room upstairs was in complete darkness, of course. This temporary one faced the backyard, and the smell of poorly maintained drains kept wafting in. Burning some incense made only a marginal difference.

Serge wanted to know what I had promised Zain to get all that information about the mercenaries, and I told him the truth.

'You are a proper little demon beneath that saintly face,' he chuckled, 'but I'll help you get Zain off as lightly as possible. All the accounts of top civil servants and party bosses will be frozen as soon as the City is in our hands. And they certainly can't leave the country by air or by road, but I fear that some key figures will escape cross country.'

Just then there was a sudden eruption of distant small-arms fire, ragged and spasmodic, the corridor having funnelled the sound to our open door.

'What in the…' exclaimed Serge, both of us looking at our watches. Still twenty minutes to go.

'Some trigger-happy goat's cousin jumping the gun!' he snarled, as we were running down the corridor to the Ancestor's quarters. He came out of his room just as we reached it and immediately asked what was going on.

We moved down the corridor to a shuttered window facing the general direction of the Palace. The sporadic firing continued. Serge unclipped his walkie-talkie from his waistband and pressed buttons.

'What's going on, Bluebeard? You have checked with the others? That's strange. Hold on.'

He turned to us. 'Ancestor, Bluebeard says none of our men are firing. It is coming from inside the Palace itself, and it's not aimed at us.'

The reflected light from the corridor showed a look of incredulity on the Ancestor's face, but he was quick to react. He reached for the walkie-talkie and shouted into it, 'Bluebeard! Order all commanders to hold their fire! Zero hour put back to 2030 hours. Repeat, 2030 hours.'

The shooting suddenly stopped, and a few minutes later all the lights in the Palace came on! We were back in the lighted southern room, discussing what might be happening, and so did not know until a soldier came running to tell us. Bluebeard and the mortar company would not have seen this as they were low down, cut off from the Palace by the wall and trees. Only the soldiers directly opposite the gate and the breach in the wall did.

We walked upstairs to the conference room with torches and went to the observation window, this time opening one panel of it. True enough, many of the Palace windows were lighted. We looked at one another in the faint reflected light. Something serious must have happened.

'This is most curious,' said the Ancestor, not wanting to commit himself to saying what we felt it all meant. 'Let's go out to the Avenue and peer through the gate.'

'Would that be wise, Ancestor? This could be a trick concocted by the mercenaries.'

'I don't believe so, Erion,' he replied, already leading the way out.

The Palace Avenue separated us from the Palace wall and stretched a kilometre or so to the left. It was wide enough for a four-lane motorway. We walked round the office building and on to it, two soldiers with assault rifles accompanying us a step behind, and then down to stand behind a double row of sandbags. A machine gun team were having a quiet smoke when we arrived, and jumped to attention once they found out who were behind the torches. Most of the street lighting had been shot off.

Through the somewhat twisted gate we could see right up the driveway to where it forked, and the Palace rose from behind the stumps of what were once flowering trees. Brightly lit rows of windows revealed smashed grills, torn shutters and splintered frames. But no figure moved across them.

Then a circle of light in the air came down the driveway towards the gate. As it got nearer we saw that it was somebody moving a torch rapidly in circular motion. At the gate he poked his arm through and went on moving the torch.

A soldier was sent across to see what he wanted. After a few minutes he returned to say that "Colonel Tufayl" had taken command of the Palace Guards and would like to speak to an officer of similar rank or higher.

The Ancestor told the soldier, who was a corporal, to run down the Avenue and summon Assistant Commander Moses. (The "Firefly" ranking was: Commander, Deputy Commander and Assistant Commander, the last being equivalent to colonel to brigadier, depending on "Class".)

Moses came on the double and was sent across to the gate. After an exchange of words he walked back the fifteen metres or so to the hole in the wall, and went through.

'This is getting more interesting by the minute!' said the Ancestor. 'Did he say the new commanding officer? That explains the shooting.'

Moses was gone almost twenty minutes, and meanwhile Bluebeard and outlying officers had been informed that the Palace was negotiating a ceasefire. We didn't want some keen officer to start shooting dead on 2030 hours.

When Moses emerged from the hole he suggested to the Ancestor that we all went upstairs to the conference room as there was much to tell and discuss. Bluebeard, Aziz and the others were recalled.

Convinced by Moses's confidence that the fighting was over, the Ancestor ordered lights to be switched on in the building, though innate caution made us refrain from opening any windows in the top rooms. Refreshments were ordered as we waited for Bluebeard and the others. Nobody said anything, and to his credit the Ancestor did not ask for a summary of what Moses was going to relate to the Council. I thought he was probably enjoying exercising his mind as to what the Palace wanted.

Bluebeard walked in as if not quite sure he had heard right

in being taken away from his command post at the last minute, but this time he managed to restrain his habitual impatience and sat down without saying a word. With the nine of us now present, the Ancestor nodded to Moses.

The story he had to tell was strange and astonishing. Just after the mortar attack the President had asked for all the mercenaries to be called in and taken them up to his private suite. They were locked in there for more than half an hour, together with the Ministers of Defence and of Finance. While in there they must have radioed for the helicopter. The mercenaries had then returned to their various posts, telling the Guards that a helicopter was bringing reinforcements, and that when they heard it coming they were to fire away in all directions to tie us down. They had already discovered that our mortars were no longer where they had been and assumed correctly that they were being moved west.

Colonel Tufayl himself was preparing for a frontal breakout, while his commanding officer, the brigadier, was with the President.

When the helicopter swept in he didn't see what was going on as he was busy in front. It was only when the helicopter took off, and the firing stopped, that he went back to meet the reinforcements. To his astonishment, he was told by the brigadier that the President, Ministers, and the mercenaries had all flown away! But, said the brigadier, they were to hold the fort for the President would send back reinforcements and also have the southern army move up.

The colonel said he knew only too well that, without the President's presence and the mercenaries, the next "Firefly" attack would take the Palace and so he conferred with some other officers. They decided to approach us for a ceasefire and a negotiated armistice. The brigadier would have none of that and before anyone knew what was happening shooting broke out, started by the brigadier firing at an officer who was going to walk out to us. Quickly the men broke up into two camps and exchanged shots. The colonel had the wider support, and the brigadier's supporters soon surrendered and were locked up in a room. Now the colonel would like to discuss terms of withdrawal either with the "Firefly" leader himself or his chief of staff.

Nobody had said a word during Moses's narrative. This was a development we had never even dreamed of, and it caught all of us completely off balance. Even the Ancestor was nonplussed. Finally he spoke.

'Gentlemen, let's not count our chickens before they are hatched. Does anyone here know Colonel Tufayl?'

Assistant Commander (formerly Major) Aziz said he had a passing knowledge of him. 'One of the better officers, from reports, with some training abroad.'

'All right. Commander Erion and the Professor will go to meet with him, one to discuss the logistics of withdrawal and the other to try and win him over to us!'

My inclusion was unexpected, but interesting.

Prior warning was given to the Palace, specifying that we would be accompanied by five armed men, and they were to provide a similar number for our protection. So when we arrived at the now open, if a bit mangled, gate their men actually presented arms, and then formed ahead of us, with our men behind looking sharply about.

Scenes of battle damage greeted us everywhere, the worst being where rifle and rocket-propelled grenades had hit. Otherwise it was bullet holes all over the facade, until we entered the huge entrance hall and saw what a mess the ZSU's 57 mm shells had done to the inside. Chandelier glass and bits and pieces of antique and glass furniture all over the place. Shame, that. Fortunately we did not have to pick our way over the debris, for the colonel came out to meet us from a room on the right. He came forward with hand extended, but neither side smiled. We were not there on a social visit. He escorted us into the room, which had escaped damage by virtue of being a middle room, leaving all our guards outside. Some of them had gone round the side and we could see them outside the windows.

Having settled down in comfortable, velvet-covered furniture, with coffee and halwa already in place being served by a maiden, Serge introduced us.

'Why are you not using the internationally accepted system of ranking? Why "Commander" instead of "General"?' asked Tufayl, seeming genuinely interested.

'The Commander-in-Chief seeks to avoid the rigid divisions that often stifle conventional armies. At any rate, he feels that the standard rank differences can lead to a confusion of command. You'll have to ask him when you meet him!' Serge ended, smiling for the first time. He asked the colonel to present his proposals.

'We ask to be provided with transport to leave the Palace, but first, as a matter of top priority, to have our wounded taken to the hospital, the military or the general, for immediate looking after.'

Serge promised that that would be attended to as soon as the meeting was over.

'And we wish our dead to be buried with full military honours, after the religious one.' Agreed.

'Then we should be free to disperse to our various towns and villages, promising not to seek to rejoin the National Army, either in the north or in the south.'

This is where I stepped in, my enquiring look at Serge having been answered with a slight shake of the head.

'We find that totally unacceptable, Colonel. If you come out your men will have to be interned until the country is firmly in our hands. You and your senior officers will be our guests for the duration. The Firefly Army is a highly disciplined army, Colonel, as you have seen, and I assure you that no harm will come to any of you if you end this senseless resistance.'

Someone opened the door and peered in, but was waved away.

I now decided to place the persuasive card on the table.

'Colonel, your head of state and superiors have betrayed you. The fact that the Southern Division, particularly the Armoured Regiment, has still not come up means one of two things: either they have given you up for lost and are fortifying the south; or they are no longer willing to die for this leadership.'

Timing my pause just right so as not to allow him to speak, I went in for the big sell.

'The Firefly Army is growing almost by the hour. This morning the 3rd Battalion joined us, and now the 2nd Battalion is on its way. We are also in touch with several other units. We promise to build up into the most efficient army in the region, ready to meet any threat from anywhere. Join us now, Colonel, and play your part.'

I had carefully avoided mentioning the consequences if he should reject the offer. On the other hand, even though we were certain to take the place before sunrise the next day, the southern armour might already be on its way. Troops had to be moved to the southern defence line about six kilometres from the City that same night.

'Give me until midnight to decide. I have to discuss all this with my officers.'

'Sorry, Colonel, but we can only allow one hour. We have deadlines to meet,' said Serge.

'Right then, Commander Erion, I will meet you at the gate at 2130 hours precisely with my answer.'

We reported all this back to the Council, and army and civil ambulances were told to line up in Palace Street, ready to move to the Avenue and into the Palace. Our own casualties had been taken swiftly and regularly to the military hospital in the north-western suburbs, and our dead promptly buried in the military cemetery not far from the hospital, as religion specified. There would be no military ceremony, nor was there going to be any for Tufayl's men. His years abroad must have made him forget that what counted were the proper religious rites; anything else was window dressing.

With almost an hour to wait, we dispersed, to meet again at 2100 hours. I went to freshen up, and then down to the canteen for a cold drink. Personally, I doubted very much that there was any fight in the Palace Guards left. They would opt for internment or to join us. Nevertheless, all units were kept on alert, ready to resume fighting.

Colonel Tufayl decided to move over to us, with 426 of his men. The brigadier and about 140 officers and men were taken away to the City barracks to be detained. The colonel was instructed to keep his men within the Palace grounds until morning, when Bluebeard would inspect them and disperse them among our units.

The siege of the Palace was over, and after an hour's rest two platoons of our Foresters armed with anti-tank rifles and rocket-propelled grenades were transported south to reinforce our defence lines.

We could now breathe easier. Some soldiers started firing into the air in celebration, but that was quickly stopped. Any celebration would be far too premature.

At the Council table we celebrated with the traditional coffee and halwa. It was going to be a good Eid! Planning the next move kept us up well into the small hours, dispersing for a bit of freshening up and rest when it was well past 2 a.m. The Ancestor remained in the building, but the rest of us went to the hotel. We were to return at about 7.30 a.m. if nothing untoward happened. We arranged for breakfast to be sent to the Ancestor at HQ, and we had our own (thanks to an obliging and probably fearful management) before making our way back.

Lady Luck was giving us an extra big smile, for early in the morning our checkpoint at the Northern Bridge reported a convoy of lorries and trucks led by two armoured personnel carriers which our soldiers said had stopped before reaching the bridge, their commanding officer asking to speak with a senior officer from our side. Deputy Commander Aziz (promoted overnight) and an Assistant Commander were immediately despatched.

They reported back that it was a contingent of the 2nd Battalion, infantry, motorised, under a Major Elba, coming over to join us with some useful vehicles and weapons. Aziz had mentioned him at the Council meeting following the helicopter incident.

They were instructed to proceed to the barracks (whose previous occupants had mostly opted for internment rather than join the Firefly Army, and were in the POW camp set up in the sports stadium), and Bluebeard would go to inspect them. Major Elba was to be brought to meet the Council. He would automatically become a member and move up to Assistant-Commander.

Practically every member of the Council was now deep in some administrative work, for there was much sorting out to do. One thing that the Ancestor insisted on was that every platoon must be led by a Forester. The Forest men (the former "Yellow Men") were the ones who could be depended on one hundred per cent, quite apart from the fact that they were first-class fighters. All of us agreed on that, and a certain number of all-Forester companies were to be maintained in the otherwise mixed army. The aim was ultimately to indoctrinate every soldier with the "Firefly" ideal.

The unexpected ease with which we had secured the Palace

– who would have dreamed that it would be handed to us on a plate by one of their own officers? – left the "Firefly" High Command in some state of confusion. We had not expected the police to put up much of a fight – police mentality and training do not lend themselves to a prolonged exchange of fire with forces larger and better equipped than themselves – but they had put up no fight at all. So we were running way ahead of schedule as if we were in a desert marathon against opponents wearing sandals, and even the Ancestor was at a loss as to what to do next. Anyone coming to Army Headquarters at that time would have been puzzled to see senior officers playing cards, drinking endless cups of coffee, or simply pacing the corridors.

It is interesting here to move two years ahead and compare the facts of the capturing of the Palace with the account given by Colonel Bertillot in his book, *War, Witchcraft and Idealism in Rivenia*. This is where he makes his strongest accusation that the Firefly Army had resorted to witchcraft to subdue the defenders. Here is part of what he says:

"Half an hour before the attack, the Palace defenders were horrified to hear the steady chanting of witch-doctors from without the surrounding wall, rising and falling as they went round the Palace complex. One of the mercenaries, a fellow countryman, who was in front of central wing, had this to say to me:

You know what these people are like. Irrespective of their religious persuasion, or education, Rivenians are an intensely superstitious lot, and I saw the men around me visibly wilt as the chanting proceeded. I was standing up with my Uzi sub-machine gun, facing the main gate, when a group of naked men wearing hideous masks pranced in front of the gate, and quickly lit a fire. Then they threw in some leaves or something which produced thick white smoke. When it blew in our direction, it smelled like incense. I did not, of course, understand what it meant, but the Rivenian crouching next to me started shaking as if in high fever.

'Are you all right?' I asked him.

'Yessir,' he said, 'but we're now doomed, doomed!'

'What do you mean?' I said.

The figures, six of them, were now dancing round the fire, waving shining white skulls on sticks, and making obscene body movements, as if fornicating in a most vile fashion!

So I asked him what effect that had on the Rivenian defenders, and he said that from then on they were petrified with fear, and fired wildly into the air. Only he and his seventeen comrades held the Firefly invaders at bay, until the President lost courage and ordered evacuation by helicopter.

One truly marvels at this account. No soldier of ours dared even run across the gate for it was covered by no less than three heavy machine guns which kept firing short bursts through it even with nobody there. The nearest thing to witch-doctors that we had were a doctor and three nurses in an improvised ambulance in a side street just off the Avenue, whose magic was dedication. The Palace Guards had actually fought harder than expected, but they would have fought back even without the mercenaries, whose contribution nevertheless we did not underestimate.

That a whole week passed without any reaction from the government forces in the south puzzled us. We had been getting a steady trickle of deserters from the Northern Division, so we were growing slowly stronger by the day, and it was not just in personnel for they had at times come down to us in company strength, in armoured personnel carriers, jeeps and other vehicles, bringing heavy machine guns and mortars. Surely the Southern Division must have realised that by delaying their attack they were making things harder for themselves?

The Ancestor come out of seclusion on the fifth day and first visited the wounded in the military and the City hospitals – it was not "Firefly" policy to advertise the number of casualties, ours or the enemy's – and then went down with Serge and Bluebeard to inspect the southern defences. Reporters and camera teams, regional and foreign, had swarmed over us from the second day, but the Ancestor had refused to be either photographed or interviewed. Too early for that, he kept saying. Come back when the whole country is under our control.

Shops in the City had started opening on the third day, though enterprising stallholders had kept going right through the battles, and done well as a result. Little bags of nuts and sweets had sold like hot cakes. Sending squads to protect the power station and water-pumping installation had ensured a continuous supply, much to everyone's relief.

On the eighth day a headline appeared in one of our local independent newspapers which took us by surprise, the paper not having informed us in advance, perhaps for fear of being stopped. Newspapers seem to have their own intelligence services which are superior at times to the official ones, for we certainly had no knowledge of what the headline blared:

PRESIDENT HOLED UP IN LAKE HUNTING LODGE!

It went on to say that with him were the Ministers of Finance and of Defence, minus their families, though the President had his.

The Ancestor immediately convened a meeting of the Military Council, and we met in the "conference room". Army Intelligence had contacted the editor and been assured that it was from a most reliable source.

'Well, gentlemen,' the Ancestor opened, 'anything we can do about this?'

The lodge was about three kilometres south-west of Granitetown, which put it way out of reach for us. We'd have to defeat the entire Southern Division to get at him.

'Nothing that I can see, Ancestor,' began Serge. 'The paper says he is guarded by the mercenaries, so even if we could send a party overland and down the Red River tributary it would have to be a pretty big one to take them on.'

Even the impetuous Bluebeard kept silent.

Actually we had been hoping that he had gone into exile in one of the neighbouring countries – something we had not wished earlier before the City was in our hands – because he must now be using his considerable personal wealth to buy loyalty in the south. We expected him to ultimately persuade the Southern Division to launch a counter-attack. We knew that the southern commander was a certain General Suleiman, reputed to be a pretty wealthy man himself, a colourful character who walked with a limp from a battle wound he got in a fight against a group of mutinous soldiers. He was known to relish the good things in life, a collector of antiques and fine wine. And mistresses.

I suggested that the general's character might explain why he had not attacked up to now. He must be reluctant to risk losing his precious armoured vehicles in street fighting, something that no commander of armour welcomes the world over. Tanks don't like having Molotov cocktails thrown at them from windows.

The Ancestor closed the meeting with the remark that the stalemate could not be allowed to go on indefinitely as otherwise there would be a de facto division of the country into two, with our half being economically the poorer.

To make matters even less comfortable for us, an article in the monthly *Military Journal* gave a quite accurate estimate of the strength of the two forces facing each other, surmising that a spirited armour thrust should be able to push our troops back into the City and then blockade us. We had nothing, it said, to penetrate the armour of the T-54s, SU-100s or the AMX-13s at a distance.

What we disliked particularly about this article was the fact that it might discourage hesitant northern units from joining up with us, and they would continue with their "wait and see" policy.

There was one of us who was definitely not prepared to wait and see, and that was Bluebeard. The Ancestor had good reason to remain cautious and not embark on military adventures, but Bluebeard thought up a scheme which he felt would not jeopardise our position. He was the son of the famous pirate after all, and was desperately anxious to get out from under the shadow of his legendary father. Without informing the Ancestor or consulting anybody, this is what he did on the tenth day:

He borrowed a despatch rider's motorcycle and made for our southern defence lines. At the first entrenched line he asked the commander to round up twenty volunteers (insisting that they be Foresters only) and have them standing by at 7.30 p.m. sharp with an APC. He then drove through the other positions and made for the enemy lines, fifteen kilometres away. He rode to within rifle range of their first barricade, assuming, correctly as it turned out, that no one would shoot at a single motorcyclist as he might be bringing a message. Here he stopped under a "cotton" tree, took off his boots, and climbed up a main branch. He took out his binoculars and peered over the sandbags laid across the road. He saw that there was an APC and two armoured cars parked by the roadside some distance behind the barricade. Way behind he thought he saw what looked like gun emplacements. Satisfied, he climbed down and roared back to our lines keeping very close to the line of trees on the left of the road, expecting them to open up with rifle and machine gun fire. If they did he was not aware of it, the noise of the bike covering up any sounds of distant firing.

At 7.30 p.m. he collected the twenty men armed with assault rifles and drove with them towards the enemy positions, much to their unease. Half a kilometre from the sandbags he ordered the driver to stop, and everybody got out. He told the men about the armoured cars and said they were out to grab them, not to destroy. He thought he saw some of the men grinning in the darkness, and he led them among the trees. He had specifically asked for Foresters because they would have little difficulty finding their way among tree and undergrowth in near pitch darkness.

They came in behind the enemy defenders, finding them eating around hurricane lamps, made them lie down and tied them hand and foot after ordering them to remove sandbags from one side of the road. Bluebeard and the lieutenant from the first line piled into the armoured cars and drove out. The men walked to the artillery emplacements and immobilised the three 76 mm guns with grenades. Then they drove out in the APC, carrying away all the enemy weapons and ammunition cases, as well as all the pack rations they could cram in.

Bluebeard had staged a first-class coup, but the rest of us did not learn about it until the following morning. He had gone straight to report to the Ancestor, who then called Serge. What the Ancestor's initial reaction was, we were never to find out. But he officially congratulated Bluebeard in front of us, and a week later at a medal-awarding parade he led six others to receive his medal.

At one stroke "Firefly" elan had been restored. I now understood why the Ancestor sometimes put up with Bluebeard's gruff manner and impatience at Council meetings, letting him off with just a rebuking look. Bluebeard represented the other face of the Ancestor, admirably complimenting his own cautious, contemplative nature. Serge, his Chief of Staff, was a pillar of strength, as he had been to me as well, but shared the Ancestor's caution.

I requested two days off to attend to my own affairs as there was really nothing for me to do during this period. I'd be available at short notice, of course. I had not been back to Bonelands since that last time to get information out of Zain, and

I needed time off for two reasons: one was to recharge my psychic batteries, for the presence of other people for long periods always wore me out, and I needed to be alone; two, I had a great yearning to see Aida. I had not even phoned her during all that time and I feared that she might feel that I was no longer interested in her. I intended to visit the Zains that very afternoon.

I had hardly had time to rest after a shower and lunch, and was looking forward to a nice lie-in with an aircraft magazine, when the phone rang. Anybody other than Aida would simply not be welcome at this time. It was Serge, curse it! I was going to be dragged back again to Army HQ.

'Hello, Prof. I have got a nice surprise for you!' he said.

'You'll have to keep it for when I return to HQ, Serge,' I replied. 'All I now want is to lie down and sleep.'

'No, this can't wait. There is a journalist here from one of the three top international news networks. She wants to speak to somebody high up. Well, neither Bluebeard nor myself can speak her language well, and Deputy Tufayl is not here. That leaves only you. She is leaving tonight, so you'll have to see her straight away. Just be your usual charming self. We must have her as a friend. I'm sending her in ten minutes.'

I cursed for a minute or two, and then roused myself to get dressed. Jacket, "Firefly" insignia and all. Even boots.

About half an hour later a staff car stopped at my gate, and I waited on the veranda. She turned the corner, accompanied by a corporal who saluted and then returned to the car.

She was blonde and fast approaching middle age, but age disappeared with her girlish smile. I noticed, however, a certain sharpness in her eyes which told me that she was not here to make friends. She was a newshound, out for information.

I settled her down in a chair on the veranda and went inside to fetch an ice-cold pineapple juice. I could see she was admiring the view. Nobody who came by was not impressed by the distant mountains.

'Lovely view. Are those the mountains where the famous battle took place?' She had been doing her homework, and I had to be careful.

'No,' I said. 'A bit further on, where the range curves in.'

Now she got down to business, looking at me with the kind of openness that our women seldom dared for fear of being thought sexually interested.

'I understand you are a professor, a history professor. How did you come to get mixed up with a gang of rebels?'

I had not expected this question, but saw no reason to explain that I was not a professor. I focussed on the "gang of rebels" element.

'We are not rebels, we are patriots. The country was going to the dogs. Sooner or later, there would have been civil unrest and widespread rioting, with massacres, burnings and looting. The "Firefly" was not prepared to see that happen. I joined him out of conviction that he is the saviour the country was praying for.'

'Saviour, eh?' she said cynically. 'Well, I'll tell you something: just four years ago I interviewed a "saviour". Not far from your country. Tears poured down his podgy cheeks as he swore that he would rather die than see his people oppressed again. They had suffered terribly, he said, first from slavery, then colonialism, then a succession of tyrannical leaders. My people are now free, he said, for the first time in two centuries. Well, his prisons are full of political prisoners, and his people are more oppressed than ever. He and his cronies are reputed to be multi-millionaires.'

I wondered who it could be, for one kept reading of coups and counter-coups, and it was difficult to distinguish one regime from another in the area, indeed the continent.

'The "Firefly" is very different, I assure you. He has made no speeches promising to restore democracy, and so on, for the simple reason that you cannot restore what was never there to begin with. His dream of returning the country to "the rule of the Twelve Elders" – to quote him – goes back to his childhood. He used to sit at his grandfather's feet and listen to stories about our Golden Age. He has no hang-ups about either slavery or colonialism, which he considers as being used by unscrupulous leaders and politicians to silence Western criticism. "Don't blame us for having to take these drastic steps," they say, "because you are responsible for having created this situation".'

'I have read of the Twelve Elders, though only in outline. I must say I am not surprised that the "Firefly" has no hang-ups about slavery. After all, Rivenia was a slave-owning empire wasn't it?'

'So were several other countries outside the empire. Slaves were bought and sold in just about every corner of the continent. The victims were from conquered nations and small tribes, just as everywhere else on earth a few centuries ago. In our empire slaves were quickly absorbed, and I challenge you to go into the streets and ask how many can point to a slave ancestor, say five generations ago. Descendants of slaves actually participated as field commanders in extending and maintaining the empire. Former slaves even rose to rule.'

All this was being recorded on tape, and she did not take her eyes off me for a minute. She must have been satisfied with what she had obtained, because she wound up the session, thanked me with another of her girlish smiles, and I escorted her to the car. She said she would be back to interview the "Firefly" and could I please, please arrange it? I promised to do what I could.

My siesta having been blown to pieces I had a cold shower to clear lingering cobwebs, and then prepared an early tea. I sat out on the veranda, reviewing what I had told the journalist, relieved that I had not given away anything I should not have.

And now to get dressed to go to Aida!

At the enchanted hour of 5 p.m., with its soft sunlight and cool breezes wafting in from the east, the mountains looking like a watercolour painting by a painter who is also a poet, I drove slowly to Aida's house. I was driving because the boot of my car was packed with half the provisions I had stored in the spare bedroom in preparation for the attack on the City. I was not going to have all that stuff waiting months to be consumed since fresh stuff was obtainable. And I feared that the Zains might be running short because of his bank account having been frozen, together with those of all top ranking civil servants and party officials.

They were on the balcony, as always at that time, and I opened the gate and reversed my way in to the front door. It was opened by the maid, cheeky as always. I told her I had brought some presents and opened the boot. Together we started carrying the boxes in, and just then Zain and Aida came down the stairs, eyes round in astonishment.

'This is a fantastic surprise, neighbour! Have you won the lottery, or something?' He and Aida helped to carry in other boxes.

I explained briefly how it had all happened and was rewarded with a lovely smile from Aida. Now that she knew how I felt about her (since my statement that I'd be proud to have Zain as my father-in-law) the look in her eyes was more intimate, though still guarded.

We retired to the sitting room, being joined by Mrs Zain, and tea and cakes came in. I described to them briefly how things had worked out, but they had known from the radio about the President's flight. Zain did not suspect that I had fooled him, so relations remained friendly. Mrs Zain, on the other hand, seemed to be eyeing me in a peculiar manner, and it made me feel uneasy. I was soon to discover the reason.

'This has been a very rough time for all of us, and poor Aisha has not been sleeping well at all,' she began.

I looked at Aida, and her eyes seemed to be sending me an appeal which I could not quite make out. What was she trying to tell me?

'My husband and I feel that she should go away to her auntie's until this horrid war is over. We are hoping to make marriage arrangements for her in the near future, for it is high time she gave us a grandchild.'

It was clear from her words that the intended husband most certainly wasn't me. So she was going to be put out of my way until the approved aspirant came along, and she'd be a married woman when I saw her next. It didn't need much guesswork to know that the man Mrs Zain (it was obvious from her husband's hangdog expression that she was the boss in the house) had in mind was our professional playboy, Zahor, the Minister's son.

I waited for Aida to say something, but she just kept looking at me with that appealing look. It is against our tradition for a daughter to oppose her parents' wishes in public, though she could air her objections in private. But if the parents absolutely insisted, to the point of threatening to withhold their blessing, then the daughter had only two options: obey or lose her family. But it very seldom happened that way, since soundings at the earliest preliminaries would establish whether the man forwarding his proposals would be acceptable to both daughter and parents or not.

In my particular instance it had been clear from the start that Mrs Z simply considered me much too old for her daughter, whereas rich and handsome young Zahor, wild or not, was just the ticket.

But I wasn't prepared to just get up and walk away. Perhaps the appeal in Aida's eyes was for me to say something.

'Mrs Zain, I may be much older than your daughter, but she

and I know that we were destined for one another. You cannot change what the Almighty may already have decreed.'

'Well, you are blaspheming when you presume to know what the Almighty may or may not have decreed. At any rate, she needs a rest, and I sincerely hope you will make no effort to track her down.'

A fleeting smile touched Aida's lips at these last words, and her eyes told me the rest. We were not going to lose contact, if she could help it.

At the door, Zain apologised lamely, but I told him not to worry. I knew that he had no objection to my marrying his daughter, if that was her wish. I had no doubt in my own mind that it was her wish, but she could still come under such pressure as to be forced to yield. For she was not the type to forsake her parents and marry by "registration". Nor should I have liked her to do so, for it would be the recipe for ostracism and increasing unhappiness.

•••••••

I was preparing dinner in a pensive mood when the phone rang. It was Serge again on the line.

'Prof, come over in precisely one hour's time. Conference Room. Something pretty urgent has come up. Come in your car, it's quite safe now, and the streets are lit. See you.'

While worrying about what could possibly have happened – had the Ancestor fallen sick? – I was glad to be saved from a long night of anxiety over Aida.

There was very little traffic on the ring road because of the blocking off of the route to the south, the only civilian vehicles being to and from the small settlements this side of the defence lines. Shops were open in Main Street as usual, and the disappearance of gangs of lounging youths encouraged families to loiter and window shop. But nightclubs were shut permanently, being considered a bad influence by the "Firefly" regime. The cinema, however, was showing movies already in stock.

Army Headquarters was going to move to the Palace in the next few days, but meanwhile we assembled in the same long room in the Ministry building. I was about ten minutes early, but found some members already there. Nobody had any idea what it was about. Soon Bluebeard came in, and then the rest of the members, including Serge, next to whom my seat was. The Ancestor, who came on the dot as was his usual custom, sat between Serge and Bluebeard. Our side was completed with Aziz on my left, and Tufayl on Bluebeard's right. Six on our side and five on the other formed the Council now.

Serge and I had only exchanged generalities, so I didn't have the faintest idea of what the conference was going to be about. The Ancestor began.

'Gentlemen, a foreign diplomat came personally to tell me this afternoon – and this is a hopeful indication of his government's attitude towards us – that our deposed President has been in contact with Presidents Gerod and Magrari, and that the latter has offered to send a mechanised brigade to bolster the Southern Division's offensive capability. Gerod has not offered any troops, but has promised logistical support.'

At this point I should pause to explain who these two men were, and the countries they represented, for they were to figure greatly in the dramatic events that lay ahead.

President Gerod ruled Xarcassia, our immediate south-western neighbour with whom we shared a border about sixty kilometres long. As rulers in the region went, he was not a bad man, and there was a measure of democracy and freedom of the press in his country. For most of the sixty kilometres we were separated by the Red River, which then curved westwards into the other country concerned: Bussota. This was President (formerly General, having seized the country in an army coup, and a pretty bloody one) Magrari's land.

Now, though Bussota was actually Xarcassia's western neighbour, and hence several hundred kilometres from us, she laid claim to a piece of rich farmland in the north of Xarcassia which was under dispute. For historic documentation showed that the area, known as the River Plain, had been arbitrarily taken away from Rivenia as recently as the First World War. In fact, the first two Rivenian presidents had pressed the matter through the World Court, and had seemed to be making progress. But, unfortunately, their successors were more interested in lining their own pockets and those of their cronies.

So to discover that Xarcassia and Bussota were to co-operate militarily was surprising enough; but to find the President of our country seeking the assistance of the tyrant Magrari, who was unjustifiably claiming land which we were hoping would ultimately be returned to us, was nothing short of shocking.

And so to proceed with the conference. Indeed, there was a shocked silence, though Serge and Bluebeard seemed to have known about it, being constantly with the Ancestor.

'Allowing for mobilisation time, transportation difficulties because of the state of their roads, general inefficiency, and so on, I'd say that it'll be about three weeks before their units can cross into Rivenia. We, therefore, have no option but to mount an attack on the Southern Division well within that period. Say, ten days from today!'

Members looked at one another in disbelief.

'Ancestor,' said Deputy Aziz, 'we have been preparing for a defensive war, letting them come to us and harrying them along their flanks. I don't see the firepower to smash into them.'

I expected Bluebeard to jump up and back the Ancestor, but even he remained quiet, running little rings on the table with his forefinger.

'Well then, that's the homework I'm giving you. You have

four days in which to come up with ideas which can be co-ordinated into a viable plan of attack. I expect something as detailed as possible, for there is no time to lose. The sooner we hit them the better. Contact your Chief of Staff here in the event of any snags. And feel free to meet and consult with one another. This is not a competition as to who can produce the best ideas; it's a team effort. I will not give credit to any particular individual. Thank you, gentlemen.' And with that, we were dismissed.

On our way down the corridor I whispered to Serge that I had never seen the Ancestor so brusque with the High Command, and he replied that it was because events were rushing him to take one action after another, right from the very beginning. The Ancestor was a careful man by nature and liked to do things in an orderly, logical way. There was no logic in attacking a force which outnumbered us and heavily outgunned us.

We left with a list of all the available combat units in battalion and company strength, and we also now had the two Bluebeard-acquired armoured cars, both of excellent calibre, one being a French AML-245 and a British-made "Ferret" scout car with a .30 machine gun. With the BTR-40 APCs and the ZSU anti-aircraft vehicle, these constituted our armour. Our anti-tank defences consisted entirely of bazooka-type weaponry. With the addition of detachments from the north and the former Palace Guards, we could now field about 3,000 men. There were about 1,000 men still dormant in the north, in a "wait and see" attitude.

Our only hope lay in their low state of morale and poor training. It was an army meant more to suppress the population than to fight another army.

On my way out I slipped into our "records" office and collected a fairly large-scale map of the region which, in my usual fashion, I spread on the sitting room carpet when I got home. Walking round it gave me the illusion of being in a reconnaissance aircraft. Then I sat down to examine features more closely. After that I moved it to the polished hardwood table and placed a sheet of tracing paper over it for marking with felt pens of different colours. I felt confident that I could come up with proposals as good as anybody else's, and then let the professionals deal with logistics.

Meanwhile, I felt desperate to see Aida again just once more before she went away. I had the ready excuse of taking them a few more cans from my stock. But first to find out if she was still there. I picked up the phone and Zain was at the other end. After reassuring him that all was well, I asked directly to speak with Aida.

'Sorry, neighbour,' he said, 'her aunt came to collect her this morning.' I thought I also heard Mrs Zain snapping something in the background.

Then a sudden idea came to me: I was going to get a photograph of her, and I knew precisely how to set about it.

'Well, it doesn't matter for now, Zain,' I said, 'but I have a couple of spare jars of pineapple jam, so send the maid to collect them any time.'

'Many thanks, neighbour. I'm sending her straight away.'

And now to think up a story to tell the housemaid. It appeared that the last few weeks had turned me into an accomplished wheeler-dealer.

The maid came soon after, and after giving her the jam I asked her to sit down as I wanted her to do me a favour. Immediately a wary expression replaced the usual flirtatious one, and she got on the balls of her feet, ready to run. This girl gave the impression that she would be an easy touch, but I saw now that she was one of those who simply enjoyed giving men ideas. She'd fight like a leopard if anyone tried to take liberties.

'No, no,' I said, reassuringly, 'this does not concern you.'

She gingerly sat at the far end of the couch, eyes still on the alert.

'You see, I paint portraits – people's faces – every now and then, and I'd like to give your mistress Aisha hers for her birthday.'

Which, I need hardly say, I did not know but it would give her the impression that we were on quite intimate terms. Her suspicions apparently confirmed, she relaxed visibly, and her knowing smile returned. She waited to hear what I had to say.

'Now, I want you to swear that this will be a secret between us.'

She hesitated for a moment, and then nodded. I'd not really mind if she did tell Aida.

'Right! I want you to get me a good, recent photo of her.'

She looked startled. 'But how am I going to do that?'

'Easy,' I replied. 'She is bound to have photo albums in her room, and I'm sure you go in and out there to tidy up. All you have to do is to wait until Mr Zain and his wife are enjoying their siesta, which should be in about an hour from now, and then go through the albums. Look for a nice, close-up photo of her, and sneak back here with it. It'll take less than five minutes to run here and back.'

I could see that she didn't like that, so I said, 'All right, then, I'll come to your gate one and a half hours from now, and you'll hand it to me through it. I promise you that I will give you enough money to get yourself a very nice pair of shoes!'

Now that made her eyes light up. A good pair of shoes would be equivalent to her month's wages. She nodded happily and ran off.

I returned to prepare my lunch, feeling quite pleased with myself. My only worry was that she might pick an unflattering snap of her. After lunch I had to resist my own urge to go and lie down, and sat out on the veranda, repeatedly looking at my watch and working out a story should by some misfortune Zain or his wife chance to look out and see me at the gate. Then it was time to go, and I put on my jogging shoes. I had a white shirt and slacks on.

I saw the maid's face at the window next to the door, and she came tiptoeing to the gate and handed me a postcard-size photo. I slipped her an envelope with the money in it, and she ran back in. I didn't even glance at the photo, waiting until I got home. I nearly ran back all the way myself!

I put it face down on the bedside table, got undressed, lay down in bed, and only then turned it over and looked at it. My heart jumped. It was a fine photo, taken with a good camera, and for the first time I could really stare at her and look at every square centimetre of her face. In my obsession, I saw nothing but near perfection everywhere.

I went to the study and returned with a magnifying glass. The image, now almost life-size, so close to my face, dispelled all doubts about the chemistry being right. When the wedding night came, I'd be ready as I had ever been. The anticipation was almost painful, and I returned to the study and put it in a drawer.

My siesta had been shot to pieces, and snatches of an ode which I had used in my youth to justify one infatuation after another now emerged like a past echo to justify this one. The name of the poet had long slipped away, but I knew that this was an English translation of the poem:

From women's eyes this doctrine I derive:
They sparkle still the right Promethean fire;
They are the books, the arts, the academies,
That show, contain, and nourish all the world.

I have a perverse streak which often throws cold water on a happy mood, and I now remembered that the composer of the beautiful melody, "Jeanie with the Light Brown Hair", did finally have his dream come true – and the marriage lasted precisely two years. “They lived happily ever after” is seldom true outside fairy tales.

The following day an impromptu meeting of the General Council was called to hear a report from our Army Intelligence chief (acting) concerning developments in Xarcassia. We knew that the present military stalemate was not going to last, and that it was quite likely to be broken by what was happening in Xarcassia and Bussota rather than in Rivenia. We were in training and preparation for a possible attack on the south in the next week or so, though not even Bluebeard was very happy about it. My plan was about ready to be submitted, and it struck me as being reasonably feasible.

‘Ancestor, gentlemen,’ reported young, bespectacled Mrad, whose nickname, for some long-forgotten reason, was “Six Eyes”. ‘Our agent in Xarcassia says that President Gerod is seriously ill in hospital and is not expected to recover. He is in intensive care at the moment.’

‘So?’ cut in Bluebeard with his usual impatience.

‘President Magrari was seen at the presidential Palace very early this morning, and left about two hours later, making straight for the airport. He did not visit Gerod in hospital.’

‘Unusual, but there’s probably quite a harmless explanation for that. After all, Magrari is no stranger to Xarcassia,’ commented Serge.

‘Yes, Chief, but he was closeted in with top-ranking Xarcassian army officers during that time. The Vice-President was not present.’

Mrad must have seen the Ancestor before reporting to us, for the Ancestor made no comment.

There was a general ‘hmmmm’ as we began to assess the implications.

‘That’s right, gentlemen,’ the Ancestor now cut in. ‘Magrari and friends are about to stage a coup. This makes me wonder whether poor Gerod's illness is a natural one. When he goes we'll be faced with a very different situation indeed, for Gerod was a restraining factor despite his occasional bombast. Given the right associates he might have made a good president, for I think he was basically a good man at heart.' And then he said the floor was open for debate as to what our reaction should be.

I was the first to speak.

'Ancestor, I think we should examine what members have submitted, or are about to submit, with regards to "Plan K" and see whether we can achieve unanimity. It seems to me that we have only two options: act or wait for further developments while strengthening our hand.'

'I suggest, gentlemen,' said Bluebeard, 'that you hand in your proposals by tomorrow evening at the latest, and then we'll decide what to do. I am all for attacking without delay while their attention is turned inwards. I am positive that we can defeat the Southern Division in two to three days, and that will not give time for Bussota or Xarcassia to send troops.'

That sounded good to all of us, and I was a bit surprised that the Ancestor did not wholly endorse it. But I was soon to know why.

'What seems to have slipped our minds is the existence of the remaining Northern Division. There are, according to the latest intelligence reports, still several infantry companies up there, with artillery and mortar squads. Even, perhaps, a handful of AFVs. And their commanding officer is a general who is related to our overthrown President. We were right not to be too worried about them, but that applies only as long as we are all here in the City and central Rivenia in strength. That will not be the case once our main force is down south, locked in combat. The token rear guard will present too great a temptation for the Northern Division, and they are bound to rouse themselves and strike south.'

I had to confess that I had not thought of that possibility at all, and nor, it seemed, had anybody else. Initial hesitation had us caught in a situation in which movement in any direction was fraught with risk. We no longer even had the option of sitting back waiting for more deserters from the north to swell our ranks.

'I think some of you must be wondering how we allowed ourselves to get caught up in this situation, so it will be good to remember that we were forced to come out of the forest and attack many months ahead of schedule. Yet in spite of that, our achievements have been quite remarkable so far. So let us keep remembering that we are no ordinary army. We are the Firefly Army and must not shrink from the task ahead.'

'Operation K is suspended as of now. I have one or two ideas buzzing around in my head which I need a bit of time to stop and examine. But for a start, Commander Erion and Assistant Elba will leave for the north tomorrow morning to the 5th Battalion encampment at Cool Springs, sixteen kilometres south-east of Marmar, in a white Land Rover with a white flag to persuade their commander to join us. They must be aware over there of the implications of what's going on down south. No Rivenian will be the winner should our country be invaded.'

'But, Ancestor, what if they should detain the Chief and Elba?' asked Mrad in some consternation.

'I don't think they'll dare to. They'd not wish to break the unspoken truce. Once we have the 5th Battalion with us the general will have to come to terms. We shall meet again when they return.'

Bluebeard had been as quiet as a mouse throughout the debate, which was very much unlike him. I wondered if he was concocting some new unauthorised move.

Back in my office my secretary said that 'a woman with a very sexy voice, Commander' had left a message. Titter, titter.

‘The message said: “She is safe and sound, and nothing has changed.” End of message.’

‘Did she leave her telephone number?’

‘No, sir.’ More titters.

I did not know any woman with a sexy voice, but it did not need a Sherlock Holmes to deduce that it concerned Aida. My heart fluttered.

Could there now be any doubt about the way she felt?

The next day Army Headquarters moved to the Palace, where we had a true conference chamber which could accommodate up to sixty people round the horseshoe-shaped grey-glass-topped table, and comfortable padded seats. There was seating for advisers and interpreters, phone cubicles, a stage with rostrum, and other regular facilities. Even a well-equipped radio room next to the chamber, which, being in the inner core of the Palace, had escaped damage from the fighting. With no windows to the outside world, it was artificially lit and ventilated. The interior had been the work of an imaginative architect or interior designer, its slender columns and decorated ceiling and concealed lighting winning even my usually critical approval.

There was a twenty-four inch television at one end of the stage, and we were just in time to watch the burial service of the late President Gerod of Xarcassia. Prominent among the mourners was our deposed President, looking much thinner than we remembered him. We, of course, had sent no representative.

On 24 March the news was announced that the two republics of Xarcassia and Bussota had merged to form the United Republic of Xarbuss, with Magrari as the first President. The Vice-President was an army general called Alexus, popularly known as “Zeppo”, who had succeeded the late President Gerod. As far as we were concerned, they were “birds of a feather” for “Zeppo” had risen to prominence when, as a colonel, he had devastated the village of Bari a few years ago when its inhabitants had refused to pay taxes.

Magrari was now on our doorstep.

Our Military Council met the following day, and came to the conclusion that we were now faced not just with conflict with the Southern Division but with a possible full-scale invasion from Xarbuss. The situation could hardly have looked bleaker. The Ancestor wound up the conference with these words:

'The idea of a military solution has now to be ruled out. Even with reinforcements from the north – 5th Infantry Battalion is on its way down, possibly with some artillery pieces – and fighting a purely defensive battle, we could not hold them for long. I suggest you return an hour after lunch to discuss an idea that has occurred to me.'

Lunch was characterised by long silences, quite different from the usual enjoyable exchange of gossip. Bluebeard kept clenching and unclenching his left fist as he ate with his right hand. Serge's eyes were focused on the flowers in the garden. Probably, like me, everybody was thinking that Bluebeard had been right after all. We should have attacked while their attention was turned inwards.

Back in the conference room I looked closely at the Ancestor, trying to read his thoughts, but he'd have done well as a poker player. His first words surprised us all, even Serge.

'Who among you knows General Suleiman?' he asked.

The general was the man commanding the Southern Division.

'I do, Ancestor. Very well indeed, as I served under him before being transferred to the Presidential Guards,' said Tufayl.

'What kind of man would you say he is? A true officer and a gentleman, or a self-seeking political appointee?'

'Well, I cannot say for certain, but he comes from a rich family and has never lacked for money. His house is a little castle. Races camels, as well.'

'Any idea as to his political views?'

'Not really, Ancestor. My impression was that he was more interested in women than politics! Still a playboy in his late fifties, early sixties. Limps a bit from an old bullet wound, sustained when he was with the foreign army.'

There was a ripple of chuckles at mention of his amorous pursuits.

'An interesting man, then. How is he viewed by his officers? And what's the quality of his aides?'

We were listening with rapt attention, for we knew that the Ancestor was leading up to something.

'We were devoted to him. Most of the officers come from a similar background to his. Been to the same schools. The Southern Division does not lack for shoes and uniforms, unlike its northern cousins. Nevertheless, it has suffered as much from "mislaid" allocations. That's why they haven't got the money to repair the worn out armour.'

'Did you ever hear the general complain?' persisted the Ancestor.

'Only once or twice in my presence. I was a captain then.'

'Tell me this, Deputy Tufayl: do you think you can arrange to meet with him?'

Ah! Now I knew what the Ancestor had in mind. Serge turned and gave me a fleeting smile.

'Well, how, Ancestor? We are enemies, with several checkpoints between us.'

'We have his Southern Command HQ telephone number, but I have a feeling that some lines between us and Granitetown have been disconnected or something. Intelligence has tried to get through and failed. Do you know anybody in Granitetown who can contact him?'

'Yes, Ancestor, my nephew. He is married to one of Suleiman's daughters.'

The Ancestor leaned back and seemed to breathe a sigh of relief.

'That is excellent! Family bonds are still strong in Rivenia, despite external influences, so there is no way he will refuse to see you. Now, this is what I suggest you do.'

Tufayl was to ring his nephew in the early evening when he'd be at home, and say that he had to see General Suleiman on a matter of extreme urgency. The nephew must personally go to the general with this request, and not say it over the telephone. (That would, of course, be on the following day, Tuesday.) The general was to decide on the best date and time to receive Tufayl, and then instruct his defence lines to let through a white civilian car with a "Doctor" sticker on the windscreen and the rear window. One hour precisely before the appointment the nephew was to ring the general for confirmation that the checkpoints had received the instructions, and then telephone Tufayl at his house. In fact, Tufayl was to ring from home and not the Palace, and drive south from there after informing us that he was on his way.

'How does that sound to you?' the Ancestor asked us.

It was a good arrangement, as we all agreed.

'But, Ancestor, what's he going to say to Suleiman?' asked Bluebeard, speaking for us all.

'I was coming to that, Bluebeard,' he replied, slightly annoyed. 'I'm going to write a personal letter to General Suleiman, pointing out the extreme danger which now faces not just the Firefly Army but the entire country. For, apart from Magrari's long-standing claim on the river plain, it is more than likely that once he crushes us and takes the City he will hang on to it and then spread out to occupy the rest of the country. And what will Suleiman's pampered and ill-disciplined Southern Division do then? Will our former President and Suleiman then say, "Thank you very much, President Magrari, you may now return to your country." He'll be more likely to put them in chains and at best install a puppet regime and station troops.'

I could see Bluebeard fidgeting impatiently with his pen. He would much prefer us to push ahead with Plan K instead of fiddling about with attempts at finding a diplomatic solution.

'I'll also point out to Suleiman what a treacherous act our beloved President committed in aligning himself with our traditional enemies, who will not only occupy our river plain – though admittedly handed over to Xarcassia by the old foreign rules – but seem to want to destroy Rivenia. I can only hope that the south will throw off its traditional lethargy and rise to the occasion this time.'

The Ancestor then went on to say that he would demand from Suleiman that he immediately put the President under arrest and then send his mercenary guards packing. But he appreciated that the mercenaries were likely to put up a fight unless they were paid large sums of money, so he was giving the general freedom of action. It was up to him to either send in the Armoured Regiment to crush the mercenaries (and risk taking casualties, for they had hand-held anti-tank weapons) or pay them off, in which case the "Firefly" government would reimburse him. He was known to be a very rich man.

As there was no going home until Tufayl contacted his nephew and we knew that the meeting with General Suleiman was on, I went to see my new office and found it to be slightly larger than my old one, with standard public service furniture and fittings, officer grade. This meant that the desk was glass-topped and had lockable drawers, and the chair was covered in grey imitation leather. The top drawer contained folders, stationary clips, ballpoint pens, and an appointments book.

I had already been introduced to my new secretary, a middle-aged woman with alert but kindly eyes, and I knew we should get on well. However, I'd have to share her with Deputy

Aziz for the time being. Only Serge and Bluebeard had their own secretaries, though the Ancestor himself did not. But that was out of choice, preferring to make use of his two senior most officers' ones whenever he needed some typing done or for arranging appointments. He had not got over the secretive ways of the forest, and typed his own top secret documents. (Later he relaxed and did have his own secretary.)

There was a large brown envelope on my desk already, marked "Confidential", and when I opened it found that it contained a brochure of assorted military equipment, from radio sets to an armoured car. I did not ask from where it came. A note from the Ancestor said, 'Note down anything we might require in due time.'

Some members of the Council drifted up to the Council lounge to watch television, a somewhat smaller set than in the conference hall, with a choice of four channels. Three of them had late evening newscasts in Arabic, English or French. (Our own TV station was expected to take off in a matter of months.) Foreign films were also shown every now and then, so for the time being we were not too dissatisfied.

When Tufayl returned after ringing his nephew in Granitetown he went directly to the Ancestor's quarters to report, then came down to the lounge to tell us.

'My nephew rang back a short while ago to say that General Suleiman would be glad to see me tomorrow morning, any time between 10 a.m. and twelve noon. I should go dressed as a civilian, in a white civilian car with a "Doctor" sticker on the windscreen and the rear window. He would instruct his checkpoints to let me through without delay. So it's on!'

It was a great relief to all of us, and we were to meet again the following morning when called by the Ancestor, which was expected to be after 11 a.m. I saw no point in hanging around any longer and made for my car. I had several times been offered a staff car, complete with a Commander's pennant, but preferred continuing with my own trusty Morris 1000, just transferring the pennant to it and having the army shield painted on the sides. Faithfulness is one of the things I value very much, and the Morris had given me years of that. The very few times it broke down it did so either at home (refusal to start, misfiring and so on), or within sight of a garage! Mind you, I maintained it meticulously.

Tufayl proceeded safely through the four defence lines and checkpoints, two on either side, in his white "doctor's" car, all checkpoints having been instructed to let him pass without a search or questioning. He wore civilian clothes, and all the soldiers must have been mystified, ours and theirs.

I drove into the Palace at 10.30 a.m. and made straight for my office, where I busied myself jotting down notes for a lecture I was to give that afternoon to a machine gun squad on the history of their weapon. It was ironic that it was the introduction of a Maxim that tilted the balance against our warriors at the Battle of the Mountain Pass, and hence resulted in our being colonised.

Two hours passed without my being called up, so I went to the mess for a cup of tea. I found Moses and Aziz there, helping themselves to cream cakes.

'I hope our Tufayl has not been put in chains by the general. Those southerners don't have the same values, the same regard for tradition that we do. It is inconceivable to us that a guest should be harmed in any way, but they see things differently down there,' said Moses.

'You are misjudging them, Moses. The general is probably showing off his new garden or latest dancing girl!' laughed Aziz.

But deep down we were all concerned, for it shouldn't have taken that long for the letter to be delivered.

We had another round of tea and cakes, and that passed the

time quite nicely, talking about everything except war and weaponry. It was almost 2 p.m. when Serge walked in and told us that Tufayl was on his way back. Aziz put out his cigarette, and we trooped slowly upstairs to the Council lounge which we found more suitable for non-operational meetings of the Executive Council. The seats were far more comfortable, for a start, and we could see the outside world; trees and the northern mountains rested our eyes.

We reserved the best seat for the Ancestor; who had not himself chosen a particular one. From this seat he had an unobstructed view of the mountains, as well as all of us full face.

We had not bothered to switch on the TV, preferring to talk. Moses was telling us about his son abroad who was asking for his blessing to marry a foreign woman and had sent her photograph. He said she looked a decent type, and he had no objection. As he spoke, Serge walked in and said that the Ancestor was studying the general's reply and would be in in a few minutes.

'Any luck, Commander?' asked Aziz.

'Have a bit of patience, and you'll hear all about it,' replied Serge.

The Ancestor came in with Tufayl, who looked dusty and tired. The Ancestor was so preoccupied with his own thoughts that he very nearly forgot to give the traditional greeting, remembering just as he was sitting down.

'Gentlemen,' he began straight away, 'our General Suleiman has ambitions of his own. He agrees with my assessment of the situation, and admits the "possibility", as he puts it, of Magrari trying to occupy the land once the Xarbuss forces defeat our Firefly Army. However, he then goes on to say – and this is truly surprising – that he believes that we, the Firefly Army, would in that case so maul and weaken the Xarbuss armies that his Southern Division would be quite capable of "shooing

Magrari off"!'

There were exclamations of astonishment. Serge said the man must be totally out of touch with reality. Another said he must be mad. Other remarks were along similar lines.

'No, not mad, for wait and hear what he goes on to say. He has sworn the oath of loyalty to the President, he continues, but given the President's apparent – his words – betrayal of the country, he, the general, is quite prepared to grant me and the entire Firefly Army total amnesty, provided we placed ourselves under his command. In that way, all Rivenians would pool together and form a common front to deter aggression.'

Bluebeard could restrain himself no longer. 'Ancestor, let us activate Plan K tonight and teach this rascal some respect! The men are fully prepared and ready to roll.'

There were murmurs of assent, some rather muted. The Ancestor looked affectionately at Bluebeard. He, more than any of us, represented the true Forest spirit.

'Tomorrow night will be soon enough, Bluebeard. First, let me finish summing up Suleiman's letter.'

Bluebeard sat down again, and the Ancestor resumed. 'Suleiman doesn't stop there, but leaves a door open. He is gambling for high stakes. He wants to make sure that whatever happens, his life and status will not be affected. He'd come to terms with Magrari himself if that could be guaranteed, but it strikes me he is not sure that would be the case. He can't help not knowing that when Bussota was part of our empire its people were the only ones who caused the Twelve Elders a good deal of trouble. They practised human sacrifice until quite recently.'

The Ancestor knew more about our history than I did. I had been far more interested in earth-shaking empires of old, and great events of the near past.

'So he is inviting me to send a top level team for further discussions. His words are: "to look deeper into the matter, to our mutual satisfaction". He ends on a hopefully comradely note with, "With confidence in our future co-operation, Yours sincerely, Suleiman".'

This surprised all of us. The level of adrenalin began to slide down, and refreshments were ordered. The Ancestor was still to tell us what he proposed to do next, but for the moment we listened to some more anecdotes about the general. A colourful figure but, despite his medals and known personal bravery, he was not a national hero like old Bluebeard Senior. Nor, of course, could he challenge the Ancestor's pre-eminence in any way. The general had given Tufayl his home number as our contacts were to remain secret. He was to be telephoned from Tufayl's house.

While we were going through the refreshments, the Ancestor let slip one of those extremely rare bits of revelations about his past. After weeks of close contact with him we knew (I exclude Serge here who, despite being subordinate to him, gave the impression of being an uncle figure, whom the Ancestor treated with utmost respect) next to nothing about his life.

'You know, I have been thinking of contacting Serranos one day soon. I notice that he has not joined in the general condemnation of our coup, though paying lip service to the demand for the restoration of "democracy" in the country. He has not called me names.'

He paused, and we waited for him to continue.

'Serranos and I shared a flat in London in our formative years and our thinking ran along very similar lines at that time. Perhaps he has not lost all the ideals that we aspired to.'

Serranos was the President of our northern neighbour, Soffenia, a large, rambling country which was almost half desert, with a population of about seven million. Much desert separated us from them, and Rivenia never considered Soffenia to be a threat at any time. In the old camel caravan days much business intercourse took place between us, but that dwindled away as richer markets were found to the east and west and abroad. However, oil had been discovered in Soffenia and that country was now poised to leap ahead. It would be most useful to have them as an ally.

'I intend to send an emissary as soon as this southern business is over and done with.'

I reflected on how practically every world leader this century had or has, at one time or another, lived in one of a small handful of cities in the world, mainly in Europe. Indeed, in some cases future leaders had actually met and even lived together in one or more of those cities in their youth or early middle years. The most prominent cities that came to mind were London, Paris, Vienna and Cairo.

'And now to return to our crafty General Suleiman. I hereby appoint Commander Erion, the Professor and Deputy Tufayl to go down and make Suleiman see sense. Tufayl will ring him at home this evening, and the three of you will go down to meet him tomorrow, early, say at 10 a.m. He will remain C-in-C, South, with no loss of privileges. There will be an exchange of units to begin the process of integration. But one thing I insist on: the President must be removed from power, and the mercenaries eliminated one way or another. I will not compromise on these two points.'

The inclusion of myself came as quite a surprise to me, but I knew better than to question the Ancestor. In fact, it was quite a compliment and one never looks a gift horse in the mouth.

Bluebeard, Aziz and Moses were to finalise preparations for Operation K, to take off the same night of our trip if it should fail.

I hung around at HQ until Tufayl made his phone call to the south, and then rang us to say the meeting was on, and it would be at 10.30 a.m., in the office of the hospital administrator of the military hospital.

We would be going as visiting medical specialists in an ambulance. Nobody would stop and question us, of course, both sides to be instructed to let us through without delay.

I spent the night in a hotel nearby to make sure to be there on schedule. We left at precisely 9.30 a.m. to clear the city traffic and get onto the ring road. Their military hospital was our side of Granitetown, so it should take about twenty minutes' driving.

The southern military hospital was about the size of the City one, but newer. (The Northern Division had to make do with a decrepit old building, with old equipment. It used to be a good hospital when the foreigners were here, but successive Presidents tended to favour the south.)

We were escorted up the terrazzo steps and down the inevitable corridor to the administrator's office, where extra chairs had been brought in. The administrator, not being in on the secret, tried to cannily find out why General Suleiman had personally sent for us, but received no satisfaction. It was clear to me that it was the general who now ruled the south, and not the lame-duck President.

He limped in a few minutes past the appointment time, his thick, carved walking-stick rubber-padded at the tip and making little sound on the polished floor.

'Welcome to the south, gentlemen,' he opened, beaming, his grip firm as we shook hands.

In his white uniform and rows of medals and peaked cap he reminded me of somebody, but I couldn't remember who at first. And then it came to me. Of course! Reichmarshal Herman Goering, the Luftwaffe boss of the Third Reich, though not as fat. A kind of sunburnt version of Goering.

Serge introduced us, and Suleiman's attention immediately shifted to me.

'It's very strange to find an academic like you associating

with rebels. One would expect you to be a staunch supporter of the Establishment.' He then swiftly pre-empted an angry remark from Serge, which he could see coming, by hastily adding, 'Don't get me wrong, gentlemen! I know that today's rebels are tomorrow's establishment. So I'm just being curious, not critical.'

I found it difficult to dislike this man. Pompous, egocentric, and not quite the model of diplomacy, but there was a feeling of integrity about him which told you that he was not the kind to break promises or stab you in the back. Though he'd have to do the latter to the President, if we were to get on. But that would be for the sake of the country, not of an individual or group.

Having established our starting points, we now got down to serious negotiating. Once he reverted to boasting about his Armoured Regiment, and I decided it was time to tell him we knew the truth.

'General, I personally took the chance of inspecting the armour that was under canvas after the parade, and I saw what condition the tanks were in. They are write-offs. So please let us be realistic.'

He was absolutely dumbstruck, and looked at me as if seeing me for the first time. And then he burst into laughter.

'This will teach me never to prejudge anyone! I had you down as having been made a "Commander" – a major-general, if I understand your rankings correctly – by virtue of your having poured a lot of money into the "Firefly" coffers. But I can see now you have done other things to deserve it. Right, let's proceed.'

And we did, for almost two hours (and two refreshment breaks). The general agreed to all the Ancestor's terms, but made a demand of his own. He was to be made Field Marshal, with salary and retirement privileges to match!

'Our President, soon to be "former", made a bad mistake

when he refused to make me Field Marshal. Apart from my record, going back to the days of the foreigners, I have had to struggle for many years to prevent the Southern Division from falling to pieces, like the Northern one. And yet he promoted his cousin, Omar, straight up from brigadier to full general to command the Northern Army. The same rank as me, can you imagine!'

Having succeeded beyond our wildest expectations, we were more than happy to sympathise with him; actually quite genuinely.

Before we left the room he said that he had to think and plan very carefully how to deal with the President and the mercenaries, and would have to consult his senior officers. So we should not expect anything for at least three days. We were amenable to that, but when we were in the ambulance on our way back we decided to advise maintaining our present level of alertness.

'Well, Prof, do you think the man can be trusted?' asked Serge.

'Yes, I believe so. His anger at not being made Field Marshal was genuine enough,' Tufayl concurred.

'Do you think the Ancestor will agree to make him one?'

Serge thought a bit, and then nodded his head. 'The Ancestor is a pragmatic man. No, perhaps "pragmatic" is the wrong word, because to avoid the shedding of further Rivenian blood he'd do anything short of giving up the "Firefly" principles. Today we really scored a major victory. He'll be extremely happy about this.'

And so it proved, and the day following that at a special meeting of the entire General Council we were applauded as if we had won the Olympic gold medal. Serge pointed out that it had all been the Ancestor's brainchild, and we had merely carried out his instructions.

'Ah, Erion,' replied the Ancestor, 'any of you three could

have put a foot wrong, and it would have put old Suleiman's back up! But let's wait until we hear of the President and his gang of killers first, before we let our guard down.'

That sobered us up a little bit, and we returned to our posts. There was no question of taking time off to have a bit of a rest in Bonelands, so I accompanied Bluebeard to watch some shooting practice and spent the night in the hotel again.

« ELEVEN »

The news we had all been on tenterhooks waiting two days for was brought to me by our acting chief of Army Intelligence, Captain Mrad. Forgetting rank in his eagerness – he had not yet learnt the laid-back ways of the Council – he came barging breathlessly into my office.

'Guess what?' he panted.

I decided to let him off this time.

'What?' I enquired, pretending to stifle a yawn.

'The President and his lot flew away in a helicopter a short while ago. General Suleiman has just been through to us, not having the Ancestor's direct line. I have just been to inform the Ancestor.'

'Well, thank the Almighty for that! We feared a shootout. Did Suleiman say how it was achieved?'

'No,' he replied, 'but he is on his way here to see the Ancestor.'

'Make sure our checkpoints are fully informed. We don't want the general to be shot on our doorstep.'

'I was about to go and do that, after telling Commander Erion.'

'Leave that to me,' I said as I accompanied him to the corridor.

Serge was not in his office, nor was Bluebeard. They were out in the fields somewhere, so I returned to my office in case the Ancestor sent for me. Some more brochures on military equipment had found their way to my desk and I busied myself for the next hour marking weapons systems which it would be highly desirable for us to obtain, if our very limited budget permitted. The Council had already decided, for one thing, to standardise as much as possible for our weapons had been bought in "jumble sales" and were of too many different types. Our heavy machine guns, for instance, ranged from the Degtyarev 12.7 mm DShK to the .30 Browning, and we had no less than four or five different types of sub-machine guns and assault rifles. Getting ammunition from different sources was already proving a problem. This applied to getting spare parts for the armoured vehicles in particular.

General Suleiman's arrival passed almost unnoticed for he was whisked straight away to the Ancestor's office. The Ancestor must have decided to exert his considerable magnetism on the general without anybody else being present, though Serge would probably have attended had he been in. He must have made the right impact, for we were secretly amused when the general joined us for lunch (which he looked at with barely disguised disdain) and his conversation was, 'The Ancestor said…' and 'I think the Ancestor would like…' and so on. The man was hooked, like the rest of us. He didn't say if he had been promised the upward leap (on paper) to Field Marshal, and we did not mention it.

He was to meet the Ancestor later that afternoon for a briefing, and then was to join us again to tell us how he had managed to handle the President and his mercenaries.

Once the tête-à-tête with the Ancestor was over, the general was brought to the lounge for afternoon tea and to meet the other members of the Council. In his usual frank way (some might call it undiplomatic) he commented that he had expected to see a wild bunch of long-haired characters bristling with knives and hand grenades. Bluebeard was about to say something, most probably uncomplimentary, but he restrained himself in time. In fact, soon afterwards he excused himself and left. The chemistry between those two never quite jelled, but the rest of us got on reasonably well.

He gave an account of how he had dealt with the President

and his mercenaries, and we discovered later that he had embellished the story a bit, though not by much.

'I drove up to the hunting lodge in my Mercedes, not my staff car, alone, and caught him having breakfast with the Defence Minister. A couple of the mercenaries were sitting under a tree a few metres away and did not bother to get up. The official bodyguards were at the end of the veranda. I joined them at table and accepted a cup of coffee.'

I wished he'd hurry and get on with the story because I wanted to go home in case Aida rang.

'They were not surprised to see me, of course, having been there several times before.

"What brings you this early to see me, General?" he asked.

"Mr President," I said, "I am afraid I am forced by circumstances to ask you to temporarily leave the country, taking the mercenaries with you. Your life is in very serious danger for I have discovered that my junior officers, with the support of some very senior ones, are planning to stage a coup should any Xarbuss troops enter the country."

"Magrari will send in troops to help us liberate the country from these "Firefly" bandits, so what are they talking about?"

"My men do not trust Magrari, Mr President. They believe he will take over the country."

"Rubbish!" he said. "We have signed a treaty of friendship. He will not break that treaty."

'For me this was confirmation of what the "Firefly" – the Ancestor – had said, and I could now act with a clear conscience. So I said, "Mr President, I have no alternative but to ask you to leave. I suggest the mercenary leader gets in touch with the helicopter that brought you straight away, to come and ferry you out. You have an hour before my Armoured Regiment and 6th Battalion surround you and open fire. I have given the orders."

"Why, you traitor! I'll have you hanged by your ears for this! Maybe I should have you shot right here and now!" And the Minister of Defence joined in with some pretty foul words, I can tell you!

"If you do that, my men will not spare any of you!" I answered back, and got up to leave.

"You'll regret this to the end of your short remaining life, you…" he shouted, but I'll spare you the words he used.

'The mercenaries, meanwhile, had collected in a group around my car, knowing that something was wrong, and waiting for a signal from the President. One of them jostled me violently, but otherwise let me pass, get into my car, and drive away. I had my second-in-command with five armoured cars and a company of infantry stationed half a kilometre away, and I ordered them to go and line up on the hills within sight of the lodge, and just remain there keeping a sharp eye on the mercenaries' movements. They tell me that a group with rocket-propelled grenades looked like it was going to engage them, and even set up a couple of mortars. But then our infantry appeared from behind the armoured cars, and that must have shown them they'd be committing hara-kiri. And if there is something a mercenary values more than money it is his life!

'The helicopter arrived about forty-five minutes later, alighting on an old landing strip just off the lodge complex, and the President and his entourage led the way, loaded with suitcases. And, would you believe it, machine guns fired on our men as it made off! Fortunately no one was hit.'

It was certainly an exciting story, and we congratulated the general. I asked him where the President had made for, and he said probably overseas to look for political support. Magrari would now have no more need of him.

And so it proved. Before long pressure was going to be brought to restore him to power and return to "democracy". But that was yet to come, and for the time being we rejoiced in almost two-thirds of the country having now come under "Firefly" control with the minimum of conflict.

We celebrated the day also for another reason – we received our first salary payment! The paymaster-general, or whoever looks after salaries in the army, came personally to deliver these brown envelopes marked with the "Firefly" motif. I suppose the other ranks had to queue up for theirs! Almost without exception we just slipped the envelopes into our pockets without opening them. We were senior officers, after all, not bothered about such little things as money.

Later, when I opened the envelope and looked at the cheque I figured that it must be about half what a major-general in another army would get, but I honestly did not mind. In fact, in all the weeks not once had I wondered whether I'd be paid or not for what I was doing.

Nevertheless, on top of my very modest pension it now put me in a position to consider fulfilling an old dream – to buy the kind of rambling old house that I was born and brought up in, with decorated niches, arched windows, slim-columned arcades, a landscaped garden, the lot. But that had been in the far north, in the town of Marmar. I had seen one or two here and there in the City, but the chances of finding an empty one for sale were slim. Old families clung to theirs, and I'd have to depend on the stream of luck that was flowing my way.

It came as no surprise, two days later, to hear that the general commanding the Northern Division (or rather what was left of it as more and more companies trekked their way to join us) had skipped the country. He was on our list of "exploiters of the people", and there was no way we would have absorbed him into our army. His second-in-command was granted amnesty, but was demoted to captain. His punishment could have been much harsher, so he did not complain.

Though we had not bothered much about the northern troops, seeing them as no threat at all, we could now truthfully tell the people that the country had a new government, the "Firefly" government.

The Ancestor now started putting into practice his lifelong dream of getting as close as possible to the form of government that existed at the time of the Twelve Elders. Elected councils were to be formed, stretching up from village level to the Supreme Council, of which the Ancestor became chairman. The system was to be reviewed every two to three years for any necessary modification in the light of modern conditions.

The expected howls of condemnation poured in from all sides, from regional leaders right up to the United Nations. But since there was precious little democracy in evidence among most of the regional countries, and a couple of absolutely vile wars were taking place not far from us, our Political Council asserted rightly that no big power would want to squeeze our throat and let off the others! The popularity of the "Firefly" was clear every time he spoke in public, as at the huge military parade in the sports stadium on the penultimate day of March. The cheering hardly ever stopped, and I was left wondering if half his words had really been heard!

Much of the existing civil service structure was left to carry on as usual, except that "Firefly Directors" headed Ministries. In addition there were "Firefly Inspectors" who saw to it that everyone did one's job in the proper manner, and with the right attitude towards the public. The typical, arrogant civil servant got very short shrift. As did the habitual bad-tempered nurses in hospitals, who made the common patient dread going to hospital. The police force was reorganised from top to bottom. All that was in the weeks and months to come, for there was a looming threat hovering on the horizon. This was from our south-western neighbours, the United Republic of Xarbuss.

On 5 May President Magrari gave a speech to army cadets which seemed to make war inevitable.

'We have unearthed historical evidence,' he roared, 'that it is not just the river plain that belongs to us and not to Rivenia as they claim, but also the area of the Red River promontory. For it was a fairly recent, in historical terms, geological upheaval that pushed the river on to our land to form a bulge.'

Now it happened that this bulge – a straight line at its base would be about twenty-five kilometres long, and a vertical to its rounded tip about the same distance – was an area of cornfields and rice plantations, providing up to forty per cent of our requirements. To lose it would cripple us economically. The bulge was directly opposite the river plain, the Red River separating the two. The river itself was fairly slow as it negotiated the curve, and so crossing it was routine for the communities of fishermen who lived on either side. Officially, the border between Rivenia and Xarcassia ran down the centre of the river, but fishermen seldom paid attention to this.

'Things are moving faster than anticipated,' the Ancestor said at the conference that followed. 'We will have to build up a whole company of artillery, and obtain river-crossing equipment without delay. I'm sending out a procurement team in the next few days to the north-west where they are bound to have surplus equipment. And I myself intend to fly tomorrow night to see my former colleague, Serranos, of the north. If he will grant us free passage through his land it will save us a lot of money, as well as speed things up considerably. Deputy Moses will head the procurement delegation. Prepare a list of what we require, and then hand it to Commander Bluebeard within two days.'

I was not sure whether I was to be involved in the preparation of the list of equipment or not, for the Ancestor's instruction had not been specific. Nevertheless, I determined to browse through the brochures just to see what was available, even though it was highly unlikely that we had money to buy new.

But much personal trouble was in store for me when I returned to Bonelands which was to cause me much heartache. It seemed that the powers that be had decided that things had been going too swimmingly for me, and I needed to be put through a meat-grinder for a while.

No sooner had I stepped out of my uniform than the phone rang. This must be Aida, I thought! It was Serge's secretary.

'Commander, Commander Erion sends his apology for having forgotten to tell you when you were here. I am to tell you that Mr Zain has been arrested in today's round-up, and is at Police HQ. He said he'll tell you all about it when you come in tomorrow, and meanwhile to take no action.'

This was terrible news, indeed. I had given Zain the impression that I'd protect him, and now they were bound to think that I had deceived them. For surely as a Commander did I not have influence enough to get him eased out of the list?

I got on to the Attorney-General straight away. He was a new appointee, a youngish man whom I didn't know, and so I had to introduce myself.

'Commander, I issued orders on the basis of lists submitted to me by the Security Chief. Zain was in "Exploiters, Category 2". First category were rounded up yesterday. Perhaps you might like to ring the police chief?'

I thanked him and hung up. Perhaps I had better wait until I discussed it with Serge, first. But, meanwhile, I wished I had Aida's telephone number in order to reassure her. I decided to go later that afternoon to see Mrs Zain who would now be alone with the maid.

I was in a much troubled state because I had been dreaming of a marriage in August, hopefully having by then found the spacious old house to move into. For some reason, my once restful bungalow had suddenly started feeling constricted. I just could not imagine living with Aida in it. The plan was too angular, the spaces too cramped. She deserved to live in a place whose spaces would flow like her long hair.

After tea I made my way to the villa, my feet feeling like they were made of solid lead. What was I going to tell Mrs Zain? She was never exactly fond of me to begin with. And now she'd have every reason for persuading Aida to reject me.

As I rounded the bend into their cul-de-sac I immediately saw three cars parked outside the house. And one of them was the Defence Minister's son's. My arch-rival Zahor was already here to commiserate.

I very nearly made an about-turn, feeling particularly vulnerable in a white shirt and brown trousers, with sandals. Why had I not come in my uniform?

The gate was wide open, and as I walked in I heard the angry voice of a woman, followed by a babble of voices. Mrs Zain must have rung up relations and friends.

I pressed the doorbell, and there was sudden silence, which to me was more ominous than the voices. I pressed again after a few moments, for I had heard no sound of somebody coming.

'Who is it?' came an enquiry from behind the door.

I suddenly realised that these people now lived in fear. Of the "Firefly" government? Somehow this struck me as incongruous. Our government was a true government of the people, and fear should have no part in it. I announced who I was, and after loud whispers which floated down from the grill above the door the door was opened by the maid. She was not smiling, and that came as an unexpected little shock.

She led the way to the sitting room, and several pairs of eyes bored into me. But worse, far worse, was the fact that Aida was there and did not look up. I was not invited to sit down, but saw an empty chair and did. Immediately Mrs Zain turned on me with eyes blazing.

'What have you done with my husband? Where is he?' she shouted.

'Mrs Zain, your husband is quite safe. I assure you that everything will be straightened out before long. I only learned about it an hour ago.'

Zahor, in his short-sleeved foreign-made shirt, showing off his biceps, jumped up in mock anger, wanting to impress Aida.

'You people are turning Rivenia into a police state! All you want is to terrorise the people into being slaves again! Why don't the lot of you pack up and go far north where you belong!'

I hadn't realised until then that there might be those who viewed the "Firefly" regime as being a northern imposition. This disturbed me, and I made a mental note to bring it to the Ancestor's attention.

'Listen, Zahor,' I replied in as even a voice as a dry mouth would permit, 'your father's government was squeezing the life out of this country. How many millions of US dollars did your father send out? And all the other Ministers? Why were the hospitals short of even aspirin when every top civil servant and party official could holiday in Switzerland and Hawaii? Need I say more?'

For a moment I thought he was going to rush at me, swinging. But then a look of cunning came into his eyes. He knew how to hurt me.

'Why is an old man like you hovering round Aisha like a dried-up old moth? What would a girl like her want with somebody like you? Why, you are old enough to be her grandfather!'

He leaned back in great satisfaction having had his chance to hit me below the belt, and hit hard! He looked across triumphantly at Aida. I looked at her as well. She just had to lift her eyes, however briefly, to exchange looks with him and I'd know that the dream was over.

But she didn't shift from her concentration on the patterns in the carpet, moving her eyes to follow each design through. She seemed miles away, and my heart lifted. Perhaps, just perhaps, she had not been listening to him at all.

I had not been paying any attention to the others who were present, and now I saw that there were three women and two men, in addition to Zahor. I wasn't going to let him get away with it.

'By the way, Zahor,' I said, with studied casualness, 'now that all the nightclubs have been closed down, where do you go to get your whores? Or do you cruise up and down some street?'

I relaxed back in my chair, knowing that he didn't have a mind quick enough to get out a convincing riposte. I heard one of the men snigger, and knew I had an ally there.

Zahor glanced quickly at Aida who, to my surprise, looked at me instead. Before I could read the expression on her face Zahor had got up and was looming over me in two quick strides. Having done some boxing in my early to mid-twenties, my left hand moved instinctively up and forward, ready to jab; my right formed into a defensive cup.

But he didn't touch me. Instead, he poured out a string of curses which, even if we had all been men there, would have startled one or two. Unfortunately for him, there were ladies present and in a family context, and as of that moment his chances with Aida dropped to zero. Or so I believed.

One of the men stood up and shouted to him to apologise immediately, which he did lamely, and then sat down staring at Aida. I actually felt sorry for him, for despite his philandering ways I think he was genuinely in love with Aida. But even looking at the whole thing dispassionately, how long would a man like him remain faithful to his wife? His type usually kept a wife in a constant state of pregnancy, while he went out with other women.

At this point I decided that to stay any longer would be counterproductive. I felt I had buried him as far as Aida was concerned, but I could, of course, be mistaken. Some women find loose and uncouth men highly attractive, and derive masochistic pleasure from the suffering they must go through.

And now I went and did something quite vindictive to rub salt in Zahor's wound. In fact, even a month earlier I'd never have dared do it. I went to where Aida was sitting, right next to her mother, and placed my hand on her shoulder, leaving it there until she looked up at me with eyes wide open in surprise. I gave the shoulder a bit of a squeeze, and then made for the door.

I had staked my claim for all to see.

•••••••

At the Palace the following day, I found that the Ancestor and Serge had quietly slipped away during the night and driven north in a convoy of three large four-wheel drive cars. President Serranos, our northern neighbour, had already been contacted and they would meet in the border town of Zaitun. Naturally only we of the Executive Council knew about the visit, and the explanation we gave for his absence was that he was having a bit of a rest in the cool north-west highlands. In fact, some soldiers were sent there to put on a show of guarding the VIP guest house. We were into June, a hot month but with the usual wisps of cloud beginning to gradually thicken, getting together to produce the Greater Rains* in a few weeks' time.

The Ancestor was expected to be away three or four days, and with Serge also gone Bluebeard was left to mind the house, which was a bit worrying because he was not the kind of man who liked to consult anybody before acting. Fortunately there did not appear to be any crisis looming. Intelligence estimated that integrating the Xarbuss forces would take another six weeks, and training would require another month. Our own

*Greater Rains: a season

programme was proceeding apace, and if new equipment started flowing in within the month we should be fairly prepared about one week before they were. Everything now hinged on how well the Ancestor got on with his old comrade.

I took the opportunity presented by the Ancestor's absence to intensify my search for the old house of my dreams, and I began by visiting estate agents. I drew a blank in every instance and returned much dispirited. Fortunately, during lunch Aziz asked me what was depressing me and I told them. Somebody mentioned seeing some old houses in the sports stadium area. One or two houses did not look well tended, but he was sure people lived in them.

I went back to the estate agent who had been most friendly and co-operative and mentioned the houses in the stadium area, asking him as a special favour to go and see whether any of them would like to sell. I was prepared to pay well, even if it meant borrowing from the National Bank. (As a Commander I could borrow quite a large amount; is there any country where rank does not convey privileges? After all, I'd not be stealing from the populace.)

The agent had a nice surprise for me when I checked with him the following day.

'A very old couple lives in one of those houses, and the gentleman can barely see and walks with difficulty. The old lady said they use only a small part of the ground floor, just four rooms in fact, and the rest is shut up. The entire first floor as well as half the ground floor. They would prefer a small house in town, but it must be near a hospital and have close neighbours they could call upon. I have no small house near a hospital. I have a house in Hospital Street, but it has a first floor. Naturally it'd cost quite a bit.'

It was a great pity my bungalow was out of town otherwise it could have been a straight swap. He gave me both addresses, and I decided to have a look at both that very day.

On the way to the stadium I looked in on the old café group and was assailed by the local equivalent of the wolf whistle because of my new uniform and insignia.

'I think I'll join the Firefly Army!' said portly Suweid, a fruit merchant.

'They'd love to have you for bayonet practice!' said another. 'Or, maybe, as a raft for river crossing.'

I left after just one small cup of coffee, and turned into Stadium Road, keeping a sharp eye on the left-hand side as instructed. The houses were quite widely separated because of their extensive grounds, and their high walls meant that one only caught a glimpse through the decorative scrolls and bars of their iron gates, some of which were badly rusted. The house I was looking for had to be behind one of these, and not the well-maintained ones. I finally found it by the number plate on the moss-covered wall next to the gate. It groaned and screeched inwards, and I made my way between bushes and weeds where once was a garden, and suddenly there was the entrance portico in front of me with three steps leading up to it. I think I fell in love with it from that moment. Never mind the crumbling plaster and the peeling paint, this house had that welcoming feeling, a psychic quality, which some houses acquire not so much by design, choice of materials or proportions, as by the character of the people who had lived in it.

For one does come across some fine-looking houses which are yet uninviting, and even forbidding. To me, at least.

Regrettably, the carved and embossed hardwood door was rotting along its base, and the threshold showed signs of termite destruction. I pressed the doorbell, but it didn't seem to be working, so I banged the brass knocker, one of those cheap modern imitations obtainable at any ironmonger's.

The door surprised me by opening almost without noise. One

moment it was shut, and the next there was a very old lady peering up at me. I was immediately struck by her very long white hair and her upright stance. And there was nothing wrong with her eyes either, for she suddenly focused them on my left breast pocket and, with a quick movement, flicked away something.

'Stink bug,' she said. 'Its juice stings if it gets in your eye.'

I formally greeted her and asked whether I could go in to discuss what the estate agent had come to see them about.

'By all means,' she said, 'please come in,' and she stepped aside. A tremulous voice asked who it was, and she said somebody come to talk about the house.

She apologised that the housemaid had not been round for days, probably ill, and the place was a mess. It certainly was, and the dust was not that of just a few days. I suspected that they could no longer afford a maid. But I looked about and was captivated; the fluted columns, the height of the ceiling, the staircase at the other end of the hall, the arched windows with tinted-glass lights, everything reminded me of the house of my childhood. I did not ever feel the need to examine any other rooms, for I already knew what I'd find there. This was standard traditional architecture for those who could afford it. And if there were walls damaged by damp, or woodwork eaten by termites or consumed by wet or dry rot, I was quite prepared to temporarily bankrupt myself to have the repairs undertaken. In short, I had already made up my mind to own this house. And as with my car, I felt a psychic affinity with it already.

But first to find out if I could persuade the old couple to sell it. The husband, who looked frail and short-sighted, stood up with some difficulty to shake my hand. He must have been in his nineties, and she a few years younger.

Peering a bit more closely at me, while she went away to make coffee, he said, 'I see you are in uniform. Old National Army or new?'

‘Firefly Army, sir,’ I replied.

‘Our radio has broken down, so I don’t know what is happening. How are you finding life in this new army?’

‘We are preparing for a possible war in the not too distant future. Our south-west neighbours are claiming our land.’

He was quiet for a moment, and then whacked the carpet with his stick.

‘If those cursed foreigners had not come we would not be having all these problems. Our empire was strong, and everyone knew his place.’

His wife then came in and I jumped to carry the small table which she was about to bring before us. She returned to the kitchen.

‘What kind of man is this leader of yours, the “Firefly”?’

‘He is inspired by the Twelve Elders, sir. He has come to save the country from being overcome by foreign influences.’

‘Ah! Too late, I am afraid. We can no longer even take a breath without the foreigners’ approval. They can make us or break us at will. They are the potter, and we the little pots they mould into shape. If a pot doesn’t look right to the potter, what does he do? Smash it and make another one! And that’s what they do to countries, and they never seem to tire! Day in, day out, they make and break.’

There was nothing I could add to that without sounding trivial, so we waited in silence for the traditional coffee of welcome. It was peculiarly comforting to be with people so much older than myself. It was like being with one’s long-lost grandparents.

The lady saved me the awkwardness of having to bring up the matter of the house by broaching the subject herself.

‘My husband and I can no longer run this house. Because of the steps, he cannot even go out to sit in the garden. The man must have told you we want a small house, with many neighbours calling, for we love company. And also near a doctor, for we are getting on, though, the Almighty be praised, I am in good health. My mother was over one hundred years old when she passed on, may she rest in peace.'

'Have you always lived in this house? And isn't it a "wakf"?'

A "wakf" is a house which is never to be sold but is to provide shelter for descendants, generation after generation, as long as it stands.

'No, it is not a wakf because our son bought it for us about thirty years go. Alas, he was our only child, and our dear grandchildren send us money every now and then. But they live abroad, and we have not seen them for five years. The house is entirely ours, so we can sell it.'

With their son dead, and their grandchildren (how many of them) out there in the world, out of sight, it was all very sad.

'Where were you before you came here?' I asked.

'Marmar, the jewel of the north. How I wish we'd never left!'

This was quite a coincidence, having been brought up from early childhood in Marmar myself. I told them so, and they looked delighted.

'Ah, you are one of us then. Did you marry before you left?' I regretted that I had not, but had married abroad.

'A great shame, that. Look at my lady wife. Could you find a woman like her anywhere else? She is beautiful now, but you cannot imagine what a bird of paradise she was in her youth! Eyes followed here everywhere she went. I kept thinking I was in some wonderful dream.'

She went and kneeled by his armchair and held his hand. I could well imagine what a beautiful woman she must have been. Perhaps more lovely than my own Aida even, I thought.

She turned to me. 'Do you remember the row of girls selling flowers from distant regions in the market? And the camel caravans, coming in and going out, day and night, their bells ringing? And the exotic fruits, and blocks of ice in sawdust? And the carpets from Shiraz, the perfumes from Arabia, and brassware from Hindustan? What is there now to compare? And the grapes, pomegranates and the figs and blood-red dates? Surely the growers must have added honey to the fertiliser!'

Time had stood still, and I was back with my grandmother, a bittersweet moment.

'Well, sir,' said the old gentleman, 'that was how I came to meet her. She was one of the flower girls.'

'Let me tell him, husband. Let me tell him, for I love telling the story. You will only tell part of it, I know you!'

I resisted the temptation to look at my watch and sat back resignedly.

'I was returning home just before the noon prayers one day, having sold all my flowers and filled the basket with sweet potatoes and fruit, with money to spare. A kindly gentleman had bought all the flowers and paid me well.'

'I think he was after you!' cut in her husband.

'Fate had meant me for you, sir, even if he had paid me the price of a camel. Anyway, I heard this voice seeming to come from the sky above and behind me. "Ho, damsel!" it said. "Hold a while!" I stopped and turned to look, and there he was, high up on his camel. How princely he looked! I think I fell in love at that instant, but I was certainly not going to show it. "I have no more flowers to sell. And I am in a hurry to go home." He made the camel kneel, and he stood in front of me, eating me with his eyes.'

The old man chuckled and snipped off another piece of Turkish delight.

"By the glories of Paradise, surely your flowers stand ashamed before you. You are surely a "houri" from Paradise!" he said.

"Do not blaspheme, sir!" I cried, but falling even deeper

under his spell. "Ask for the Almighty's forgiveness before He punishes you." But he was not disturbed by any of that, and asked me to tell him my name, and whose daughter I was. "I do not give my name to strangers," I said, and turned and walked away. He climbed back on his camel and followed me some paces behind. I knew he wanted to know where I lived, so I led him a merry chase, up and down the streets, but my arms were beginning to ache from carrying the basket, and in the end I had to go home. He tethered his camel to a tree outside my house and returned to sit there after prayers, looking at the house. He left only after the afternoon prayers.'

I was swept along by their pleasure in reliving that day, and I wanted to hear how they subsequently married. So I said, 'And then?'

This time the old gentleman took over.

'She and her mother and younger brother must have been watching me through the window slats, for when I arrived early next morning to take up my vigil this young boy came up to me, most respectfully, and said, "Sir, my mother says you are making my sister afraid to come out, and if you have anything to say to please wait until Father returns in three days' time God willing, and then speak to him." I dug into my pocket and gave him two coins, and blessed him. I was only about twenty years old myself. I went away.'

She cut in, 'When Father returned, the first thing he said was, "Have you been encouraging that young man out there?" He was very stern. Mother told him the whole story, and that the man must have returned only that day. Then the two of them went to another room and shut the door. They seemed to be in there for hours, and I knew they were discussing me and him.'

His hand was shaking slightly as he lifted the small, handleless coffee cup and she steadied it with hers. I had a feeling that the memory was more responsible for the shaking than the usual weakness. When he did not say anything, she asked him if she should tell the rest of the story, and he nodded.

'So when they came out of the room, straight away Father asked me how I felt about the young man. I didn't know what to say! I was afraid to say anything! So Father said, "He has asked for my permission to send a marriage proposal." So they had already talked! Everything was happening so fast that I broke into tears. Mother said, "Let me talk to her, husband. You go and have your bath." I told Mother that he must love me to have done all that he had done, for there was no shortage of pretty girls in Marmar. And that I liked him, too. She agreed. Father went out and told him – sitting patiently under the tree, poor man! – and the next day his uncle and a cousin came with a formal proposal of marriage on his behalf. A month later we were man and wife. And will be to the end of time.'

I was so affected that I decided then and there to "adopt" them as my grandparents, and to help them in any way I could. I promised to find a suitable house for them in town, and to send a handyman that very day to tidy up the place. I wished they had been in their eighties and not nineties for very soon they were bound to be gone.

I looked forward to taking Aida to see them, and knew she would take to them, as I did. After we were married, of course.

Which reminded me to start pulling a few strings to get her father released on bail. But not before the Ancestor returned from the north which we expected to be in the next day or two. For security reasons, even Bluebeard had no idea as to the date and time. Nothing could be easier than to ambush a convoy of three cars on the open road, and, not for the first time, I had a premonition of what was going to happen. For I saw him choosing, or on the insistence of his old mate Serranos, to return by helicopter. And so it proved the following afternoon when I was fast asleep in mid-siesta.

Any expectations of a major breakthrough in our relations with the northern neighbour were quickly squashed by the Ancestor with his very first words.

'Gentlemen, I regret to say that my old friend and fellow idealist, Serranos, has become a comfortable, rich head of state, who has lost interest in the great universal struggle that used to reduce him to tears. Of our small group then, he of all of us seemed the most revolutionary, the most dedicated.

'And yet from the very first moment I hardly recognised him! Was this plump, pinstriped suited man, with his gold watch and custom-built luxury car, really Serranos? I only became certain when he called me by the nickname known only to our intimate circle. None of the others made it to the top, two of them losing their lives trying.

'He wanted us to talk alone, so we went out and sat under a tree in the garden of the private villa. He congratulated me – off the record, as he pointed out – and the upshot was that he was prepared to tone down any resolution that was passed against us by the region, but could not go so far as recognising our government yet. He assured me that he was waiting for an excuse to do so, and the speeches being given in Xarbuss, threatening us, were being followed closely by his government.'

Later there was a business lunch, at which Serge had presented our request for military equipment to be allowed to pass through his territory. Discussions had continued after dinner, and the end result was that the northern government would allow "tractors, generators and other heavy goods" to use their roads and be provided with a police escort.

The Ancestor was satisfied with this, for the military equipment bought in the far north would now take but two days to reach us instead of up to two weeks by devious routes. So in one important aspect the visit was a success.

But without an official ally, and diplomatic pressure on us

steadily mounting – countries going by the book and ignoring the obvious national support that the "Firefly" regime enjoyed – we were still exposed and vulnerable. A single major country had to suggest intervention to restore the deposed President and, as with a snowball rolling downhill, an avalanche would be upon us.

The Ancestor then took the unprecedented step of asking each member of the General Council to swear to stand by him to the death, if necessary, adding that anyone who was not prepared to do so would not be censured but on the contrary be given every assistance to emigrate with his family. If there was anyone who was tempted to pull out, he did not show it. Nevertheless, the Ancestor, a keen judge of character, must have detected a slight hesitation in the case of an Assistant Commander for he was quietly posted north.

No wonder it is said that one's best friend may prove to be his worst enemy and vice versa, for it was our arch-enemy Magrari who was now coming forward to check, or at least mute, the mounting regional demand for our restoration to "democracy". (Which to most of the regional leaders meant retaining the status quo for ever and a day, the same dominant, and domineering party continuing to rule.) And he was doing so by reiterating his claim on both the river plain and the river bulge. He started a series of manoeuvres close to our border, on a progressively larger and larger scale. Naturally this began to make some regional leaders a bit worried that an arms race could be in the offing. Many of them had armies only meant to fight rebels or subdue the population.

And then the official media in both Xarcassia and Bussota began to print articles in weekly installments on the history of the region, going back centuries, to show, as they claimed, how Rivenia had "built its empire on the backs of slaves" under the rule of the Twelve Elders. They studiously avoided mentioning that the Elders included representatives from all the countries in the region that belonged to the empire. And that slavery, a few centuries ago, was a worldwide phenomenon.

The Ancestor asked me whether I'd like to reply to these articles with one of our own, not in our pro-government papers but in the independent ones. I thought about it, and decided not to make corrections to their version of history, but to take the emotional sting out of their propaganda by showing the universality of slavery at one time. I remembered a book I had at home which had a treatise on the purchase of slaves, which, despite the grim subject, was surprisingly funny.

I gave this idea to the Ancestor and he approved, saying only that he hoped it was in good taste. I assured him it was.

Back in my study I took down the book, an anthology, and turned to the treatise I had mentioned.

Back in the tenth century there was a ruler call Kai Kaus. He ruled the regions round the south shores of the Caspian Sea. To prepare his son to succeed him, he wrote a book called *The Book of Kaus*. It had forty-four chapters on a wide range of subjects, from how to govern to falling in love. One of these subjects was slavery, and in a long chapter entitled "The Purchase of Slaves" he gives an astonishing assessment of the character and suitability of different races as slaves.

Just how radically different the thinking was in the past to what it is today (barely over the last hundred years, in fact) can be gauged from his opening remarks:

> …Most people imagine that buying slaves is like any other form of trading, not understanding that the buying of slaves, or the art of doing so, is a branch of philosophy…

Then he gets down to telling you how to judge suitability from the face, eyes, nose, body, and even teeth, before going on to look at different races in turn and the number of diverse nationals regularly available for sale in the open market. The universal belief is that it was only Africa that provided slaves, but for many centuries slavery knew no race or country. Kai Kaus, for instance, gives advice in purchasing the following: Russians, Turks, Central Europeans, Alains (whoever they were), Indians, Ethiopians, Armenians, Byzantines, Nubians, and even Tibetans! Kai Kaus himself admits that were he to describe every single race it would require an entire thick volume, so he restricts himself to those most commonly available. He gives the good points and the bad points of each, mostly restricting himself to men.

For fear of boring the reader, I shall quote briefly on only a few:

> The Turks… are blunt-witted, ignorant, boastful, turbulent, and without a sense of justice… Their merit is they are brave, free of pretence, open in enmity, and zealous in any task allotted to them. For the domestic establishment there is no better race.
>
> Slavs and Russians are near in temperament to the Turks, but are more patient.
>
> The Byzantines… are artistic… but are prone to theft, disobedience, betrayal of secrets… indolence, hostility to their masters, and escaping. Their virtues are that they are soft-natured, agreeable, and quick of understanding.
>
> The Armenians… are mischievous, foul-mouthed, prone to flight, disobedient… From head to foot, indeed, they incline rather towards defects than to merits…

He goes on to warn against the Hindu, who, he says is not only evil-tongued but is a menace to any slave girl!

He has praise for Abyssinians and Nubians, who, he says, "are freer of faults, with the Abyssinians being considered the better".

His analysis goes much deeper than I have indicated, and his eye for physical detail was acute. And he even suggested a pretty thorough medical examination! But in conclusion, he urged that slaves be treated decently, as befitted one's dignity.

The *Sunday Chronicle* accepted my article and serialised it over a period of three weeks. Their circulation went up, and they asked me to prepare a similar "enlightening" article.

But critical events started happening the very next month, and I never got round to writing it.

Finding some free time I went to have a look at the one-storey house in Hospital Street which the agent had mentioned. I'd have to be buying two houses, instead of just the old Stadium Road house, and I'd have to borrow heavily from the bank on top of the money I'd get for my bungalow. But I was even prepared to lose out on the deal in order to secure the old house. It fitted Aida in my mind like no other house I had seen in town. And with a loving couple like those remarkable old people having lived in it for so many years, the psychic atmosphere was bound to be good.

The agent had been misled; the house was not in Hospital Street but off it, in Olive Street. Still, it just meant a five-minute walk to the hospital, and the house was separated from its neighbours on either side by a low brick wall. The plot was small, but there was room for a nice front garden and a yard in the back. The only problem was the extra floor which they would have no use for. I wondered it they'd like to take in tenants, perhaps a young couple just starting out.

I noticed that there were two steps at the front door, but they were lower than the ones at the old house. I rang the doorbell.

The man who opened the door reeked of alcohol and didn't look too steady. But when he spoke his voice was sober enough.

'Yes? What can I do for you?'

I explained the purpose of my visit, and he invited me in. As expected, the sitting room was like a junk shop, though clean enough. I had hardly sat down when he burst out that life had treated him very badly indeed. And as he went on with the story of his life, confiding in someone old enough to be his father, I had to admit that he certainly wasn't the luckiest man in the world. One misfortune after another had struck him in quick succession in the last few months. At work, and even at play (he was limping from a broken leg sustained playing tennis of all things); a burglar had walked off with his expensive hi-fi equipment, and his investments had crashed. And finally, last month his wife left him, calling him a "jinx".

So now all he wanted was to get out of the house, get out of the town, and get out of the country. He had even contemplated suicide. Well, that explained to me his drinking, and I was thoroughly ashamed of myself for having viewed him with contempt.

We got down to talking business, and he said that he was prepared to lower his price considerably if I could pay him in one lump sum within two weeks for he didn't think he'd survive another month in that house.

His misfortune proved to be my good fortune (and, truthfully, I received no joy from this fact), for the sum he mentioned was actually smaller that I expected to get for my bungalow. Being a town house, fairly recently built, it should have fetched almost twice the amount.

I promised to fetch the money within four days and get all the documentation formalised that same week. I could not yet sell the bungalow, of course, but I could just manage to cover the purchase of this house. Strangely enough, it had not occurred to me that the old people might very well accept a straight swap, their house for this one. All the time I had been thinking in terms of having to buy both houses. I rejoiced when the realisation finally hit me, but first to get the Olive Street house all nicely tidied up, including the garden. (But what if they said they didn't like this house?)

I had not had lunch and was well into my siesta time, but the good thing about having to endure a whole month of fasting every year in the month of Ramadan, taking neither food nor drink from just before sunrise to sunset, is that one never panics when missing either breakfast or lunch. So I drove straight back to the stadium house (as I had taken to calling it in my mind) to tell the old Marmar couple about having found a house for them. They were cautious in their response, asking me to describe it in detail, as well as the area. I even suggested that it would not cost too much to provide an external timber staircase in the back leading up to the first floor, so that tenants would not have to use the front entrance. This would bring them a steady income. They were not sure about sharing the house with other people, but said they would consider it after moving in. There was one bedroom downstairs, and two upstairs, with own "family space" and bathroom. But a kitchenette would have to be added which should be adequate for students or a young couple.

When I looked at the large pieces of antique furniture they had in the sitting room, my heart sank. There was simply not enough room in the other house, unless they used the first floor for storage purposes. But I blocked my mind to that particular difficulty, determining to cross that bridge when we came to it.

I left the house considerably less sanguine than I had entered it, going straight home instead of calling at GHQ on the way. Outside my front door I saw a plastic carrier bag, with a small covered dish in it. I was not going to open it until I had had a nice shower and then a pot of tea, for I knew it had to be something good.

Out on the veranda (I had not bothered to make lunch) with my tea and biscuits, I delicately opened the dish. It contained honey! But one lick told me that it wasn't just ordinary honey;

it was the very rare and very expensive "three-flower" honey, which is reputed to have great medicinal value, and is used by healers and herbalists in many of their concoctions. Apart from having a superb taste.

But who had sent it? There was no note attached. I could think of only three people who would have sent it – the Ancestor (as a present from the north) Serge, or... Aida. No need to tell you which of the three I wished to the Almighty had sent it!

Well, I'd find out soon enough the following morning when I went to the Palace. We were to meet to discuss organising nationwide demonstrations in support of the "Firefly" government. Foreign news teams would be invited to see for themselves that the entire nation was behind us. And why should it not be? Roads were being repaired, hospitals being stocked with long-missing medicines, salaries were being paid on the dot, fewer electricity cuts, no muggers in the streets, and most of the little concerns of ordinary citizens were receiving attention.

The first instalment of my article on slavery having appeared in that Sunday's paper, I searched my mind for another subject of relevant interest, again based on the views of centuries ago, and came up with an article I remembered reading when I was desperately trying to give up smoking. I located it among my books, and after going through it twice I started jotting down bits and pieces for a first draft. How many people know that smoking was a contentious subject centuries ago? That it even carried the death sentence in the Turkish army? Soldiers were executed for smoking and otherwise suffered many other forms of punishment, depending on the character of the commanding officer. And yet this did not succeed in eliminating the habit!

The famous Turkish writer, Katib Chelebi, who died in AD 1657, wrote at some length on smoking. In his book *The Balance of Truth* he covers many aspects of smoking in considerable detail, and his grasp of psychology is quite astonishing. He begins with its very first appearance in Turkey in 1601, and then plunges into its impact on society, almost immediately causing much debate and contention and leading on to violent attempts to repress it.

I shall give very brief quotations to give a flavour of the debate that raged throughout the land.

> From its first appearance… various preachers have spoken against it… and many of the learned Ulema have written tracts concerning it… The eminent surgeon, Ibrahim Effendi, devoted much care and attention to the matter, conducting great debates in the Abode of the Sultanate… giving warning talks at a special public meeting… He troubled himself to no purpose. The more he spoke, the more people persisted in smoking!

Is this not true today as then? And he goes on to say:

> As to its harmful effects, there is no doubt. It ends by becoming a basic need for the addict, who does not consider its evil consequences… it is medically noxious in that it makes turbid the aerial essence…

But, remarkably, he concludes by coming down on the side of free choice, people to be left to decide for themselves after all the warnings had been given. He even touches on the economic aspect of the tobacco trade.

Voices from the distant past, as relevant now as they were then. Left to gather dust in archives, accessible only to the odd scholar.

But as already stated, the chance to submit this article to the *Sunday Chronicle* never arose, for we were overtaken by dramatic events soon after the third instalment of my slavery article appeared.

As I walked up the marble stairs in the Palace on Thursday morning I felt some weakness in the knees, and a slight tightness in the eyes. Lifelong experience told me immediately what it was: the ever-present old enemy, *plasmodium*, was perpetuating the species in my bloodstream. This astonishingly cunning creature has the knowledge, the cunning and the patience to hide safely in the liver, once it has been introduced into the body by a mosquito and wait for its chance to come out. Should its "blitzkrieg" be beaten back by drugs, the survivors stage a disciplined retreat back to the liver and bide their time. If reinforcements arrive by way of another mosquito bite, or the host body suffers from acute fatigue or is generally indisposed, the plasmodium battalions come charging out again in an orgy of feeding and reproduction.

Depending on the type of plasmodium, the symptoms can vary from little fevers and weaknesses which drag on and on, to an overpowering of the body's defences, leading to death. The best thing is to go immediately for a blood test of course, but personally I always kept two types of pills in my medicine cabinet at home, and wasted no time taking one or the other. Occasionally the slight feverish feeling would still be there a week later, in which case I'd repeat the single dose. Only once in my life was the attack exceptionally violent and I had to be hospitalised.

So I went to my office with my mind somewhat preoccupied, especially since I could feel my temperature rising steadily. I asked my secretary to hunt around for pills, single-dose variety, and also for a thermometer, and I went to see Serge about getting Aida's father out on bail.

Serge hated paperwork, but as Chief of Staff he found he was having more and more of it to do. I suggested that he delegated some of the work to an appointed administrative assistant, not necessarily a high-ranking officer. His worry was security clearance, but I believed a Forester of captain rank could be trusted.

Then I got down to the ticklish problem of bail for Zain, and he said he would have to be moved to a lower category of "defaulters" first. Only then would bail be considered. To begin making exceptions would undermine the "Firefly" ethos. Nevertheless, he'd consult the AG, and the charges against him would be looked at. For my sake, he hoped that Zain had been left out of the "big deals".

Serge had not sent the dish of honey, and he said that among the presents given to them up north he didn't remember seeing honey, so that ruled out the Ancestor. Which left… Aida? How wonderful if it were so!

My secretary had gone out to the nearest pharmacy to get me the pills, plus Vitamin C in 1,000 mg tablets. Then she fetched me pineapple juice from the mess. A nice, motherly type who would have made a nice nurse. But she had forgotten to buy a thermometer, and as I felt my temperature still rising (the feeling in the eyes is a good gauge) I rang Serge to be excused from the afternoon meeting concerning the proposed demonstrations. I was relieved to hear that the Military Council was not to be involved, after all, all the organising work having been handed over to more relevant councils. He explained that since our Council had been closest to the Ancestor, his automatic response when anything came up was to put us in charge. But the formation of other councils – political, economic, public relations, and so on – would now leave us free to concentrate on purely military matters.

A "Supreme Council of Elders" was expected to emerge from the multi-layered council elections scheduled for September.

When I got home the thermometer confirmed what I already knew – the mercury was past 39.6°C So I had a sponge-down, and took to bed with an aircraft magazine, a source of unfailing pleasure totally free of any bad associations.

Fever and fatigue combined to make me dead to the world until almost sunset. The pills had been doing their job, and so had the long rest, and I woke up feeling hungry and thirsty. It would take another day or two to fully recover, but unless it was one of those particularly resistant strains of malaria the worst was probably over. My temperature was almost back to normal, and I had tea and sandwiches. Later I went through a pretty heavy dinner of beef curry, rice, mushrooms and olives, followed by a dish of mixed fruit. I realised then that I had been half-starving myself the previous two or more weeks with quick and haphazard meals, grabbed at all manner of times.

I devoted the next day entirely to the matter of purchasing the Olive Street house, taking the seller in my car to the bank, and then the various government departments where forms had to be signed and sealed, each with a charge of its own. I wanted to get the whole thing over and done with that same day, and it took right up to office closing time. The owner then promised to be out by Saturday, two days away. He offered to sell his furniture, which was standard "modern" but in fairly good shape, for a small sum and I accepted. If the old people didn't want it and insisted on bringing all their old stuff, it would be locked away in the garage and put out for sale. Frankly, my secret hope was that the couple would want to sell their massive antique furniture to me, and settle for the stuff already in place and which was easy enough to move about.

With that big load off my mind, I could now relax and get back to routine, planning to take the Marmar couple to view the house on Sunday. I wanted them to move in as quickly as possible so that I could get the old house repaired and renovated. As for purchasing their house, I was now confident that if they liked the other house they would be agreeable to making a straight exchange.

We were now into July and Friday was the first. And we had our first foretaste of the rains to come. In a very short time indeed dark clouds emerged from behind the mountains and joined up with others which seemed to have materialised out of nowhere. Thunder roared, reverberating from all sides, and that was the signal for the downpour to start. On the roof it sounded more like hail than rain, and I kept an anxious eye on the ceiling panels, on the watch for wet spots to appear. As the rain was coming almost vertically down I sat out on the veranda and soaked in the obvious relief of all the vegetation around. Drought was something that every living thing dreaded, and it was a constant seasonal anxiety. A delay of more than a month could mean not getting a drop of rain for months. Or, in the worst case scenario, even a whole year or longer.

Actually, these rains could not have come at a worse time as far as the region was concerned because the regional football competition was scheduled to start on Monday, 4 July, just three days away. So there must have been many prayers being said that these premature rains go away and return another day, in August!

The first match would be between the "Spearheads" of Xarcassia, and our own "Blue Wasps", to be played at the sports stadium. Eight teams were fighting for the cup, so other teams were playing in other capitals on the same day. Our "Blue Wasps" had won the cup only once before, many years ago, whereas the "Spearheads" had won it three times, though they were not the current champions. So everybody expected a pretty tough fight.

It was good to put politics on the back burner, if only for a while. But not quite! For in the usual, quite illogical way, how the team performed would reflect on the "Firefly" regime. This put an enormous mental burden on the poor players.

Members of the Military Council were no more immune to the general excitement than the man in the street, and the Ancestor (having, like me, been out of the country for so many years) listened with interest to stories of past matches. The universal appeal of soccer is really quite astonishing. Freud would no doubt see the scoring of a goal in sexual terms, pointing to the giveaway gestures of the scorers, and the way they pull off their shirts to expose their bodies; Carl Jung, on the other hand, would see it in quite other terms, having to do with archetypal triumphs and ancestral rites. The answer probably lies somewhere in-between the two.

Because of the planned demonstrations, it was almost critical that our team should win against Xarcassia. This led to sober reflection at the Saturday meeting, and the idea of holding those demonstrations was dropped for the time being. At any rate, the entire region was aflame with football fever and would be for the next three weeks if the rains allowed.

On Sunday I took my adopted grandparents to see their new house, all nicely tidied up, with a bit of new paint here and there, and the garden cleansed of weeds. Even the gate was freshly painted and greased.

Before opening the gate they stood in silence for a few minutes, and I knew they were saying the appropriate prayers for the occasion. His wife and I came to an unspoken agreement to let him lead the way in, so leaning on his stick he reached for the gate and pushed it. The smoothness with which it swung in caught him by surprise and he staggered forward, grabbing on to it! But he recovered before I got to him, and turned round and laughed.

'This is a merry-go-round, not a gate,' he said, making us join in the laughter. The path up to the front door was paved with concrete slabs, so he had no difficulty hobbling on, surveying the house from end to end, while she seemed more interested in the garden. As far as I could make out, the expression on her face was one of approval.

Now we came to the critical part – the steps up to the small porch. She moved forward, and with a bit of support he managed them all right. I had already given him the keys, but he stood and looked back at the garden, a riot of colours after the recent rains. They he opened the door, with a bit of difficulty because of his arthritis, and we followed him in.

I left them alone to look from room to room and sat out on the front steps. Some minutes later she called me in and asked me if the furniture was going to be taken away. I said not if they wanted it, and to my great relief she said they did, except for two or three items which she didn't like. Also, they wanted their favourite chairs and some other small items to be brought in.

'What about the bed, the wardrobes, divans, and your other things?'

'Oh, no, no!' he said. 'Too full of memories for us. We want to start a new life. You keep them if you want. Otherwise sell them.'

And now I was forced to bring up the matter of whether they would accept this house in exchange for theirs. He replied by asking a series of questions.

'Is the roof here sound? And the walls free of damp? No problem with water supply? And the wiring, what state is it in? How far is the hospital? Are the shops near?'

I assured him on all those points, and then mentioned the option of making the first floor self-contained, with its own stairs. Very shrewdly, my "granny" said, 'Well, if you will do the work to the first floor we will accept a straight swap.'

'Done!' I said, thoroughly satisfied. The work could be easily done with them in the house, since there was no major structural work involved. The timber stairs at the back would be self-supporting, and just tied into the wall. The central "family area" window would be cut out to make a canopied door. The kitchenette would pose no problem, the bathroom being next to it.

Weight number two was now off my shoulders, and the

future seemed to be taking shape nicely. I rang engineer Adam, of our café group and gave him charge of doing both the Olive Street and the stadium houses, the latter to start as soon as the old people had moved. He said he would require about a week for the first job to be done, if I'd get all that was needed for the kitchenette delivered on site within four days. I'd then take him to the old house and show him what I needed doing. Sketches would help.

The talk was all about football that Sunday evening on the local radio, and though I was quite looking forward to the match the following day as keenly as anybody else, I grew rather bored after a while and switched over to short-wave for the rest of the evening, playing my clarinet in-between, for I always got more fun playing than listening.

Army HQ had decided that we should all go by staff car in convoy with the Ancestor's, so I was at the Palace by 3 p.m., forty-five minutes before we were due to leave. Members chatted in the Council lounge until a messenger came to tell us the Ancestor was on his way down. We caught up with him at the front entrance, and I was surprised to see that he was dressed traditionally, in robes and turban, looking like a sultan from a bygone era. And very impressive he looked, too, and I reasoned that he wanted to get away from the military image to down play the nature of our regime. Until the council elections produced the right calibre of civilians we remained, of course, a benevolent (we tried our best to make it so) military dictatorship to all intents and purposes.

The Ancestor rode in the back in a civilian convertible (I was not sure what kind it was, but definitely in the luxury class), with Serge by his side in uniform. Bluebeard was in the front passenger seat. This made a good impression on the people, for it signalled the end of the demi-god President who was too high and mighty to permit anyone else to ride with him.

We followed behind the two security cars, another preceding the Ancestor's behind a motorcycle escort.

The stadium was already packed, with hundreds milling about outside the gate creating quite a problem for the scores of police. And posing a grave security threat to the Ancestor who, much against advice, was already standing up in the car waving to the people outside. So the roar of cheers started even before he entered the stadium, becoming absolutely deafening when we were inside. With nice timing, the police band then struck up the national anthem (the new one, still very unfamiliar) and we made our way to our seats.

As at HQ, Serge was on the Ancestor's right, and Bluebeard on his left. I sat next to Serge, with Moses next to me. Some of the well-dressed men and women nearest to us, behind and in front, were no doubt security personnel. We were in the third row up.

Cheers again as the players came out of their dressing rooms and the Ancestor went down to shake their hands. Cameras all over the place, a very tense time for the bodyguards, I was sure. A cameraman trying to get too close found himself flung to the ground and frogmarched off the field.

Events were only too soon going to show that the anxiety of security was well justified.

I have often wondered who composes national anthems, and how they come to be approved. Most of them seem to have one thing in common – dreariness. They drag on and on, aimlessly and yet predictably, moving towards a climax somewhere in the third octave, so high that only sopranos can sing it. Or so low that women give up, and men croak embarrassingly. Surely there should be a local, or even international, competition before one is selected by popular acclaim? Being expected to go into battle and die singing something that is uninspiring, and sounding like a tricky exercise for a trumpet student, is surely not conducive to nationalistic fervour.

The Ancestor returned up the steps to his seat after the two anthems were played, and the humming of the audience beehive changed into one of anticipation.

Players went into formation, blues on our left (our boys) and greens on our right. The whistle blew, and the game was on.

There is no point in describing how the game went as it had no relevance to what happened afterwards. Suffice to say that our "Wasps" gave as good as they got, but there was a touch of overconfidence in the beginning which cost them a goal in the fifteenth minute. A penalty levelled the score just before the whistle blew for half-time, which restored life to the stadium.

But then the second half started, and that's when it happened, transforming the situation in a split second.

Above the shouting and cheering I heard a sharp sound behind me, just off to the left, like a coconut being cracked open with a hammer, but mushier, followed by a gasp and a low cry. Remember, I was sitting on Serge's right, and he was next to the Ancestor. The crack came from behind them.

I leaned back to look behind Serge's head. He was already bending over the Ancestor. To my horror, I saw that the security man behind him was sprawled halfway out of his seat, his head hanging back so that I could see his throat and the underside of his chin. Craning my neck and looking at the Ancestor I saw that he had his hand covering his right ear, and blood was trickling down between his fingers.

What happened next was a confusion of sound and movement as somebody shouted and a woman screamed, and all at once we were jostled back into our seats by the security men as somebody called the army doctor a few seats away. I had one brief glimpse of the Ancestor as the security men made space for the doctor, and was horrified to see that the top of his ear was missing, leaving a jagged gash. The bullet had missed his skull by barely a centimetre and hit the man behind him in the forehead.

In a very short space of time all eyes in the stadium focused on where we were sitting and a hush fell. Play stopped abruptly as the players turned to look, and the referee blew his whistle for some reason.

There was now acute danger of panic breaking out, with people tumbling down the seats to get away, but suddenly the public address system crackled and Serge's voice came over.

'This is Commander Erion speaking. A bottle of fizzy drink behind the illustrious Chairman of the Supreme Council exploded in the heat, and pieces of glass cut his ear. The wound has been attended to and our leader is perfectly all right. Referee, please let the game resume!'

There was a slightly uneasy cheering as the game got going again but soon the incident seemed to have been forgotten as excitement took over. Fortunes swung to and fro and our boys, the underdogs, managed to hold the "Spearheads" to a 2:2 draw. There would be a rematch the following week.

But for us round the Ancestor the waiting for the game to end was nightmarish. It was obvious that he was in pain, but did not want to attract further attention by receiving further treatment. Fortunately the blue colour of his robe and turban hid the bloodstains, making them virtually invisible at a distance.

While all this was happening, a low-key but intensive search was going on for the assassin, and the stadium was already surrounded by a combination of security units. The bullet had come from the stands opposite, and it should not have been too hard to work out the exact spot from where the shot was fired. Obviously it would have been in such a manner as not to be obvious, a silencer being the most basic requirement.

There was another security man behind us who kept informing us of the search for the assassin. He was in touch by walkie-talkie.

I can't really say I remember much of the football game after the event, but judging by the roars, the cheers and the sing-songs the fans got their money's worth. In fact, I believe my fellow council members themselves got carried away at times, briefly forgetting the hair's breadth escape from disaster. How often the course of history has been drastically changed by the death of just a single person.

Strictly speaking, the Ancestor should have been bundled away out of the stadium altogether, as the plot might have involved more than one man. But nobody seemed to have thought of that and, to be honest, I do not see the Ancestor as having agreed to be rushed off.

The final whistle came as a tremendous relief to every one of us there, and I was surprised to find that when I stood up that my knees felt weak, revealing the high state of tension I must have unknowingly been in.

All the chiefs of the various branches of Security were to report to the palace immediately with their progress reports. Obviously they had not succeeded in catching the assassin and this was disappointing and disturbing.

The Ancestor became almost angry when everybody insisted that he transfer to another, bullet-proof car, so we had to yield. He left as he had come, standing in the convertible and waving to the crowds.

'The Hour can neither be advanced, nor delayed,' he quoted to us when we were back in the conference hall. 'It was the Hour for the poor security man behind me, may the Almighty rest his soul in peace.'

The security chiefs came in to make their reports while we were unwinding with refreshments. We deliberately kept away from the subject of the attempt on the Ancestor's life, mostly talking about the performance of our boys, and the reaction of the crowd. But the Ancestor seemed to be in some pain, wincing every now and then, and that made the laughter a bit forced. He was still wearing the same clothes, being keen to hear what Security had to say without delay.

The security chiefs – army, stadium, police – trooped in with long faces soon after. That there had been a major breach of security, there was no doubt. They knew that they would have to come up with a full explanation as to how it could have happened, otherwise heads would roll.

The story that emerged revealed such a lack of co-ordination between our various security bodies, including the Central one, that we were left aghast. From the time the assassin (which is what we must continue calling him, for though he had missed his primary target he had killed a man) handed in his ticket at the gate, bedecked with cameras and carrying a travelling bag, to when he was seen setting up a camera tripod behind the top row of seats, almost directly opposite the Ancestor's seat, no information about him had been passed on to police or army.

For instance, when the travelling bag was searched it was found to contain several steel tubes of various sizes, and other steel objects with holes, nuts and screws which were easily explained away as being for the heavy video camera stand. In fact, as the reader will long have guessed, they were components of a custom-made sniper's gun, and would have made anyone who frequented the movies or watched television immediately suspicious. However, our security men on the ground had not had that advantage, and it was a pistol, a bomb, or some obvious weapon that they were on the lookout for. The gate did not report the presence of this lone "reporter" to the stands, nor did the latter to central control.

And the reason was that the man was a European, with the letters of a famous, internationally renowned news network emblazoned on the back of his motorcycle jacket, and on his baseball cap. Who would suspect such a person? Wasn't the country keen to present a good image to the world in a bid to be accepted? He had openly set up his camera and lethal contraption, with security men just a few paces away, and even chatting with one or two who passed by; waited for them to drift away, seized his chance and fired! Had not Providence made the Ancestor move his head a fraction just as he fired, the "Firefly" era would have ended then and there.

But how had this foreigner then got away, when he could easily have been picked out in any crowd? He had left the gun-camera where it stood and his jacket and cap were discovered later in a lavatory cubicle behind and under the stands. Since there were dozens of foreigners among the audience, he'd have mixed in with them while the security men were trying to establish where the shot had come from. A silencer was fitted.

I must say we were all appalled by what we heard. Did this man belong to an antagonistic foreign service, or had he been hired by our deposed President? Professional killers of that calibre didn't come cheap, and the Ancestor said that from his knowledge of the man, Magrari wouldn't part with that kind of money to eliminate him. Magrari would get far more satisfaction and prestige in the region if he defeated the Ancestor in the field of battle.

After the chiefs of security had been told to keep check at all border crossings and of course the airport, not hesitating to question any likely suspect, Council members had a chance to air their own views. My own instinctive feeling – and I had learnt to trust it more than logic – told me that the assassin would not be among those leaving the country straight away. He had probably come to the country as a tourist and would remain until his visa expired. No doubt he had changed his appearance while throwing off his jacket in the lavatory, and was now plus or minus a moustache, toupee, or whatever;

perhaps even the colour of his eyes.

Serge had been sneaking anxious glances at the Ancestor, and now said that he was taking him to the military hospital for a closer look at the ear, despite his pretended annoyance. It was obvious that he was in some pain, and there was a trace of blood on the bandage.

Delayed shock hit me when I was undressing at home. Our new world had come so close, so very close, to being utterly destroyed. For neither Serge nor Bluebeard could have held the country together had he died. It would have broken up into factions, at war with each other, and then been swallowed up by our south-western neighbour, Xarbuss. Rivenians would wish they had never heard of the "Firefly", and remember the old days of corruption and exploitation as "the good old days".

It all didn't bear thinking about.

The attempt on the Ancestor's life could not be kept secret of course, and it was headline news in all the regional papers the next day. It also became international news, and there was much speculation as to who might have been behind it: the former President, the regional mafia, foreign intelligence, Magrari, or even a faction within the administration?

The police raided a guest house on a tip-off and found a foreigner in bed with a local woman. But it had been a false and embarrassing lead because the man happened to belong to an NGO and had been in the country for over a year.

The Ancestor's covert "semi-diplomatic" contacts failed to come up with anything useful and our lack of "legitimacy" in the eyes of the international community meant that we could not call on such as Interpol for assistance.

At the hospital, quite a bit more work had to be done to the Ancestor's ear, the army doctor having done only a field job. He had to spend the night there in case the bullet had been tipped with something noxious.

I was much touched when I dropped in at the café and the group showed great concern about his condition, pressing me for details. Pillars of the old establishment had been won over to us, and surely this was proof enough that our "undemocratic" system had the support of the majority of the people of all classes. In fact, spontaneous prayers of thanksgiving were given in all places of worship throughout the land.

When the Ancestor came out of hospital he sent for the "inner circle" – Serge, Bluebeard, and myself – to meet in his office. It was a remarkably sparsely furnished room, with just a large antique desk and chair against the picture window facing the northern mountains; a long, low cabinet with four door panels and three telephones on it, and two tall filing cabinets. A beautiful Persian carpet covered most of the mosaic-tiled floor, and that's where we sat, leaning on cushions. Only a privileged few were received in this office, there being another one with a long table and chairs for visitors decorated like a standard boardroom with all the facilities that went with such a place. It was three doors away, and it was where his secretary (finally accepted with great reluctance) was stationed in her own cubicle, separated by a framed glass partition.

I sensed that something had changed in the Ancestor, and it wasn't just because he had a bandage round his head. It was something in his eyes. They looked distant and preoccupied, which was never usually the case when he was with his closest companions. With the three of us he did not begin with, "Gentlemen", but either "Brothers" or "Comrades", which set us apart from the other members of the Council.

'Brothers,' he began, 'I have reason to believe that Magrari is receiving covert military support from a fairly major foreign power with the ultimate aim of making Xarbuss the dominant country in the region. When we took over Rivenia we put a spanner in their works, for the previous government – I will show you the documents recently found in the safe of the Foreign Affairs Minister who, as you know, managed to flee the country - was beginning to move towards uniting with Xarcassia and Bussota to form a three-nation United Republic.'

The startled look on Serge's and Bluebeard's faces showed that even they had no knowledge of it, and a look of disapproval crept over Serge's face, which the Ancestor was quick to spot.

'I am still in the process of studying the documents and frankly did not consider them to be of more than political interest, making no difference to the military situation.'

Satisfied that he had mollified all of us, he proceeded.

'I mention it now because I have come to believe that the professional foreign killer was sent by the same country, quite possibly without Magrari or our former head of state knowing anything about it.'

'But, Ancestor, why would this country go to that extent, risking being caught out and exposed to the world?' I asked, but then quickly corrected myself. 'Of course! No connection with officialdom would ever be found!'

Bluebeard was a soldier through and through, and normally he was only concerned with military aspects of any situation. But he knew enough about the "puppet-masters" in foreign capitals to ask the question as to the ultimate aim of forming a tripartite republic which would merely precipitate an arms race in the area which they could not hope to sustain against the oil-rich north and mineral-rich south.

'Well,' smiled the Ancestor, 'billions would be spent on arms to begin with, keeping the military industrial complexes in some countries laughing all the way to the bank. Secondly, you know that a good percentage of my friend Serranos's oilfields are just forty or fifty kilometres from our northern border.'

He paused and let that sink in. If Magrari were to occupy Rivenia, politically or militarily, the oilfields could come under artillery fire within an hour of the start of hostilities.

'And that's not the end of the story as far as oil is concerned. Prospecting is proceeding apace for offshore oil in Tamaria which, as you know, is separated from us only by northern Xarcassia and the river plain, which we stand a good chance of having restored to us by the World Court in the not too distant future.'

'Aaah!' said Bluebeard, nodding his head.

A "tangled web" and no mistake, I thought. We had to do something to put off for a few more weeks the inevitable attack from Xarbuss (whose manoeuvres close to our borders seemed to be gaining in size and proximity), for our procurement teams were still out searching for what we badly needed and, more importantly, could afford. And then there would have to be the unavoidable weeks of training.

'Xarbuss is obviously receiving foreign backing, though still on a fairly moderate scale. Unfortunately, we have so far failed to attract a major backer. Perhaps it is too early yet, and one or two are sitting on the fence. As far as I can make out, at least two countries are fairly well disposed towards us – one feeds us with bits of intelligence – but I place little value on friends who will wait and see how we shape up against Xarbuss forces before speaking out at the United Nations! The time to issue an international warning to Xarbuss is *now*, before lives start being lost. I must confess I never expected to have to worry about an invasion so soon. Quite sickening. Why will they not leave us alone?'

I thought I detected a note of near hysteria in the Ancestor's voice. So many years of planning and dreaming seeming about to go up in smoke because of some tinpot dictator's greedy ambitions.

I saw for the first time just how vulnerable the Ancestor really was to people who did not play by the rules of the game. He had believed that the international community would see that the “Firefly” regime had the welfare of the people at heart, an efficient and honest administration having replaced the series of corrupt and oppressive ones. He had expected the major democratic countries to be the first to be the first to recognise this, choosing to overlook the basic truth that countries acted according to national self-interest. Rabid tyrants have been tolerated as long they benefited their powerful backers, and lip service was paid to concern about the people's welfare.

An unusually long silence followed the Ancestor’s outburst, and I could see a look of pain on Serge’s face. And the way Bluebeard was hunched forward, a clenched fist resting on the table, I had no doubt that he would have sent our poorly equipped forces hurtling against Xarbuss if given half a chance.

At this point an unexpected development took place. The Ancestor suddenly turned to me and said, ‘Professor, as of this minute I appoint you my Military Adviser’, and leaned across to shake my hand. The surprise on his two Commanders’ faces must have rivalled mine!

‘Ancestor,’ I spluttered, ‘I don't know what you mean. I am not sure I am qualified. Surely...’

‘You will accompany the two Commanders on inspections and sit on planning committees. At all times you will discuss and assess situations with my two Commanders and report to me. A knowledge of history is a great help in anticipating situations, and that is why I expect you to be of assistance to Erion and Bluebeard on a regular basis. Your rank of Commander Second Class remains.’

I sneaked a look at Serge and Bluebeard, fearing to see disapproval or even anger, but the Ancestor must have discussed it with them beforehand because they were beaming!

Warfare is a costly business, and has been from ancient times. The deplorable thing is that governments with starving populations have yet diverted national resources to creating and maintaining armies. Hospitals may lack the most basic of facilities, and children may lack even notebooks, but you can be sure the armed forces will have the latest radio equipment and abundant munitions. What is so depressing is the fact that human nature will have to be changed first before every country can feel secure. The territorial imperative seems to have been part and parcel of Evolution, and the sweetest-sounding songbird is out to enclose its claimed territory.

So how can one blame a small country which feels constantly threatened for maintaining an army? The terrible thing is that a small handful of small countries develop military capacity far in excess of defensive requirements, and then begin to threaten and oppress their neighbours. Conflict then becomes a way of life and, indeed, one can think of regimes which actually depend on conflict for their survival.

So we embarked on securing equipment for our forces with considerable reluctance, and it was only after much discussion that we finally decided to add to our defensive weaponry. Artillery and assault-guns, for instance, in preference to tanks. Our procurement team went to the usual "bargain basement" sales depots up north, looking for more of the old SU-100s and 76mm artillery. The abundance of arms for sale allowed for an astonishing variety of small arms and mortars.

We had long come to the conclusion that there were two logical points for Xarbuss to send in their tanks, and these were: the River Bulge and the Southern Bridge which linked us with Xarcassia. They were the only possible crossings as the Red River was too wide or deep or fast elsewhere. So this is where we began to build bunkers and machine gun nests. We just hoped they did not have any serviceable aircraft of any description!

« TWELVE »

On Monday morning the mystery of who had sent me the "three-flower" honey was solved! No, it was not from Aida but from the divorcee I had met at Adam's place! Obviously they had discussed me with her and, it seemed, even hinted that I was interested. It was a real shame because she seemed a very nice woman, and but for my utter preoccupation with Aida she certainly would have come top of the list.

A nephew of hers came to collect the little dish and I gave him a box of chocolates to take to her, with a polite note of thanks. I had actually meant the chocolates for Aida.

Another thing that happened that week was the rematch of our Blue Wasps with the Spearheads, and to everyone's joy our boys won 2:1! Needless to say, this was a nice bit of propaganda for the "Firefly" regime! But it was still only the quarter-finals. Nevertheless, groups of little boys went round waving banners and singing the soccer anthem ("Blues have wings, Blues can sting") whose composer remained unrecognised. Newspapers had offered a reward for him to come forward but nobody had. Since the anthem went back some six years he must either be dead or had left the country. It was a delightfully catchy little number.

The following week the Military Council thought of sending me on a diplomatic mission to our eastern neighbour, Sebaqia, to see if they would be prepared to recognise our government, but a high-level official in their foreign ministry offered, over the telephone, all manner of excuses not to see me and we realised that while they were not antagonistic they preferred to remain in the background. Actually they were neither rich nor strong, but we, as beggars for recognition, were no choosers, and it confirmed our isolation.

A quick visit to the café on Wednesday morning came up with yet another offer of a meeting with a potential wife prospect. I was not much interested, of course, but Abubakr, a clothes merchant, was so insistent that he would have lost face if I had turned him down. As he lived just a few houses down the main road crossing the Bonelands' western end I agreed to drop in that same evening. The woman was a distant cousin of his and was a widow. Her husband died in an accident some years before. Widows, it seemed, were almost invariably more choosy about their next husband than divorcees, and she had turned down a couple of proposals. He said she was about forty or so.

Since I neither expected nor wanted anything to come out of the meeting I drove to his place with dragging feet, so to speak (even my Morris sounded unhappy and spluttered a few times), and I was busy drafting excuses all the way.

Living in a one-storey modern house, Abubakr had three daughters and one son, and I noted how pretty the eldest was. I caught myself reflecting guiltily that had I been some thirty years younger I'd have made a play for her straight off! As for the woman I had gone to see, she definitely was a very attractive woman. Tall and still slim (our women tend to put on weight in their late thirties, but often retain their good looks for many years) her hair was cut short and styled by a hairdresser. A smart woman, all right, and probably educated.

Human nature being perverse, I found myself getting increasingly annoyed as she virtually ignored my presence. My pride was receiving a beating, and though at no time would I have considered exchanging her for my Aida, to be treated like one was invisible was a painful experience. (One who has lived in a country where racism exists will know what I mean.)

I was feeling pretty dejected when Abubakr walked me to the car but my pride was immediately restored when he said, 'I am really sorry to have bothered you, Prof, but the woman simply has no wish to marry again. My wife told me but I took her lightly. She mentions her late husband in every conversation.'

I drove back wondering if Aida would be like that if we married and I passed away.

Being appointed military adviser was already proving to be a very mixed blessing indeed. On top of a programme of giving lectures to the troops, going on field exercises and standard administrative work in the office, and sitting on committees, the Ancestor was getting into the habit of letting me deal with correspondence with "foreign connections" of an open nature, if it had military relevance.

•••••••

I had completely lost touch with Aida. This posed the danger of her thinking that I was losing interest in her, so I had to do something soon. Being now back with her mother, she was no longer free to ring me, and nor could I ring her. So I had to find an excuse to visit them.

This came in the last week of July when Serge walked into my office at GHQ with a smile on his face.

'I have good news for you, Prof! Your future father-in-law is out on bail, so the kissing can resume!'

Since I had offered to stand bail for him, I assumed that I was now responsible for his conduct. If he skipped the country I'd be in an awkward situation indeed. But it turned out that he had co-operated fully with Army Intelligence, revealing deals unknown to them, and the bail was his reward. Nobody could accuse the "Firefly" government of going by the book! Pragmatism was the key word in these dangerous times. Survival was the name of the game.

Naturally I was much relieved and delighted, planning to drop in at the Zains' that very afternoon.

The day continued to be good, for the procurement team had managed to locate an arms source that would provide us with everything from pistols to 122 mm and 155 mm artillery pieces, in good condition, "used in a short war"; and there was an astonishing array of armoured fighting vehicles available. Surely this easy availability of weapons of all kinds must be the main reason for little conflicts constantly breaking out all over the world. A head of some small state reviews his array of tanks, armoured cars and the intimidating long gun barrels, and the thought that comes to his mind is not, "We must seek a peaceful solution to the border problem!" But, "I will blow the son-of-bitch's head off, and then he will see reason!"

When the ever-enchanted late afternoon came, and I made my slow way to Aida's house – it was still quite hot and humid, the Greater Rains being about two weeks away – I marvelled at how much my life had changed in such a short time. Barely six months ago I was quietly rusting away, my sole aim in life having been to complete my book on the Mongol invasions, and then search around for another subject. I had almost given up social life, apart from a pleasant hour or two with my café group every other morning or so, and despaired of finding the right calibre of woman to marry. And here I was, "Action Man" himself, with hardly the time even to play my clarinet, a thousand and one things to be attended to, the mind busy day and night. How I wished all this had happened years ago!

There they were on the balcony, as always, enjoying the scenery and the gentle breeze. The old terror whenever I approached that villa still lingered, though no longer to the extent of making my knees quake a bit. I had decided to always visit them in uniform, just in case that numbskull Zahor was visiting. It gave me a psychological edge.

Aida got up and disappeared inside. She was at the door when I reached it. I was taken aback when I saw no smile on her face, but then understood why.

'Hello, Commander. I thought you had gone abroad.'

Ah! She was annoyed with me for not having got in touch. The time for beating about the bush was long past.

'Aida,' I found myself saying; the words came out like a new, unplanned melody sometimes comes out of my clarinet, 'I missed you every minute of the day and night. I wanted so much to see you, or at least to ring you and hear your voice.'

She tried hard not to show her feelings, but failed. She could not hide her delighted surprise and, for the very first time ever, reached up and touched my face with her hand. But before I could make a move I heard her parents coming down the stairs, and she quickly skipped away to the bottom of the stairs and looked up.

'Take the neighbour to the sitting room, Aisha,' floated down her father's voice.

The stairs were in two flights, and they were coming down one step at a time because Zain's legs occasionally gave him much trouble, depending on the weather. They had not yet reached the landing, and so couldn't see me.

Aida ran back and led me to the room, with her left arm round me, so that her head lay against my shoulder. I could hardly believe it! My words seemed to have removed every single doubt from her mind, and I knew now that, God willing, this woman was going to be my wife. Let the likes of Zahor flex their impressive biceps or send her all manner of presents, this woman's mind was made up.

Words from the "fifth place" of Hexagram 63 (After Completion) of the *I Ching* came to mind:

> The neighbour in the east who slaughters an ox
> Does not attain as much real happiness

As the neighbour in the west
With his small offering!

I expressed my pleasure and relief to Zain for being out of detention, and he said that "your boys" had treated him decently. His only complaint was that they had put him in a room with a man who snored all night! Mrs Zain was also, naturally, far more friendly towards me. Perhaps they believed that I had had something to do with his release, though they never formally thanked me for it.

As for Aida, we were in eye contact practically all the time. Seldom had I felt happier.

The time was coming for me to formally send the marriage proposal. Our marriage procedure was quite involved, with fixed stages. But, first and foremost, to get the old Stadium Road house repaired and renovated without delay. Which meant getting the old people and their things out at the earliest opportunity.

Things were growing increasingly ominous in the south-west, and all I could do was to hope and pray that some diplomatic moves would diffuse the situation.

At the Council meeting my carefully prepared analysis proved totally unnecessary, for Bluebeard (and Deputy Tufayl, his number one disciple) had overnight moderated his stand, and the consensus at the end of an unexpectedly short meeting was that we should concentrate on defence, but retain a limited offensive capability.

General Suleiman, who attended about one Council meeting out of five (without being particularly missed, it must be said) this time made a significant contribution by suggesting that we obtain more anti-aircraft self-propelled guns, just in case Xarbuss did possess the rumoured gunships. We had only two, the ZSU-57s, in the country.

The General Council was then presented with the programme for immediate implementation, and the procurement team left in the same week with a new list.

Army HQ was now a hive of activity as marker pens slid over maps, and gun emplacements, lines of trenches, bunkers and blockhouses were marked on. There were only two areas where the enemy could cross in force:

A. Across the Red River where it was slowest and shallowest, and that was off the left curve of the river bulge, near the base, where the water slowed down and eddied before straightening out.

B. Over the short (about sixty metres) but massive stone bridge which linked us with Xarcassia, and whose road led directly to our southern capital, Granitetown, barely forty kilometres away. On their side the road divided into two, farther in, to connect with several small towns.

Since bridges can be blown up, opinion in the Council tended to favour the Red River bulge as the most likely to be the main front. There was a stretch of almost one kilometre where suitably fitted up tanks could cross. And if they had amphibious vehicles the choice of landing places extended by another two kilometres.

The small fishing community living on the river bank was moved to the northern side of the bulge, being recompensed for the inconvenience.

While the construction work was proceeding in the bulge, our "new" equipment arrived in measured lots over a period of several nights, some being taken directly to storage sites among the plantations, with the full co-operation of the farmers, who had been offered compensation for any damage done to their buildings or crops. After all, if Xarbuss forces occupied the land they would lose everything, wouldn't they?

All construction work was greatly inconvenienced by the

Greater Rains, which virtually coincided with their start. Pumping water out of excavations became a day and night affair, and mixing concrete had to be done on timber platforms, under canvas or palm-leaf tents. Programming phases required both ingenuity and patience. Transportation was a particular nightmare, all the minor, untarmacked roads having turned to mud, ankle-deep or deeper.

One Saturday – the days and weeks were slipping away like they were on greased rails – I simply told my secretary I'd be unavailable for the rest of the day and made for the stadium house. My adopted grandparents were delighted to see me, and I told them to prepare to move in two hours' time if they could. "Granny" said they were already packed, and had been for days. To my surprise and pleasure, they had decided to leave most of their heavy furniture behind ('We are already overburdened with memories,' she explained), and what they wanted to take could be accommodated in a small van.

I drove back to the city, found a removals company, stopped off at the café to restore contact with the group and kill time, and after lunch at The Hideaway escorted the removals van to the old house.

I had expected to see them leaving the house where they had spent so many years of their life with great regret, and even tears but on the contrary the old man was the first one down those steps, nearly tripping on the last one in his eagerness to leave! At the gate, she looked back once briefly, shrugged her shoulders and stepped into my car, joining her husband in the back. I had had to help him get in.

With their stuff all in the van, I said a silent prayer of protection before locking the massive door. The house was now mine. Aida's and mine.

By 4.30 p.m. my Marmar "grandparents" were safely installed in their new house, and she hugged and kissed me on both cheeks as they saw me off at the door. I saw their adjoining neighbour peering over the low brick wall separating the two houses, and I shouted, 'Come and meet your new neighbours!' I saw her going round as I drove away.

When I got home I rang my engineer friend, Adam, and asked him to collect the keys to the stadium house (surely my mind should have come up with a more romantic name?) from my office, and get his team on site to begin internal repairs, starting with the roof if anything needed doing. Bits of external works could be squeezed in on the odd dry day later. With my promotion to "adviser" my salary was beginning to look respectable.

At my bungalow I now had to tread carefully every time I stepped on to the veranda lest I squashed a frog. On some nights I could hardly hear the radio for the croaking, and I noticed that when I played the clarinet in the lower register the croaking would at first diminish, as if the frogs were trying to figure out if a revolutionary new species had stepped in. After deciding that it posed no threat to their amorous activities the mating calls would resume from where they had left off. High notes did not seem to bother them. Occasionally there would be that very different and unforgettable cry of a frog in the fangs of a snake or a rat, the former being much more drawn out as snakes squeeze and swallow, slowly and carefully.

As July drew to a close the government had to resort to the first unpopular measures, like raising income tax and introducing petrol rationing. The importation of "luxury" items – from cars to perfumes – was forbidden, though those already ordered and paid for were allowed in. But a price freeze was imposed on all "basic necessities" (which were defined in the decree), so the new austerity would take a bit of time to hit the lower income groups. More measures were being contemplated, if necessary, so the "Firefly honeymoon" was now at some risk of ending.

We, who knew the true situation, could only hope that the people would be prepared to make much greater sacrifices when our country was invaded.

Under pressure from the Political Council, the Ancestor agreed to swallow his pride and make another trip north to persuade Serranos to officially recognise our government. It might lessen the undeclared economic squeeze on us which, even if there were no war, would begin to bite in a matter of months rather than years.

He left for the north with political and economic advisers on 3 August, this time from the airport in one of our two surviving military aircrafts, a DC-3. Our hearts fluttered a bit as the two engines successively spluttered into life; it seemed to take ages to leave the ground!

We returned to our cars with a heavy heart, especially when we observed the massive black clouds to the east, and towering thunderheads to the north.

With the Ancestor and Serge away, and Bluebeard always out on exercises, my administrative load increased. In the end I complained to my secretary and she, an experienced civil servant, said I could delegate non-confidential stuff to this or that departmental head. Which I let her do without reference to me, having complete faith in her judgement. This made life a lot more tolerable until the Ancestor returned three days later. Serge was gone even longer, one whole week, but kept in touch with him by direct line.

That we had enemies within, as well as without, was revealed while the Ancestor and Serge were away.

On the morning of 5 August, at about 11.30 a.m., Commander Bluebeard was returning to the City from a visit to the 5th Infantry Battalion encampment at Salamander Creek, eight kilometres north. He was in a staff car, Commander's pennant flying, with only the driver (who had a sub-machine gun lying on the passenger seat by his side) for company. They had just crossed the Northern Bridge and were some way into the ring road, but had to slow down where the heavy rains had once again created potholes on a short stretch of hastily repaired road. It was raining steadily, and the holes were filled with water, making it impossible to gauge their depth, so one had to weave gently between them, avoiding going into any if possible. There was a shallow ravine on the right-hand side, and bushes on the other side of the road.

It was from these bushes that a man suddenly appeared and threw something at the car. The driver, a trained bodyguard, instinctively hit the accelerator and the car surged forward, twisting to the right as the front wheel dipped into a pothole. That lurch probably save Bluebeard's life for he fell forward and sideways in the back seat. There was a terrific clap behind the car and the rear window blew in, globules of safety glass shooting inside the car to smash the windscreen and burying themselves in the roof. The hand grenade must have exploded on or close to the ground, about two metres behind the car, making quite a mess of the back of it, shrapnel punching through the boot and its underside, and stopped only by the iron plate that formed the back-seat support. Had it been a civilian car it was unlikely that either would have survived. Shrapnel was later found to have punched through the roof, having come through the rear window diagonally upwards.

The driver's steel helmet saved him from most of the glass globules, but some hit him in the left shoulder as he too lurched to the right, clutching the steering wheel. The exhaust pipe and silencer having been torn off, the car gave one loud howl and the engine stopped. Bluebeard, recovering from the shock, crouched on the car floor and peered up cautiously over the back window-sill and saw the man walking slowly towards the car, a pistol pointed with both hands. He whipped his Walther P38 out of its holster, pulled back the slide, and with both knees on the back seat reared up and let off a string of shots, none of which hit the man but confused him long enough for Bluebeard to empty the magazine with better controlled shots. Two shots hit the man as he started firing in turn, and he whirled round and fell.

Meanwhile, the driver had got out of the car and was coming round in a crouch with the sub-machine gun; he opened fire at the still-moving figure, who seemed to have been trying to twist round to fire again.

'He was a pretty tough *hombre*,' narrated Bluebeard later, 'and I had a sudden terrible feeling that he might be one of our own Foresters.' Bluebeard used the Spanish word to emphasise the toughness.

And so it proved to be. The man was identified as Sergeant Farouk, who had gone to the forest to join up about six months before the "Firefly" broke out, claiming to be a deserter from the National Army. Bluebeard was particularly shocked and saddened by the fact that he had shown officer qualities, and was scheduled for commissioning in the near future. Obviously he must have been the enemy agent who had been radioing out information from the forest until the discovery of the radio set, and he must have continued making contact with his masters after the country had come under "Firefly" control. It was a pity he had died and not just been wounded, for there was no doubt there was a ring of conspirators operating in the country which our security forces had been unable to crack. At least now they had someone whose movements in the last few months they could trace back.

The driver's shoulder, down to his elbow, was badly lacerated and while they were waiting for a passing vehicle to pick them up he lost quite a lot of blood. He was rushed to the military hospital probably just in time. Bluebeard had escaped with just glass dust embedded in the skin of the left side of his face and neck, which had to be virtually scraped off – in the operating theatre, not with a razor blade!

We decided not to announce the attempt on his life and just let out that he had been involved in an accident.

Bluebeard himself swore to crush "the whole rotten lot" though nobody had any real idea who were behind it. But in his mind it had to be connected with our neighbour, Xarbuss.

The old DC-3 Dakota brought the Ancestor safely back that Friday and after a brief rest he called us to his office. We waited to hear what he had to say first before mentioning the attempt on Bluebeard's life. He looked quite relaxed this time (we were beginning to get used to the slightly lopsided look caused by half his right ear missing, but it was really noticeable only when he took off his beret, which he now pulled low over his ear), and we knew he had some sort of good news.

'Serranos, gentlemen, has agreed to stick his neck out and be the first to recognise our government at the first opportunity. He has to consult his cabinet, of course, but I don't anticipate disagreement. I suspect what finally persuaded him were the photographs I took with me of our old gang in London!'

He was lost in memory for a while, his eyes far away. I remembered the song, "Those were the days, my friend; we thought they'd never end…", and shared his nostalgia. It was a time in one's life when the future looked bright, and nothing was impossible.

After congratulating him, we had the unpleasant task of bringing him down to earth by telling him about Bluebeard's near brush with death, Bluebeard seeming unwilling to mention it.

'I have a shrewd suspicion that our beloved President is behind it, thinking that once he eliminates the leadership the people will rise and clamour for his return. People like him live in a fantasy world of utter egotism and delusion. They oppress and bleed the country dry, and yet continue to believe that the people love them,' commented the Ancestor.

'Could it not be that the same foreign intelligence that sent the professional killer to get you is also behind this attempt?' I asked.

'Possible, but unlikely,' replied Bluebeard this time. 'Sergeant Farouk joined us when no one on earth gave us the slightest chance of being able to overthrow the government. He must have been the agent whose radio was discovered. No, he is the President's man all right.'

Serge was still down south, and Bluebeard expressed his concern about the commander of the Southern Division, General Suleiman.

'Ancestor, rapid action is not one of the general's strong points, and yet he is sitting on the only armour in the country. We must ease him out of the way somehow. I must take charge of the Armoured Regiment.'

We all agreed, but decided to wait for Serge's report first.

•••••••

The forbidden matter of discussing the Ancestor's private life was unexpectedly raised by Deputy Aziz one afternoon in the Council lounge, and it began with a simple question.

'Why don't we get Commander Erion to persuade the Ancestor to marry?'

There was a sudden hush. We looked at one another, not knowing how to react. Bluebeard, the only polygamous one among us, actually looked up with interest, but it was Moses who broke the silence.

'Careful, Aziz. Dangerous ground!'

'No, seriously. The leader has been under terrible strain for years, and his only relaxation is doing a bit of painting every now and then. I have seen the paintings, mostly views from one of his windows. Only the Almighty knows how high his blood pressure is. Surely a suitable wife would do him a world of good.'

'The emphasis is on the word "suitable". A bad wife can ruin a man's life in no time at all. I had that experience, and so did the adviser here,' said Deputy Moses.

'Well, even Adolf Hitler and Benito Mussolini needed a woman behind them, except that they were mistresses, not wives. Hitler had the undying love of Eva Braun which was proved when she chose to die with him in the bunker. Mussolini's mistress also was with him to the last, when they were strung up together by partisans. And Napoleon had his Josephine, of course,' I recounted.

'I hear Japanese women make the most devoted and the most faithful wives in the world. So what about importing one from there?' quipped Mrad, the intelligence chief, facetiously.

This brought a few smiles and chuckles.

'True enough,' I added, 'the number of Japanese wives who chose to commit "Seppuku" with their husbands in defeat was quite remarkable. But let's not write off all our own women, modern trends to the contrary. Foreign influences have not yet penetrated to the roots, as those of you who have been happily married for years will testify.'

'Being the leader, why not play safe and marry two or three?' asked Bluebeard, mischievously. Or perhaps he really meant it – and I did not hear laughter from the others either! After all, we were legally allowed four, subject only to the religious stringency that they should be loved and treated equally. One who failed to do that was committing a sin. Also the first wife had to agree. Add economic considerations, and you begin to understand why monogamy was the rule even among the well-off. At any rate, if the relationship with the first wife proved satisfactory, there would be little desire to upset the apple cart, as the English would say.

In the end, Bluebeard suggested that I should be the one to suggest it to the Ancestor, after remarrying as everyone knew I intended to do shortly.

'Just sing out your new-found happiness and peace of mind to the Ancestor when you return from your honeymoon, and fill him with envy. That should do the trick!' concluded Aziz.

'Just one honeymoon?' smirked Bluebeard, 'why deprive yourself of the pleasure of two or three? You could afford it, couldn't you?'

It was a real pleasure seeing the other side of Bluebeard's character for the first time. The world saw him as a stern, humourless and aggressive military man who found music only in the sound of gunfire.

As we got to know one another better, the lounge get-togethers became as enjoyable to me as the gatherings of the café group, even when our Chief of Staff, Serge, rejoined us two days later. He was quick to notice the change of atmosphere and joined in with gusto. However, when we were there for official discussions strict military protocol was maintained. As indeed it was outside the lounge at all times.

Serge's report on his southern inspection confirmed Bluebeard's fears that General Suleiman was too lax with his officers. Many of them were relatives or sons of old friends, and he hated disciplining any. Serge said he attended one gun-firing tank exercise in which the tanks scored an average of one hit for every five shells, and against stationary targets! Also the armour had no idea of how to attack in formation, getting in each other's way in a dangerous manner. The anti-aircraft units had no aerial targets to shoot at, firing at targets on hilltops instead.

I could see that the Ancestor was much troubled by the report, as was everybody else. But what was he to do? In ordinary circumstances he would simply have transferred the general to another region for a while and sent down Bluebeard and Tufayl to straighten things out. But the circumstances were far from ordinary in an army which was, in essence, two separate armies.

To my horror, the Ancestor turned to me and said, 'You are my military adviser, so what advice can you give to sort this thing out? Persuasion won't succeed, and force is out of the question.'

'Ancestor, give me until tomorrow afternoon to try and come up with a solution. It is a complex problem.'

'Right, then. We meet here tomorrow at 3.30 p.m.'

I wasted no time getting back to Bonelands to be by myself. My psychic batteries were badly in need of recharging again and perhaps my books might come up with a hint or two on what could be done, often quite indirectly. Another way of solving a ticklish problem was to slot it into the mind, and then get on with something else. Often the subconscious would come up with something.

On an impulse I rang the Zains, hoping that Aida would answer the phone, but I gently put the phone down when her mother's voice came over. I got down to domestic chores and passed the rest of the day in the routine manner. While having the afternoon tea on the veranda I saw in the reflecting mirror Zahor's BMW passing the gate, having heard a car coming. That man wasn't going to give up to the end, but I felt more annoyed than anxious. Aida was not the kind of woman who would nestle her head against a man's shoulder if she did not care very deeply for him. I could stake my life on that, in spite of much experience of the fickleness of human nature.

I returned to the study and just sat looking at my row of books, keeping my mind a blank. And a volume on the history of the Luftwaffe stood out. I did not have to take it down, for the multi-dimensional computer of the human mind had already worked out its permutations. What came to mind was the secret training of combat airmen in the earliest formation of the Luftwaffe in the early 1930s at a time when the Treaty of Versailles was in force, forbidding Germany to rearm. This training took place, ironically, in the Soviet Union, with the connivance of the Soviet government.

So what did this have to do with solving the problem of General Suleiman and his lackadaisical Armoured Regiment? The answer lay in the training carried out in another country.

I was going to propose that once President Serranos fulfilled his promise to officially recognise the "Firefly" government, we should come to an arrangement with him to send all the officers and men of the Armoured Regiment, and the anti-aircraft units, to our northern neighbour for "advanced training", and include among them a goodly number of our Foresters. The training need not last more than about six weeks, and meanwhile we would send more of our men down south "to receive basic training, and to keep the vehicles in operational condition" until the return of the advanced trainees. When that happened, we would mix up the crews and the armour would no longer be the reserved domain of General Suleiman and his cronies. An added bonus would be that our troops would return much improved all round, for we knew that Serranos's army was well equipped and run thanks to the oil money.

I sat down at my typewriter and put all that in a two-page report to be photocopied for each member of the Council. I reread it several times, then and after dinner, but it still struck me as a feasible solution. The general would simply not dare oppose the idea either of advanced training or of integration, for he would be challenging the head of state himself.

Nevertheless, there was one major danger, and one possible setback, in my proposals. The danger was if Xarbuss were to attack while our tankers and gunners were still up north; the possible setback was in Serranos turning us down.

Well, nothing ventured, nothing gained, so I shrugged off all the nagging little worries by the simple expedient of playing my clarinet for half an hour. I went to bed hoping to dream of Aida, but it seemed that the dream world felt it had done its duty in virtually creating the romance, and now had no need to put the icing on the cake.

The following morning I was so anxious to present my proposals to the Council that I nearly went up to the Ancestor's office. But he now did not favour surprise visits except on matters of immediate urgency. Unlike us, he had a hundred and one other matters to attend to, though the Military Council was still his favourite. He probably did not feel much at home with the political, economic, diplomatic, or other councils.

The Supreme Council consisted of the chairmen of each of the nine councils so far formed. It was intended to add another two so that, including himself, there would be twelve "Elders". The man remained an idealist and a dreamer, even in the harsh light of reality.

When I entered the lounge, deliberately delaying going there until just five minutes before the appointed time to avoid getting involved in conversation, I was the focus of several pairs of curious eyes. Obviously nobody else had come up with a practical idea, so there must have been great curiosity as to whether I had, and what it could be. In fact, I noticed the odd guilty look of people who had been talking about me.

I had the photocopies in my briefcase, but did not open it until the Ancestor, arriving dead on time as always, had formally greeted us and specifically asked me if I had anything to report. Only then did I bring out the copies and distributed them around, beginning with the Ancestor and Serge.

Silence reigned for several minutes, broken only by the shuffling of papers and the odd "Hmmm" and cough. The Ancestor, as usual, read it through twice, the second time very slowly, piece by piece, as one after another finished and looked up. As far as I could make out from carefully controlled facial expressions none was antagonistic to my ideas, but the glint in

"Uncle" Serge's eyes was congratulatory. But what about the other powerful figure, Bluebeard? After looking up briefly at me he bent down to the document again. All were waiting for the Ancestor to comment. The minutes dragged. When the Ancestor looked up with a hint of a smile I knew that all was well, but he turned to Mrad.

'How do you assess the likelihood of Magrari attacking within two months? What is the state of their preparedness?'

Mrad was caught by surprise, having, like the rest of us, expected the Ancestor to address me first.

'Well, Ancestor, they have moved away from our border, and my information is that the armour is exercising in Bussota itself instead of near to us in Xarcassia. I can only presume that they are testing some new tactics or weapons as far away from us as possible to remove them from observation.'

'That doesn't answer my question. We have the two to three weeks of the rainy season still left, so we can count on about a month of safety. Could it be that they have moved to Bussota simply to get away from the rain and the mud?'

'Not really, Ancestor. Conditions are no better in Bussota; if anything, they are worse because of the forests and the marshlands,' he replied.

'Interesting,' said the Ancestor. 'Get more detailed information, if possible, from our agents there by this evening, and give me a positive statement as to how quickly they could turn their forces round and get back to our borders.'

At last he got down to my proposals.

'I personally think the adviser's idea could work, but I'll welcome other opinions.'

'Ancestor, the matter of the armour coming under my direct control has not been tackled in the adviser's exposition. Even with a mixed crew, General Suleiman will still be in control,' objected Bluebeard.

This was true enough; I had not thought it out to the end. I just could not come up with an idea as to how to ease the general out of the way.

'Leave that to me, Commander. Once we have an integrated armoured force and war threatens, I'll appoint you Supreme Commander, Southern Front, and bring up the general to Central Command. He will be in the operations room with the Chief of Staff and myself. I'm sure he will be delighted to be at the centre of the command structure, though whether he will have anything to contribute is another thing.'

Bluebeard's face lit up and we shared his delight. The Ancestor said he would contact Serranos that very night. The plan was definitely on, and if intelligence said we didn't have two months then we would just have to shorten the training period, though he hoped we shouldn't have to do that. Even six weeks was really too short a period to train an effective armoured force. He would ask Serranos to put them on his older tank models, the kind we had, and not on his latest acquisitions. That applied to assault guns and armoured cars as well. (We had acquired one more British "Ferret" and one French AML-245 with the 90 mm gun, but financial strictures had forced us to add two venerable old Soviet SU-100s. No new tanks were bought, the money being spent on artillery of various calibres.)

My part in what came to be coded "Operation Interchange" being over, I was free for the rest of the day and went round to see how the repairs were proceeding at stadium house. (Every time I passed the stadium I remembered that terrible day when we so very nearly lost the Ancestor. Our dream of holding the cup final in that stadium had been shattered a week previously when our "Blue Wasps" were stopped in the semi-finals by the Eastern "Wanderers" in pouring rain.)

I returned home to start arranging for my proposal of marriage to be submitted to the Zains, and a dower agreed on.

For that I'd require the co-operation of two or three of my fellow Council members, preferably led by my "Uncle" Serge. There wasn't time to waste.

Much work seemed to have been done during the night because I woke up to the glad news on the radio that our northern neighbour had now recognised the "Firefly" government as being the legitimate government of Rivenia, and full diplomatic relations were being restored. I knew even before I went to the Palace that "Plan Interchange" was on, though on the advice of intelligence the training period was to be shortened to five weeks instead of six. It had to be very intensive indeed to produce tangible results, but the mood at GHQ was buoyant.

There was only a brief meeting of the General Council in the afternoon in the conference hall, at which tasks were allocated. General Suleiman was present, and, survivor that he was, expressed full agreement. Deputy Tufayl was to go south with him to do the donkey work, accompanied by some middle-rank officers; and Bluebeard was to proceed north to look after that end of things, with Assistant Petres (signals) and support staff.

It was decided that to save time the commanders and senior officers would fly in the DC-3 the following morning, and the 250 or so junior officers and other ranks would drive up the north road in armoured personnel carriers, an arduous eight-hour journey in wet conditions for almost half of it. (At the eleventh hour however, it was decided to send them in lorries instead.)

GHQ was a beehive of activity all day, and there was a feeling of optimism which had been lacking since the attempt on the Ancestor's life. The number of our female staff had also been steadily going up, and it was refreshing to enter offices where one smelt perfume instead of stale tobacco. But there was no mixing of men and women, and budding Casanovas had to watch their step!

Being preoccupied with my own romance, I looked for a chance to have a private word with Serge, and this finally came when I bumped into him in the corridor returning from a field visit. I was on my way to the mess for a cup of tea and I asked him to join me for a few minutes. He looked at his watch, and then accompanied me.

'I hope you haven't discovered a terrible loophole in "Interchange" or something, Prof. I don't think I could survive any shocks at the moment,' he muttered. He was really being asked to do far too much for a man of his age, and I was sure the Ancestor realised that. As Chief of Staff he was automatically a member of the Supreme Council of Elders, and should now rightly disengage from military activity. But at this stage he was virtually indispensable so he had to carry on.

'It is a personal matter, Serge, and one which I'm sure will please you.'

He looked much relieved and quickened his step to the mess. I chose a corner table and wasted no time getting to the point.

'Serge, I want you to lead my delegation to the Zains. I intend to send my marriage proposal as soon as you are available.'

'Ah, well,' he said, smiling broadly, 'now that will be a pleasure! I suppose you are absolutely confident of her feelings for you?'

'Absolutely, Serge. Would you believe it, she even guided me to the sitting room with her arm round my back when her parents were still out of sight on the landing!'

Now why did I have to tell him that? It was such a silly thing to boast about.

'Really?' he said, arching his eyebrows. 'I dread to think what she will do to you on the wedding night!' His very light brown eyes were full of amusement.

There had been such a mixing of blood in Rivenia and countries which had belonged to the empire that one hardly noticed differences in hues and features, and all credit was due to the wisdom and culture of our ancestors who determined centuries ago that a child's race was that of its father's, and no other. Thus there was no word to describe one of mixed race, and this applied right up to the Middle East. (There is no Arabic word for one of mixed race, and anyone who adopts one from another language is going against culture and tradition.)

I compared this eminently sensible and humane tradition with the harsh and demeaning practice found in other types of societies, where there is a welter of divisions, sub-divisions and sub-sub-divisions, as if human beings were a collection of bacteria. Thus you have words (to quote from just two languages) like mulatto, mestizo, half-caste, castizo, quadroon, octaroon, half-breed, morisco, torna tras, and so on!

Our society is totally free of that preoccupation. Your father's is your race and that is all we are concerned with.

Serge said that most of the senior officers would probably be unavailable, but he would find someone to form a delegation with. I told him in advance that while negotiating over the dower, which was done by the head of the delegation conveying the marriage proposal since the hopeful suitor himself would not be involved in the preliminaries, he was to accept whatever dower figure the parents mentioned because I was prepared to pay it.

'Now wait a minute, Prof!', retorted Serge. 'You may be madly in love with this woman, but she is not a royal princess, you know. She is a girl from a good family like several thousand others, no better, no worse, as far as I'm concerned. If you show yourself ready to pay anything Mrs Zain will skin you alive. You can add a bit more to the standard rate but that's all.'

'Okay, Serge. Just remember – I want that woman!'

In the end we arranged that Serge should come on Friday at 5 p.m., subject to Zain agreeing to the time and day. I picked up the phone and rang Zain. I did not want to give Mrs Zain a chance to interfere, so I simply stated that I was sending my delegation on Friday at 5p.m., and to please extend the courtesy of receiving them.

'Why, certainly,' he said, without any particular enthusiasm knowing what Mrs Zain would say.

It did not matter a hang to me what his feelings were as long as he received my delegation. I was determined to ride roughshod over anyone's feelings to get Aida, and the usual niceties be hanged. It was a peculiarly intoxicating feeling which was almost sensual in its intensity.

« THIRTEEN »

The very first example of a "Firefly" officer accepting bribes came to light the following week, and the fact that he was a councillor made it that much more disturbing. Further investigations incriminated two senior clerks in his department.

It would have been naively idealistic to expect a few months of "Firefly" rule to change human nature, which so easily takes to greed and covetousness, but to have it happen so high up the ranks came as something of a shock. The council was one which dealt with trade, and had recently been expanded as the undeclared embargo on us (never fully respected by a handful of countries) sprang sizeable leaks. In fact, petrol and other forms of rationing might soon be eased.

The Ancestor was furious, and though he did not comment publicly it was taken for granted that an example would be made of the men. I can't say I felt sorry for them because none of them lacked for the necessities of life.

I asked the Ancestor whether I should submit an article to the *Sunday Chronicle* on bribery and corruption, drawing inspiration from the views of the legendary Sari Mehmed Shah who was the Treasurer of the Ottoman Sultan Ahmed III, who reigned from AD 1703 to 1730. Shah practiced what he preached, bringing much prosperity to the land. In his *Council for Viziers and Governors* he devotes a whole long chapter to bribery, and among the many things he says (which in my newspaper article I would quote at some length) is this paragraph:

> Bribery is the beginning and root of all illegality and tyranny, the source and foundation of every sort of disturbance and sedition, the most vast of evils and greatest of calamities.

He goes on to call it, "an act which is entirely destitute of benefit… It causes a decline in the productivity of the subjects, and in the revenues of the Treasury". He recommends that a watchful eye be constantly kept on public servants, and that appointments and promotions be made strictly according to merit.

Another remarkable figure from the past, Nizam-al-Mulk, the long-serving Vizier of the Seljuk Sultans, Arp Arslan and his son Malikshah, looked at the problem from a different viewpoint: that from the top. In his *Book of Government* he has this advice for heads of state:

> It is the King's duty to enquire into the conditions of his peasantry and army, both far and near, and to know how things are. If he does not do this, he is at fault, and people will charge him with negligence, laziness and tyranny, saying: 'Either the King knows about the oppression and extortion going on in the country, or he does not know. If he knows and does nothing to prevent it and remedy it, that is because he is an oppressor like the rest, and acquiesces in their oppression; and if he does not know, then he is negligent and ignorant!'

Corruption at the bottom often mirrors that at the top.

Experience had taught me that articles in the papers, speeches and general appeals to human nature seldom have more than a passing impact on those predisposed to bending the rules, and that, regrettably, fear often succeeds where persuasion has failed. Or, resorting to the psychological trick of repeating the same message over and over and in different, subtle ways, so that it sinks in and forms part of one's behavioural pattern. But whatever one does there will always be resistant minds, and they don't call money "the root of all evil" for nothing. It may not be true that every man "has his price", but that could be said for a very high percentage. People tend to follow the example of those who lead them, so much depends on the type and calibre of leadership. "Greed" can spread faster than influenza and is not seasonal.

Over the next two, three days our armoured troops were ferried north, and Serge had to come back on Friday from the south to lead the marriage proposal delegation. He came with Moses and Saleh. Mrs Zain was the only possible fly in the ointment, and she could delay things by asking for a week or more to consider. Contrary to foreign belief, in our society the wife and mother is usually the captain of the household, for every married man will tell you that a disgruntled wife can make life well nigh unbearable!

They were there much longer than anticipated, beeping their horn at the gate almost forty-five minutes later. As they didn't come in I went out to meet them.

'Sorry, Prof, but we have to rush back.'

'Well?' I asked with a sudden attack of anxiety.

'There was a bit of a tussle with your sweetheart's mother. First she said the proposal was premature as her daughter intended to go abroad for further studies. Then she said that they would need a month to give it full consideration. Zain was stammering and stuttering all over the place. That woman is tough enough to be a matron at our public hospital.'

'So what happened? Come on, Serge, get to the point!'

'Zain suddenly found some courage from somewhere and took her to heel. I had already stated that to save time we should discuss the dower at this visit instead of on yet another visit of acceptance or rejection. "As her father," he said, "I accept the proposal on behalf of my daughter, and as I know her feelings, and the high reputation of my neighbour, our answer is we are in agreement." He then went to another room and came out with a sheet of paper. Here it is. The dower is on it. I did not haggle.'

I looked at the dower figure and breathed a sigh of relief. It was no more and no less than I'd have paid for any other bride from a good family. I had a feeling (which was later confirmed) that Aida herself had had a word with her father, pointing out that I was not rich, though holding high public office. It was not uncommon for the bride-to-be to have a say in what her parents considered a suitable dower. Depending on how she felt about the suitor, she could suggest raising or lowering it. The dower should rightly go to the bride-to-be, but cases of parents helping themselves to a goodly portion of it are not unknown. Actually, tradition disapproves of excessively high dowers but vanity, and sometimes pure greed, had made a high dower a mark of status. Much more reasonable are dowers for widows and divorcees which, it must be said, has its beneficial side, many a young man often having to save for years to marry a virgin from a good family. A high dower could result in an abundance of "wall-flowers", as in fact is happening in some countries in the Middle East. To the point where government has been forced to intervene in one or two countries, fixing the highest figure permissible.

The lower the social scale the lower the dower, of course, but it still tends to be relatively high to keep in fashion. Nevertheless, there have never been rigid class barriers as such, and even in the old days there was no bar to crossing over. For obvious reasons, it tends to be men from the better-off classes who marry "below". (Class is determined not by race so much as by family status, wealth or education.)

I thanked Serge and my colleagues profusely, and invited them to be my "Witnesses" at the next, conclusive step, and that was the "Akdi", or religious ceremony. This is really what makes a man and a woman "husband and wife", and the wedding celebrations that follow are mere social functions. Some strict sects dispense with all celebration, the husband simply collecting his bride after the Akdi and taking her straight home. But to most people this is considered to be the mean act of those not prepared to spend money to entertain guests. And even among the poor, friends and relations invariably pitch in to help hold a function attended by fifty or more people, with food and soft drinks for all (with usually some left over for those seen hanging around, looking in).

From the time the proposal was handed in and was accepted, Aida and I would not be allowed to meet or even see one another. This old custom no doubt had the purpose of ensuring that there would be no change of mind at this eleventh hour, and to reinforce this the bride-in-waiting was never allowed to go out unchaperoned. And also to avoid conversing in the street with any man not closely related to her! The bridegroom-to-be also had to watch his step – any tête-à-tête with a female could be reported!

I paid a call on the Zains and we arrived at a date for the Akdi – 7 September. All the other functions would take place the same day: Akdi in the morning; wedding feast for the men guests in the afternoon after prayers; and the big do for the women in the evening. It is the women who really do the celebrating, with choirs, song and dance. At a suitable time I would go to collect my bride.

Zain and I planned for about one hundred and fifty male invitees, and let Mrs Zain prepare her list of guests, which we expected to be longer.

•••••••

While returning to Bonelands, late Tuesday afternoon, I had a most disturbing experience. As I emerged from Mountain Road on to the ring road I noticed a police car parked at the junction. There was nothing unusual about that, but when I was several hundred metres down the road I saw in my rear-view mirror a car coming up very fast. I was doing about 90 kph myself, but this car caught up with me in a matter of seconds, and then swept past. My Morris 1000 was flying a Commander's pennant and had the High Command shield painted on each side, and this always commanded the immediate respect of all forces, military or police. This driver, wearing dark glasses, turned to look at me as he passed, but no hand was raised in salute or acknowledgement. Because of this I looked at his number and memorised it. He soon disappeared from sight round a bend.

I was about to turn into the access road to Bonelands when I chanced to look farther to the right and saw the car tucked in by the side of the ring road under a baobab tree. And it faced this way, not away towards the south. I felt that something was not quite right here, so I braked to a halt about fifty metres from the road mouth. I opened the glove compartment and took out my Smith and Wesson .38, loaded it and waited. Sure enough, the police car slowly came into view and started coming down towards me, but almost immediately stopped on spotting me.

What could he possibly be after? Had he meant to shoot me he'd have done so as he passed me on the ring road, or even pumped in shots from just behind. We remained locked in position for what must have been five or six minutes, and then I decided to go and confront him. On foot it would have been far too risky, so I started the car and pulled across the road to the right in order to reverse and turn round.

I was facing up again when he reversed back into the ring road and took off with tyres screeching. My Morris simply didn't have the power to give chase so I returned slowly and thoughtfully to my bungalow.

I picked up the phone and rang Police HQ. The Commissioner was not in, but I reported the incident to a lieutenant to be passed on to him, giving the car number. I demanded an immediate explanation.

While I was having dinner the Commissioner rang to say that no police car in the force had that registration number, but they were tracing the movements of all cars in the City at the time. It would have been an easy matter to switch plates of course.

On Wednesday morning I told Intelligence about it, and the few remaining Council members not involved in Operation Interchange took it very seriously, but none came up with a possible explanation. Later the Commissioner rang to say that three police cars had been on or within proximity of the ring road, and the drivers were being questioned. I requested everyone to make sure the Ancestor did not get to know about it.

The rains began to ease as we moved to the end of the month and now a whole day, or even two, would pass without a drop falling. The vegetation had had more than their fill, and even the normally desolate landscape of Bonelands was a wonderland of colours. The mountains had lost their painting-like quality of delicate greys, browns and greens, and were a solid mass of green, even where they were steepest. There was an area between the mountains and our houses which had turned into a sizeable lake which, in the morning, shone like silver.

The incredible profusion of living things, each perfectly structured and integrated into the overall life system, surely must cast serious doubts on the theory of evolution as being due to chance factors automatically reacting to environmental demands. What team of artists and scientists was put to work to design a part of an orchid which not only resembles a rare type of wasp, but has the texture and perfume of a specific female wasp? How did the plant come to learn such intimate details of this wasp, and then construct a replica accurate enough to fool a male wasp? The wasp pollinates the plant.

Nature is full of literally billions of such examples, and they are to be found everywhere one looks. To believe in "natural selection" – i.e. there is no guiding hand – is like accepting that a coin can be flicked a million times and come up heads each time.

As there was a lull in my administrative work – I had not seen the Ancestor for over a week and knew he was busy with non-military matters – I took to putting on my combat camouflage gear and accompanying several commanders on their exercises. Once I had to pull a field commander up short for excessive zeal. To have a heavy machine gun firing over the heads of raw recruits was something which I considered to be unreasonably dangerous at that stage of their training. The poor chaps had not even learned to shoot properly! And yet another was pushing his men to the point of utter fatigue, while he stood or sat under a shady tree, occasionally munching on a bar of chocolate. I had a chance to fire various weapons myself, and I have to confess that I enjoyed every minute of it. Guns are incredibly seductive things, and I reflected that this fact alone made peace on earth a forlorn dream. The only highly evolved human beings must be those who cannot stand the sight of guns, big or small. Or, indeed, of anything specifically designed to kill, for before guns men loved their swords and spears and bows and arrows.

I rang the Commissioner on returning from one of these exercises on Thursday, but he said that all the men questioned could account for their movements that afternoon, and the precinct chief himself had been in the area at that time. They were now looking into the possibility of the car having come from the north or the south.

I had a feeling that the police were treating the whole thing with far less seriousness than it deserved. Since army and police seldom got on, even under the "Firefly" regime, I could imagine them treating the whole thing with a great deal of mirth. After all, nothing had really happened, had it? But after the attempts on the Ancestor's and Bluebeard's lives I could not help but see something sinister in it. I was fourth in line in the High Command.

'Commissioner, please have the precinct chief come to see me in an hour's time, if possible. There are one or two things I'd like to ask him.' He didn't like that; I was interfering in police affairs and also showing a lack of confidence in him.

'Adviser, I have already personally investigated the matter. I assure you I left no stone unturned. You would be simply wasting your time.'

I had no wish to antagonise him or make him feel small, but at the same time I had to get to the bottom of things so as not to start worrying every time I saw a police car behind me.

'Commissioner, since it was quite a minor incident it is quite possible that your officers gave it low priority and gave you a casual report. Personally, I'd not have given it a thought but for the two assassination attempts. So perhaps you could send me a copy of the precinct chief's report just to reassure myself.'

He could not deny me that, so he promised to have it on my desk within the hour. It was actually time for me to go home, my secretary having already left, but I had to wait.

When it was delivered, in a large brown envelope stamped "Strictly Confidential", I closed the office and took it with me. Over a cup of tea on the veranda I slit open the envelope and pored over the report, which actually consisted of two or three paragraph statements by all the officers operating in the area at the time of the incident. None claimed to have spotted my car on the ring road.

The report was countersigned at the very end by the precinct chief. His name was: Captain Alfon Zuki.

Surely it could not be the same Zuki, the pride of the "Special Squad" who as Lieutenant "Strongarm" Zuki had come so close to discovering the "Firefly" plan of operations and whom I had so very nearly come to shoot? With a reputation for brutality in the poorer districts, how would he have slipped through the net and continued in service, even to the point of being promoted? I had not known his first name, so surely it had to be another Zuki.

Serge was down south again, and the Commissioner would

be at home so I had to wait until I got back to HQ the following day to ring him.

When I arrived at the office I rang Army Intelligence first, but the chief himself was out so I asked his deputy to come round. He was a relative newcomer, a young man whose "Mexican" moustache was, I was sure, meant to make him look older and fiercer. I began by asking him how the police had been processed to weed out those known to have exceeded their authority, or been corrupt or brutal. He said that was done by the previous Commissioner and his investigative team, after nothing had been found to incriminate him personally or his deputy. The army had let them to their own devices and had accepted their recommendations. Several police officers had been submitted for trial.

'Have you come across Captain Zuki of the Third Precinct?' I asked.

'Yes. He is one of those looking into the stadium incident in co-operation with Army and Central Intelligence.'

'Sounds like a bright lad,' I said, my thoughts in a whirl.

'Yes, sir. He has come up with one or two good leads.'

I had to weigh what I said next very carefully. I didn't want this as yet unproven young man to rush off sniffing about like a bloodhound, treading on sensitive toes and warning off whoever might be involved in some form of conspiracy.

'Is this the same Zuki of the old Anti-Terrorist Squad? Used to be a lieutenant then. I knew him well, and was just wondering what had happened to him.'

'Oh yes, sir. The same man. The former Commissioner recommended him to us.'

'Any idea why he was replaced? I mean the Commissioner?'

'I am not really sure, but he was getting on a bit in years. Probably retired.'

'And how far have the investigations into the two attempted

bumping-offs of our leaders got?'

'Pretty far, as far as the foreign assassin is concerned. We know he slipped the country and is now moving openly in Xarcassia, but always in the company of fellow mercenaries. About ten of them still hanging around, the rest having probably returned to their countries. I am afraid we can't touch him.'

'And our sergeant who attacked Bluebeard? As a Rivenian you should surely have discovered all about his movements and contacts by now?' I continued.

'The police have done much work on that and should come up with a full report any day now.'

I was astonished by this answer, but then had to accept that door-to-door enquiry was not for Army Intelligence to do, even though he had been an army man.

I briefly considered seeing the Ancestor and telling him of my suspicions, but feared I might only be making a fool of myself if it had all been just a prank to bring a bit of amusement to the department. With crime having dropped to an all-time low, a policeman's lot had become a very boring one. They could see all those army types whizzing about in armoured cars and APCs, armed with all manner of exciting weapons, while the police remained looking on, with truncheons that were seldom used, and old AK-47s which were fired twice a month in target practice. No wonder they resented us.

Much of the old police force remained in place, despite changes here and there, and promotions and demotions. This also, inevitably, applied to the civil service. There was really no alternative to doing that. One didn't throw away people who knew their job and had years of experience, and most of them adapted fairly easily to the new philosophy. So it was not inconceivable that even such as Zuki had mended their ways, for his old brutal ways had been tacitly permitted by an oppressive state. He could not now be the old swaggering bully terrorising the poorer districts.

And yet, remembering his devotion to the former regime and hatred for the "Firefly", nagging doubts assailed my mind. Could a leopard change its spots virtually overnight?

The following Saturday a police constable was found stabbed to death behind some bushes on the open ground next to the stadium. He was discovered by a group of boys playing football. Just one stab through the neck, nearly severing his head off. Enquiries revealed that the man had been fooling around with somebody's wife, so the husband was immediately arrested on suspicion of a revenge killing. The constable had belonged to the Third Precinct.

Serge returned from the south on Sunday and after about an hour at his place came round to mine. I was delighted to see him, and we went out on the veranda for tea and chocolate biscuits like in the old days.

'I see that my bungalow is still standing,' he said, 'but I wonder what I'll find when I come next.'

'Probably an entire swimming pool with frogs nesting on your furniture,' I offered.

'I'll leave the keys with you so that you can check it out every now and then. I don't think I'll return to live here – I'm looking for a house in town – but I want it to be in reasonable condition when I sell it.'

Then casually I told him about the police car shadowing me, the failure of Police HQ to identify it and finally mentioned Captain Zuki.

'What! Zuki promoted?' he exclaimed.

'Not only that, he is liaising with Army and Central Intelligence in the investigations into the two assassination attempts.'

His eyes opened wide in surprise, and then just as quickly narrowed to slits.

'Zuki. Of course you must remember that not everybody had the experience we two had with him. Perhaps when he was not beating people up, or intimidating somebody or other, he was a good, conscientious officer.' He paused reflectively, then added, 'Nevertheless, there is something going on in the Third Precinct that is not quite right. A police car follows you, and a week later a policeman is found dead. Coincidence? And who should happen to be the chief? Zuki. Another coincidence. Well, let's not get carried away and start imagining things. This is work for those whose job it is. Let's meet tomorrow morning in my office. Say 10 a.m. I'll have the Attorney-General and our intelligence chief there.'

'What about the Commissioner?' I asked. 'We can't go behind his back. He has received clearance, hasn't he?'

'Yes, of course. I think he is a "firefly".'

We then talked about the infinitely more pleasant subject of my coming wedding, and Serge's recommendation that we keep it small and low key was very much in line with my own feeling. Lavish affairs would not quite fit in with the times, an austere lifestyle being what was demanded of the populace. All I was interested in was to run home with my bride!

At the meeting the following morning I felt sorry for the young and inexperienced Commissioner. He was shocked and distressed, and we had to reassure him that no fault was attached to him. Serge and I left the three of them to work out a plan of action of their own, but the end result was that the retired Commissioner himself, as well as Captain Zuki, would now be investigated. Also their contacts with army personnel.

We all felt somewhat guilty and a bit nervous about keeping the Ancestor in the dark about all this, but we agreed that there was no point in merely wasting his time with half-baked theories and suspicions. He had more than enough on his plate, as it was.

One unusual phenomenon that made the Bonelands community quite different from most others in the country was the scarcity of children. I could not understand this, for most of the inhabitants were married couples, many of them young. I knew that some of them did have children, but to my knowledge none had more than two. During my afternoon strolls down the "street" I never saw more than four or five playing outside. In just about any other area in town one would see at least a dozen, with football matches going on wherever there was a bit of room for one off the street, or even on it where there was only residential traffic.

I wondered why this should be. Why did Bonelands attract only people who did not want many children? Admittedly some of the residents tended to be in their middle years, with children studying abroad or at some academic institute in a nearby country (Zain's son was somewhere in Europe), but what about the young couples?

Personally, I very much missed having children running in and out of the house, and to tell stories to. But my life had taken a peculiarly twisted course, and could not be said to be typical.

Well, it was not too late yet… If I am not mistaken, a great Middle Eastern king, of modern times not way back in history, fathered his last child close to his ninetieth year. So there was plenty of time for me yet, God willing! Losing a father early need not prove catastrophic for a child, and one can name a great number of historic figures who lost their fathers very early in life.

There was no bar to my visiting my future parents-in-law, so on Wednesday afternoon (at the "magic hour", I need hardly add) I took a stroll to their place, knowing of course that Aida would disappear from view the moment she saw me. They were up there on the balcony, as always, but as I went through the gate, eyes fixed on her, she did not jump up to run inside.

Instead, she actually flaunted tradition by stepping forward to the balustrade, smiled down at me, and then turned and went inside! Her mother said something sharply, but I didn't think she would be too bothered. I found this combination of traditionalism and rebelliousness quite enchanting.

Suddenly a feeling of terror swept over me, so strong as to make my knees wobble. The thought struck me that things seemed too good to be true. I had been altogether too lucky in just about everything. Surely something bad was bound to happen to interrupt this cycle of incredible good luck?

The Zains came down and greeted me most cordially, and led me to the sitting room. The maid brought a glass of ice-cold passion fruit, and we got down to discussing wedding arrangements. Had I female relatives they would have looked after that, leaving me only to select the guests and provide the cash. They agreed with some reluctance to a small wedding, not yet having adjusted to the new situation.

I mentioned the house I was having renovated in Stadium Road and Mrs Zain, not the most tactful of persons, said, 'Thank the Almighty for that! At least my daughter will have somewhere decent to live.'

I did not rise to that, having myself written off the bungalow as not having the right family atmosphere. But it was by no means a "shack".

Knowing that there was no chance of Aida coming down, I took my leave. At the gate I stopped and looked up at the upper windows but saw no sign of her. She was now sticking to convention.

The fears and anxieties that resurfaced over the number of things that could happen between now and the wedding day, barely three weeks away, kept me awake and dry-eyed for much of that night. The cicadas, which were taking over from the frogs, sounded abnormally loud.

And the mind refused to shut them out, as it usually did after a while. I dropped off just before dawn and, as a result, overslept. I was almost an hour late for work and my secretary said she had nearly rung me at home because the Ancestor wanted to see me. It had to happen today of all days!

I ran up the stairs and then slowed down a bit as I hit the corridor. I took several deep breaths outside his office door and then knocked. The guard was standing to attention, looking straight ahead. Only members of the High Command knocked. All others had to have an appointment and be announced by the guard. We could just walk in after knocking three times. I expected a rebuke or at the very least a look of disapproval, but he replied to my traditional greeting in the normal way, showing no sign of irritation at my delay. I noticed he had removed the insignia from the epaulettes and now just retained the golden fireflies on the lapels and the one on his beret. His opening remarks caught me completely by surprise.

'Did you know, Professor, that ants have first-class memory? Entomologists really know so little about these tiny creatures. I have been carrying out experiments on the sill of this window, where you can see a line of them coming from outside and then up to that tiny hole in the ceiling panel frame.'

I went closer and saw that they were the harmless tiny black ants which were tolerated because they never bit, unlike the tinier red ones.

'First of all, I do not accept that they find their food by pure chance as a result of spreading all over the place. You will observe that their double column takes a fixed, regular path, and you see none venturing out on to the wall. Two or three may be seen meandering over the windowsill every now and then, but otherwise their movement is very restricted and disciplined.'

Having come to the same conclusion myself long ago, I listened with interest to what else he might have discovered.

'Now, I was having some bread and honey last week when it came to me to put a dab of honey, just a fingertip, on the wall here, almost half a metre from the column and well out of their sight, and see if they would find it. Would you believe it, in a few minutes three or four of them broke rank and got on to the wall, seeming to meander aimlessly. Then one, as if by accident, came across the honey!'

He looked at me to see if I was still paying attention and, satisfied that I was not getting bored, he continued.

'It hesitated for a moment, then apparently tasted it, and stood back, rubbing its antennae with its forelimbs. Surely it must have been sending out a signal, because the other "scouts" soon zigzagged their way to the honey, and the discoverer raced back to the column. Now these ones stayed and supped away, but in a very short time indeed others broke rank and came skittering towards the honey.'

He paused before making his first point.

'Now, since the accepted scientific explanation is that an ant, on finding food, leaves a trail of saliva or something for others to follow, how to explain the coming down of the other "scouts" from different directions to begin with? Secondly, the other ants which soon joined them did not – I repeat not – make for the honey in a single, orderly line as if on a marked path, but came individually, spaced out. In fact, none moved in a straight line but just in the general direction of the spot of honey. So where were all these spots of saliva they were meant to be following?'

'I have noticed that myself, Ancestor, and I share your rejection of the scientists' contention. Whenever they can't find the true explanation they come up with a clever theory which then goes in the textbooks as fact. Scientists have been demolishing other scientists' theories for centuries, and will no doubt continue to do so to the end of time.'

The Ancestor was delighted that I shared his interest, and now he concluded with his discovery that ants had a good memory.

'On the following day I repeated my experiment in the same place and at the same time. Again the same thing happened. And now comes the interesting bit.' He paused and rubbed his hands in glee. 'On the third day I put nothing on the wall, nor on the fourth day. But on each occasion I saw a handful of "scouts" wandering about on the wall at the time I had placed the honey. Doesn't that show they remembered not only the place, but the time? They hung around for over half an hour on each occasion before rejoining the column, and on the first day two or three kept returning throughout the day. Doesn't that show sustained memory, Professor?'

Considering the lifespan of an ant, twenty-four hours must represent a long time indeed. It really is quite remarkable.

'So what did you do next, Ancestor?' I asked.

'Oh, I now put a dab of honey on the windowsill every morning as a regular breakfast. Just enough so as not to make them too lazy to look for dead insects and things. We have an excellent relationship.'

I knew that he hadn't sent for me just to tell me about the ants, of course, but using "Professor" instead of "Adviser" meant that it was off the record, and I wondered if it was in connection with the secret meeting in Serge's office concerning security matters. Or was it about my coming (God willing) marriage?

But he wasn't through with the ants yet!

'Do you know, I wonder how these tiny black ants have survived through the millennia, if not millions of years, when they seem to have no defences except to cut and run. In my entire life never have I seen them strike back at their nasty red cousins, or at any other insect. The reds, with their vicious bite and aggressive nature, simply move in every time they see the blacks carrying or feeding on something and take over. The reds will overpower even a live insect, a giant in comparison, if it is too slow to escape. I have seen a housefly land on the table with a red ant clinging to a leg. The fly must have been in great agony because you know how *we* feel when bitten by one! I keep hoping that no red ant discovers the honey breakfast on the window sill because it will be goodbye to my friends.'

He then made for a newly installed map table with four chairs and I joined him. He stood looking at a medium-scale map pinned on, and it was of the entire region, right across to Tamaria on the western coast.

'Professor, Intelligence tell me that Xarbuss armour is manoeuvring in this area here, thirty kilometres from the border with Tamaria's coastal strip. That is almost two hundred kilometres from our Red River bulge. I am beginning to wonder whether Magrari's speeches against us are not just a blind to cover his real intentions. He has laid claim to the Tamarian coastal strip a few times, but always in low key. You know there is a foreign company prospecting for oil there this very minute, with high promise of success. So what better time for him to move in than now?'

I looked at the map and saw how this coastal strip was roughly rectangular in shape, about twenty kilometres by twenty-five in size, and obviously artificially carved out of what should rightly be Bussota land. The foreign rulers had created many artificial and illogical geographic divisions, and this looked to me to be one of them. Magrari and his people had every reason to feel badly done to by being unnaturally cut off from the sea, and the finding of oil deposits off their stolen piece of land must seem all the more galling.

'But, Ancestor, why then has the man been threatening us when his claim on the coastal strip is far more justified than on bits of our territory? Tamaria is a small and weak country, so why not try to frighten them into making concessions?' I asked.

'Because Mal-Zarasta, Bussota's other western neighbour,

also lays claim to the coastal strip. Except that they have been doing it through the international courts for many years now. And Mal-Zarasta has the armed forces to move in first and keep Bussota out.'

'I see what you mean. But surely if Magrari invades, Mal-Zarasta will send in her troops to drive him out?'

'Oh, yes. But the element of surprise will give Xarbuss forces time to dig in, and I doubt if they can easily be dislodged then. Mal-Zarasta, with a modest, non-militaristic president in power, may not find it easy to mobilise and plunge into war. But that would not be the situation if Magrari had started tipping his hand months ago. Hence his verbal attacks on us and all the manoeuvring off our borders.'

'The beast is much cleverer than I thought!' I said.

'Yes. If this assessment is correct, it means that we have been panicking for nothing and can take our time preparing our forces.'

'Preparing our forces, Ancestor? Surely there is no need for that now? Xarbuss will be locked in a long drawn-out war with Mal-Zarasta and Tamaria for months, if not years.'

'Quite possibly, but we cannot rule out an attempt to fulfil all his ambitions at one stroke. Occupy the coastal strip, fortify it, and then race back to sweep us out of the Red River bulge while the region and the United Nations debate as to what to do. They will be presented with a *fait accompli*!'

'But surely Mal-Zarasta and Tamaria must have been informed by their intelligence services, or by friendly foreign intelligence, long before now?' I asked.

'Undoubtedly,' he replied. 'And they must be in emergency session this minute. But put yourself in their position. What do they do, declare a state of war and mobilise only to discover that Magrari is bluffing?'

'The man had everybody fooled when until only last week

his forces were exercising off our border. Remember that even the famous foreign intelligences have been fooled before, or have failed to interpret developments correctly. Personally, I think Magrari is going to move into Tamaria in the next two to three days, and it is too late for Mal-Zarasta and Tamaria to check him.'

I made a quick mental calculation, based on the supposition that Xarbuss forces would overrun the Tamaria coastal strip in a week or so, and then require at least two weeks' rest and regrouping before dashing back to our border, and I came to the happy conclusion that we were not likely to be in a state of war until a week or so after the wedding.

'So you agree with me that we should now allow our men in the north to complete the full six weeks of training?' the Ancestor was saying.

I did. Their return would coincide with my wedding but would not affect it in any way.

'Right then. I'll call a meeting of the full Council when we receive news of the invasion of Tamaria. No point in saying anything before then, so don't mention it to anyone. Erion will be back from the south tomorrow, and I'll whisper into his ear.'

From the Palace I went directly to my stadium house to see how work was progressing. The building had to be ready and everything functioning at least three days before the wedding date, for extra furniture and things to be moved in, including items from my bungalow.

That evening the President of Mal-Zarasta issued a solemn warning to Magrari to refrain from "military adventurism", and that of Tamaria appealed to the United Nations to warn the United Republic of Xarbuss not to infringe on Tamaria's territorial rights. So there was still hope that Magrari would be persuaded to pull back.

But on 28 August came a frantic broadcast from Tamaria

that Xarbuss forces had crossed the border at several points after an artillery bombardment, and heavy fighting was going on in the coastal strip. Enemy armour was already on the outskirts of the small town of Kiseria, twenty kilometres inland.

The Xarbuss government spokesman went on television an hour later and stated that Tamarian artillery had fired on Xarbuss troops which had been "on routine exercises" five kilometres off the Tamarian border. The serious provocation could not be ignored, he said.

The world was kept in the dark for several hours as no reporters were allowed in. However, those trying to get to the battlefront from the Tamarian side reported hearing distant gunfire. Apparently the small Tamarian army was not going to give up without a struggle. Reinforcements were being sent.

We were at the Palace, clustered in excited groups round radio sets. The TV in the lounge had nothing to show yet on any of the four channels, and their news bulletins were less detailed than those from the major international broadcasting stations which, in their usual miraculous fashion, already had reporters within cordite-smelling distance of the fighting. There was not a word from either Bussota or Xarbuss since that first rebuttal of Tamarian charges.

Having been expecting to be called to session all morning, we were puzzled that lunchtime arrived without a word from the Ancestor. We knew he was all right because his secretary had told us so. Since the Chief of Staff himself was with us and Bluebeard was up north, who was he conferring with?

We went to lunch with a portable radio on our table. Foreign reporters were still talking of hearing distance gunfire and seeing columns of smoke billowing up from the town of Kiseria.

While we were having coffee in the lounge the Ancestor sent for Serge and me. We hurriedly put down our unfinished cups, and somebody said, 'At last!'

The Ancestor had the look of one who had just finished performing prayers and meditation, with a calm, clean look.

'Let's sit on the carpet,' he said.

As always, we sat forming a V and not directly facing him. When people faced one another, even the best of friends, a certain element of confrontation sometimes arose quite unwittingly. In nature animals tend to commune at an angle to one another. Head-on means a challenge, and one tries to dominate over the other. I read this in a psychology book a long time ago, and the Ancestor might have known about it, though more likely it was the result of tradition, which itself must have had sound reasons.

'I have not called a meeting because certain alternative courses of action keep coming to mind as the day progresses. This morning I expected Kiseria to be in Magrari's hands before lunchtime. As of this minute, Xarbuss troops have not yet taken the town. The port of Hopston is ten kilometres north-west of Kiseria, through hilly country. It is a bigger town, easier to defend because of the restricted access to it between the hills, and has a contingent of marines – a small one, about one hundred and fifty strong, but said to have received foreign training at the time they bought their three patrol boats – in addition to an army barracks. So Xarbuss forces are going to find it a somewhat harder nut to crack.'

I was not sure what he was driving at, and nor, it appeared, was Serge who then commented, 'The Tamarian forces have shown far greater heart than anyone anticipated, Ancestor, but Xarbuss forces are bound to defeat them. It is just a matter of time. They'll bring up their armour and artillery and raze the port to the ground if resistance continues.'

'I agree entirely, Erion. But it may take them a week or more and not just the two or three days we expected.'

'Forgive me, Ancestor, but what difference does that make

to us?' I cut in. 'At the end of it Xarbuss will still be strong enough to return east and threaten us.'

'True enough, Professor. But they'll require more time to lick their wounds. I do not now see them roaring back to our border before the end of next month. And that has given me an idea which I wish to discuss with the Executive Council as soon as Bluebeard returns. I have radioed to have him back with the other Council members in the north and down south to a Council meeting tomorrow evening at 7.30 p.m.'

'Could you give us an idea of what you have in mind?'

'Ah, Professor! I require more time to think. I may wake up tonight, or tomorrow morning, and be glad that I never mentioned it to you.'

With those enigmatic words we returned to the lounge to tell the others about tomorrow's meeting, but saying nothing about the Ancestor's speculations. All attempts to wheedle some more out of us failed.

The rest of the day was spent listening to the radio and watching Xarcassian TV, which at last began to acknowledge that there was a war on and showed troop movements. The artillery barrages and tank movements struck us as having been filmed during training and exercises. The soldiers were simply too relaxed and casual for real warfare. Later during the early evening other channels showed film of real action, taken from the two internationally best known services. It certainly looked like the invading troops were taking casualties. Magrari must be gnashing his teeth. Tales of atrocities being committed by Xarbuss troops were already beginning to emerge. There were reports of Tamarian prisoners being summarily executed, women raped, and men being forced to dig trenches and carry ammunition boxes and other heavy items. Magrari's Bussota contingents were the ones most blamed for these acts, though the Xarcassians were guilty of a few.

If there was any sympathy for the Xarbuss forces because of Bussota's justifiable claim to the coastal strip, this started evaporating. And the people of Rivenia were having a preview of what would happen if our turn came next.

Later in the evening Mal-Zarasta announced full mobilisation, but stopped short of declaring war. We were not impressed.

Bluebeard arrived in a Soffanian Westland helicopter, courtesy of Serranos. Our old Dakota, which had been sent to fetch him, would follow later after collecting the other top-ranking officers who were in scattered locations. He was in a pretty bad mood, having independently surmised that, since we were obviously no longer in imminent danger, the troops would be allowed to complete the course. We were not in a position to enlighten him ourselves, and the Ancestor had left strict instructions that he was not to be disturbed until the meeting in the evening.

The town of Kiseria had fallen during the night, with some sections of it on fire. Xarbuss forces were now racing towards the port of Hopston. The UN called for an immediate ceasefire and for the Xarbuss forces to withdraw from the coastal strip. No report yet of troop movements in Mal-Zarasta towards the border.

By 7 p.m. most of us, anxious to hear what the Ancestor had to say, were already in the conference hall, passing the time chatting about various things, depending on which standing group you happened to be with. Serge and Bluebeard arrived separately with about ten minutes to go, and at long last the Ancestor walked in to the nearest second. (What a showman! I thought irreverently.)

After greeting us he took his seat at the top of the long, U-shaped table, and we took our hierarchical positions. There was no sign of tension on his face, and his eyes were clear and placid. (Rumour had it that he communed with the ancestral rulers before making grave decisions, but not even his closest companion, Serge, would admit to having seen him do it.) He looked slowly round the table at each individual in turn, something I had never seen him do. It sent shivers down my spine. It was like the premonition of a death sentence.

'Gentlemen, what I am going to propose is something I have gone deeply into since the opening hours of the invasion of Tamaria, examining it from every angle, fully realising the possible consequences to our people and nation.'

The atmosphere had suddenly turned very tense, and not a finger moved. I could hear the breathing of the auxiliary services chief, who was slightly asthmatic. He was six chairs away from me.

'The Xarbuss forces, which outnumber their opponents by as much as three to one in armour, and by even higher factors in infantry and artillery, are having to fight for every square metre of ground. Not because they lack training or are low in morale, or the Tamarians have superior weapons. No. The reason is twofold, namely the terrain favours the defenders, and the sheer guts of the Tamarians.'

This we had already surmised and it had been discussed everywhere from the officers' mess to the lounge.

'I may be proved wrong, but I expect the port of Hopston to hold out at least five days. No armour likes to get tied up in street fighting, as you know. Since Magrari is after the coastal strip only, my belief is that he will simply seal off the northern line and not venture into the rest of Tamaria. And Tamaria, in turn, will regroup round the capital and wait for the international community to take action.'

'Which we know from experience will take many months, if at all,' added Serge.

'Right,' continued the Ancestor.

'But what about Mal-Zarasta? Surely they'll not let Magrari get away with it? After all, they have a claim on the strip themselves.' This was from Deputy Aziz.

'Mal-Zarasta has one of the very few leaders in the area whose primary concern is the development of his country. His defence force is precisely that, and he'd have to be attacked to get involved in a war. No, he will not send troops to Tamaria,' answered the Ancestor.

The countries north of Tamaria belonged to a different political bloc and were not likely to more than just issue statements of condemnation. It looked like poor little Tamaria was on her own.

The Ancestor looked at each member of the Council in turn, with a deep, penetrating look. I had a feeling that something dramatic was about to happen.

'I have, therefore, come to a decision that we should go to Tamaria's assistance.' The voice was calm, the eyes placid.

'I beg your pardon, Ancestor. I am not sure what you mean.' Deputy Tufayl was speaking for us all, for even Serge and Bluebeard looked nonplussed.

'We are going to reclaim our river plain. By force of arms,' said the Ancestor.

'You mean invade Xarcassia? Declare war on Xarbuss?' asked Bluebeard, with what I thought was a tinge of eagerness.

'Yes, gentlemen. This is the chance of a lifetime to do it. Furthermore, we have every reason to believe that Magrari will turn towards us as soon as the coastal strip is in his hands. So why leave all the initiative to him? We'll also be giving Tamaria a chance to survive, for if he has to divide his forces and fight on two fronts the port of Hopston will be able to hold out very much longer. Perhaps long enough for the UN to put an end to the invasion. Magrari has no friends anywhere at the moment, and the world knows that the river plain is legally Rivenian territory.'

The silence that followed was of deep thought and not of rejection of the idea of going to war with Xarbuss.

'I am with you, Ancestor.' Bluebeard smiled, and thumped the table.

'Planning begins straight away. Get cracking, gentlemen,' the Ancestor wound up.

The very hastily prepared plan of operations for "Operation Daybreak" had all the weaknesses that came with haste, as we were to discover in the days to come. But this could not be helped as there was no time to lose. The Ancestor was right that this opportunity would undoubtedly never rise again. And taking the initiative, after weeks of seeming to have wallowed in indecision and near despair, was exhilarating. "Who dares, wins" was a sound motto, for the soldier as for the lover.

As military adviser (what a laugh, I told myself; never served a day in any military organisation, let alone gone through staff college, yet here I was advising on the basis of indirect theoretical knowledge) I visited one group of detailed planners after another, and found shortcomings in several. So pure book knowledge was yet again making its contribution.

The plan called for just two major thrusts, north and south of the river plain: via the bridge in the south, to be seized by a coup,* and across the Red River from the bulge.

The armour would use the bridge to cross into Xarcassia, and then turn sharply right and race to the river plain, followed by APCs and artillery, which would be located to check counter-attacks down the three interior roads. On the northern front, infantry with mortars and hand-held anti-tank weapons would cross the river under covering fire from the already entrenched artillery in the bulge, to be followed by the lighter 76 mm guns on heavy rafts. It was considered that the northern sector was the more likely to bear the brunt of Xarbuss armour, the land between it and Tamaria being almost dead flat bushland with sparse vegetation.

Two couriers carrying a personal message from the Ancestor

*Coup: a military term for cunningly seizing an objective by a swift, unexpected move to the President of Tamaria had already been despatched by different routes. In the letter was the simple message that help was on its way, and to hold on. For security reasons nothing else was said.

Bluebeard was appointed Supreme Commander, with Aziz commanding the north and Tufayl the south. As yet General Suleiman had not been informed, nor anybody else apart from the Executive Council and officers directly involved with planning. But that afternoon the Ancestor rang the general and informed him that Deputy Tufayl was being despatched south on a special mission. He would first go to Regimental HQ, which was not far from the bridge, and then would "give the general a report". Actually, nothing of the sort was intended as the Ancestor decided that I should go down south and personally tell the general what was being planned, and that he was to join the Ancestor and Bluebeard at Central Command. Meanwhile I, as Commander, was to remain with Tufayl and (in confidence, just between the Ancestor, Serge and me) "supervise" his command. I was to use my "tactical judgement". I had actually resigned myself to seeing the campaign out in the operations room at Central Command, so this assignment was quite a surprise, and a thrilling one.

As a full Commander I could override decisions made by all field commanders, accounting for my actions only to Bluebeard.

Operation Daybreak was scheduled for 2200 hours on 3 September. That was just three days away.

It then hit me that my wedding was to take place on the seventh of the month! I was having coffee with Assistant Petres in the lounge when that happened. The cup fell on the carpet as my hand jerked, leaving a black stain on it. I hurried to the washroom and returned with tissue paper and a glass of water, and proceeded to clean the carpet.

'Anything wrong, Adviser?' asked a startled Petres. I told

him the truth.

'That's terrible, Adviser. What are you going to do? Could you not speed things up and marry straight away?' he asked.

I stood still, and hope flooded into my heart. 'Petres, you are an evil genius! You have just saved my life! Go tell my secretary I have to rush out on most urgent business!'

And with that I ran all the way downstairs and to the car park. I was breathing hard as I slipped the car into gear and, not bothering to spare engine or tyres for the first time, roared out of the Palace, narrowly missing a staff car coming in. I didn't look to see who was in it.

On the ring road I calmed down a bit, berating myself for having behaved like some crazed teenager, and did my usual steady 90 kph. I drove straight to the Zains' villa, knowing in advance that Mrs Zain would oppose any bringing forward of the marriage date, let alone one so drastic. Even the tolerant Zain was bound to be shocked.

The door was opened by the maid who gave me her usual cheeky smile, and I saw Zain right behind her. We greeted one another and I was the one who led him by the arm to the sitting room this time, much to his astonishment. I wasted no time getting to the point as soon as we were sitting down.

'Zain, I want the Akdi to take place tomorrow afternoon as a matter of very great urgency to me.'

A look of utter disbelief came over his face, and his mouth opened wide, showing several fillings in the lower teeth.

'What! You must be joking!' he croaked, beginning a smile which he quickly stifled when he saw that I was dead serious. 'But how can that be? Impossible! Absolutely impossible! Everything is arranged for the seventh, everything. That's five days away. And the guests! The caterers! The dressmaker! It simply can't be done!'

Mrs Zain, who had come into the room, asked what it was

all about, and her husband repeated my demand. Strangely enough, she did not burst out with an encyclopedia of admonitions and rebukes but asked, as he should have done, why? I asked her to sit down first, as what I had to say was of grave significance. And also, I added, it was absolutely top secret, and I asked them to swear solemnly in the name of the Almighty not to whisper a word of it to anyone except the bride-to-be herself. They began to look frightened, looking at one another, and then moving closer on the sofa.

I could not very well tell them about Operation Daybreak, so I had to give them another convincing explanation, though that too would justify swearing them to silence.

'We have information that Xarbuss is going to invade us in the very near future, perhaps in a matter of days, and I am going to be posted away the day after tomorrow. Only the Almighty knows how long that'll be for, but I feel it in my heart that Aisha would want us to face the uncertain future as man and wife.'

Mrs Zain saw her chance here to put off the wedding indefinitely, and perhaps even end the whole business.

'I am not sure that I'm happy at the idea of my daughter being turned into a war widow so early in her life. If you love her, why not wait until the whole thing has blown over and we know you are safe and sound and able to look after her?'

The trouble was, she made sense. I could very well get killed or incapacitated, and that certainly would not be fair to Aida. But pure selfishness prevailed. One who desires deeply fears no consequences. I could not visualise the future without her, and my rival Zahor may have been disgraced and sidelined but the potential for a comeback was there, egged on by Mrs Zain.

'Mrs Zain,' I said, 'please go upstairs and ask Aisha herself to decide whether to marry me tomorrow or to wait an indefinite period. I'll accept her decision.'

This was where Aida's true feelings would be severely

tested. She'd frankly have to be lacking in common sense to say yes, and my own conscience was already beginning to bother me. I had no right to bring possible grief and misery into her life and should call the whole thing off right here and now.

'Zain,' I said after his wife had gone upstairs, 'please go and tell them that I have decided it'll be better to wait after all. We hope it will be a very short war, so there should not be much waiting.'

Zain was actually at the foot of the stairs when Aida ran down, followed by her mother more staidly.

I had just got to my feet when she swept into the room, her skirt swirling and hair tumbling over her shoulders. She held out her hand and I grabbed it with both of mine.

'Commander, what is this about going to war? You are not a soldier, just go and tell them you are going back to teaching. They can't just send you off like that!'

'Sit down here a minute, Ai… Aisha,' I said, sitting her by my side on the couch. Her parents were standing at the door. 'The Ancestor has great trust in me. I cannot let him down. I must go, but perhaps I'll be in some headquarters kilometres away from any scene of fighting. Still, I'm beginning to think that perhaps I was wrong in thinking we should marry before I went. It would not be fair to you if I were to get killed, leaving you with the grief and burden of widowhood.'

She was a respectable distance away on the couch, as convention demanded, looking at her parents who were standing absolutely still. She turned towards me and there was some moistness in her eyes.

'Of course you won't get killed. What rubbish you talk, Commander! The Almighty preserved you from the machete, He will protect you from bullets. I am sure of it.'

Actually, I kept getting the feeling that I was putting on an act and felt a tinge of shame. I knew I was going to be at

Regimental HQ, safely behind the frontline. Unless, of course, the enemy counter-attacked and broke through…

Suddenly Aida stood up and looked down at me. My heart sank. She was going to return upstairs after agreeing that we should wait, I was sure of it.

'Well, Commander, you decide for us if it is tomorrow or another day.'

'Tomorrow,' I said, the word slipping out on its own.

'But my wedding dresses are not ready,' she replied. The Zains might as well not have been there, for we had forgotten them.

'You'll wear them at the celebrations when I return.'

'All right. Tomorrow then, God willing.'

And she turned abruptly and walked out of the room, with Mrs Zain trailing after her.

Zain came and joined me at the couch. We had to discuss details.

'What am I going to tell the close relations who will be attending? I'm sure even if I swear them to silence someone will open his or her mouth and panic will break out.'

I hadn't thought about this, and it posed quite a problem.

'Just tell them I'm going on a journey and may want to send for Aisha to join me should the assignment be extended. After all, they'll know the real reason in a few days' time.'

'Yes, that's it,' he agreed.

'I'm returning to the office to arrange for my Witnesses, and should confirm the time tomorrow within the hour. What about finding a sheikh to perform the ceremony? Will you find one?'

'Sheikh Rashid officiates at all our family weddings. I'll go and see him.'

With that settled, I drove back to the Palace, marvelling all the way at the calm way Aida had handled it. The Zains had brought her up well, and she seemed to have taken more after her father than her mother.

Back at the office I rang the Ancestor's secretary (not wanting to abuse my privilege over a personal matter) to ask him if I could go round as soon as possible. Within a minute she said I could go straight away.

The Ancestor was at the map table when I entered and after the formal greeting he asked me to join him there. As quickly as possible I told him what it was all about, and requested the presence of Serge and another member of the Council to be my Witnesses at the Akdi. He agreed without hesitation.

'Ordinarily, I'd have said you were being over hasty and impulsive, and that it would make far better sense to wait. But times are by no means ordinary, and I most certainly do not want one of my top commanders worrying about his love being snatched away when there are bullets flying around! Also having a wife to think of will stop you from doing anything silly, like leading the men in a charge. I want you to keep yourself out of harm's way. I have no other official historian lined up.'

I assured him that I had no intention to earn a posthumous medal and got up to leave. But he gestured me to remain seated.

'Do you know, Prof, I had thought that once the country was in our hands I could get straight down to development projects and send my young men to train as craftsmen, engineers and agriculturists. I was going to scale down the entire army to just a single professional division, equipped with the best we can afford, secure behind good defensive lines. But then I never expected that Xarcassia and Bussota would actually unite to form a militaristic bloc. This was totally outside my calculations. So do not get the idea that your chairman is a rabid militarist, now about to rampage. I'm simply reacting to circumstances.'

'The course of action you have chosen is the logical one under the circumstances, Ancestor. We are all with you,' I said. And I meant it.

'I'm relieved to hear that. And now go with my good

wishes.' I was almost at the door when he called out, 'Professor!' and I turned. 'I was going to mention this to the Council but it slipped my mind. I might as well tell you now.'

Wondering what it could be – and he was smiling in a pleased way, so it had to be good – I returned to the table.

'I have just received, at long last, a letter of endorsement from the southern village Elders. It would appear that when some of them went on a pilgrimage two months ago, they got together during the resting period and there was much argument and debate as to my piety and integrity, because of my having attacked in the Holy Month and over Eid. They finally concluded that I must have been forced to do so, and no impiety had been intended. So when they returned they went from village to village to explain their new stand, and now I have the full endorsement of all the southern and eastern Elders. I received that of the northern ones at the very beginning, as you know, many of them there having known me from way back.'

I was certainly delighted to hear this and congratulated him. I then went to Serge's office and found him talking with some middle-rank officers. I sat down and waited, and they soon left. I quickly brought him up to date with developments, and he chuckled and punched me in the arm.

'That's the kind of daring commando action which I like!' he said. After thinking a bit he added, 'I'll come round for you at 4.45 p.m., if that's all right with you. Unless you have been to a "seer" and he has given you a different time.'

This was quite common practice to find the "most auspicious" time for a wedding, though it was frowned upon by religion. I said it would suit me fine.

I then told my secretary to cancel all appointments for me the following day, giving her the good news. She was delighted and insisted on an invitation to the wedding celebrations. I regretted there would be none until a more suitable time, only the religious Akdi being performed this time.

I had visualised taking my bride straight to our stadium house with its much more romantic atmosphere, but renovation work was still continuing, so my austere bungalow would have to do. It would only be for one night anyway.

This single-night limitation imposed a heavy mental burden on me. For in our society one can be sure that a well brought up woman will be a virgin. Unlike in Western or similarly organised societies, girls do not allow boyfriends to explore their bodies, even if stopping short of intercourse; nor do they ride bicycles or do exercises which tend to stretch the hymen. As a result, it provides a pretty tough physical obstacle which, not infrequently, defeats many a strong young man initially, requiring several attempts over two or three days. Often this is the result of anxiety, nervousness, or simple ignorance of the female anatomy, but even a skilled approach still requires a bit of effort and determination. And it is no fun for the woman, either, for there is quite a bit of pain involved which lingers two or three days, eased by periodic douches with warm water.

(It never ceases to amaze me when I read of so many instances in Europe and America of little girls of ten and twelve being raped in their own homes by some close relation, and yet the parents – the mother in particular – not noticing anything wrong with their little girl. Weeks, months, years pass before the truth emerges. At that age, no pain, no discomfort, not a drop of blood? Either the parents must be half-blind, or those innocent little ones had been experimenting with boys over a period before the rape.)

Having been "out of action" for almost four years, and not getting any younger, I viewed the wedding night with trepidation, almost wishing we could keep our love purely spiritual! I kept trying to put it out of my mind, but the harder I tried the more anxious I became. Mysterious little aches and pains began to manifest in obscure parts of the body, and I started getting ectopic heartbeats, the heart rising to my throat and then rolling over. Playing my clarinet helped, but I could not go on playing all day.

After a light, tasteless lunch, I took to bed with a tranquillizer and a book on great naval battles, from Jutland to Leyte Gulf. I woke at twilight, which at that time of the year lasted about forty-five minutes, feeling much refreshed. A very late tea and chocolate biscuits cleared away the cobwebs, and prayer put me in a philosophical frame of mind. I decided to devote the entire evening to my Mongols book, wishing I had a television. There was really no reason why I should not get one, but a strange lethargy kept putting me off buying one. I'd have to have one when Aida moved in, at any rate.

A quick dinner, and then back to the book (or rather the notes) until almost midnight. One never ceases to be shocked by the Mongols. Listen to this, for instance:

"Yet there was also an element of sadism in the Mongols," says Sir John Glubb *(The Lost Centuries)*, "who invented innumerable ways of killing. Some of their victims, bound hand and foot, were used as targets for their archery. Some were cut in half, some were suffocated by having earth pushed down their throats, some were trampled to death by horses."

All this in addition to the "standard" methods of killing, like hanging, decapitation, and so on. Even the ritual killing of an animal for food had to be peculiarly sadistic, for it had to be laid on its back and have its heart torn out! They were truly the Devil's Horsemen.

Having dropped off to sleep surprisingly quickly, perhaps due to sheer emotional fatigue, I woke up on the wedding day to a cool, drizzly morning. The secret terrors of the previous day gave way to a feeling of anticipation, even of eagerness, and soon after breakfast I drove into town to buy Aida a special gift box of select chocolates. I passed the time as much as I could window shopping. I did not go to the café to meet the group, being in no mood for idle chatter.

A light lunch, a brief siesta (taking care not to fall asleep), and I had tea on the veranda in full uniform, waiting for my Witnesses. They arrived promptly at 4.45 p.m. and had a cup of tea while Serge told me about what had been going on at HQ, making me feel pretty guilty about putting my personal affairs before public duty.

Being unable to find any of our Council members, Serge had brought a senior administrator by the name of Abdul-Hamid, whom I had met two or three times in the general office. He had to come in his normal office wear of shirt and trousers, there having been no time to go home and change. Serge and I were in full dress uniform.

I was most relieved to find when we got to the Zains, that the sheikh who was to conduct the ceremony had already arrived, as had Aida's two uncles and a cousin. So no time was wasted in getting down to the procedure, and the sheikh first went upstairs to personally ask Aida if she was marrying willingly. On receiving this confirmation he returned downstairs and we sat in a horseshoe on the sitting room carpet, my Witnesses facing hers. Beginning with extracts from the Holy Book, he moved on to the subject of marriage itself, its religious and social significance, my responsibilities as a husband, and so on. Zain having already expressed his consent to the marriage and conferred his blessings, the sheikh asked me to move forward and sit facing him. Right hand gripped, I repeated the marriage vows after him, after which he recited prayers in blessing.

And that was it. Aida and I were now man and wife in the eyes of God and man. I could hardly believe it! After black coffee and halwa it was time for me to go up to see my bride led by the sheikh, whose job was not finished yet, and trailed by the two parties.

Aida was sitting on a couch in the master bedroom, cleared of other furniture to make space for all the participants, for there were also quite a few of her relations there, a blur of smiling faces. A white muslin veil covered her head and face, but before lifting it to gaze on my bride I had to place my hand on her head in personal blessing, while the sheikh recited more verses from the Holy Book. I felt my hand trembling slightly on her head, and I was sure she was quite amused by my nervousness.

The last little ceremony over, the women were now free to ululate, sing or do whatever pleased them as I lifted the veil and sat by her side. She was wearing an embroidered indigo dress with just a simple gold necklace and earrings. (Not the one she had really meant to wear, she later told me, as it was still at the dressmaker's, together with the formal bridal gown and veil meant for the wedding celebration. But she could have worn a cheap white cotton dress, for all I cared.)

We could now hold hands in public, and it had the thrill of doing something forbidden though it wasn't. No kissing in public, of course, but what was the hurry? One group after another then joined us on and behind the couch for photographs, beginning with her parents sitting on either side. (Serge and Abdul-Hamid had to stand in the back, not being family.)

As somebody downstairs put on a record of wedding songs I decided that it was time to go and whispered to Aida that I'd come for her after the evening prayers. She nodded her head and squeezed my hand. When I turned at the door to look back at her she was surrounded by her relations and I couldn't see her. A hug from Zain and mother-in-law, and I was out of the house. My colleagues were already in the car.

'Has your wife got any divorced or widowed female relatives? I saw some pretty nice faces there!' was Serge's only comment as I got out of the staff car at my gate.

‘I’ll find out for you, Serge,’ I replied, winking.

I sank into my favourite armchair with a feeling of great relief. It was done, and yet I felt no particular triumph. There was a certain inevitability about it, and had been from the start.

When I went to collect her in the evening I found her ready and waiting, clutching a small bag. She looked calm and composed, though her smile had a touch of nervousness. And she was wearing that black dress with yellow flowers, whose significance was known only to the two of us.

In the short drive to my place she sat up rigidly, looking straight ahead. I put my arm around her and gave her a brief hug. It was raining fairly heavily, and as we walked from the car to the house under an umbrella, bodies touching and her delicate perfume battling with nervous perspiration, the first urgent signals began to flash in my body. It was like a broken down electric grid being reactivated, beginning with secondary switches, tentatively, and working up to the entire system. By the time we were inside the bungalow, and she was in my arms, I knew that I had no reason to fear failure.

At this point a veil must be drawn over the events of the night. Religion and custom forbid us to divulge what happens between husband and wife in the privacy of the bedroom. So I will just sum up the night with this verse from Hafiz’s “Ten Odes”:

A rose blooms within me, wine is in my hand
And my Beloved embraced.
This day the world’s king is my slave.
Bring us no candlelight at dark
Because the moon-face of Love is full.

A hot shower just before the dawn prayers, followed by a bleary-eyed light breakfast, which she insisted on making, and only too soon it was day. I had to force myself to return her to her parents, and for the first time caught myself cursing the Ancestor with his war games. Why not just resign and return to civilian life, now that I had Aida? It was out of the question, of course.

Both the Zains were out of their front door the moment I opened their gate, faces full of anxiety. For their honour was at stake, should I have found their daughter not as she should be. Aida moved to embrace her mother as Zain and I shook hands. The women quickly disappeared indoors, and I could hear the babble of female voices inside. Obviously her aunts had stayed overnight.

Reassured that family honour was intact, Zain invited me in for a coffee, but I had to rush to Army HQ for the 8.30 a.m. meeting.

Traces of her perfume lingered in the car, and I shut all the windows to retain it for as long as possible.

« FOURTEEN »

The Ancestor, Serge and Bluebeard were at the map table when I entered, three enquiring pairs of eyes facing me. In a way it was a tense moment for all four of us, for there could very well be conflict between honour and duty. The Ancestor tried to make light of it by saying, 'Well, Professor, that leaves only Erion and myself unattached – and I am not quite sure about Erion, for he is a devious sort! I suppose it must feel like coming home after a long absence? I have been told that you have chosen well, which pleases me. One can so easily pick the wrong sort nowadays, thanks to our young women coming under the influence of cunning foreign brainwashing.'

As I thanked him Bluebeard could not restrain his curiosity about how the wedding night had shaped out, and went about it in a crafty way.

'I suppose you'll want to return home for lunch with your bride today, to get better acquainted?'

In view of the imminence of Operation Daybreak there should have been no question of taking any time off from then on, but had I failed that first night, tradition demanded that I be allowed a second chance straight away, honour taking precedence over duty.

'I wish I could, Bluebeard, but she is now back with her family. Time for a bit of rest!' I replied, smiling.

Serge punched the air, and came and embraced me, all faces smiling.

'The Armoured Professor has done it again!' he guffawed. 'I bet you had it all worked out in advance, complete with diversions!'

It was a good moment, and one which I shall always treasure. The other two shook my hand, and it was now down to business.

'Adviser,' started the Ancestor, 'there has been a merry tussle between Erion and Bluebeard as to whether you should remain with us in the operations room or be sent out to one of the two fronts in a sort of supervisory capacity. I had some difficulty deciding myself, for I have assigned Tufayl to the south and Aziz to the bulge, and your presence might cause some resentment. Either might feel that I lacked confidence in him.'

Bluebeard took up from here. 'You must understand that we do have full confidence in Tufayl for he showed in the battle for the Palace that he is not a man to shrink from making hard decisions, and he remained cool under fire. However, we came to the conclusion that whereas the enemy will more than likely counter-attack against the northern river plain, and try to break through to the bulge, the terrain in the south is conducive to tricky little thrusts down three roads from the interior. So there is where minute-by-minute tactical decisions will have to be made. We believe that your presence there will be a source of strength.'

'Surely not as Tufayl's deputy? I'm not prepared to accept that,' I said.

'Not at all, Adviser. Not at all,' cut in the Ancestor. 'On the contrary, you'll be answerable only to Bluebeard as Supreme Commander. Feel free to overrule Tufayl – or indeed Deputy Aziz, should the two fronts overlap – any time you are convinced that a wrong tactical decision has been made. I believe you can do it without arousing resentment.'

'Ancestor, you are making me virtual front commander while all credit for a successful campaign would go to Tufayl. Not very fair, is it?'

I was surprised to find myself openly arguing with the

Ancestor, something which even my two seniors dared not do, at least with others present. Well, I was beginning to flex my muscles as a member of the Inner Circle without being disrespectful to the leader. In a way I was putting myself before country, and they'd have been justified in pointing that out. Bluebeard intervened here in a most unexpected way.

'As Firefly military adviser you represent the chairman of the Supreme Council of Elders, of which even I, as Supreme Commander, am not a member, though the Chief of Staff is. Need I say more?'

Unless I was mistaken, the Ancestor tried very hard to hide his surprise. Apparently he had not quite thought of my position that way, but he was quick to recover though I detected a certain uneasiness.

'Commander Bluebeard is right. You have my full authority behind you, and I have every confidence that you will use it wisely.'

To save him from further embarrassment, I asked technical questions. I could not get over the reflection in Bluebeard's words that politically I was virtually his peer. Had the Ancestor realised this when he appointed me his adviser, which in our unusual and experimental system meant a kind of Secretary of State? I myself had had no idea. So where did it leave me? And what was Bluebeard's motive in pointing it out?

'Ancestor,' I asked, 'do we have full information on the strength of the enemy? What are we up against?'

'Intelligence are still sketchy about things, and only give an estimate of some three and a half divisions between the two countries, including a full compliment armoured regiment, amounting to some twenty AFVs, excluding APCs. They are also supposed to have an anti-tank battalion, though I doubt it myself. In short, we are outnumbered and possibly outgunned, but I wouldn't say the odds are too prohibitive. We should be able to give a good account of ourselves.'

I was infected by his quiet confidence, and looking at Serge and Bluebeard knew that I had worthy *kameraden.*

'Right, then,' said Bluebeard. 'Here's your copy of Operation Daybreak. Tufayl has already left for the south, and you'll find him at the Regimental HQ, not far from Rivxar Bridge. See what things are like there before proceeding to see General Suleiman at Division HQ – not the Southern Command HQ in Granitetown – and explain the programme. I don't have to ask you to be diplomatic with the general because you know what he's like. But it is imperative that he be made to come up here.'

We went on to discuss Operation Daybreak for another half-hour or so, during which I noticed that the Ancestor said very little, leaving all the talking to his top commanders. This puzzled me at first, but then I surmised that he must gradually be withdrawing from too much direct involvement in military planning in order to turn towards being head of state, who should not interfere too much in the minutiae of operations, though retaining the last word.

'One important thing to remember,' said Serge, 'is that the Rivxar Bridge must be in our hands about half an hour before H-hour.'

As I got up to leave the Ancestor said, 'Oh, another thing. I don't want to lose my military adviser in the attack, so try and resist the temptation to charge into machine gun nests! I don't want to award you a posthumous "Firefly" Star of Valour!' And he was not smiling, either.

I was to drive down to the south in the afternoon, so I had time to return to Bonelands to prepare for the journey and get some rest. The first thing I did on arriving was to ring my wife. The sexy voice of her Auntie Amina came over, and I heard her saying, 'Your hero on the line.'

'Why, Commander, what a surprise!' came Aida's voice.

'How are you feeling?' I asked.

'Fine, fine. And you?'

'Ready for a repeat of last night,' I replied, forgetting that her auntie, and maybe others, must have their ears peeled. I heard several giggles. Aida did not take up the offer.

'Where are you ringing from?' she asked.

I decided not to tell her I was back at Bonelands for she'd resent it if I did not visit her, and my mind was too full of military concerns at the moment.

'From the office. Listen, I will bury the bungalow keys in a small plastic bag at the foot of the front court mirror. I'll be gone a few days, so help yourself to anything you want.'

Her voice turned serious as she tried to find out where I was going, what I'd be doing, for how long, and so on. I couldn't tell her, of course. In the end she told me to take care, and not do anything silly!

Driving down in a staff car (minus the Commander's pennant, not wanting to advertise senior staff movements), in full combat gear with my GI-style steel helmet on the seat beside me, I felt divorced from reality. It still held the feel of a game, or of a dream from which I'd wake up any minute. And yet in a strange way I was enjoying it immensely. It was certainly making up for years of excruciating boredom.

The way scrubland and widely spaced trees gave way almost imperceptively to lush green vegetation never ceased to amaze me whenever I drove south, something which I had actually done but rarely. I had taken more flights to distant countries than trips to a flourishing part of my own country. It was so different from going north, where the change to near-desert conditions was quite abrupt, and the villages were isolated little oases. It must have to do with geological factors rather than rain patterns, for some rain did fall in the north right up to the irregular desert line.

One also observed the change in the physical characteristics of the inhabitants – lean of face and figure in the north, stiff-jointed; round-faced and taking to fat, loose-jointed in the south. These physical differences also expressed themselves in behaviour. The northerners considered the southerners to be lazy and immoral, whereas the latter thought of their northern brethren as being humourless and rigid in outlook. The City folk, on the other hand, shrugged both of them off as being "peasants and camel-herders". All this created lingering resentment which had historically erupted into periodic little clashes but of a minor nature.

Regimental Headquarters was about two kilometres from the Rivxar Bridge, so named because it linked Rivenia with Xarcassia. It was built of solid granite and was one of the foreigners' major achievements. The river was just about fifty-five metres wide at this point, but fairly fast-moving and deep, and so must have presented some engineering problems those sixty years ago.

The HQ was really a trio of barns round a grass court, in the middle of which was an old baobab tree. (For some reason this type of tree is regarded with superstitious awe in the entire region and farther afield, figuring prominently in nocturnal magical practices. Its exceptionally massive trunk, huge exposed roots and often contorted shape must form an important part of the myths surrounding it. You won't find many people brave enough to sit under one at night!)

The scene could not be more peaceful. Cows were grazing on the rich green grass round the barns, and groups of soldiers were lounging under trees, talking and smoking. I was directed to the smallest of the barns, and that was where I found Tufayl, sitting round a table with some officers, studying a map. He looked up in surprise when I entered, stood up and came to meet me.

'Why, Prof!' he said, trying a smile which did not quite come off. 'No one told me you were coming.'

Without saying anything I took him by the arm and led him outside.

'You are to address me as "Commander", Deputy Tufayl. This is not a social visit.'

He was taken aback for a moment, but recovered quickly.

'My apologies, Commander. Force of habit. Let me introduce you to my officers. They are southerners, so they don't know you.'

'Not yet,' I replied. 'I see only a couple of staff cars and some jeeps and a lorry. I expected to see rather more than that.'

'There was a bit of administrative confusion at Division, but they should be arriving any time now. First, the infantry battalions and then in the afternoon armour and artillery.'

'Have you told the men yet about Operation Daybreak?'

'Not yet, Commander. Not generally, that is. The senior officers in there know about it. I intended to do so when everybody was here.'

'Good. But before we settle down, get someone to drive us to the bridge.'

He seemed about to argue, having already been to inspect the bridge, but changed his mind. This was obviously not "good old Prof" talking. He went inside and came out with a captain, and we hopped into a jeep. I had asked him to bring binoculars, and from behind some bushes, fifty metres or so from the bridge, I surveyed the distant end. Our men had strung rolls of barbed wire across the exact centre of the bridge (which I considered to be a very token gesture, but perhaps useful in further misleading the enemy), otherwise I saw no other defensive measures. They'd now have been put in place had not the Ancestor decided to go on the offensive. I wanted to see what was on the other side.

'Can this bridge bear the weight of armour?' I asked.

'Up to medium tanks, I think, but we'll have to send them well spaced out, just in case. And slowly.'

My inspection was to produce unexpected dividends. Indeed, we should have been in for quite a shock had I not troubled to carry it out.

'What are those grassy mounds beyond the bridge? What are they doing in the middle of the road?' I asked.

'They are not on the road. They are like an island. The road forks around them,' replied the captain.

'Why is that? What for, and since when?'

'I don't really know, sir. Our map doesn't show them, so they must be fairly new.'

Tufayl was looking disturbed. It was something he should have queried, and had not.

'We'll find out from Division, Commander,' he said.

We drove back in silence.

We contacted Division, but they had no information to give, other than that our guards had reported construction work going on there some weeks previously, mostly behind a corrugated iron fence. Nobody had really thought anything of it since it was not considered a threat. They could do what they wanted on their side, after all.

Tufayl was a good officer with a quick mind, and when he turned to look at me I could see that he shared my concern.

'Could be pillboxes,' he said.

'Yes,' I confirmed, 'and probably with anti-tank weapons and machine guns, the slits being cleverly camouflaged.'

We had no option but to send a commando unit across to investigate and destroy. We had to get the pillboxes, if such they were (and by now we were absolutely convinced) out of the way before the 2200 H-hour.

I had to drive to Division to see General Suleiman, so I left

Tufayl to get the raid organised. It would have to be by inflatable rafts as crocodiles forbade swimming across.

Division HQ was roughly halfway to Granitetown (not to be confused with Southern Army HQ in Granitetown), and I had already radioed the general to meet me there. I was relieved to find that he had arrived.

'Well, well!' he gushed in his usual expansive fashion. 'Somebody is paying attention to us poor southern boys at long last! The Chief of Staff was here not so long ago, and then Deputy Tufayl, and now you, the "Firefly's" military adviser!'

I did not permit myself to get rattled. My instructions were to inform the general about Operation Daybreak but not in detail. The important thing was to get him away from the front so as to give Tufayl a free hand, and to do this I'd have to use all my diplomatic powers. He was a touchy and suspicious man, and we did not want to put his back up. He commanded the loyalty of most of his officers and could only too easily put a spanner in the works.

'Come, let me order some coffee. You must be tired.'

We chatted about this and that, and I saw that he really had no idea of what was going on. Which was reassuring, because the southern army had its own intelligence section. It also meant that none of the southern officers under Tufayl's command had radioed or rung Army HQ. Coffee and almond lozenges over, it was time to broach the subject of the general's transfer.

'General,' I began in what I intended to be authoritative tone, 'we are going to move into and occupy the river plain under Operation Daybreak, tomorrow night. It is our leader's, the Commander-in-Chief's express wish that you join him at Central Command from tomorrow afternoon, in fact, and be with him throughout the campaign. We'll be making a two-pronged attack, from the Red River bulge and up from the Rivxar Bridge.'

The general was slow in digesting it, and I decided to throw in the sweetener. 'He wants you where major decisions will be made. Your copy of the operations plan will be delivered to you as soon as possible. Certainly before you leave for Central Command. The printing machine broke down, and even I have not received my copy. Just verbal instructions.'

The glib lies came out smoothly.

The general looked astounded, and sat down heavily in his chair.

'Why was I not informed long before now? Surely you must have been planning this for days, if not weeks?' He looked most offended.

'General, as you know, all our initial plans were towards putting up a solid defence. It was only two days ago that the Ancestor himself decided to gamble on offensive action, feeling that the time was right.'

He sighed, and then said, 'I suppose just about everybody else knows about it already?'

'On the contrary, even Deputy Tufayl was sent down here simply with instructions to ensure that things were shipshape. I'm going to issue his final instructions when I visit Regimental HQ after having seen you.' Which, of course, was another lie.

The general started seeing the good side of it all. He stood up and strutted about the room.

'Central Command, eh? That should be an interesting experience. I hope the "Firefly" – the Ancestor – will not be long in making me a Field Marshal. Can you think of anyone else better qualified?'

I was going to point out that in the "Firefly" system Commander, First Class, was the highest grade, but that would have to come later. He had to be humoured to ensure his full co-operation.

'No, General,' I replied, and he beamed. How much he

reminded me of Herman Goering!

'Anything I can do in the meantime?' he asked.

'I was coming to that. Please order the 1st Armoured Regiment to roll down to Regimental HQ at 1600 hours sharp, and place itself under Deputy Tufayl. Complete with supporting services and enough gas for a two hundred-kilometre journey. And not to forget to load up on ammunition.'

I should not have added that because he looked offended.

'Adviser, we are not amateurs down here. We are a professional fighting unit, always fully prepared for all eventualities!'

I hoped so, but had to apologise.

As he sent for his second-in-command I made my way out to find a good hotel to spend the night in, for I was not due to meet Tufayl again until the following day, the third.

I was on the stairs when the general called down. 'Oh by the way, Adviser. Would you like to have dinner with me and spend the night at my place? If you'd like to have refreshments in the mess and meet some of my officers I'll come to collect you in about half an hour's time.'

Apart from being on its own extensive ground, large enough for his stable of four or five horses, the general's mansion was quite modest in size by the standards of our well-to-do, many of whom had become very rich under the overthrown regime. He, on the other hand, had inherited most of his wealth, though his hands were not spotlessly clean either. Its design was simple and traditional, with thick stone walls and arched windows, and the interior was quite simply decorated. None of those golden freezes and column caps that one saw in some other mansions. Even the chandeliers were moderate in size and splendour, but the walls were covered with old swords, daggers and long rifles, grouped round various types of shields. He introduced me to his plump, benign-looking wife (long-suffering, according to the grapevine, as her husband was known to have had a succession of mistresses) and teenage daughter, who seemed to be taking after her mother. I did not see them again thereafter, as was the custom with a first-time visitor.

We spent the time before dinner in his small library, well stocked with some rare old Arabian and Persian books, beautifully illustrated. He was obviously a collector of rare and beautiful things, and his garden was said to have exotic plants from as far away as Indonesia. I was fascinated by his war games board, with its blocks of little metal infantrymen and mounted officers. He said they were French soldiers under Napoleon, who rode in front of the cavalry. I picked up the piece for a closer look, and it was Napoleon all right, complete with telescope!

After a very good dinner we sat in the reception room (the women were in the TV room on the other side of the entrance hall) and talked about our experiences with regards to women.

'Foreign women consider orgasms to be like money in the bank – the more, the merrier! It's quantity they are after, not quality. Our women are satisfied with a single, really good one!' he guffawed. He was really quite incorrigible where women were concerned, but apparently he always treated his wife most affectionately and never flaunted his affairs. My thoughts kept turning to my own new bride, and I swore that she'd never have to worry about my taking a mistress.

I got up early the following morning and asked a hovering head servant not to wake his master. He attended to getting me breakfast while I was getting dressed, and then found a chauffeur to drive me in one of the general's cars to Division HQ. There a staff car took me back to Regimental HQ. The morning was spent on discussions on how best to employ our various units, and also inspecting groups of infantrymen which arrived at intervals. We were to attack with two battalions of them, but by early afternoon barely a battalion was in place. This was the inevitable result of everything having been rushed. Battle plans must be made well in advance, but it appears to be the fate of the "Firefly" forces to be rushed into one thing after another. (It would be unfair to blame the Ancestor for impetuosity!)

It was well after 4 p.m. when the rest of the infantry (minus one company) rolled in, in armoured personnel carriers. The initial groups had come in lorries, straight from Granitetown. These APCs must have been from outlying districts, but we were too relieved to see them to waste time on questions. Each group had to be sorted out and given specific instructions, and the response ranged from gloomy acceptance to joyful cheers.

Then the artillery – 76 mm and 122 mm guns on carriages, five of them – loomed up to ragged cheers. Just after we had chewed off all our fingernails, and the sun was beginning to dip behind the distant forest, the tanks and assault guns thundered in, preceded by four armoured cars.

We asked the Armoured Regiment's commander why there were only ten vehicles in all when we expected fourteen, and he simply said they were still in the workshop.

'We should have been told at least some days earlier,' he said testily. Tufayl and I looked at one another and let it pass. He had every right to be annoyed. We'd just have to make do with what we had.

Pack-dinner was served in the "office", and during it a lieutenant came in to say that the inflatable rafts had arrived and the raiding party of twelve was ready to go. I looked at my watch: 8.30 p.m., still one and a half hours to H-hour. The rafts were to be inflated half a kilometre upstream and then drifted down to a patch cleared by animals coming down to drink that was nearest to the suspected pillboxes. The men would disembark and approach from behind. The whole operation should not take more than half an hour, but I felt that it would be safer to begin straight away. I had to be careful not to assume direct command, so I suggested it to Tufayl. He agreed and told the lieutenant to begin operations.

'It'll be on your neck, Commander, should H-hour be cancelled or postponed with the enemy already tipped off,' he said with a nervous smile. I shrugged. It was not in the Ancestor's (or Bluebeard's) nature to pull back at the last moment.

Field lines had been laid between Division and Regimental HQ during the day, so we were now in direct contact with Central Command. At 9 p.m. Serge rang, wanting to speak to me.

'Everything shipshape, Prof?'

There could never be formality between us, though demanded of everybody else.

'Just about, Serge. The raiding party is on its way.'

There was a slight pause. 'What raiding party?' he asked.

I looked at Tufayl, who was standing by my side and could hear every word. He winced and cursed softly. He had not informed Central, as I had assumed he would do. He grabbed the phone off me.

'My apologies, Commander Erion. I had intended to let you know but was diverted.'

He then he proceeded in short, terse sentences to tell Serge about the possible pillboxes. He was asked to hold on. Many minutes later Serge came on again, asking for me.

'Good thing you found out, Prof,' he said, which was an open rebuke to Tufayl who winced again. But he recovered when Serge went on to say that the southern army had had weeks to investigate the matter but had chosen to ignore it. On the other hand, there had been no state of tension and traffic had been flowing between Rivenia and Xarcassia, so it was difficult to really blame anybody. All is well that ends well, Serge concluded, and to let them know the minute the commandos reported back. He suggested that we send a couple of armoured cars for back-up, just in case.

We immediately despatched a "Ferret" and an AML to lurk behind bushes just short of the bridge. The near-full moon was some way up, so they could drive on dipped headlamps once they got close to the bridge.

There was a customs building just off the bridge, in addition to the checkpoint on the bridge itself, and it was their radio set that sent us a message in code with just twenty minutes to go to H-hour.

"CROCODILE SAYS FALCON THREE CAN NOW RELAX. PLEASE ACKNOWLEDGE."

Muted cheers broke out in the general office, and some officers found the excuse to hug the female staff. It was quite a relief for we were beginning to worry. (Later it turned out that they had had problems inflating one of the rafts, wasting over ten minutes.) Central Command was immediately informed, and dead on 2200 hours came "Daybreak" over the radio.

So there it was. Time for action, and a green flare went up into the air. Engines rumbled into life as men piled in, dark silhouettes until suddenly illuminated by headlamps. With the clanging of steel hatches they disappeared into the bowels of their steel monsters, glinting dully in the moonlight. The noise was nearly deafening as they lined up and crunched off in initial low gear, rusty exhaust pipes contributing to the din. The air was thick with diesel fumes, through which we watched their receding tail lamps.

Armoured cars raced ahead, followed by the tanks and assault guns. When they were out of sight the armoured personnel carriers, six of them, started their engines, with troop carrying lorries in close chase. And then blessed silence descended, and we returned to the office. We were due to lead the artillery at dawn the following morning. We had an AMX command vehicle, which had a map board and extra radios with operators. There was just about enough room to move around inside, but at least it was reasonably quiet inside, what with the padding and an efficient silencer. It was probably one of a handful of meticulously maintained vehicles we had.

I ordered refreshments, told Tufayl I was going for a bit of a lie-down on the divan in his office (he meekly accepted this takeover) and to be woken up with the dawn prayers. A slight abuse of privilege is permissible for a senior officer every now and then, I think, in order to function better. Anyway, Tufayl was younger than me and should be able to doze off just about anywhere, shouldn't he?

I was woken up as I had directed and shivered at the very cool morning air. I was directed to the officers' washing facilities in one of the bigger barns, where water had been brought in in buckets from a nearby well. It felt freezing cold. The water had a strong metallic taste, but was crystal clear. No doubt in future some enterprising chap would start bottling it and sell it as highly beneficial "mineral water"!

After breakfast, the sun still not up though it was lightening rapidly, I was told that the enemy prisoners captured at the bridge were behind the canteen having their own breakfast, and I went round to see them sitting on whatever largish bit of rock they could find in order to avoid sitting on wet grass. They were tucking into their metal bowls of porridge and buttered loaves of bread with gusto, looking up only when I was right on top of them. About three or four of them stood up and saluted, including the sole officer among them, a young lieutenant, while the rest simply ignored me.

'At ease, Lieutenant,' I said, and sat down on a flattish rock vacated by one of his men. I wanted to get as much information as I could about the garrison which we knew was fifteen kilometres inland, but he absolutely refused to say anything at all. Even a packet of cigarettes made no difference whatever.

Nearby I saw a sergeant who was clutching his stomach in obvious pain, and I went across to him. I had not heard of anyone getting shot, so it had to be something else.

'What's wrong, Sergeant?' I asked him.

'Just of a bit of pain, sir. I get it every now and then.'

I deduced it must be an ulcer and waved to one of our soldiers who was keeping guard. When he came I told him to get someone to go to our medics and see if they had any antacids.

I returned to the admin building to find Deputy Tufayl preparing to order the artillery to start moving, and just waiting for me to arrive.

'We are ready to roll, Commander,' he said, to which I just had to nod, and we piled into the "Véhicule de Commandement", an AMX variant fitted with all the requisites. With armour of 10–30 mm we should be fairly safe from the casual sniper. An APC led the way with us just behind it, and then the artillery followed, with another APC at the tail end.

On the way Tufayl filled me in on the details of the commando raid, confirming that the mounds were indeed a pill-box and a bunker with accommodation for fifteen men, though they found only nine, half-drunk, and playing cards by hurricane lamp light, or listening to music. Both the two structures had a 47 mm anti-tank gun, peering through a wide camouflaged slit.

Our armoured cars would have been taken out one by one at that close range. We had had a very narrow escape. Our commandos had done a professional job, with not a shot being fired.

I asked Tufayl if he had any information on how things were working out on the northern front, and he said not very much, except that the infantry had suffered casualties while crossing and the heavy guns in the bulge had had to bail them out. Northern Command had asked for armoured assistance, and he had despatched three armoured cars, which were being followed by tanks. Then I said I was driving to the northern front HQ, and he said he was returning to see how the artillery was being emplaced.

Driving on the river plain I saw for myself what a valuable bit of land it was, with its lush greenery and extensive plantations. Just about anything could grow there, and in abundance. The foreign colonialists who had between themselves chopped Rivenia up in a most arbitrary manner had certainly deprived us of fine agricultural land. But was Xarcassia ever going to accept its loss, whether we had a historic right to it or not?

All along the way I saw little groups of plantation workers sitting by the roadside, men, women and children, all looking very sulky and unfriendly. To them we were invaders, of course, and not liberators. Later we would reassure them that their jobs were safe, but it was up to the "Firefly" government to determine policies and not us.

It took almost an hour to get to northern headquarters on the badly potholed road, and a tank would have probably made better speed! It was in a large farmhouse, surrounded by smaller buildings which used to be servants' quarters, stores and so on. The plantation owner must have been a pretty rich man. (He had fled with his family at the sound of gunfire a few kilometres away, taking away his station wagons and tractors, and some of his staff.)

Much to my delight, I found that Bluebeard had already arrived, and we hugged one another like long-lost brothers. As the northern salient was, as I have already described, directly in line with the Xarbuss forces in Tamaria, with only a line of low hills to disturb the flattish landscape, it was where an armoured thrust was expected, and Bluebeard was having most of the artillery pieces of various calibres ferried across from the bulge. It was a risky thing to do, since if the enemy broke through the two lines of defence being prepared they would be at the river within less than an hour.

Deputy Aziz was the front commander but I did not see him as he was away on an inspection tour. Two lorryloads of Xarbuss prisoners rumbled by as we stood talking, making for the river. I asked Bluebeard about our casualties, and he said, 'Rather more than anticipated, but not prohibitive.' To a general, every battle is like a chess game; to begin to think of soldiers as being human beings, somebody's father, husband, uncle or son, would make it impossible to send them into battle.

After telling me that the Ancestor was very pleased with the way things had worked out in the south, I left to return to our HQ. I saw a group of men and some women milling about in front of the building whilst still some distance away, and knew straight away that they must be reporters and camera teams. As my car got closer and they noticed the Commander's pennant flying from the bonnet they started filming away, and then assailed me as I stepped out. They were actually our own media personnel as the outside world was yet to know what was happening. In fact, even Radio Xarcassia was yet to announce our incursion, which was surprising given that it was almost mid-morning. Perhaps they were under the impression that it was a hit-and-run raid, being far more concerned with what was happening in Tamaria.

Being news people, they were rather disappointed that we had nothing dramatic to show, but I said they would have better scope up north, and also to return to Southern HQ subsequently to get the story of how the bridge was taken. That cheered them up considerably.

No sooner had I taken off my combat jacket and boots, and was enjoying a cup of tea and biscuits in Tufayl's office, when there was a knock on the door and a woman from the radio room came in.

'Sir, the Supreme Commander has just radioed that you are to report to Central Command at your earliest convenience.'

I cursed. 'Did he say anything else?'

'No, sir.'

'Are you sure he said "Central" and not "Frontal"?' I persisted, still hoping that she had not heard right. I did not fancy the long journey on bad roads again, having been on the road virtually without a break since dawn.

'He repeated it, sir,' she replied patiently.

I finished my tea, put on my boots again and asked for the staff car. The driver looked no more pleased than I felt, and I snapped at him when he gnashed the gears. He apologised, and thereafter he drove carefully enough for me to scrunch down on the rear seat and catch forty winks.

This is like coitus interruptus, I thought. I was sure there would be more action soon, and I was going to miss it.

Well, there just might be a chance to visit Aida when I was back at Central.

From about three kilometres to the river I began to see the first signs of the fighting that had taken place. Our 122 mm guns in the bulge must have carried out a creeping barrage because there would be a smashed enemy APC or truck, with uncollected bodies sprawled about; and then other groups of enemy dead, spread farther along across the landscape, mortar barrels flung all over the place. Then another APC, still smouldering, and lines of zigzag trenches, the soft earth all dug up around them by shellfire. I did not count the bodies I could make out (many were badly mangled, or simply bits and pieces hanging on shrubs) but there must have been at least one hundred and twenty to one hundred and fifty along that stretch. I wondered what our own casualties were.

I told the driver to wind up his windows because of the stench that was wafting in. I had to tell Central to send a burial unit. Hyenas, vultures and other scavengers had been scared away by the gunfire, but they would soon be back.

I sighed with relief when we were actually on the raft ferry, one of several in operation, being poled across by six hefty men. This was where the river was fairly wide but slowest and shallowest. Ramps of hardwood logs and boards had been built on the banks, sloping right into the water. Army engineers seldom receive credit for the vital work they do to keep combat machinery going.

It took about twenty minutes to cross the river, and we passed a couple of 76 mm guns being ferried the other way. Also more infantry in inflatable rafts. It was intended to erect a pontoon bridge later, and also survey the river bottom to see whether tanks could cross, for there was always the possibility of Xarbuss forces proving stronger than anticipated and pushing our forces right back to the river.

We crossed the bulge, with its extensive defence lines built when a new hotel was said to being constructed, and were down Mountain Road and into Main Street as the sky was turning pink. Everything looked perfectly normal, people shopping and exchanging gossip in the streets as if absolutely nothing was happening barely forty kilometres away. They should be thankful, I thought, that air power played no part in our regional conflict.

I asked the driver to stop when we passed a newspaper kiosk and I collected three evening papers which seemed to view our moving into the river plain in very different ways. You could tell from the headlines: "FIREFLY TAKES ON SCORPION MAGRARI!"; "FIREFLY INVADES XARCASSIA"; and "WE ARE AT WAR WITH XARBUSS!"

As we were soon at Army HQ (Central Command) I only had time to glance swiftly through them, mainly to try to gauge the general reaction in the region. It struck me as being pretty straightforward reporting, without showing any particular bias. I had no doubt that the reaction would have been very different had not Xarbuss been at that very moment engaged in subduing a small, peaceful country, not to mention the reported atrocities. Xarbuss had no friends in the region, and some might even have approved of our action.

I went directly to the operations room and found only Serge and General Suleiman, who embraced me like one who had been given up for lost. Even the general, who seemed to be enjoying his "promotion". Serge filled me in on how the river crossing had gone, saying that mortars several hundred metres inland had poured in shells, until silenced by our bulge artillery. Nevertheless, they had caused us casualties. I heard that Magrari had at last appeared on Xarbuss TV and had threatened Rivenia with demons straight from hell!

'He swore that he would summon Shaitan himself and raze Rivenia to the ground! In fact, he sounded pretty much like your old friend, the Mongol warlord. Not even a tree, he said, would remain standing!'

'Magrari is really his own worst enemy,' said the general. 'I'm sure that his foreign supporters are beginning to have second thoughts about him.'

My instinct that I had been dragged away from the south salient just as some action was in the offing was proved correct within the hour. Deputy Tufayl came on the air with a 'Falcon Three to Falcon One' and was told to hang on while a guard was sent running to fetch the Ancestor. When "Falcon One" acknowledged (actually the code name applied to Central Command as a whole, but it was taken for granted that when "Falcon" was mentioned it meant something very important was concerned), Tufayl proceeded:

'Enemy infantry, estimated battalion strength, started attacking our P-2 Section an hour ago, coming down the central side road. Our 76 mm got two of their APCs and one or two lorries, setting them on fire. Then as it got dark they must have crept forward among the thornbushes because we are now coming under intense mortar and machine gun fire. We still have a few flares left, and have twice caught them on the open ground between, mowing them down. But one of the 76s has been knocked out by a mortar shell, and we are down to two. Request permission to call up armoured cars from Regimental HQ.'

This was very disturbing news, indeed, for we had neither expected nor made any contingency plans for an early enemy counter-attack in that sector. Our minds had been fixated on an armoured attack in the northern sector, and we had even sent our two 122 mm guns to Northern Command.

The radio communication was all in the clear, there having been no time to work up a code system, so we could only hope that the enemy did not have the equipment to intercept.

'Falcon Three, we are sending you reinforcements but pull back the unit from P-3 and tighten the ring round the 76s. They must not be allowed to fall into enemy hands. Destroy if necessary.'

The Ancestor then asked the radio operator to raise Falcon Two, who was Bluebeard, and turning to General Suleiman ordered him to go down immediately to Division HQ and round up anyone and anything available to send to defend the Rivxar Bridge. The general nodded, and hurried out.

Just then Bluebeard came on the air, and without wasting a moment on explanation the Ancestor told him to rush down to Section P-2 with armoured cars and a mortar squad.

Returning to the map table, it was clear that if the enemy broke through P-2, they would be at the bridge within less than twenty minutes and at Southern Command HQ in half an hour.

'I'm afraid our military intelligence seriously underestimated the size of the garrison fifteen kilometres inland. Listening to

Tufayl I had the distinct impression that they were under attack from *at least* a battalion. And we have no idea of the size of their reserves clustered around the capital.'

I do not think an army like ours would have lasted a day against a really professional army, for despite the sizeable infusion of regular army personnel we remained in essence very much a guerrilla army. Our good fortune was that we were surrounded by regimes which maintained an army purely to put down uprisings and suppress public discontent.

That night was a very long one as we listened to the messages being exchanged down south. Our line of defence was along a range of hills which, regrettably, faced yet another range a kilometre away, which allowed the enemy to hide his vehicles and regroup after every attack. We should rightly have moved right up to that second line of hills from the beginning, for there was only open space beyond. It was the Ancestor's strict observance of legal boundaries that stopped us at the first line, for that was the line shown on the old maps as bordering the river plain. And land beyond was Xarcassia proper, and the Ancestor did not want to occupy even a metre of pure Xarcassian land.

But tactically, the line we occupied was going to be very difficult to defend, and I knew it was just a matter of time before one of the commanders pointed this out. I hesitated to do so because of its legal and political implications. We could rightly claim the river plain as belonging to us; but then, what were we doing occupying some five square kilometres of Xarcassian territory? So I kept my mouth shut.

At about 1.30 a.m. the radio operators changed shift, and the Ancestor said we should all go and have an hour's lie-down and then come back for refreshments, for he had a feeling that there would be no resolution before the end of the night.

He returned to his quarters, and Serge and I made for the

lounge where the seats were well padded. It'd certainly be no worse than trying to sleep in an airport transit lounge. My offer to return south to see what was happening was bluntly rejected by the Ancestor.

No sooner were we in the lounge with a nice cool breeze blowing from the west, having crossed many rivers, when all sleep evaporated. So we started talking again, beginning with a discussion of the battle situation, and then moving on to other subjects. I asked Serge a question I had not thought proper before.

'Serge, how is it that with your varied and long length of service in two armies you were never commissioned?'

He had always bluntly avoided revealing his past, so I was prepared for a shrug of the shoulders and a non-committal grunt. I was pleasantly surprised.

'I was commissioned in the Foreign Brigade, Prof. In fact, I was the very first local ever to rise to captain. Doesn't that surprise you?'

It certainly did. It explained much about his easy air of authority and that unmistakable "officer quality". And he had been with "cavalry", the elite of the foreign army.

'For heaven's sake, Serge! So why did not our National Army make you at least a colonel, straight off? Indeed, even a brigadier.'

'Ah, Prof. I did a very naughty, naughty thing and made lifelong enemies of my superiors. I was demoted. Skidded down from colonel to sergeant-major quicker than you'd say "camel's tail"!'

He laughed mirthlessly, and this time shrugged his shoulders.

'Remember, that was thirty-five years ago, and I retired after four years. As sergeant-major, though I dislike the "major" bit. Excess baggage.'

'But what naughty thing was that to cause such punishment? It'd have to have been something extremely serious for such a drastic demotion. Was there a court martial?'

'Not exactly. Too much would have come out. Just a directive from the Commander-in-Chief, claiming to be "in the interests of national security", unquote.'

'Serge, please tell me what you did. You know I'll never tell anyone.'

He gave me the familiar look of a grown-up having to deal with a persistent child.

'There is an old Moroccan proverb which says: "If you are a peg, endure the knocking; if you are a mallet, strike!" Well, I have endured my knocking and am now a mallet.'

One of these days I was going to go through the military archives and find out what "naughty" thing Serge had done all those years ago. Assuming, that is, that it was on record, for no court martial had taken place.

When we returned to the operations room an hour later it was to be told that the Ancestor had just been in and gone out again on receiving a message from Bluebeard that things were under control, and he would be personally returning to give a full report early in the morning, probably between eight and nine o'clock. We were to retire for the night until then.

Serge made straight for his quarters in the left wing of the Palace, and I went to our usual hotel (not The Hideaway) round the corner, commandeered by the army from the beginning and open twenty-four hours a day. With most senior officers away I had no trouble getting a private room and I fell asleep immediately, and soundly.

•••••••

When Bluebeard walked into the operations room just before nine o'clock we were shocked to find that the right sleeve of his combat jacket had been cut off, and his arm was in a sling, swathed with bandages. There was a three-day stubble on his cheeks, and dark half-moons under his eyes.

The Ancestor gave him a formal, light embrace, and Bluebeard carefully eased himself down in his usual position next to him. With Suleiman gone, and the other executive members out in the field, only Serge and I were present.

'I see you cut yourself shaving!' said Serge, to hide the anxiety we all felt. Nevertheless, we all smiled, including Bluebeard himself.

'I bring bad news, I'm afraid,' he said in a slightly slurred voice, probably caused by fatigue and maybe morphia. 'Elba is dead.' Adding, 'And so is Tufayl's second-in-command, Captain Murtaza.'

Elba was the major who had brought in the 2nd Infantry Battalion during the Palace siege, a quiet, popular officer.

'May they rest in peace,' said the Ancestor. 'How did it happen?'

'When I received your message I rounded up three armoured cars – my "Ferret" and two AML-245s, one of them Elba's, and raced down to P-2. It took us half an hour to get there, and we found a pretty critical situation. An enemy company had actually broken through a section after eliminating two machine gun nests, and our headlights showed a group of them right on our road. They scattered right and left, flung themselves down among the bushes and started firing. We closed down the hatches just in time, having at first thought they were our men. They were wearing the same type of combat gear as our men, and only their helmets were different, being of the Soviet kind.'

Serge seemed on the point of asking a question but then remained silent.

'We slowed down and kept firing short bursts into the bushes until there was no more return fire. Assault rifles, no bazooka. A platoon of our men came down from the hill on the right and joined in, taking some prisoners. It was a pretty confused scene, with just a bit of light from the sinking moon.'

‘How far from our artillery?’ asked the Ancestor.

‘Barely a quarter of a kilometre down, and the enemy had really infiltrated through the depleted P-3 sector, moving down to get to the guns. When we got to P-2 all hell was breaking loose, with mortar shells falling right on the road at the rate of about one every three minutes. There might have been a whole regiment of them attacking, for all we knew.’

‘Anyway,’ he continued, ‘we found that Tufayl had formed a proper little hedgehog round the 76 mm guns and was confident that he could hold until reinforcements arrived. But he was running short of flares, so I did not share his confidence. Not after seeing that enemy group on our road.’ His arm was obviously giving him pain, and he gingerly rested it on the table.

‘So I decided that the only thing to do was to try to get behind the enemy and sow some confusion. We raced down towards the bridge and took the main road to the interior. You know that it branches off into secondary roads about six or seven kilometres in, and the one on the right links up with the three dirt tracks, the middle of which the enemy APCs had come down on. We followed in their tracks and, surprise, surprise, there were their APCs and trucks tucked away behind the second line of hills, one kilometre from our front lines!’

His sheer delight was infectious, and for a brief moment I wished I had been there with him.

‘Well, I let the 90 mms of the AMLs have their say. It was a beautiful sight, believe me!’

He forgot his arm as he started laughing and tried to gesture with it. A wince brought him back to earth.

‘And how did *that* happen?’ I asked.

‘By trying to play hero, that’s how! We pushed on past the burning vehicles, sending the personnel running up the hills, and came right up behind the attacking force, scattered over quite an area. We spotted their mortar squads through binoculars, located clear of the bushes. We took out each one in turn with the 90s, spraying whatever moved with our machine guns. And that's when poor Elba and I got it.'

The elation felt earlier now evaporated; grim reality had reasserted itself.

'You see, we were virtually sitting on top of our turrets to enjoy the sight, when a machine gun fired on us from behind a bush, barely sixty metres away on our right. Elba received two bullets in the head and one in the chest. And I caught two in the arm. We raced back to Regimental HQ, but the medics could do nothing for Elba. I was lucky, no fracture.'

'Good work, Bluebeard. Good work. Professor, take Bluebeard to the military hospital straight away. At least with you I know he will be safe.'

On the way I asked him how bad the hits were, and he said that he feared that quite a bit of damage had been done to his biceps. He wondered if he'd ever be able to lift something heavy with that arm again. I told him they could do all sorts of repair nowadays, so they'd probably fix him up in no time at all.

'But not in Rivenia,' he replied gloomily. 'The old government chased away one skilled surgeon after another by paying them the kind of salary a nurse gets in Soffenia, our northern neighbour, let alone in more advanced countries. And yet their abundant and totally useless members of parliament, so called, received all manner of allowances on top of their exorbitant salaries.'

The handouts didn't stop with the "lawmakers" but percolated down a whole pyramid of politically appointed "officials" of remarkable number and diversity, whose necessity and usefulness no one ever really found out. One knew of their existence only when applying for permission to build, or raise chickens, or whatever, for one then discovered that one had to secure the signatures and rubber stamps of a whole long line of them. And if just one of them took a dislike to you, that was your bad luck!

The hospital refused to release Bluebeard, and I returned to the office to the surprising news that the Ancestor and Serge had gone south. My secretary was emphatic that they had not left a message for me to join them, so I decided to wait an hour and then radio Southern Command.

In the operations room I asked for "Falcon Three", and Tufayl was soon located. I began by asking him to give me a report on the situation, conversationally, not semi-code, and he said daybreak had revealed well over one hundred enemy dead, and many more too wounded to move. A ditch-digger was coming up from Granitetown. Our own dead were already buried in separate graves at the foot of the hills. Their families would be informed. Assistant Commander Elba's body had been taken to his family graveyard in the eastern village of Qamara at the request of his family. The captain was buried with the men, where they fell.

I did not ask how many men we had lost, but I wanted to know where the Ancestor and Serge were.

'Have the visitors arrived?' I asked cautiously.

'Come and gone. To the next line of hills.'

'What! Why didn't you stop them, for heaven's sake? There could be snipers or wounded enemy around!'

To my astonishment, he laughed.

'They went in the command vehicle, crunch, crunch, crunch! Right through the bushes to the hills! I'm beginning to think Bluebeard is not the only daredevil in the family! But listen to this: he has taken the entire defence line with him! Yessir, we are now on the inner hills! I stayed behind to see to the dismantling of the 76 mms to move them forward.'

Well, the Ancestor had certainly wasted no time agonising over pushing into Xarcassian territory! "In for a penny, in for a pound," as the English would say. We now had a defensible line, and to hell with them.

When an hour later General Suleiman rang me to say the "guests" would stay with him for two days, I thought of making a beeline for my wife but then, on a sudden impulse, decided to begin moving to the stadium house that very day, and then go for her the following day. So I went straight to the removals agents and got a furniture van to follow me to Bonelands.

With the removals people helping, and with not much left to pack in addition to my books, magazines and small items, we managed to complete everything in just over an hour. I was going to leave most of my furniture, including the two beds for now, but was taking the new mattresses.

And there was the stadium house – *our* house, looking serene in the late afternoon sun, surrounded by tall trees, the garden neatly laid out, discreetly landscaped. How lucky I had been to find it! I went up the three steps of the portico, selected the largest key on the ring, and one side of the carved double door opened as noiselessly as on my first visit. The hinges must have been made by a watchmaker, for I saw no trace of grease or oil.

Into the hall, with its slim columns and plain caps, and the curving staircase at the end. Adam's craftsmen had done an excellent job of redecorating, for I could not even see where broken floor tiles had been replaced. The money had been well spent, and it was a house worthy of my Aida. And for me the bonus was in reminding me of the family house in Marmar, in style if not in size.

After the men had dumped individual items where I wanted them – the boxes of books in the room at the far end of the hall, the mattresses upstairs in the large bedroom over the sitting room (there is no such thing as a "living room" in our traditional architecture as there is always at least one "family area" and even bedrooms in traditional houses are large enough to be put to other uses, like sewing and knitting, reading and writing, and so on), in the kitchen, store, etc. – I tipped them handsomely and retired to the easy chair at the end wall facing the hall. I had brought coffee in a flask, and now relaxed to sample the atmosphere.

And a small cloud of depression began to descend on me, like some tangible thing, growing steadily in strength. Perhaps all the coffee I had been drinking lately was sending my blood pressure soaring up, and that was why I was feeling that way. I poured the coffee back into the flask, and went out to sit on the front steps, to enjoy the profusion of flowers, wild and uncultivated. I took several slow, deep breaths, each full of the fragrances of rose and jasmine. What a lovely garden it was. I must ask Adam to send me that gardener again. Dusk was beginning to fall, and I hurried back in before the miniscule vampires woke from their sleep.

I switched on the lights and took the radio out of its case. I went back to the kitchen to make tea this time and opened a packet of chocolate biscuits. I returned to the easy chair, from where I could look into the garden through no less than four narrow but tall windows, with arched, coloured glass toplights. In the old days no window ever had iron bars or iron grills, but "modern progress" made them a necessity. Even these protective measures proved of no avail if the owner was known to be away for many hours at night, with nobody else in the house. Needless to say, all that ironmongery destroyed the delicacy and beauty of even the finest windows.

'Now come back here!' It was a little girl's voice, and seemed to come from the entrance hall. Just above a whisper, but quite distinct. My first thought was that I must have left the front door open and the neighbours' children, seeing the lights, had come round to see who had moved in.

'Come in,' I said, expecting to see them appearing from behind the short bit of wall that hid the door from view, for there was a wide arch between the sitting room and the entrance hall to create a continuous space. There was silence, so I got out of the chair and went to see. The front door was locked and bolted, so they had to be outside. I unlocked the door and peered out. Beyond the lighted portico I could see that the gate was shut and bolted.

Well, I must have dozed off and imagined it. I sat down and switched on the radio, beginning with the local news and moving on to international ones. I felt like ringing my wife, but the phone had not been installed yet, so it was back to the kitchen for a dinner from tins and then an early night.

The bedroom was long and high-ceilinged. I had had the walls repainted from light blue to a light cream, and the heavy old four-poster realigned north–south and moved from the centre to nearer the end wall, a much cosier arrangement. After replacing the mattress, I hopped in after switching the main lights off and the bedside lamp on, settling down with an aircraft magazine. I should have been feeling relieved and contented at being in the house I had wanted so much, but even the magazine failed to prevent a recurrent of transitory fits of depression like the echoes of a sad memory. It was a warm, humid night, and yet I felt sudden little chills. Not malaria again, surely? Ah! Of course! It was all due to trying to suppress the fear that Bluebeard, the pillar of the Firefly Army, would probably lose the use of his right arm. And at a most critical time.

Utter fatigue took over and I must have dropped off while still holding the magazine, for when I was suddenly roused from sleep the lamp was on and the magazine was on my chest. I looked at the bedside clock, with its barely audible tick, and saw that it was just 1.35 a.m. A faint breeze was seeping in through the windows, and a pair of bush babies seemed to be exchanging insults, for they were making the crudest of sounds!

This small, big-eyed and big-eared animal, with its squirrel-like bushy tail, has an impressive repertoire of cries, from deep, throaty chuckles to staccato rattles, and long drawn out moans like the baying of a wild dog at full moon. It has the misfortune of having become associated with witchcraft and is thought to be used as a "familiar" by witches. The superstitious get very nervous when a bush baby spends too long on their roof, or on a nearby tree. This makes this pretty little animal unwelcome anywhere, but I think this is a blessing in a way – nobody wants to keep it as a pet!

I put the magazine on the side table, switched off the bed lamp and settled myself down again, with the resolution that I'd go straight to the military hospital first thing in the morning to see how Bluebeard was doing before going to the office. And then collect my beloved straight from work and bring her here.

And that's when I heard the whispering, seeming to come from the door. I then saw that I had not really shut the door after all, for there was a darker line down the edge where there should not have been. I switched on the lamp, and sure enough it was slightly ajar. So it must have been the wind whistling through it. I got up and strode to shut it when I heard a name, quite distinctly: 'Maryam!' followed by more whispering of an urgent nature. The voice was of a little girl, like downstairs.

I opened the door and stepped out into the corridor, calling myself all manner of idiot for letting my imagination run riot, but as I went out I had the distinct impression of a faint rush of air, like something moving down the corridor. I checked the corridor window but it was tightly shut, and passing my hand over the frame felt no trace of wind. I went and switched on the staircase lights and looked down, knowing there would be nothing to see. There wasn't, but the whispering continued, now coming from the entrance hall.

Now I should point out that there is no belief in ghosts as

such in our culture. Whatever unusual happenings of a possibly psychic nature that are observed – and it is almost taken for granted that old houses must have a "presence" of some sort, though manifest to only a sensitive few – they are caused not by the spirits of those gone by, but by psychic entities which exist in their own right. The reason for this belief has to do with religion, for it states that no soul that leaves this earth ever returns again. Though it must be said that there are those among the learned who dare disagree, pointing to certain obscure verses that to them suggest otherwise. A few even see a hint on reincarnation in one verse, but applying only to very specific cases. Personally, I have tried all my life to avoid dogma.

I went slowly down the terrazzo steps, one at a time, making sure I was not just dreaming by concentrating on the smooth feel of the polished hardwood handrail. When I reached the bottom step I sat down on it, turning my head slowly from side to side to locate the occasional whisper. What a lovely entrance hall it was, with its slim white columns! The house must have belonged to one of the old emirs, and one with good taste.

'All right, children. Come on out and let me see you,' I said, feeling rather foolish. But then was startled to hear giggles! Nothing happened, and after a while I went round the stairs to the kitchen for a glass of warm milk, which is known to promote sleep. I returned with it to the stairs and sat down again. And with the first sip I felt such a wave of despondency that I literally could not swallow it for a minute. I knew then that I could not bring Aida to this house. The feeling of love and peace which I had experienced on my first and subsequent visits here had been created by the presence of the old couple. When they left, it went with them, allowing an older, infinitely less happy atmosphere to resurface. Despite the giggling little spirits or entities, or whatever they were, something dreadful must have happened in this house. Even if Aida experienced nothing, I could not live in it.

I climbed the stairs with dragging steps, already planning to have my things returned to my old bungalow. The search for somewhere else would have to begin all over again, and I felt devastated. Did I not know that things were going too well for me?

On the middle landing I stopped and looked back. And I saw them! Not two but three little girls, the tallest one, about ten to twelve years old, in the middle, and the younger ones on either side of her. They did not look "ghostly" at all, but continued to appear out of focus however hard I stared.

'You must be Maryam,' I said to the middle girl, with a feeling of wonder. Who was going to believe my story? Not even Aida or Serge, I was sure.

She just smiled, and the two looked up at her.

'Who are you? What happened to you, children?'

They went on smiling and were gone. I sat on the landing until my eyes grew heavy, and I staggered to the bedroom.

I was up with the first cockcrow and returned downstairs to re-pack my things. I included only two items from the house: the antique Swiss/French clock, and a small ivory inlay coffee table. Only when everything was ready to go did I make breakfast and then packed up the kitchen things.

I was out of the house at 7.30 a.m. sharp, and did not look back. I made for the military hospital.

The military hospital, like all other in the country (apart from two private ones), was short of essentials and was in a state of disrepair. The "Firefly" government had health care at the top of its list and basic repairs were already in progress. I even received a smile from a nurse, but perhaps that was because I was obviously "brass".

To my surprise I found the Ancestor and Serge by

Bluebeard's bedside. They looked equally surprised to see me. No sooner had I offered the traditional greetings and asked an obviously sedated Bluebeard how he was feeling, when the Ancestor rounded on me.

'Where on earth were you the whole of yesterday? We went as far as contacting your wife, and had our military police joining in the search!'

I did not blame him for being most annoyed, for my disappearance on top of Bluebeard being knocked out of action reduced the Inner Council by half. They feared I might have been kidnapped or assassinated.

'I did not expect you to return yesterday, Ancestor, the general having told me that you'd be his guest for a couple of days. So I took the opportunity to move to my stadium house.'

'I did not return yesterday. In fact, we arrived here about forty minutes ago. But I wanted you to join us down south for discussions. Well, you missed making your contribution!'

On top of the shocks and disappointment of the previous night, this strong rebuke from the Ancestor plunged me into deep gloom, and I could think of nothing to say. Serge came to my rescue.

'Are you now settled in your castle?' he asked kindly, for once casting a disapproving look at the Ancestor, who to his credit placed a placating hand on my shoulder.

'With Bluebeard out of circulation for a few weeks the burden of overall command now rests on the Chief of Staff and you.'

'Not a few weeks, Ancestor; a few days,' mumbled Bluebeard. 'I'm returning to duty as soon as they stop pumping all this stuff into me. They'll turn me into a drug addict if I let them.'

The chief surgeon who was hovering nearby came forward sternly.

'Now look here, Commander! Do you want to have half an

arm or a full arm? Or maybe you are left-handed? If you are, then I'll release you tomorrow, if you want.'

That silenced Bluebeard.

'Anyway,' the surgeon added, 'a team of gunshot wounds specialists should be arriving from Soffenia this afternoon, and I want you to be nice to them, do you hear?'

The three of us tried hard to smother our grins, for nobody else would have dared talk to Bluebeard that way.

Outside the hospital the Ancestor said he wanted to see me after lunch, and I told them then that I had decided to move back to Bonelands that same day. They looked astonished.

'Why?' asked Serge. 'Something structurally dangerous?'

'No,' I replied, wondering how to put it. 'I heard and saw things all night. The place is inhabited.'

'I see,' said the Ancestor. 'Ever had this experience before?'

'Not since I was about twelve years old in our old house in Marmar. Granny told me it was nothing to worry about.'

'So why worry about the new house?' he asked. 'They usually mind their own business, whatever it is.'

'Because there were three little girls who seemed to want to attach themselves to me. And there was a terrible feeling of sadness, though I saw them smiling. I fear they'll come between me and my wife should we move there.'

I had no fear of ridicule or cynicism, for psychic phenomena were commonplace. It was taken for granted that life existed in other dimensions, and we were separated from them by a thin veil, the corners of which could be lifted when the circumstances were right. Occasionally forcible entry was made and this resulted in "possession".

Until fairly recently the scientific world tended to sneer at anything termed "psychic", but there are now research establishments the world over devoted entirely to the phenomena. But the ground rules do not yet seem to have been laid, and it may be that the "scientific" approach will never produce tangible results. Acceptance of clairvoyance, telepathy and precognitive dreams is only a small step towards understanding the manifestation of these dimensions, not the principles.

'I remember hearing something, may years ago, about a house in Stadium Road. There was—'

I immediately cut Serge short.

'Serge, please never, never tell me what happened. Never!'

He looked seriously at me, and said, 'Right,' as we walked slowly to the car park.

'Professor, get your things back to Bonelands and come directly to my office tomorrow morning. I have something very important to tell you.'

I drove straight to "Express Deliveries" and the manager looked startled to see me.

'Anything wrong, Commander?' he asked, fearing I had come to report a missing article or something.

'No, but I want my things taken back to Bonelands.'

His eyebrows went up all the way to the hairline, but he was too good a businessman to ask questions. He picked up the phone and told me a van would be at the house in about half an hour.

I did not go inside the house but sat outside on the portico steps, the beauty of the garden tugging at my heartstrings. Again and again I nearly changed my mind and decided to stay and stick it out, though I knew with terrible certainty that the children would do their best – or worst – to make life unbearable for Aida. I don't know what gave me this conviction, unless it was that they had wasted no time in revealing their presence to me. In the vast majority of houses with "presences" the odd, fleeting appearance is all the indication one receives that they are there. (Poltergeists are a different thing altogether, and our "healers" or exorcists treat them the same way they would as in a case of possession.)

When the men arrived I went in with them, and with practically everything already packed this time we were out in less than fifteen minutes. I remained at the entrance and said a prayer for the little girls before shutting and locking it. Again I did not look back from the gate.

My old bungalow maintained a discreet silence while I restored things to their former places. What sounded like a brief chuckle was, of course, due to the wind.

After a hasty shower I put on a fresh shirt and trousers, and still in sandals drove to the Zain villa. The maid opened the door and a furious wife came charging out.

'Commander! What in heaven's name have you been up to? Even your office didn't know where you were! Really, husband, this—'

'Let's go to the bungalow and I'll tell you all about it,' I said, grabbing her by the arm and leading her to the car whose engine I had left running.

'But I can't go like this? I'm in my house robe.'

'Never mind that,' I said. 'Nobody will see you. I'll bring you back tonight.'

I took her back the following morning on my way to the office.

I had not told her about the three girls, but had simply said that the roof was full of bats and it would take ages to get rid of them. Also the marshlands nearby were infested with rats. That was more than enough to put her off!

'Thank the Almighty you found that out before I moved in! I'd have run back to Bonelands the same night!' She had then added that her father had friends in the hotel business and they might like to convert it to a guest house. 'Let's look for a house nearer Bonelands,' she suggested, wanting to remain within easy reach of her parents. I had no objection to that.

As the days passed, with only periodic sniping action being

reported in the south and all evidence pointing towards Xarbuss reinforcing its Tamarian front, the Council came to the conclusion that there now appeared to be a distinct shift in Magrari's strategic aims. The Ancestor even speculated that perhaps his next target was the deep-water harbour in Skandiland, north of Tamaria, though he would be mad to try it.

Meanwhile, Bluebeard had been flown north to our neighbour Soffenia's new military hospital to repair the extensive tissue damage in his arm, and the Ancestor followed him a couple of days later, finding the excuse for another talk with President Serranos. The whole region had been flung into a state of unease, and it was the "Firefly" government's hope that we would be invited to send observers to the next meeting of regional heads.

When he returned he called a special meeting of the General Council and declared that he felt it was now safe enough for our forces to be stood down. There was much work to be done to the infrastructure and the fields and the bulk of our troops should now be released to help out. The villages and plantations needed their young men back, though it did not mean demobilisation. Arrangements were also being made for some officers to go abroad for further study and training.

On the diplomatic front, Xarcassia was being offered compensation for the five square kilometres of their land – all useless, dry scrubland – which we had had to occupy for defensive purposes. We surmised that Xarcassia, though a part of the now three-nation Xarbusstam Republic, would not be averse to the idea, since the alternative would be taking it back by force. With a share in the Tamarian oil, even the loss of the river plain could be taken on board. But for us in Rivenia, our economy was greatly strengthened by having the plain back.

After the meeting the Ancestor took me aside and said he wanted to see me the following day as an urgent matter concerning me personally had come up.

Aida had moved in at the bungalow, and for the first time in years I was enjoying a normal, routine married life. I felt that I had at last rejoined the human race, for family groups with children now dropped in, and we exchanged visits. It all seemed strange and wonderful.

I also finally found out why Aida had looked in a state of shock that night of the storming of the city. I never asked her what had made her take interest in me, for I had learned from experience that one should never look a gift horse in the mouth. Many couples make the mistake of probing and prying into one another's thoughts and feelings, and the result is often to drag things out of the unconscious which were best left alone. As long as something works, leave it alone!

So it was with a certain amount of unease that I heard her suddenly say, one afternoon on the veranda, 'Do you know what made me absolutely sure you were the man meant for me? When I saw you in that hunting jacket of yours with your badges and revolver. You see, in the dream I had seen you in military uniform. When I first saw you, in shirt and sarong, you just looked familiar somehow, but I was left in doubt. The second time, you were nearly there! But that night I *knew* it!'

Is ours to reason why?

« FIFTEEN »

The Ancestor looked relaxed and in good humour as he left his desk and came to shake my hand. His few days in Soffenia, no doubt spent mostly talking of "the good old days" with Serranos but also perhaps receiving reassurances of concrete support in the political and military fields, had done him a world of good.

Without warning he sprang his bombshell.

'How would you like to go abroad for a year or two?'

Serge's words had made me wonder whether I was going to be transferred to another Council, perhaps that of education, politics or culture, to allow one of the returning Rivenian exiles who had served with the UN and been through staff college or military academy to take my place. Being sent abroad had simply not figured in my thinking.

'Where abroad? What for?' I asked.

'Do you remember Mr James, who came to ask about the Mongols? You'll have gathered that he was no journalist but was our head of military intelligence. Well, I can tell you now that he was, and is, much more than that. I can tell you now that without him the "Firefly" movement might have died in its infancy. He funded the organisation in its first year, and it was he who roped in Erion who in turn brought in Bluebeard.'

This was a revelation indeed!

'This is astonishing, Ancestor! Why is he the same rank as me, then? Surely he ranks even higher that Serge and Bluebeard?'

'Rank really means nothing to him. He is totally outside the military, or even political, structure as you will discover when you join him.'

'Join him? Where? What for?'

'He travels a lot, but he is based in a European country, one very familiar to you. Which is why he is asking specifically for you to help him in his work, apart from the fact that he considers you the most suitable among our Council members. And it is extremely important work, for remember no major country has so far come out to recognise our government.'

I was beginning to suspect that I was about to be plunged into politics, and I said so.

'Surely, Ancestor, a senior member of our Political Council would be eminently more suitable?'

'Do you know any with knowledge of the machinery of war?'

Ah! Things were now beginning to sound interesting! He took my smile as meaning acquiescence.

'We have no embassy there, so you will be going as my "military envoy", a vague enough title to get you places without diplomatic complications! You'll be attached to Mr James' company.'

I was satisfied with that, and he said he'd let me know as soon as all the arrangements were completed at that end. I'd be accompanied by my wife, of course, he added, smiling.

I was out in the corridor when an idea struck me, and I returned to his office. And the idea very nearly proved disastrous.

'Forgotten something?' he asked when I entered.

'I was just thinking, Ancestor, that since I'm bound to meet all manner of people there, what about interesting a pharmaceutical company in our mountain flower? It could bring in a lot of foreign currency.'

The way his expression changed was frightening. I'd never have imagined he could look so icily menacing.

'What mountain flower, Professor?' he asked, not looking at me directly.

'Why, the yellow one that is so insect repellent.'

'Who told you about it?'

By now I knew that I had said something terribly wrong, though I couldn't figure out what.

'Surely it is now common knowledge that our men daubed themselves with it to survive in the forest?'

'No, Professor, it is not common knowledge. What is known by the Forestry Department is that both the leaves and the flowers are very highly toxic. But so are some of the other flowers in the area. So who told you?'

'I think you are being very unreasonable, Ancestor. Surely all the men who collected them and those who prepared the mixture must have known about them?'

'Yes, they did. But they had sworn the Oath of Blood, and remember, they were collected at night and taken to the still. The other men never knew where they went at night, nor saw what they brought back.'

For the first time I felt I was in some sort of danger, and the continuing icy look in the Ancestor's face did not reassure me. What was he going to do? I then had a sudden inspiration to tell him the full story. But first I found the courage to rebuke him.

'Ancestor, may I remind you that I am a member of the Inner Council? So why should any secret be kept from me, especially one which is no longer of the slightest importance? If I do not have your full trust, please accept my immediate resignation.'

Like one who had been sleepwalking, his distant and glazed eyes slowly refocused on me, and the ice in them dissolved. It had been a frightening experience, almost like at that episode of possession.

'Professor, please accept my sincere apologies. For two years I – we – lived in terror of someone discovering and revealing the secret of my men's yellow paint, so my reaction just now was as it would have been then. Of course it no longer matters who knows about it, but do tell me who told you or how you found out.'

I gave him the full story, leaving nothing out. He listened most attentively, and in the end shook his head.

'Strange indeed are the ways of the Almighty. But how you joined us is no stranger than how I came to learn the secret prescription that turned a deadly poison into a source of protection. You see, just before I was arrested – and incarcerated for four years, without trial, as you know – I was preaching my message in the northern village of Qurtur when a man came and said a certain sheikh, a healer, wanted to see me. My reaction was that the man must have thought I was possessed or something and was going to suggest "cleansing" me! I went, nevertheless, out of curiosity and after the customary round of sips of coffee, he asked me a strange question. "Are you going into the forest?" he asked. I had heard of the "forest people" but they were hardly the kind for me to preach to! Then he said, "Come and see me before you do!" I politely promised to do so, and left with relief. Obviously he was not quite right in the head.'

He was gazing out at the distant mountains through the long, low picture window as he talked, seeming almost to forget my presence.

'I kept remembering his words in my last year in prison, though I did not know that it was my last year, but even then the idea of forming an armed resistance force was beginning to take shape in my mind. It was in London, in the year that I returned to Rivenia, that the forest seemed to call me, as one day I told Mr James. For reasons known only to the controllers of our destinies, he offered his full support from that moment.'

The feeling of wonder was still with him as his shining eyes turned to face me.

'I had a letter of introduction to Erion, and when I had managed to locate him we went together to Qurtur to see the sheikh, praying that he was still alive. He was, and when I told him I was going into the forest he went to an inner room and came out with a yellowing, rolled up sheet of paper. "You will need this – study it carefully, and preserve it with your life." I burnt it the day the whole country was under our control so that it would not to fall into the wrong hands when I die.'

'But Ancestor, why isn't that plant included in our book of Rivenian flora?'

'Oh it is! Except that it is shown as having green leaves. The book was compiled six years ago, so the red leaves must be a recent mutation of some kind. The green-leafed type is still there, though hardly noticeable among the other bushes.'

He rose from the carpet as a sign that the session was over, and I followed suit.

'By the way,' he said, 'you were extremely lucky not to apply your scientific concoction on any part of your body. It attacks skin like acid, even when heavily diluted. Your three tablespoons of oil to one drop of sap would have left you with deep burns. You see, the yellow colour of the men came from the solvent, not the yellow sap!'

Suitably chastened, I was turning to go when he restored my pride by saying, 'It is much to your credit that you did not seek favour with the government by reporting your finding, for you would have been handsomely rewarded. You see, even though your assumption was wrong, it would have directed attention to the flower which until then had escaped notice. At least the possibility of the yellow daub being the result of it would have been investigated, and an eye kept on the mountains. So even though their labs would not have come up with a safe formula, the result for us would have been the same. Sooner or later they'd have seen our men gathering the flowers. Can you imagine what would have happened had we been discovered even earlier?'

We looked at one another with great seriousness for a moment, and I said, 'So I suppose even if I had taken the sap abroad it would have been a useless exercise?'

'Oh, with their incredibly advanced technology they, no doubt, would have worked out some suitable formula, even if not the same as ours. But there are so many much easier and safer concoctions on the market that they'd not have bothered. We used it because it was immediately available and *free*. Mind you, it could also be that most of the insect repellents available would not have scared away the green spiders. The mountains must remain a nature reserve. The "green demons" are the guardians and must remain a source of dread.'

Aida's response to our being sent abroad was one of resignation. 'At least I'll know where you are most of the time. No dashing off into bushes and things!' She never believed me when I said that I had never been in any danger from start to finish; she kept pointing out what had happened to Elba and Bluebeard.

Towards the end of the month Bluebeard returned, still bandaged up and looking much thinner. Weeks of therapy still lay ahead, but the prognosis was good. At a special ceremony he and the late much missed Elba were awarded the "Firefly" Star of Valour, which was the highest. Others, including myself, were given various other types and grades, mine being the same as that awarded to Tufayl and Aziz, for distinguished command.

Aida wore mine as a pendant everywhere she went, much to my delight but slight embarrassment since both Tufayl and Aziz had come under fire, whereas I had not.

•••••••

Our flight to Europe was to be in the second week of November, the exact date to be confirmed when Mr James returned to base from the Far East. That meant waiting some nine or ten days and Aida and I were already so keyed up to go that every day seemed like a week. The last Council meeting had taken place a week previously so that meant it was my last one, the next one being due towards the end of the month. As usually happens, once somebody is known to be leaving he very quickly gets sidelined and for some strange reason ceases to be considered of the "in" crowd. So I tended to get left out of informal little gatherings, and nobody rushed to my office with a juicy titbit of gossip. I have never been able to understand this phenomenon, for it was not that I was being sacked. Perhaps the secret belief was that I was being "pushed out of the way" for somebody else to be appointed in my place. Well, they were going to be disappointed, because the Ancestor had hinted at a promotion when I returned, which could only be to Commander, First Class.

I kept going through the motion of reporting at my office, going over the old brochures again and again (and even had a go at redesigning an armoured car) and then going across to a nearly empty mess. For it would appear that it was in times of war, when there was much to do, that officers spent much time in the mess. The highlight of the week was an outing with Bluebeard to watch a new batch of recruits being put through their paces. Bluebeard was disgusted.

'What sort of young men are we getting nowadays? Look how much fat they are carrying around with them! Look how clumsily they run! Why, the ragged bunches of layabouts and drug addicts I started off with in the forest were better on their second day of drill than this lot will be after a whole month of it!'

I was amused by this universally held belief (throughout the centuries) that yesterday's men were superior to today's. Every successive generation is seen as being inferior to the previous one.

With about three days to go I took Aida to say goodbye to the old Marmar couple in Olive Street. We were delighted to learn that the old man had had a cataract operation in one eye and that he could now see quite well with it.

'Aah!' he said when Aida went to greet him, after embracing the old lady and kissing her on both cheeks. 'You have indeed chosen well. I can see now that she would have given my dear wife some competition.'

'You would still have preferred me, sire. My hair was longer and my dress had little jingling bells,' his wife said, flirtatiously. She said he now walked much better and even did gardening. I did not tell them that we were not going to live in their old mansion after all.

'When the Almighty brings you back safely from those heathen lands you will find our pear trees ripe with fruit,' he said at the gate. 'And my second eye will also have been fixed.'

We wished them long life and drove away with some sadness.

On arriving home HQ confirmed that we were booked on a flight leaving at 10.30 p.m. on the fifteenth.

Serge had received three weeks off to look after the harvesting of his pineapple crop in his plantation down south, but he came up the following day for lunch with us to wish us bon voyage.

On the fourteenth I was called to the Ancestor's office, and he reminded me that I was his military adviser and not to get sidetracked into politics. We were going to build our forces into the best military presence in the area, because only that way could we ensure our survival as long as the likes of Magrari were around. He had no designs on anyone's territory, and it would be a purely defensive force but able to go on the offensive if necessary. His parting words were: 'And don't start experimenting with gunpowder while you are there. If you want to become a scientist we'll fix up a scholarship for you – when you retire!' I was going to miss the Ancestor.

A message in my office said that Bluebeard wanted to see

me, and that Deputy Tufayl had rung from the south to wish me a good journey. I had already seen the other members of the Council and had specifically asked them not to come to the airport. I dislike formal partings.

Bluebeard had managed to acquire several books on armoured warfare, and I saw the pile as soon as I entered his office.

'Just received them,' he said. 'From a friend abroad.'

I glanced briefly at them and saw that they included Liddell Hart's, Fuller's, Guderian's, Konev's, Patton's, and so on.

'Well, Bluebeard,' I said, 'you should be a tank expert by the time you have been through this lot.'

'We have to know what we are doing and how Prof. We can no longer get away with just being an enthusiastic rebel army.'

This emphasis on military development, coming first from the Ancestor and now Bluebeard, made me feel uneasy. We seemed to be drifting away form the "Firefly" ethos of peace and plenty.

'I'm sorry to see you leaving us, Prof, even if only for a year or two. I now realise that we have more in common than appears on the surface.'

I did a quick bit of soul-searching and wondered if he could be right. I had always thought of myself as being on Serge's side.

I gave my secretary, whose eyes were moist with tears, a quick hug, kissed her on both cheeks and made my way out of the Palace.

On the way I dropped in at the Corner Café to say goodbye to the group, but found only three present. I left after a single cup of coffee. Group psychology was at work here as well. To all intents and purposes I had ceased being a member weeks before.

I found Aida at her parents' surrounded by several female relations, including the sexy voiced Auntie Amina. My heart sank when I saw all the presents they had brought her, thinking of excess baggage. When we got home I was going to persuade her to leave most of them behind. She certainly was not going to take that bright green cardigan, and the box of choice dried figs weighing several kilograms!

Mrs Zain asked if I'd let her spend the rest of the day with them and I agreed. But I had to turn down their invitation to lunch, saying I had a report to complete, being the penultimate day.

I collected my wife at sunset, and she seemed in high spirits. I had expected her to feel somewhat dejected but she was looking forward to the "winter wonderland" of shopping that lay ahead.

'I hope it'll snow this December!' she said, as thrilled as a child at the prospect.

That night the wild dogs came down very early from the mountains. At 10 p.m., almost on the dot, they started that shivering, mournful howl which I called the "death howl". I knew it well, having heard it in Rivenia as well as in other countries I had lived in abroad, from the domestic pets of owners about to die or move away from the area. Unlike the baying at full moon, this howl did not rise as a smooth, uninterrupted note but was full of a kind of sobbing gloom. It was a most desolate sound, and when I explained its significance to Aida she shivered and said, 'But these are wild dogs. Why should they feel sad that you are leaving? You have not been feeding them, have you?'

I said, on the contrary; I often threw stones at them during their mating season when they congregated behind the house and started fighting. And once I interrupted what seemed to be an important conference of theirs. So they really had no reason to love me.

'Well, they do. You must have been a comforting presence to them in some way.'

Then it struck me that the lights in my house must have

served as a distant beacon to them, an aiming point in the dark.

We lay in each other's arms that night, but did not make love. We soon fell asleep, right through the periodic howling, in solo and in chorus, and the rain that fell.

« SIXTEEN »

Bluebeard, Aziz, Mrad and Saleh had ignored my request not to bother coming to the airport and were there to see me off. I was quite touched. And then there were Aida's relations and friends, hugging and kissing, so that it was quite a relief to get on board the aircraft, a twin-engined Fokker, which was to take us to our northern neighbour's international airport to catch a jet to Europe. Our own airport was being expanded and re-equipped, so that only short-take-off-and-landing aircraft could use it at present. There were about thirty passengers, mostly businessmen with briefcases, and foreigners.

Seatbelts had to be left on for practically the whole forty-five-minute flight because of bumpy weather, but both of us were seasoned travellers. We arrived at our final destination at the customary unearthly hour (I absolutely detest those dawn breakfasts, the invariably tasteless food made even worse by sleep), but Mr James was there to meet us, immaculately turned out as always. We accompanied him to his Jaguar and he whisked us away to what looked like a well-to-do suburb. I was in the front passenger seat, and he never stopped talking from the time we squeezed into the traffic stream away from the airport to the time we arrived. He seemed starved of conversation in Rivenian, and with one of similar age and rank, but I was suffering from a bit of jet lag (I looked back and saw that my wife was fast asleep) and caught only snatches of what he was saying. It sounded like just idle chatter and bits of gossip. '...Never invite the Principal Secretary of... And all the time his hand... so you just remember... But perhaps next week…' and so on. I was going to have to ask him to repeat some of the things when we met next.

The house was a semi-detached, with the usual well-kept front garden. He helped carry in the suitcases, and Aida immediately disappeared upstairs. It was with relief that I heard him say he couldn't stay but he was going to send someone to fetch me in three days' time, when I'd have settled down a bit. There was much to do, he said, and was glad that the Ancestor had been able to spare me. I looked at his Jaguar saloon roaring off and wondered what car I'd be given.

Aida spent hours in the bathroom and came down all wrapped up in towels. The house was centrally heated and was well furnished.

'Nice bedroom,' she said, 'but the usual tight bathroom. The one in your bungalow is bigger.'

I pointed out that it had to do with climate and tradition. Heating the bathroom was a fairly recent innovation. Going to the bathroom used to be considered a necessary evil.

No sooner had I had my turn in the bath than she said, 'I hate to say this, husband, but there's nothing to eat in the kitchen!' So it was on with the heavy clothing again, and out into the biting winds, carrying her list of necessities. There were little shops at the end of the street, so I didn't have to take a bus, thank heavens.

A choice of good programmes on television had us well contented for the rest of the evening. (No doubt later we'd start getting bored with the usual fare, but for now we were satisfied.)

Three days later I took a bus and, carefully following the map, managed to find Mr James' office with some difficulty. You see, I had pictured it as a modest little office with a secretary and a couple of typists (or even a computer), in line with others of the same calibre. Instead of which, it occupied half the third floor of a prestigious building! I went up in an almost silent lift and was confronted by a wall of glass with thin anodised framing and a discreet copper plate engraved with "James Financial Services". Behind it I could see glass cubicles and rows of computers, and potted plants and stylish space dividers. No wonder everyone called him *Mr* James, I thought!

He was not in, but his private secretary came forward and must have been well briefed.

'Welcome to our office, Commander! Let me show you to your office.' She was a foreign woman, with a slight French accent. Most of the staff seemed to have been locally recruited, with a scattering of Rivenians, as I was to find out when I was introduced later.

My office was of medium size, with its obscured-glass sides beginning at chest height. But it was against the back wall, so that a long, low window gave me a view of the outside, and down into the busy street. I was not going to be a goldfish in a bowl after all. Good of Mr James.

The plate on my door said: "Director Auxiliary Services". It smacked of somewhat devious activities to me!

The real business of the firm was, indeed, financial services, so it was not just a front. But at the same time Mr James had been acting as a sort of "ambassador at large", and as I pored through the documents from a locked drawer, some stamped "Confidential", others not, my respect for him grew.

When he returned just before lunch break he said he was going to start introducing me to a few people in the diplomatic community and asked me whether I drank. Not really, I said, and he said not to worry. There was a "function" at an embassy on Saturday night, and he would come and collect my wife and me and to dress fairly formally.

Aida was no stranger to official functions, having attended some in Rivenia as well as abroad, so she knew how to dress for each occasion. But she confessed to me that she hated them, having been virtually forced to attend them in the company of her parents.

That Saturday night she looked absolutely dazzling in a Rivenian-style black dress and headwear (I can never learn the names of the hundred and one items that women ornament themselves with). I expected her to be the centre of attention, and she was. I started getting butterflies in my stomach as one distinguished diplomat or dashing young tycoon after another hovered around her while she was chatting with some woman or other, noting one or two trying to hang on to her hand when introduced. I went on sneaking glances at her, carefully noting how she was reacting to all this attention, but refrained from acting possessive and hanging on to her all evening. It was with considerable relief, therefore, that halfway through the evening she made her way to me and slipped her hand in mine.

'I have a terrific headache. Do you think we could go home?'

I looked at her and saw that she did look in pain, and we went and apologised to our hosts and left. We said goodbye to Mr James and took a taxi.

When we got home she continued feeling unwell, and then rushed upstairs to the bathroom, where I heard her being sick. I was debating whether to ring our doctor or take her to the hospital about a kilometre away, when she came out and walked downstairs.

'Ah, that's better!' she said, smiling.

'It must be something you ate,' I said.

'Perhaps,' she murmured. 'Let's see what's on telly.'

Her pregnancy was confirmed two days later, and things were never the same again. (Once she sent me out at almost 11 p.m. in pouring rain to an Indian restaurant to get her a hot curry.)

I took her out only three more times in the next two to three months to diplomatic dos, after which she refused to go. I continued making contacts and drove several hundred kilometres in the course of time to attend air shows, and even twice that year having to fly to a neighbouring country to an armaments display, spending three days there. Aida had come to make friends with our next-door neighbour (who had maintained her distance for many weeks before being reassured by our own conservativeness) and she was a well-informed, energetic widow, so I didn't worry so much about being away. I must say I was enjoying my work thoroughly, my monthly reports to Mr James being forwarded to Rivenia by special courier.

With about two months to go to baby's expected arrival (her pregnancy had had its worrying moments, but things seemed to be under control), Mr James finally decided to tell me something about his relationship with the Ancestor and his part in the "Firefly" movement. This was after a particularly delicious dinner prepared by Aida, and with the television turned low he sat back and took out one of his fat cigars. This immediately made Aida ease herself up and say she had some knitting to complete upstairs. (Later she would come down and open all the windows for half an hour, nearly freezing me to death!)

'You see, Prof,' he started, 'about thirty years ago I was one of those young men in government service who became totally disenchanted with the regime and began to meet secretly with members of the Defence Force with a view to planning a coup. You know the strange way in which like-minded people tend to be drawn to one another, a word here, a look there, and suddenly you know that you are "birds of a feather". That was the time of the notorious "Python oppression", when a single word of criticism against the government could find you flung into one of their "comfort chambers", and you'd consider yourself lucky if you came out with a quarter of your teeth still intact. Many simply disappeared, never to be seen again.'

His smile was more of a snarl, and I noticed that he was not so much smoking his cigar as chewing it.

'Our group seemed to be winning slow but steady support among junior officers, but we had to move higher if we were to stand any chance of success. A senior officer of at least major rank. And we found one. Or believed we did.

'One night there was a frantic knock on my door near midnight, just as I was preparing to go to bed. When I opened the door one of the officers, a Lieutenant Kassim, stumbled in, breathing hard. He immediately burst out, "Jonathan, get out quick! We have been betrayed! They are out hunting for us! They'll be here any minute."'

The memory was still very much alive with him, and the hand holding the cold cigar trembled a bit.

'I was panic-stricken for a moment, while thanking God that my wife and children were visiting her parents in Xarcassia – where I had met her, incidentally, while on holiday – and we were living in a rented house. But I had to withdraw my money, even if not all of it, from the bank the following morning otherwise how was I going to live?

'"Where are you running to, Kassim?" I asked him.

'"To join my brother abroad. I have been buying foreign currency for years, and so I have enough to get to him. Must run. Goodbye, Jonathan, till we meet again, if the Almighty wishes. Get moving, brother!"

'And he ran out into the street. Well, I thought of a trick to suggest I had fled, and therefore have them searching the neighbourhood while I remained in the house until morning. And then I'd write a cheque and have my uncle who lived two streets away go and cash it first thing in the morning. I knew he would not hesitate.

'So I went to the bedroom, opened the wardrobe and drawers, and left a tumble of clothing on the bed and on the floor. I took away my passport, cheque book, and small items, and put a change of clothing in a travelling bag. Then I left the front door slightly ajar, placed a chair under the loft hatch in the corridor ceiling, and flung in the bag. Before heaving myself up I gave the chair a strong kick which sent it tumbling into the front room, and then closed the hatch. About ten minutes later I heard a vehicle screeching to a stop in front of the house, and the heavy stamping of boots and angry voices as they saw the signs of flight. They called me all sorts of names, and I heard them smashing things. But then someone shouted, "Come on, you're wasting time, fuck you! Spread out in the neighbourhood!"

'They returned about two hours later, as I suspected they would, helped themselves to my radio, cutlery, and other items, and then carefully shut the front door!'

He laughed mirthlessly at this single civilised act on their part. Then he proceeded. 'I waited for daybreak and then made for my uncle's, knowing he was an early riser. I did not have to do much explaining as they had been to his house soon after leaving mine the second time. Auntie-in-law was up as well, and after breakfast she offered to go to the bank to fetch the money. And then Uncle exchanged much of it into the foreign currency in his possession – it was obtainable on the black market at that time, there being currency restrictions – adding a bit extra. I shaved off my moustache and, dressed in gown and turban, caught a bus for the north. I spent a day in a hotel in Mirage, then crossed the border into Soffenia where I obtained the necessary visas to join Kassim's brother here. Two weeks later saw a happy reunion with Lieutenant Kassim himself. But not for long, alas, for a few months later he died in a car accident.'

I waited for him to continue, but he was staring off into space, so I said, 'But how did you come to get so well established here? Not an easy thing for anyone, let alone somebody from our area.'

'What?' he said vaguely, before returning to the present. 'Oh, I was a qualified quantity surveyor, and there was a building boom on in this country. I had no difficulty getting a job with a small company which soon doubled in size. Over the years I rose to become a partner, and the firm started branching out into other lines. Financing projects was one of them, and in it I found my true métier. Ending up with "James Financial Services"! When you associate with sharks you develop extra teeth, as the old people say.'

'How did you come to meet the Ancestor?' I asked.

'I met him at a get-together of Rivenian exiles, soon after he was released from prison and was helped to come here. He struck me as being different from the others. Sadder, more intense. He seldom said anything, but when he did his eyes would flash and his jaws would clench. He struck me as a man who was being moved by some very deep forces. I took to inviting him for tea or coffee every so often, and one day he suddenly said he was a man with a destiny to fulfil. At times he sounded quite mad, as when he insisted that he was in constant touch with the Twelve Elders. But only to me, not to the others. The real turning point for me came when he suddenly said, about four years ago, that he was returning to Rivenia to organise a liberating force. He said he was going into the forest and knew who he must first contact. Like one hypnotised, I offered him full financial support and any other kind of assistance. I introduced him to Erion by letter; and he, in turn, roped in Bluebeard. And that's how it all started.'

He looked at his watch and gave a start. It was nearly midnight, and he stood up to leave. At the door I asked him if his wife and children were in Rivenia. He laughed.

'You are forgetting we parted thirty years go, and they were in Xarcassia. Well, when I had enough money to send for them to join me, she wrote back to say she wanted a divorce as she had fallen in love with somebody else! No amount of persuasion could make her change her mind.'

He looked at his watch again and said he must be going. There was nothing I could say without sounding banal.

I found Aida fast asleep and slipped gently into bed. But she was not so gentle with me the following morning! I stepped into an icy-cold living room, smelling strongly of room freshener.

'I wish you'd ask your friend not to smoke his horrible weed in here! He is welcome to do it out in the garden!'

I looked at the dressing gown bulging out in front and understood her feelings.

« SEVENTEEN »

When Colonel Bertillot's book, *War, Witchcraft and Idealism in Rivenia*, came out, Baby Leila was almost one year old. In addition to having inherited her granny's ears (a bit on the small side, though not unshapely) she was already exhibiting a trace of her stubbornness. It took several smacks from her mother to stop her flinging her toys at the television. (Perhaps she simply didn't like the standard children's fare.)

After we had both read the book, with similar outbursts of anger, Aida said I had to write one in reply, setting the facts straight. Frankly, I didn't think it would do much good as the majority of Bertillot's readership would believe him rather than me, but I gave the idea serious consideration. The problem was that an official history was already in the process of being compiled, a foreign historian having been commissioned to do so in my absence (and with my approval, on condition that I did the final editing), so there would be a certain amount of repetition. Unless I made it a purely personal account which had its risks. But Aida said she wouldn't mind if I mentioned our romance, discreetly. Well, we had gone strictly according to convention and tradition, so there was nothing to worry about there, was there?

I mentioned my intention to Mr James at the office, and after some hesitation he gave me the go-ahead on condition that he read the manuscript before submitting it for publication. I could work on it in the office during slack periods in order to finish it quickly. And it was just as well, because I was about three-quarters of the way through it, weeks later, when on Wednesday

28 October I received an unexpected long-distance call from Rivenia. It was Serge on the line, the second time in less than a week. Serge and I had been keeping in touch by ringing one another every two months, so I had a feeling that it was not just a social call.

'What's up, Serge?' I asked, trying to smother a pang of anxiety. 'Adding another wife to your harem?'

'Nothing so exciting, Prof. I have a little message for you. From "Falcon One".'

This use of our war code immediately told me that it was a grave matter, and I waited for the message with anxiety.

'Falcon One says, quote, "The red ants are about to muscle in on the window breakfast." End of message. He wants you back here as soon as possible. When can you come?'

Now, whereas "Falcon One" might have suggested impending war, the reference to the ants ruled that out. It hinted at something much closer home, in Rivenia itself. A conspiracy? Perhaps even at Army HQ?

'Serge, I have to discuss it with Mr James first. You will know when after I have seen him.'

He said he was going to ring him as well.

To my wife's enquiry, I said, 'Something appears to be not quite right. We have to return to Rivenia as soon as possible.'

I went and joined her in front of the television, and she put her left arm round me, looking up with worried eyes.

'Can you tell me what it is? Is Magrari on the prowl again?'

'No, I don't think so, but I'll check with Mr James tomorrow. He is bound to know, though he said nothing this morning. So it must be a new development.'

But then she suddenly perked up.

'Leila is going to see her grandparents at last! They'll pamper her to death, and ruin all the discipline! I can hardly believe it! But oh!' she suddenly recollected, 'we are going to miss all the Christmas shopping!'

Aida always maintained that it was the only time in the year that she did not miss Rivenia.

The following morning Mr James had a meeting which lasted until almost lunchtime, so he suggested we went to his favourite restaurant and talk over lunch. I was never one for eating out myself, preferring to be doing something else while eating, like reading a paper, listening to the radio, or watching TV. Also, being under the watchful eyes of hovering waiters was something I disliked, feeling that I was being "processed", greedy eyes already assessing the possible size of tip I was going to leave.

Mr James confirmed that Serge had rung him the night before but he'd not be in a position to know what was happening until the special courier arrived the following day. I decided not to mention the ants as I could be wrong. But one thing he did assert: there had been no report of troop movements on the Xarbusstam side.

I returned home more convinced than ever that it was an internal problem of quite serious magnitude. But if so, surely Mr James should have been the first to know?

Feeling that the next few days might not allow me any time to finish my personal narrative of the historic "Events" of the previous four years in Rivenia, I told my wife I was going to lock myself away in the bedroom and finish those last two chapters, and to disturb me as little as possible. Later I'd come downstairs after baby Leila was taken to bed and continue in the living room most of the night if necessary, because I wanted her to start typing it out the following day in between minding Leila.

'Yessir, Commander!' she said, with a salute.

During the evening she sat watching TV with the volume turned low, and I got on with it. She retired upstairs at about 11.30 p.m. after making me a cup of tea and a slice of fruitcake, and I pushed on until almost 2 a.m. I could have squeezed in a few more pages, but decided I had said enough. I ceremoniously presented the manuscript to her in the morning. As the daughter of a Permanent Secretary I believed her when she said she had not taken a peep at the bits and pieces I had left on my desk in the process of putting it together.

'If I didn't love you I don't think I'd be able to decipher your handwriting!' she said, thumping me on the chest with the manuscript. Baby Leila at her side looked up in surprise at this unusual spectacle of Mummy thumping Daddy, but was reassured when I received a peck on the cheek afterwards.

The courier from Rivenia arrived late in the afternoon, and Mr James came into my office soon after instead of sending for me. One look at his face and I knew that something pretty serious had been in the message.

'Prof,' he began without preamble, 'I am afraid something none of us ever anticipated is happening. Let me just tell what has taken place these last two weeks.'

As he sat down I noticed that my door was slightly ajar, and I went to shut it.

'Under pressure from Bluebeard and some of the new members of the Military Council, our Chief of Staff, Commander Erion, may be forced to announce his resignation at the special meeting of the General Council on 3 January, next year. The Council has swelled to forty men since you left, and a new system has been introduced – that of formal voting by secret ballot on all important proposals. The Ancestor still has the veto but, Prof, his overall control is being steadily whittled away.'

I was shocked to hear this. How could all this be happening? And not once in my occasional conversations on the telephone with Serge and Bluebeard had there been the slightest hint of anything being amiss. More importantly, why was it happening, and who was behind it?

'I don't understand this, Mr James. Surely whatever is happening must be with the full consent of the Ancestor?'

He hesitated for a long time before replying.

'Prof, I can hardly bring myself to say this, because it sounds so monstrous, but Bluebeard is making a bid for power. He has steadily been building a power base in the armed forces and in the police. It was Aziz who first tipped me off, barely four months ago, in a secret memorandum. The trouble is, the Ancestor still trusts Bluebeard implicitly. Or did until now, for he would not be sending for you otherwise. Bluebeard has been stocking the Council with his supporters, and you will see many new faces when you go.'

'What do you mean "supporters"? You do not mean they are contemplating a coup? Why, the Ancestor could dismiss the whole lot of these newcomers if he wanted.'

'And what would happen then? These are commanders of brigades and regiments. The army would split down the middle, and remember that the Foresters now form only a quarter of the army, and they are the only ones who would fight to the death to defend the Ancestor.'

The full implication of the situation now facing us began to settle on me like a terrible black cloud. The Ancestor's dream of a prosperous, peaceful and happy land was well on the way to being realised, and the "Firefly" government was now recognised by some countries. And yet the ugly spectre of selfish ambition had to rear its head! It seemed so grossly unfair after what we had been through.

'But what does Bluebeard hope to gain that he does not have already? He has the love and trust of the Ancestor and can do just about everything he wants. In fact, you know that I support his ambition of building up a comprehensive armoured division, and have been sending back full details and price lists. The Ancestor also approves of a three-division army, plus helicopters. What more could he want with our limited resources?'

'He wants to invade Xarcassia, Prof, and even move into Bussota.'

'May the Almighty protect us! The man is an imperialist. The Ancestor never contemplated going even a quarter that far to restore our empire, being content with the river plain. Are you absolutely sure about that, Mr James? Not once did I hear him mention anything like that, even in jest. Let us not misjudge the man on the basis of some idle tongue telling tales.'

'I had it from Mrad, our intelligence chief, when I visited Rivenia five months ago. He begged me to convince the Ancestor that Bluebeard was perfectly serious about it, and it was not just a general's wishful thinking. But you know how the Ancestor loves Bluebeard like a son, and all he said was, "Don't worry. He'll give up the idea when he gets down to planning it. Bluebeard must be given freedom to exercise his mind. He is a great asset to us." I must say I left him convinced that Mrad was worrying himself for nothing.'

A sudden suspicion seized me. What if the Ancestor shared Bluebeard's dream, or even indeed had put him up to it? Well, I'd be returning soon and would find out for myself.

'Just one more thing, Mr James. Why do you think the Ancestor is sending for me? I have no power to swing anything one way or the other. If his mind is already made up, or Bluebeard is planning a coup to sideline him, there's nothing I could do about it, is there? I do not command a brigade to throw in.'

'You have more influence than you think. You are one of the Inner Circle, aren't you?' he said, smiling for the first time. 'Go and prevent your friend Erion from being pushed aside. Ride roughshod over the new militaristic clique. As the Ancestor's adviser you have considerable political clout as well.'

Then he said we had a vital meeting with a Secretary of State on 15 November and therefore I should arrange to return to

Rivenia after that. I set 19 November as the date of departure.

Aida finished typing the manuscript on 16 November, three days before the planned date of departure. She had made absolutely no comment throughout the typing, and her remarkable self-control never ceased to amaze me. But that explained how she had been able to resist one enticing proposal of marriage after another, much to her mother's displeasure. Or was it all a matter of destiny? Even then, it seems to me that one has to be correctly positioned and equipped to fulfil one's destiny.

That evening, after putting Leila to bed my wife came down the stairs looking at me with some unease, and I knew that she was now ready to comment on the manuscript. She came and sat by me in the couch and held my hand. Here it comes! I thought, and it is not going to be good news! 'Well?' I asked. 'Do you think it'll silence Bertillot?'

She didn't smile but looked earnestly at me.

'Husband, you cannot possibly submit this for publication. It is far too intimate. You are revealing too much. We will be the subject of much gossip, vicious gossip. And the Ancestor, your colleagues – how will they view it? It shows them up as well. They will resent some of the things you say, though all are true. My family will be most embarrassed.'

There were no two ways about it. She was perfectly right in every respect. I had allowed myself to be carried away by enthusiasm, too eager to prove that I had done nothing machiavellian or underhanded. But why load it with intimate personal details, laying my mind bare? The simple truth was that I never thought of the possible consequences of my candidness. This was a personal journal, not a political rebuttal.

'You are right, my sweet,' I said. 'Let me throw it in the incinerator.'

'Oh no, no!' she exclaimed, hanging on to me. 'We'll wrap it up and put it in the old trunk for our descendants to read. I wish my grandparents had left a record of their time and thoughts, and their parents before them. What wonderful reading it would make! They'd come alive and be so much closer.'

In a way I felt a strange feeling of release. I'd have been mad to undress myself in public, and I had come so near to doing it.

Even worse, undress the Ancestor.

Later when we were in bed listening to the rain spattering on the window panes, a lovely sound when one is nice and warm in bed, she suddenly said, 'Do you know, Commander, you are a most devious man!'

'Devious, my flower? What have I done?'

'Not done, but would have done!'

'I have no idea what you are talking about,' I said, quite genuinely puzzled.

'My housemaid.'

'What about your housemaid?' My mind quickly scanned what I had written about her.

'The way you write, if she had given you half a chance you'd have been in there like a… like a…'

'A raging bull?' I offered, much relieved.

'No. More like a…like a rhinoceros!' she corrected, triumphantly, and then pinched me painfully in the arm.

I did not make the mistake that Shakespeare, with his remarkable knowledge of psychology, identified as a sign of guilt – protesting too much!

What surprised me was that she never mentioned "the other woman" who I had come so close to marrying. But then, I never mentioned Zahor either in our conversation.

After the manuscript was deposited in the family trunk, that was that as far as both of us were concerned.

We flew back to Rivenia on 19 November, as scheduled. Baby Leila gave us no trouble at all, the nomadic genes in her taking as naturally to travelling as a duck takes to water. In fact, she showed very little interest in what was happening *inside* the aircraft but spent most of her time gazing at the swiftly passing clouds, or peering down at the land far below whenever it became visible. Perhaps she will take to flying when she grows up.

« POSTSCRIPT »

When we landed at the expanded and much more attractive Rivenia International Airport, bypassing customs as was my privilege, I was astonished to see what appeared to be a large military delegation. I discovered that the entire General Council, some forty strong, had come to receive me, led by Serge and Bluebeard. Both embraced me with undisguised delight, and I wondered if Mr James had not been misinformed. I detected no signs of tension within the Council, and the two top leaders seemed to be on excellent terms. Aida and Leila were soon lost among a crowd of relations, and Zain came up to say we'd be returning to Bonelands in his station wagon.

After being introduced on the spot to the new Council members Serge accompanied me to Zain's car and struck the first discordant note.

'Prof, much is going on below the surface at Central, so when you come to the office tomorrow morning to see the Ancestor drop in and see me first.' He seemed to have aged quite a lot, and I felt a stab of pity for him.

It was a relief to be sitting next to an obviously happy and contented father-in-law, who started bringing me up to date on all that had been happening in the country. I was relieved to hear that most of it was good. He, himself, had been promoted to director in the Council of Culture and Arts and while complaining about the salary said that he was enjoying his work.

I asked him if he had heard of any rumblings of discontent among the populace, and he said no more than in any other democratic country. The old nightmares of constant power cuts and water shortages were a thing of the past, and schools now had books and pencils.

The laughter and chatter coming from the back seats was like a balm to my troubled mind. From the way I was greeted at the airport, it seemed to me that if the Council was split down the middle with the Ancestor wavering, then both sides saw me as coming to provide the decisive reinforcement. What was at stake was not just the future of Rivenia but of the entire region. I must take a firm, unshakeable stand one way or the other.

And that was where my personal nightmare lay – I was torn between ancestral yearnings and modern realities. Had the Ancestor lost the power to commune with the Twelve Elders, to receive guidance from them?

I suddenly found myself dreading the meeting with him the following day.

The Wordly Hope men set their hearts upon
Turns Ashes – or it prospers; and anon,
Like Snow upon the Desert's dusty Face
Lighting a little Hour or two - is gone

Omar Khayyam

END